AN ARROW'S FLIGHT

ALSO BY MARK MERLIS

American Studies

AN ARROW'S FLIGHT

MARK MERLIS

ST. MARTIN'S PRESS ✷ NEW YORK

Design by Bryanna Millis

Library of Congress Cataloging-in-Publication Data

Merlis, Mark.
    An arrow's flight / by Mark Merlis. — 1st ed.
      p. cm.
    ISBN 0-312-18675-4
    1. Trojan War—Fiction. I. Title.
PS3563.E7422A89 1998
813'.54—dc21   97-53088
                                                            CIP

First Edition: August 1998

10 9 8 7 6 5 4 3 2 1

In the Last Episode

Paris, prince of Troy, visits Sparta and departs with Helen, wife of Menelaus. A Greek army, led by Menelaus's brother Agamemnon, sails in a thousand ships to recover her. After ten years, the best warriors on both sides are dead, and the Greeks have settled in for what looks to be a permanent siege of Troy.

The Players

Achilles, father of Pyrrhus (A-**kil**-eez)
Admetus, an ancient sailor (Ad-**me**-tus)
Archias, an impresario (Ar-**ky**-us)
Corythus, a young sailor (Cor-**ee**-thus)
Deidameia, daughter of Lycomedes, mother of Pyrrhus (Day-ee-da-**may**-a)
Deucalion, a recreational slave (Doo-**kay**-li-on)
Gelanor, a queen (**Gel**-a-nor)
Lamus, a trick (**Lah**-mus)
Leo, a restaurateur
Leucon, a youth (**Loo**-con)
Lycomedes, prince of Scyros (Ly-**com**-e-deez)
Nereus, a young officer (**Nare**-ee-us)
Odysseus, a Greek commander, husband of Penelope (O-**diss**-ee-us)
Paris, prince of Troy, son of Priam
Peleus, father of Achilles (**Pel**-ee-us)
Philoctetes, an exile (Phil-oc-**tee**-teez)
Phoenix, counselor of Achilles and Pyrrhus
Priam, king of Troy (**Pry**-am)
Pterelas, a barkeep (**Tare**-e-las)
Pyrrhus, or Neoptolemus, son of Achilles and Deidameia (**Peer**-us, Nee-op-**tawl**-e-mus)
Thetis, a miscellaneous sea goddess, mother of Achilles (**The**-tis)

ARCHER'S BODY

Start with the boy, Pyrrhus. Clambering onto the bar at the Escapade, swaying lazily with the music as he unbuttoned his shirt.

Pyrrhus was wearing his standard ensemble, the white oxford button-down and the pressed, snug khaki trousers. The other Golden Boys wore less — just cutoffs and a T-shirt, or maybe some kind of one-piece elastic number that disclosed the merchandise prematurely. Less starting out and less to shed, because hardly anyone tipped you till you had it all off. Yet Pyrrhus insisted on his incongruous straight-boy outfit. For someone whose job description consisted of the single word *undresses*, he was uncompromising about the crease in his trousers and the starch in his shirts.

Maybe he understood the memories that outfit evoked for the older men pressed close to the bar, the ones quickest with their dollars. He might have been their first high-school crush: the baseball player, maybe, just stepping into the locker room, joking with his teammates, now so casually unbuttoning his shirt. Above the crisp collar Pyrrhus's face gleamed, somehow chaste despite the faint, reckless smile that stole over it as the music overtook him and he began to dance.

He had to stretch to hang his shirt on the hook over the cash register. His khakis, teasingly unbuttoned, drooped as he stepped nimbly over the cocktail glasses and the beer bottles on the bar. He pulled his pants off, hopping on one foot and then the other as he struggled to slip them past his huge, many-featured sneakers. When he was down to his briefs — as far as he would go till the next song — he closed his eyes, lost in his . . . dance, to be generic, though it was just a random series of wiggles and jerks to the rhythm of the music. Here again, he wasn't like some of the boys, who had elaborate routines, or as elaborate as one could manage while slaloming amid the glasses and bottles. As if anyone had come to see choreography. Not to mention that, if you danced all over the place, you inhibited the gesture that was now occurring and that made Pyrrhus open his eyes: the hand sticking a dollar in his white sock. He rewarded his benefactor with a wink and a single thrust of his pelvis, almost too restrained to be called a bump. He earned another dollar.

The Escapade — the Café Tip-and-Grope, Pterelas called it once — was a brick box in the warehouse district, windowless, with an old neon sign that showed, absurdly, a dancing girl. Maybe they'd bought it used, from some failed Escapade somewhere else. This Escapade was doing just fine, already jammed with men at ten-thirty, even though the neighborhood was scary at night and there had been that incident, a month or two earlier, between the high-school principal and the profoundly misunderstood sailor.

You'd pay your six bucks, pass through the metal door and into the crush of men. The crowd was always younger than you'd expect. Yes, a few grizzled fairies at the bar, at the feet of the dancing boys, but also, right next to them, kids in their twenties cruising one another. As if the dancers weren't the star attraction, but just decoration, or background noise, like the string trio at brunch at the Park Court Hotel. In the corners of the room, away from the bar, the customers hardly glanced up at the Golden Boys. The parade of naked flesh just above eye level was even a little embarrassing. Child, does your mother know what you're doing? And of course the regulars could be picky. Where did they get this one? they'd say—too skinny, too stoned, too . . . little. Not that they'd throw him out of bed on a snowy night. But really, for six bucks . . . Or that one—he tried too hard, as if he were in the talent competition at a beauty pageant. You practically had to look away.

No one looked away from Pyrrhus. Some people just stared at him, open-mouthed. Others glanced intermittently, or sidewise, as if not deigning to seem too interested. A few had come just to see him. There had been word of mouth: Honey, I know you haven't been to the Escapade in years, but . . . The most popular Golden Boy in a long time; the owner was thinking of extending his run, though the first song was almost over and he was still technically decent. Even the regulars, who were already fully acquainted with what lay hidden under his residual garment, glanced at him now and then.

At the far end of the bar was Tydeus, who had undressed too rapidly—not teasing, more as if he were just heading to the showers. He jogged in place to the music, his anticlimactic penis wobbling up and down. Tydeus had danced in other cities. He told Pyrrhus it was different there, you had to keep your shorts on, and in one straitlaced burg the customers couldn't even stick a tip in the waistband, they had to just hand it to you as they might tip a doorman. Only here, in the capital, were boys naked—except for shoes, to keep from slipping on the wet bar, and socks, for the tips. This liberty was bestowed unintentionally: the lawmakers wanted, in the clubs they frequented, to see pussy. Accordingly they never got around to writing the rules other cities had, ordinances lasciviously specific about whether a pastie had to cover the entire areole, or about where the leg ended and the cheek began.

Tydeus would as soon have kept his shorts on. Tydeus was (he insisted) a straight boy, just up there for the money; he was putting himself through computer-repair school or something. He almost never got hard. He greased himself, with the little tin of lube he carried in his sock, he worked at it, but he just didn't get hard with men looking at him. Pyrrhus got hard, helplessly, with men looking at him. As for the money: of course it was gratifying to have people mindlessly shoving bills in his socks. Mainly, though, he was there to feel their eyes on him.

They obliged; the men in the room were transfixed as he slipped off his shorts.

He was a dilute divinity. His father was Achilles, of course, so his grandmother was a B-list goddess. Making Pyrrhus only a—what?—a hemidemigod, shoulders mortally narrow, visage human. The genitals he now revealed were of ordinary size. (Not tiny, as the gods' are, sheltered in their massive loins as if to protect the divine seed.) Only his hair, the flaming red of a warrior's, hinted at his origins.

He paused before a squat dark man with no hair at all except in his ears. A conventioneer, maybe, strayed far from the downtown hotels but still wearing his suit, with his tie loosened and his collar open and even his face slack. He looked up at Pyrrhus sullenly, as if Pyrrhus's very existence were the source of some grievance. Still, you don't sacrifice to the gods because you are fond of them. It didn't matter what he felt, envy or contempt or frustrated desire; after Pyrrhus smiled down on him for a few seconds, he gave up the buck. Almost involuntarily, as if to propitiate some elemental spirit.

Next to him sat one of the very young ones, and good-looking—certainly Tydeus's equal, if not Pyrrhus's. You had to wonder what brought them to the Escapade, when they could have been meeting their peers at the Barracks or the Lighthouse. Pyrrhus danced before him, back turned, but watching his expression in the mirror behind the bar. The boy bit his lip and made himself stick a dollar in Pyrrhus's sock. Pyrrhus stood still as the boy diffidently caressed Pyrrhus's calf.

Now Pyrrhus squatted down before him; he reached forward tentatively and began to stroke Pyrrhus's inner thigh—not holding it but grazing it with the hairs on the back of his hand. The kid came up with a couple more dollars: he was entitled to a good feel now, and he reached for the prize. Pyrrhus granted it, arched his back and smiled down at the boy,

5

who gingerly grasped Pyrrhus's human-sized offering as if it were something fragile.

Pyrrhus's grin looked artificial at first: I'm supposed to smile as if I were enjoying myself while I let you do this. Yet his eyes were so bright and his smile so very broad that one could believe it wasn't put on. He gazed down at the kid almost affectionately, as if to say: Yes, isn't it wonderful, I don't know how I came by it, but here it is, all for you. For these few seconds. Though he kept the smile fixed in place, Pyrrhus was already sizing up the next customer. A little man with white hair and a perfectly tailored suit. Still, he didn't move on just yet, let the boy keep holding him. And really: what was the difference between touching Pyrrhus there for a few seconds and having him for a night, or a lifetime, what except mere duration?

The boy was pumping in earnest now, evidently imagining that two bucks gave him the right to conclude Pyrrhus's performance for the evening. Pyrrhus gently withdrew, still smiling, and sidled down the bar to confront the little white-haired man. He regarded Pyrrhus with pursed lips and furrowed brow, as if he were scandalized by Pyrrhus's nakedness, as if he had not driven all the way down to the warehouse district to partake of it. These were Pyrrhus's favorites, the accusers. He liked to kneel in front of them, presenting himself at eye level, inescapable. Sometimes they turned away, ashamed of themselves. More often they lunged for it. Pyrrhus would playfully scramble to his feet to elude them. Then they had to laugh and pretend that they, too, were only playing. They had to feign a laugh and give him a dollar. Pyrrhus would laugh, too, or at least chuckle, rather distantly. With the ice broken, he would kneel before them again. Now that everybody understood that it was all in fun, everybody was having fun, they would touch him freely. And feed him bill after expiatory bill.

The little man ignored the object proffered two inches from his nose and looked straight up into Pyrrhus's face. He studied Pyrrhus as if they'd met and he couldn't remember where. Maybe they had. Pyrrhus would have thought he'd remember, such a tiny man with his perfect suit and his fussy pocket square. Still, maybe he was once a trick, and maybe he would be again. Pyrrhus would have to speak to him.

Usually he didn't; he disapproved of the colleagues who squatted down and had long conversations with customers, breaking the spell as surely as if the actors in a play were to step down into the audience and chat about the weather. Archias, the owner, said he'd get more tips if he'd only talk to the customers. "They just like to get to know the boys," he said. This wasn't so, of course: they only wanted to know that the boys were exactly what they seemed. And Pyrrhus had the obstinate conviction that he wasn't what he seemed.

Just this once he broke the mute, precious anonymity of nakedness. "How you doing? Haven't seen you lately."

The man looked startled. "I shouldn't have thought you'd remember me."

"To tell you the truth, I'm not sure I do. I should, though, huh?"

"I don't suppose so."

Pyrrhus was afraid the guy was offended. "Oh, I know we've met. But it's been a while?"

"Yes, a good while."

This was enough talk. "Good to see you again," Pyrrhus said. He straightened up and danced, more or less, to the other end of the bar. Tydeus looked annoyed: wanton Amyclas, a legendary tipper, was at his end. Still, he had to pretend it was okay, as if they were supposed to switch sides just then. He gave way, headed over to try to rouse some interest from the little white-haired man.

Pyrrhus smiled faintly at Amyclas, then looked away; he scarcely glanced down even when the old goat stuffed a five in his sock. He was still looking at the white-haired man, who in turn was placidly surveying the room, as if oblivious of Tydeus's gyrations just above his shoulder.

They hadn't tricked; Pyrrhus would surely have remembered such a strange, icy little man. After a minute Pyrrhus gave up trying to place him and looked down at Amyclas, who rewarded his renewed attention with another bill.

Too far along, singer. We can't be here already. Pyrrhus on the bar, the diminutive emissary come to announce that the Fates had scheduled him for a career change. Practically at the end already.

Of course, if you take the grand view of things, you're always practically at the end. I could start this song with Earth rising up and shaking the drops of Chaos from her gown, and before you know it we'd be here, Pyrrhus ready to step down from the bar and embark on his adventure. If you take the large view there isn't much story, everything just hurtles toward the end that was laid out at the start of things.

No wonder our epic poets wind up repeating themselves, filling the empty pages with digressions and catalogues and, when there's no other way to finish Book XVII, one more sequence of A beheads B while C exposes D's gastrointestinal system to public scrutiny. Just to postpone the predestined conclusion. As if we didn't know how the Trojan War turned out.

On the same principle, I suppose I could make my word count just by listing every one of Pyrrhus's tricks, back when he was in the city and people had tricks. Yet even the number of Pyrrhus's tricks was, though impressive, finite. We'd still get to the end, to Lemnos, much too quickly.

We already live in the world after the end, we are all post-Lemnos: the disco there still rakes in money every summer, but the mirrored ball at tea dance hurls its splinters of light at ghosts. What's the hurry to get where we are? Why does every chronicle whiz through the age of heroes, barely pausing to sniff the poppers, in a headlong rush to get to the important stuff, to the island and the snake and everything after? We'll get here; we have ineluctably gotten here.

The only reason to break the silence at all, singer, to recount for the thousandth time how Pyrrhus made history, is to take on for a few consoling hours his god-given ignorance. To see how he lived, oblivious to what Destiny intended for him. Blind as we are, caught up in the quotidian, the little excursions that never divert us from our fated course, but that seem like life.

He did not feel, any more than you and I, Destiny's hand at his back. Destiny is indifferent to the small details of our lives. It is her myopic sister, Necessity, who tends to them. She never looks very far ahead: just herds us ruthlessly from day to day.

Even Necessity came rather late into Pyrrhus's life. She first nudged him back when he was still a waiter, just a few months before he stepped up onto that bar where we have discovered him. Making herself known through the adenoidal voice of his roommate, Leucon.

Pyrrhus was shaving, getting ready for his evening shift at Café Leo. Leucon was out in the living room watching the five-thirty news. The announcer happened to mention the date, and Leucon called out, "Hey, it looks like the first of the month."

Pyrrhus said, "Oh, right. Okay," and continued shaving. He cut himself—he wasn't like his father, he could be wounded easily enough. So he had to dig in the medicine cabinet for the styptic pencil and then work up the nerve to use it. He instantly forgot that Leucon had, however diffidently, asked him for his half of the rent. Which he didn't have.

And wouldn't earn, if he tried to wait tables with blood all over his white shirt. Valiantly he picked up the styptic pencil and stanched his wound.

A few nights later Leucon came home with groceries. As Pyrrhus always ate at Café Leo, Leucon paid for the groceries alone. Even though Pyrrhus drank his coffee most mornings without offering to contribute. Leucon was reminded of this as he removed a fresh can of coffee from the sack. Life with a roommate seemed compounded of such small inequities.

A larger grievance came to mind. He called out to Pyrrhus, who was putting on his waiter's uniform of white shirt and black pants, not khaki yet. "Don't forget about the rent."

Pyrrhus said, "No, I won't. Look, I'm late for work, catch me in the morning."

It's hard to catch a waiter in the morning. Pyrrhus worked double shifts the next few days; Leucon hardly saw him. In the mornings Leucon had to tiptoe through Pyrrhus's bedroom to get coffee from the kitchen. Pyrrhus was asleep, or pretended to be. Though the days were falling away and the unpaid rent loomed larger and larger in Leucon's world, he could not bring himself to wake Pyrrhus up. He would stand for a few moments looking down at the extraordinary creature who lay tangled in the sheets. And could not find the voice to rouse him and bitch about the rent.

On the tenth of each month the landlord taped up yellow notices next to the front door. Leucon had seen these their first few months in the apartment. Always for other people—#7 once, #5 every time. They began **No-TICE OF DELINQUENCY** in a menacing gothic. The tenth of the month exactly, starting the legal process. The sight of those notices always made Leucon feel smug and prosperous.

Even this month he almost sailed by the notice addressed to one NE-OPTOLEMUS. He was halfway into the vestibule before he recalled that Neoptolemus was Pyrrhus's legal name. He had only seen it once, the day they signed the lease. "Nobody calls me that," Pyrrhus had said. "Not even at home." Except the landlord called him that. When Leucon tore the notice off the doorpost and unfolded it, there were the two names: NEOPTOLEMUS AND LEUCON. Linked in ignominy.

Leucon was a quiet and orderly youth. He had always obeyed his mother, studied hard in school. He went dutifully every day to the job for which his studies had overqualified him, running the copying machine at the law firm. True, what he did on Friday nights with the fellows he brought home from the Lighthouse or the Barracks would have made his mother's heart stop. But he was otherwise a good boy who had never, not once, served detention at school. The sight of that yellow notice, with his name typed beneath the sneering word **DELINQUENCY**, made him feel like a criminal.

He didn't understand how routine and trivial it was, merely the first arrow let fly in a process so protracted that he might grow a long gray beard before he was evicted. Nor did he see that, if the worst happened and he and Pyrrhus were actually thrown out on their asses, they might possibly go on to live full lives. He crumpled the notice in his hand, ran upstairs, opened the door, and beheld Pyrrhus. Watching television and drinking Leucon's beer. In his underwear.

Pyrrhus sat around in his underwear all the time. Leucon wasn't used to this, and of course never joined him. As a boy, Leucon had always grabbed the catalogue from the mail-order department store the day it arrived, and hurried up to his bedroom so he could turn at once to those pages where groups of men in different styles of underwear sat around chatting, smoking pipes, admiring fishing rods. Was there ever a place on earth where men actually did this? Even in Leucon's college dorm, in pre-coed days, guys pretty much wore clothes. Well, perhaps they didn't where Pyrrhus came from. Or maybe Pyrrhus just didn't want to spoil his waiter's costume.

One explanation Leucon could rule out: Pyrrhus wasn't trying to provoke him. Of course not; Pyrrhus wasn't at all interested in Leucon. They were just roommates. Pyrrhus's near-undress practically shouted that there was no erotic possibility in this apartment, less even than in the innocent pages of the department-store catalogue, where the men's crotches were airbrushed to display not the slightest convexity.

Over time Leucon had gotten used to sitting around fully clothed while Pyrrhus wore only his briefs. The layered meanings of this tableau, all about freedom and constraint, nature and artifice, the bohemian and the bourgeois, stopped worrying him. Even the deliberate nonprovocation of it didn't bother him after a while, if only because you can't stay bothered all the time. Perhaps it was just some defense against frustration, but Leucon nearly began to feel that Pyrrhus's body wasn't enticing at all, that there was something cold and inert about it. Like the perfect torsos on one of those aggressive billboards you see nowadays, so lifeless and unreachable they might as well be the splayed corpses in newspaper pictures from the war front.

This one evening, though, Leucon burst into the apartment. It was hot—the landlord was overheating, an excess for which he would compensate in January—so hot the air just clamped down on every surface of him the minute he stepped into the room. He was out of breath from running up the stairs, and still warm with shame from the rent notice; on top of this, the startling heat of the apartment all but suffocated him.

And made his glasses fog up. There was nothing before him but an ivory glow; for an instant he thought he might pass out. Slowly, as if materializing, the image of Pyrrhus reemerged. Pyrrhus, shiny with sweat and bulging a little down there, most unlike the catalogue, as if he'd been sleepily playing with himself. He hadn't shaved; the premonition of his red beard painted his jaw a spirited rose.

Everything Leucon had managed to suppress came to the surface: here he was properly indignant about the rent and yet helplessly dazzled by this deadbeat.

Which of course was why he'd let Pyrrhus share with him in the first place, instead of lining up some sensible guy with a steadier job.

He'd been so lucky to find the apartment: two bedrooms, right downtown, and so cheap he could afford half of it. That is, he wasn't going to have to share it with three or four guys as if it were a tent at Troy; he could get just one other person and he'd have a room all by himself. True, it was laid out funny. You had to go through one of the bedrooms to get to the kitchen, and the other bedroom had no windows; who would have thought that was even legal?

He put an ad in the free weekly: *Respons GM share spac 2 bdrm dwntwn, $250 + util, call Leucon 9–5,* and his office number. He almost put *non-smok,* but it didn't really bother him that much. Better a smoker than, say, multiple cats. The main thing was *respons.* They were making him do a year's lease, and he wanted somebody who wouldn't just skip out on him.

Of course most of his callers wanted to share his *spac 2 bdrm* for about twenty minutes and were happy to offer details about what would happen in that interval. It was eerie, standing at the phone next to the copying machine—while lawyers waddled by and secretaries importuned him to do their rush before everybody else's rush—standing there and listening to the most graphic offers of lunchtime ecstasy. He never accepted, but he never hung up, either.

His heavy-breathing suitors aside, the very afternoon the paper came out he already had two serious prospects. He arranged to meet them after work. The first guy who showed up, Linus, was already perfect. A business student, neat, quiet, parents helping out with the rent. Linus had, amazingly, a car, which meant maybe they could get out to the supermarket in the suburbs instead of being gouged by the places downtown. He said he already had a lot of furniture; was that a problem? Of course it wasn't, because all Leucon had was one suitcase, back at the hostel where he'd been staying the first couple of weeks in town.

All told, just what Leucon was looking for, as far as you could tell in five minutes. A business student—that meant he had no interior life. Leucon had rather imagined a roommate who would join in collegiate bull sessions about books and movies and the cosmos. But the other guy was late, probably wouldn't show up at all. Leucon and Linus shook hands and that was it.

Leucon waited a couple of minutes after Linus left, so if the other guy showed up Leucon could tell him the place was taken. He just wandered around the apartment, and he realized he and Linus should have decided then and there about the bedrooms. Leucon was the one who'd found it; he should probably have had his pick. Still, they hadn't talked about it, and now Leucon was going to have to go through some kind of negotiation with an apprentice entrepreneur who was supplying all the furniture. Leucon figured he was getting the room without windows, and he was standing there trying to figure out how he'd furnish it when he heard somebody out in the living room. The other guy. Leucon stepped out to meet him and give him the bad news.

"Hi, I'm sorry I'm so late," the guy said. "I just got off work." He stuck out his hand. "I'm Pyrrhus."

"Leucon."

Do you know how sometimes you see a man, and you're not sure if you want to get in his pants or if you want to cry? Not because you can't have him; maybe you can. But you see right away something in him beyond having. You can't screw your way into it, any more than you can get at the golden eggs by slitting the goose. So you want to cry, not like a child, but like an exile who is reminded of his homeland. That's what Leucon saw when he first beheld Pyrrhus: as if he were getting a glimpse of that other place we were meant to be, the shore from which we were deported before we were born.

"You got any takers yet?" Pyrrhus said, withdrawing the hand Leucon had been too awestruck to shake.

"No," Leucon said. Feeling despicable right away, he and Linus had a deal, but still—"Um, no. I mean, somebody's interested, but it's nothing definite."

"Great. Let me look around."

Leucon waited in the living room while Pyrrhus inspected the place, thoroughly, running the water from all the faucets, flushing the toilet, trying all the lights. Leucon was almost dizzy, heart thumping at the thought that this divinity might find the place unsuitable and dematerialize. And at the same time trying to puzzle through what it could possibly be like to have a divinity in the same apartment. Well, decorative. But also tormenting, being a mere roommate and keeping his hands to himself. He needed to be sensible. Linus was perfectly suitable, and anyway they'd shaken hands on it.

When Pyrrhus had finished his tour, Leucon said, "What do you do?" As if Pyrrhus's black pants and white shirt weren't sort of a clue.

Pyrrhus stuck his hands in the back pockets of the black pants—a pose that always knocked Leucon out—and looked down at the floor, boyish and shy. "I . . . I just got a job waiting tables. Place called Café Leo."

"Oh, yeah, I've seen Café Leo." A little grill in the gay neighborhood that served passé entrées named for divas. Leucon had peeked in once or twice; it had always been deserted. "This is going to be two-fifty each."

"Yeah, the ad said."

"Plus utilities."

"Uh-huh. Look, I'm doing lunches now, but they're going to let me have some dinner shifts next week. I should make, I don't know, thirty or forty a night. There shouldn't be any problem."

"Oh, no," Leucon said. "I didn't mean there was a problem." There was. Waiting tables in a queer restaurant hardly anybody went to seemed to promise a rather spasmodic cash flow. But he had a job, anyway; this plus his other evident virtues settled it.

"Great." They shook hands brusquely, just roommates. Pyrrhus said, "Oh, I smoke, is that a problem?"

"No," Leucon said. It wouldn't have been a problem if Pyrrhus built bombs in the kitchen. Still, this was no way to start. "Well, it is, kind of. Maybe if you could just do it in your room."

"Okay, no big deal." Pyrrhus smiled. "Any other rules?"

"Nope. Anything goes."

"Wow. Hot times."

Leucon accepted the mockery. "Not so far."

"Me either. Course I just got here. How long you been in town?"

"Few weeks."

"That's not long," Pyrrhus said. "Things'll pick up. It'll be fun, living here."

Yes, fun. They'd be pals. "Which room you want?" Leucon said.

"I—look, you found the place, it's your choice. But I don't know, I'm sort of claustrophobic. I'm not sure I could handle that one without the windows."

"That's fine. I don't care." Leucon was a little angry with himself the minute he said it, as if this were the first in a stream of surrenders to his new pal. But he didn't care very much about the windows; there would be plenty to look at indoors.

No, of course *pal* isn't the word. There is no word for what Leucon thought lay ahead of him. Our very language is not chaste enough.

If pressed to articulate it, Leucon could have offered only a glimpse, from so long ago, of a pair of boys playing catch. Leucon watching, from behind a bush, two boys playing catch. Lazy and silent on a spring morning, in perfect communion.

Such as, let's face it, Leucon could never have had, not with either of them or with any boy, and not just because he would never have caught the damn ball. We're all grownups here, we know there's no phase of pregenital innocence, we know what Leucon really wanted when he dreamt of being one of those boys. Throwing and catching; I can scarcely write the words without a smirk.

Even Leucon knew better. He was out now, out in the big city, the years of smothered longings and mortified masturbation over. He was, as they say, *sexually active*, with all the bunnylike zeal the phrase suggests. Couldn't he see things for what they were, call a hard-on a hard-on, acknowledge that he just plain wanted to get into Pyrrhus's black waiter trousers? The other thing, for which there was no word, the playing-catch thing that was anterior to or inarticulably different from sex: he ought to have known as well as you and I that it didn't exist.

Certainly there was nothing chaste about Leucon's feelings as he clutched the rent notice and regarded Pyrrhus. Pyrrhus's hair stood up in shocks of flame. His pale skin was damp, glazed like porcelain.

Leucon could scarcely remember what he was angry about. One glimpse of the divine freeloader and he turned into the attorney for the defense. Oh, he's having a hard time; he doesn't mean to screw you. He's working double shifts, he's doing his best to make it up. How does he get those lines in his stomach without working out?

It was with a feeling of overcoming this idiot inside that Leucon said — screamed, almost, spitting with fury — "Did you see this?"

"Yeah. It's no big deal, don't worry about it."

"Don't worry about it? Are you crazy?"

"It takes them months and months to throw somebody out. They're just trying to rattle you."

"Well, it's working."

"Yeah, I see that," Pyrrhus said, with a tolerant and infuriating smile. Somehow he had turned himself into the good guy. While Leucon, waving the yellow notice, had wound up on the landlord's side. Dressed in his shirt and tie while Pyrrhus sat in comfortable abandon.

"Don't be so uptight," Pyrrhus said, a locution of those years that has happily passed out of use. Leucon was always being called uptight whenever he exercised normal prudence. Pyrrhus frowned. "I finally get one night off, I can't worry about this. You'd be a neat guy if you just didn't take everything so seriously all the time."

Leucon thought, Sure, if I were you I wouldn't have to take anything seriously. Though he wasn't clear about how this might be so. Didn't Pyrrhus care that they might lose the roof over their heads? How could Leucon become a neat guy? And if he did, if he could only relax, would they be pals then?

"Come on, loosen up," Pyrrhus said. "I think there's a beer left."

Yes, Leucon would get a beer and at least take his tie off, if they weren't going to be a picture from the catalogue. He would show Pyrrhus he could loosen up and then they'd be pals and tomorrow he would still have to ask Pyrrhus for the rent.

"Somebody's got to be responsible here," he said.

Pyrrhus shrugged and turned back toward the television. Who could blame him, what was left to say? Unless Leucon cared to issue an ultimatum. He did not.

He went to his windowless room. It was so hot, if he had been an egg he would have hatched. If he weren't too uptight. What he would have liked to do, what any sane person would have done, was strip to his underwear, get the last beer, and sit out there where Pyrrhus at least had the window cracked open. He couldn't: he just sat fully clothed on the edge of his bed—mattress, rather—on the floor, so that his knees nearly touched his chin.

It wasn't supposed to be this way. He had escaped from college, that monastic outpost in a small town where it was always February. He had alighted in the city, found his dead-end job and his cheap apartment, found his way to the bars. Life was supposed to start now.

But he was responsible: he responded to every directive from the lawyers at the office, from the landlord, from his parents when he went home to visit, from the little facsimile parents he carried inside. He had done everything he was supposed to, and his reward was to sit here in a sweltering cell and listen as beauty and freedom got up, went to the fridge, and took the last beer.

"Leucon?" Pyrrhus called through the door. "I really am sorry about the rent. I know it's a drag. But things are picking up. You know, we get a half-decent crowd at Leo's this weekend, I should be all set."

Leucon felt he shouldn't answer, that Pyrrhus shouldn't get off this easily. And he knew how improbable it was that Pyrrhus would come home suddenly rich from Café Leo. He said, "Okay."

Later, when he couldn't sleep in the heat, it occurred to him what a great concession it was for Pyrrhus, how solicitous of Leucon's feelings he was, to offer those wan promises. Still later, maybe having slept a little, Leucon lay in the dark and wondered—as so many men would wonder— how he might hurt Pyrrhus.

2

Pyrrhus was not his father; he could be wounded. Even if you credit the old yarn, about how the goddess Thetis dipped her son Achilles in the river and rendered him invulnerable, everywhere but the heel by which she grasped him — this has always seemed too pat for me — she didn't try the same trick with her grandson. He could be cut, or stung by bees. He could catch diseases. But Thetis gave him something else. That made him, somehow, harder to hurt than his father.

One could write a book about Thetis's pathetic efforts to confer immortality on her various semihuman offspring. A cookbook, even: more than once she popped a newly hatched demigod in a 350-degree oven, imagining that she had found a thirty-minute recipe for apotheosis. When the kids came out a little too well done, she moved on to the marination-in-the-Styx technique. And finally — most demented — she tried hiding the little suckers. Achilles and then his son Pyrrhus. She tried to find some place on earth where Destiny would lose sight of them.

Achilles first, when he was eighteen or so, a few years before the war was scheduled to begin. The gods were already settling down with their scorecards and popcorn — they'd been waiting for the main event for centuries — when Thetis hustled Achilles off to the island of Scyros. About as far from the whirl of things as you could get without having to learn a foreign language. She was fond of the kid, but she didn't overestimate him.

Even at eighteen, Achilles was a pretty big object to hide. The story has grown up — you may have heard it this way — that Achilles literally wore drag during his years on Scyros. Hid out in the harem of Prince Lycomedes, the doddering but lascivious monarch of the place, until the Greek recruiting officers came along and noticed something martial about the third girl from the left. It is rubbish like this that gives historians a bad name, makes some people wonder if the war happened at all. Imagine Achilles in a little cocktail number: you might as well have had him wrapped by that artist, the one who covers temples and palaces in muslin. The musculature of the edifice, stylobate to architrave, only shows more clearly through its shroud. Achilles couldn't have passed for a bull dyke, much less the little debutante who minces through the traditional account.

No, when Thetis decided to hide him, she was at least cleverer than that, came up with a disguise that should have been impenetrable. She dressed him up as a prole.

It was a trick she'd learned from the other gods. The gods, when they come to earth, never manifest themselves as princes or even as dentists, because people *notice* the upper and middle classes. They would say, So-and-so sure is divine-looking, or That guy sure can move a mile a minute, and pretty soon the secret would be out. Instead, visitations are always in the form of a fieldhand, or a bus driver, or—a favorite of Hermes—a bellhop. No one of a higher station looks closely at such people (well, queers do, but queers look at everybody). As for the other workers: they may sense something exceptional about their fellow drudge. But they know that whoever it is can't be so very special, else he wouldn't be down in the mud with everybody else.

Achilles' stupefying muscles were hidden in the bags of a mechanic's loose and begrimed coveralls; his flaming red locks were tucked into a baseball cap that said *Acme Transmission*. He bathed rarely and shaved less. He affected a slouch. For someone as self-regarding as Achilles, this imposture was more painful than exile itself. Still, people pretty much fell for it.

All except the princess Deidameia, who noticed him right away. One day, just a few weeks after Achilles' arrival on the island, Deidameia was headed downtown to return a dress. As a princess this was her chief recreation; she returned more than she bought. On the way, she happened to pass a churl loitering at a street corner. Any of her sisters would have ignored him, but Deidameia had sort of a thing for churls, a not unheard-of overreaction to the enervation of palace life. She dropped her package and just stared at him, thinking: What a stud.

This was an error. Of course he was perfect, as perfect as a half-mortal can be. Beautiful, though perhaps not exactly what you or I would call hot. He was statuesque, yes, but not an Apollo or a Perseus—more the Antaeus type. Powerful, defined, and yet: someone you didn't want to do anything with, couldn't imagine doing anything with. No part of him seemed made to interlock with any part of you, no matter what gender you were. He was quite plainly modeled directly by the hands of Zeus, but not for the bedroom, not for anyone's.

When he followed Deidameia to hers, he went through the motions, which presumably resulted in climaxes that were adequately gratifying. But it was just something to do, to fill in the dead space between real events, like the band playing at half-time. Even his famous histrionics over Briseis, the woman King Agamemnon expropriated from him during the war, had nothing to do with her, just with his pride. He didn't sulk in his tent for months because he was horny.

He would have given up every night of lovemaking in his life for one more morning of battle. The sensation of his tiny semidivine organ wandering around in some capacious mortal twat was nothing like the feeling of the blade at the end of his arm as it overcame the defiance of armor, plunged through the unresisting welcome of the layers of fascia, accepted finally the taut, exquisite surrender of the vitals, letting him in.

Any woman over the age of eleven ought to have picked this up instantly. If Deidameia didn't, maybe it was that she was too thrilled at having penetrated the disguise: all the gratification was in tearing off the wrapping paper, and she never, or not till it was too late, sat down and looked steadily at the gift she had acquired. By then she had already moved him into her wing of the palace, like a house pet. Which was fine with Achilles, even though she did want to screw pretty often. Because one of the things you had to do if you were disguised as a workman was actually work. This was not Achilles' strong suit. He could get into polishing armor and stuff, but rotating strangers' tires got old pretty quickly.

Thetis showed up one day, disguised as an upstairs maid but betraying herself with her usual put-upon look. She pointed out that living in a palace and wearing, as Achilles had taken to, karate-style pajama suits made for a rather unpersuasive facsimile of working-class life. Achilles obediently moved to a bungalow and reverted to coveralls or the even more convincingly proletarian display of butt cleavage. Deidameia was appalled, but she was also pregnant, so she followed him. There they dwelt, in simulated poverty.

Soon joined by the infant Neoptolemus. (Who was, by the time he was a toddler, called Pyrrhus: the Redhead. Because the toddler couldn't say Neoptolemus, and it was kind of a mouthful even for Achilles.)

They lived ten years in that bungalow. Achilles sat around the house drinking beer or went off to the woods to practice some manly art or other. Even though he obeyed his mother, even though his whole life was ostensibly devoted precisely to keeping out of war, he stayed in practice. His great martial body expected to be used, just as the missiles in the silos were designed to fly, no matter how often their creators protested that they intended nothing of the kind.

Deidameia shopped. She couldn't just trot downtown to the nice stores any more. No one in her new neighborhood stepped off the funicular in the afternoon wearing a knockoff of the latest Trojan couture and toting a load of packages from the best boutiques. But she had to shop, her very name meant "born to shop," so she took to watching the Shop-at-Home Network, brought to Scyros by the satellite dish. She sat all day clutching Lycomedes' credit card. Ordering everything they sold, from acrylic blouses to zirconium bracelets. Achilles would watch with her, apathetically, wondering if it wasn't time for her to buzz off to the kitchen and heat him up some canned soup and a couple of TV dinners.

It was into this parody of domestic life that Pyrrhus was born; in it he lived his formative years. If there are such years, if we aren't pretty much formed by the time we see light. For example: if Pyrrhus wasn't born a sissy, he certainly was one by the time his father first playfully wrestled with him, when he was two or three. He cried when real boys were supposed to laugh; he ran away from frogs and even butterflies; if you threw a ball at him he covered his face with his hands instead of trying to catch it. There are fathers who try to remedy this: "At-*ten*-hut! We will play catch now!" All they get is sons like Leucon, who nurse permanent grievances and still can't catch. Achilles took the other course: washed his hands of the boy, ceded him to Deidameia.

Not that Achilles would likely have been much of a father if he'd had a little tiger cub or whatever it was he wanted. He didn't, of course, have much love to squander on anyone but himself, and his real problem with Pyrrhus was merely that he was inappropriate, not the right son for a hero in the same way that, say, a midsize sedan would not have been the right car. He just ceased to acknowledge the child. Pyrrhus understood, tiny as he was. If he had to pass through a room where his father sat, he tried to make himself tinier still; he would have made himself invisible if he could have.

The war came. The Greek generals arrived on Scyros, spotted Achilles almost instantly, and lured him away. Silly Thetis: this was always going to happen, there had never been anything she could do to prevent it. All she had done was squander ten precious years of her son's brief life, holding him captive a million miles from home.

The war came, and Pyrrhus's father was gone. Before Achilles' ship had disappeared over the horizon, Deidameia was already packing. By the end of the day she and Pyrrhus had moved back into her father's palace. By the end of the week it was as if Achilles had never been with them.

Pyrrhus found himself suddenly in a world that was Pyrrhicentric, a whole fiefdom that revolved around his pleasure. Doted on by Deidameia and Lycomedes, treated as . . . what he had been all along, a prince, the next prince of Scyros.

The difference between a prince and the rest of us isn't, of course, the palace and the money. It's that, when a prince is asked what he's going to be when he grows up, he doesn't have to fumble for a reply. He is already what he is going to be, a walking tautology.

Not that Pyrrhus was supposed to be idle. He was expected to master a set of accomplishments of certified inutility: swimming, swordplay, hunting, siring a bastard with the gardener's daughter. The usual diversions of the rural gentry. Unhappily, Pyrrhus spent most of his time listening to his mother's original-cast recordings of forgotten musicals and leafing through her fashion magazines. Worse, as he came of age, he tended to disappear for long intervals, not with the gardener's daughter but with the chauffeur's son.

If Achilles had stayed around, these failings would have been re-marked upon. (Indeed, most of Achilles' recorded utterances have to do with other men's deficient virility.) But he was happily gone. Deidameia and Lycomedes didn't seem to notice Pyrrhus's many deviations from the princely ideal.

Or maybe they did notice, and these small disappointments were tol-erated; such a one appeared sometimes in the best of families. Probably his mother was even pleased that he was nothing at all like his father. One Achilles was plenty in this world; at least Pyrrhus didn't track mud on the rug or soil the slipcovers. Grandfather Lycomedes sometimes looked at him with a distant curiosity. No evident distaste, just a certain wonderment, about how Pyrrhus—when the time came and he was prince of Scyros—was going to carry out the cardinal mission of that office, the production of the next prince of Scyros.

Pyrrhus didn't wonder. Partly because this was a good while ago: kids like Pyrrhus bumbled into adolescence without a name for what they were. It never occurred to him that what went on with the chauffeur's son had any possible bearing on the ultimate likelihood of his procreating. Besides, his future duties were far away. For the time being, he had only one mission, a negative one. Never to go. Never to think, not for one minute, of leaving home.

His family never said that: "Oh, Pyrrhus, never leave us." They might as well have beseeched the mountain at the center of the island not to pick up its skirts and flounce into the sea. It never occurred to them that he could go. And it wasn't just them. Everyone on the island—the servants, the shopkeepers in the village, the farmers and their roughshod boys—regularly communicated to him the same heart-sinking message: that he belonged to Scyros, that he practically *was* Scyros. His destiny was certain; everybody knew all about it. He almost believed it himself.

He knew there were other worlds, their images beamed into the palace through the satellite dish, or shimmering indistinctly in the backgrounds of the fashion spreads. He knew the daily ferry went to a great city, though he had no idea just how short a hop it was. And on sunny afternoons, when Grandfather Lycomedes was full of appalling suggestions for healthful recreation, he hid in his room and stared at his dog-eared, treasured picture book of Troy.

Troy. Was there ever a young sissy who didn't dream of Troy? Its floodlit bridges and temples at night, by day the sun-splashed sidewalk cafés and teeming markets, the chanteuses at the supper clubs and the black-clad widows walking their terriers in the parks and the cobbled streets. Troy, center of gastronomy and fashion—every sort of fashion, from the newest ism to the fall couture. Pyrrhus had memorized every landmark. Daedalus's tower, with the three-star restaurant at the middle tier and the dizzying elevator ride to the observation deck. The temple to Apollo, Priam's alabaster palace, the walls—the walls most of all, soaring above the suburbs and the plains beyond.

He would play his records, over and over, and he would stare at his book. Though he understood it was just a picture book. He couldn't step into it; he wasn't going anywhere. He knew this even before he learned that Troy in particular was an improbable destination, as his father was at that very minute camped on the plain beneath its gleaming walls and planning its demolition.

He couldn't imagine going anywhere, but he had sometimes an itch. Just sometimes he would be sitting in the empty throne room, where it was so cool and the breeze teased the damask curtains, or on the terrace looking down on the village and out to sea—he couldn't imagine any better life, any place more pleasant to be . . .

Then the itch, or more precisely the sensation that there was a sort of vacuum in his chest, round like a bubble of emptiness that was right next to, pushing against, his heart. Starting tiny and then, if he just sat a few minutes, growing enormous, squeezing the air from his lungs and still growing, until soon there would be nothing else inside him and he would be just a shell. Like everyone else on Scyros, a little crust surrounding a vacuum.

Not this, he felt. He couldn't describe it any other way; there wasn't anything he wanted exactly. Just not this. He was going to escape.

Hence, perhaps, his grandmother's very last intervention. She appeared one day when Pyrrhus was eleven or twelve. She didn't step up and ring the doorbell, no; nor had she bothered to call ahead. She was just there one afternoon in their midst, at one of Mother's garden parties. Pyrrhus had had a couple of cups of champagne punch slipped to him by a servant who probably hoped he'd do something entertainingly goofy. He stayed off at the edges of the party, mainly to avoid the biddies who would ask how he was doing in his studies and whether he had a little sweetheart yet.

It was one of those days on Scyros when everything was hot and still and, even after a couple of cups of champagne punch, painfully clear. Pyrrhus was absolutely where he was, looking at the statues and the shrubs and the people that he would be looking at for the rest of his life. Then he felt, maybe for the first time, his not-this. Startled awake, perhaps, by the champagne, emptying him out so suddenly he could scarcely breathe.

Just as suddenly, there she was: a new face. No one, neither guest nor servant, paid any attention to her. Which was especially remarkable, not just because she was a stranger, but because she was the most beautiful being Pyrrhus had ever seen. Past anything in the magazines, a creature of serene perfection, her elegantly modeled face marred only by a certain redness about the eyes, as if she had just left off crying and might resume any time.

Everyone but Pyrrhus ignored the party crasher. He gawked at her, until she took him in hand, had a servant bring along two ices in silver bowls, and led him to the far end of the garden, where a bench encircled the trunk of an ancient oak.

He hated that oak, felt a true animosity toward an insentient tree, because the other boys would climb it and he couldn't or he didn't dare. Even as he sat down with the stranger, he imagined that he could hear the real boys overhead—teasing him or, worse, taking no notice of him at all. Just being boys, in their merciless collectivity, taking possession of a piece of the landscape that would never belong to him, not even when he became the landlord of Scyros. He could almost hear them snickering, the little sissy having an ice cream with some old lady.

Who wasn't even tasting hers, just turning it over with her spoon and looking a little queasy. After a minute she set it aside and watched Pyrrhus. She made him self-conscious: he took the tiniest spoonfuls, was ever so careful not to get any on his face or his summer suit, so he didn't really taste it, either.

When he had done, she spoke. "I am your grandmother," she said.

Pyrrhus shook his head in confusion, and she amplified: "Your other grandmother. Your father's mother."

"Oh."

"Do you remember your father?"

"Yes." Of course he did; Achilles had only been gone a couple of years. Though when she said it only one picture came, the very last time Pyrrhus had seen him, that night they came for him. Achilles, naked on the front porch of the bungalow, waiting for Mother to bring out his armor. The moonlight gleamed on his enormous chest and terrible arms. His balls hung low beneath his tiny divine cock. Pyrrhus was mortified, having this uncouth picture suddenly before his eyes as he sat in a bower with— they'd told him this, he knew it, but he hadn't really understood what the word meant—a goddess.

"Do you know where he is?"

"At the war." Why was she speaking as if to an infant? Unless maybe she just thought all mortals were infants.

"That's right. Your father is a great soldier."

"I know."

"Would you like to be a soldier when you grow up?"

"No." She seemed so proud of Daddy, Pyrrhus was afraid this wasn't the right answer. But he had a feeling there wasn't much point fibbing to a goddess. While he had no idea what he wanted to be, he was quite sure it wasn't a soldier, camping out somewhere in the rain and playing with the rough boys.

If he couldn't please her by wanting to be a soldier, maybe he could mollify her by professing the nonambition every other grownup he knew apparently approved of. "All I want to do is stay right here." Even as he

said it, he didn't know why he had thought this fib would be more persuasive.

"Here?" She looked around the bower with an expression that suggested that if she had to spend more than twenty minutes there she would
slit her wrists.

"I mean home. Scyros."

"Ah. Home. You like it here?"

Of course he'd learned in temple school what her home was like; he
could imagine how humdrum Scyros must seem to her. Still, he felt a
little put upon. Even if he wasn't telling the truth, even if he'd felt the
very minute before she'd appeared that first bubble of not-this, he grew
defensive — the way you do if somebody says something snotty about your
hometown, no matter that you once ran from it as fast as you could. "It's
okay."

"I think it is a dreadful place. If I had to stay here I would go out of
my mind." She said this without vehemence, just matter-of-fact, and she
didn't look at him, but gazed off into space like a fortuneteller. "If I were
you I should want to leave. As soon as I possibly could."

It was what Pyrrhus had been thinking the instant before she arrived.
She went on: "You can't be what they want you to be."

He was elated. How astonishing, to have a grownup — even, allegedly,
a member of his family — see all this so unerringly. As if anyone couldn't
have seen that this little, fidgety apprentice faggot in his summer suit with
short pants would make an odd prince of Scyros, reigning over an island
of hog farmers and sheep shearers.

"When you are old enough," she said, "you will leave." This wasn't
insight any more; it was an instruction.

"How? I . . . I don't know how to do anything. I mean, where will
I go?"

"To the city, I should think."

"Will I? What will I be there?"

She just looked at him a minute, as though scarcely understanding
the question. Be? Be there? Oh, he meant like a carpenter, a plumber.
She couldn't be troubled with this question; she had no interest in what
mortals were or did in this ugly quotidian sense. She said, rather airily:
"Oh, in the city, you know, it scarcely matters. They will take you for just
what you are."

"Oh."

"And no one will know anything about you."

25

The city, Thetis must have thought. They'll never find you there.

She was trying again, the ninny. All of the other gods understood that there was no toying with Destiny. They could delay or complicate, raise false hopes or make the appointed winner temporarily despair, but they could not prevent anything, change anything. Thetis alone kept trying to interfere. Was she just dim? Or was it because she had married a mortal, Peleus, Achilles' father?

Gods could accept the notion of fate because nothing really mattered: they themselves would never be hit by a truck, and—while they occasionally had a crush on some mortal and wanted to intervene—their mourning, when they failed, was briefer than a child's when it's time to flush the goldfish. Only Thetis was stubborn, or stupid, enough actually to marry one of the poor creatures. Even she lost interest pretty quickly, after a taste of daily life with Peleus: repetition, farts, a monotonous diet of plant and animal products. Childbirth with a fumbling mortal midwife instead of Lethe.

She drifted back to heaven soon enough. But she kept returning to meddle in her descendants' lives. Not because she was a slow learner, but because she was a slow forgetter: she couldn't put the pathetic little mortals out of mind and go on to the next divine amusement.

Scyros was too small; Achilles had been too easily discovered. This time she would hide the kid in the big city, and they'd never find him.

As happens in these cases, Pyrrhus immediately forgot the visit from his grandmother. If it even occurred, if it wasn't just that a mischievous servant had slipped him a cup or two of champagne punch. He was left only with a voice inside, as if the words had come from within him, promising that the city would open its arms to him just as he was. Even this voice faded as he discovered the homely pleasures of Scyros. It is not for nothing that our poets sing about shepherds and their staves. Pyrrhus sojourned with them so often that his grandfather once swore he could smell the boy before he came into a room.

This pastoral interlude ended abruptly on Pyrrhus's twenty-first birthday. Much was made of the event. Mother insisted on a big party, and she invited all the people she thought ought to be Pyrrhus's friends, the children of the local gentry. Of course none of them were his friends; his real friends were off tending sheep or tending one another. No, that wasn't exactly right: they weren't Pyrrhus's friends any more, either. He had thoughtlessly run through every available man and boy on the island—he hadn't meant to, he wasn't totting up conquests, and it had taken a few years. But it was a small island; there were only so many guys who wanted to play, even counting the priests.

So on the night of his majority Pyrrhus was suddenly feeling, in place of his occasional inexplicable bubble of not-this, a more general and rational sense that maybe he'd about exhausted Scyros. On top of that, he noticed that Mother's "Why won't you dance with that nice Nephele?" had taken on a new insistence. It wasn't any more the casual "Stop moping around, what will people think?" followed by "Oh, there's Pelopia, I must talk to her," and instant relief for both parties. Instead, she was right at Pyrrhus's elbow, all evening long. At last pulling him aside and declaring, softly but ominously: "You will have to dance with someone. You're a man now."

Pyrrhus feigned illness and went to bed. The shrimp mousse was under suspicion, but no one could be sure, so its maker escaped punishment—a disappointment to Lycomedes, who rather enjoyed dispensing justice, perhaps because he was less and less able to dispense anything much to his several consorts. In the morning, Pyrrhus crept out with just a duffel bag and the surprisingly large amount of money Mother kept in her purse. What did she do with it all, when she would proffer a credit card for anything more costly than a cup of coffee? Such an innocent country boy; he couldn't imagine that his mother's gentleman friends sometimes enjoyed small gifts of cash.

No matter: he had the money, and he was aboard the ferry so early that even most of the servants were still asleep. He resolved not to look back, went straight to the bow. But there was nothing ahead; he couldn't see anything.

After a minute or two he ambled back to the stern and looked at Scyros, which receded so gradually it seemed as though the ferry were hardly moving. The village, the palace at the top of the hill, the woods beyond it, the mountain. All looking like the postcards the tourists bought during the standard five-hour stopover of the cruise ships: shopping, lunch, tour of the public rooms of the palace for those spry enough to manage the hill.

The vista as flat and unreal as one of those postcards. Everything to which Pyrrhus had at last said not-this. Getting smaller by the minute as

27

he headed into the unknown this-instead. Of course he was a little scared. He *had*, after all, been Scyros, and now he was nobody at all. Even the crew on the ferry, who must have stopped at Scyros a thousand times, had no idea who he was, hardly noticed him. Except one sailor who winked as he walked by.

Pyrrhus turned, his back to Scyros now; the sailor looked back over his shoulder and grinned. Pyrrhus grinned, too, so wide his face practically split open; his heart got bigger and seemed to squash the bubble forever. The whole world was before him and he was nobody in particular.

All as Thetis had promised. He was swept up by the city the instant he stepped off the ferry. He never even got out of the terminal: he checked his duffel bag and stopped for just a minute in the bar, to have a soda before venturing forth. There he was greeted so vociferously it was as if the patrons knew a near-divinity had arrived. Numerous well-dressed gentlemen wanted to buy him cocktails, and more than one was gracious enough to offer him a domicile for the night.

Just as easily there had come to him a job, an apartment. Even if he couldn't make the rent just now, things would work themselves out. The future held no dangers, only scary mirages that dissipated into mist if you stepped forward to take them on. Pyrrhus stepped forward and kept his eyes focused on a spot not one minute ahead. Surely not the months that would elapse before the landlord could actually do anything. It would work out.

Perhaps it had not taken Thetis to impart this to him; perhaps he had even dreamt Thetis as the incarnation of his central sense of unrecognized entitlement. Actually, I'm not sure *entitlement* is the right word. Or maybe it is, but I'm not sure I can see the difference between entitlement and utter helplessness. You give yourself up to the Fates either way; either way you get what you don't deserve.

3

The matter of the rent, and similar clashes in a dozen other households, were side manifestations of a central calamity: Café Leo was dying. Maybe Pyrrhus should have been able to figure this out from his own surprisingly rapid ascent from untutored busboy to senior night waiter—everyone who'd been there when he'd arrived was gone.

Restaurants are like people: they don't decline in a straight line, from opening night to the day they hang up the *Closed Temporarily for Renovations* sign. They hum along until middle age, then sink gradually, then—it can happen in a single night—they plummet, go into multiple system failure. Things can be kind of slow for a while, lousy weeknights but an okay lunch crowd and a pretty full house on Fridays and Saturdays, almost enough to make up for the rest. Until there comes one evening when a couple walks through the door, looks at the wide choice of tables available to them, and turns around—figuring the rest of the world knows something they don't. From there, the death spiral.

Pyrrhus had scarcely even been in a restaurant, back on Scyros. How was he to know the signs? He didn't understand what was going on until he came in a little early, one evening a night or two after his skirmish with Leucon, and found Leo pouring cheap vodka into the premium bottle.

Leo had to have been the oldest queen Pyrrhus had ever encountered. His face was hatched with countless tiny lines, almost as if he had scales; from its midst peered tiny reptilian eyes that gleamed with an eerie glassiness. By now Pyrrhus had learned that these were just cornea implants. But they still looked to him like the eyes of a doll. Leo was like a doll, or—what with all the lines—like one of those stuffed baby crocodiles, dressed in human clothes and with little glass beads for eyes, people used to bring home as souvenirs from vacations on the Nile.

He looked up at Pyrrhus with no expression, as if daring him to say something. Pyrrhus wasn't going to, but then he couldn't help asking: "Can't they tell?"

"No. Vodka especially—little smart-asses order these fancy names, but it's all just vodka. By the time they mix it with three fruit juices it might as well be grain alcohol."

"Have you . . . have we always done this?" The question softened, Pyrrhus hoped, by the solidarity of the *we.*

Leo was indignant. "Of course I haven't always done this. I used to have some principles."

"Oh."

"I wonder why," Leo said. "I mean, how about, 'Let the buyer beware?' That's a principle. And how do I know the importers aren't filling their own bottles with the cheap stuff?" He put the ersatz import back on the premium shelf and hid the gallon jug. "You know, you just go on doing things automatically the way you're supposed to, until there's some extremity."

"Is there some extremity?"

"We're going down the proverbial tube."

"We are?"

"My child, for you they could have invented the word *hick.* I'll bet you're even going to be surprised when you don't get a paycheck this week."

"That is a surprise."

"Well, I could write one if you promise not to try to cash it."

"You're not paying anybody?"

"Kitchen help, that's it. Don't be hurt. But you know, they walk, it's over. You go, I can always wait tables myself."

"I guess."

Leo put a hand on Pyrrhus's shoulder. "You know how, when it snows, they have these announcements, 'Nonessential personnel need not report'?"

"That's me, huh?"

"This is not to say, mind you, that you're not ornamental. But you'll notice I don't have fresh flowers any more, either."

Pyrrhus sat at the bar. "I guess I didn't know how bad things were."

"Let me tell you how bad things are. I pay the suppliers COD. I mean, I want a chicken, I got to have the cash, and the guy hands me the precious bird with one hand and takes my bill with the other."

"Oh."

"Plus I let them cut off the phone."

"I thought it hadn't rung in a while."

"No, in the supremely unlikely event that someone should wish to reserve a hot table, they will be greeted by a that-number-is-not-in-service. As will my creditors."

"I guess I should go."

"What's your hurry? Have some vodka with me — tomorrow you can look for work."

"I only like the imported stuff."

"Ha! As if you could tell."

Phylas, the other waiter, came in the front door, nominally late. He was puffing from his hurry getting there. He stood for a minute at the front of the dining room, looking perplexed. The restaurant was empty, of course, not underpopulated but literally empty at almost seven.

He'd only started on Friday, when there'd been a few customers. Now he must have been wondering if he'd made some mistake, if the place was closed that night. He peered back and saw Leo and Pyrrhus in the gloom of the bar.

Pyrrhus murmured to Leo, "Why did you hire a new guy, the way things are?"

"I thought you needed company. Like you never buy one goldfish."

"Thanks. He's going to be a little surprised when you don't pay him."

"Ah, that one's so fresh he's surprised when the sun comes up."

Phylas joined them at the bar. "Where is everybody?"

"Lost," Leo said. "Everybody was coming but they got lost. They thought we were on East Orchard when we're on West Orchard."

"Oh. Slow night, huh?"

"Friday was a slow night. This is a night in full arrest."

"Well, it's cold, maybe people don't want to come out."

"Maybe so."

"Funny, it's almost hot in here. You should turn it down, maybe."

"I'm splurging," Leo said. "The electric company's giving the stuff away."

"They are?"

"They don't know it yet, but they are."

After Phylas, the front door opened twice that evening. The first time was just someone peeking in. The second set of intruders might have slipped away, too, after one look. But Leo was on them with astonishing speed. "Good evening, good evening. Table for two?" He sat them at the table nearest the window, as bait. Pyrrhus's station, as it happened. He might make a few bucks.

It was a couple of middle-aged men, with cowboy hats they positioned precisely at the two vacant places on their four-top. No, they didn't want drinks; they might look at the wine list later. Pyrrhus nodded at this laughable concept, handed them the menus, and discreetly retreated. The menus were handwritten by Leo, that day. They offered a selection of various things Leo had found in the freezer, plus a variety of possible destinies for the chicken Leo had ransomed that afternoon.

After a minute the larger of the buckaroos called Pyrrhus over. "Is this the whole menu?" he said. "Or just the specials?"

"That's it tonight," Pyrrhus said. Then, improvising, "We have a lighter menu during the week."

"This menu could practically float away. I guess I'll just have the stuffed flounder. What about you, Perdix?"

"Oh, the same, I guess," Perdix said. "Are you sure you don't have the surf 'n' turf? I used to get the surf 'n' turf here."

"Not tonight, I'm very sorry."

Pyrrhus reported their order to Leo, and he said, "Oh, shit, I should have told you. I've just got one portion of that."

"Oh, no."

"It was in the freezer. Took me twenty minutes just to figure out what it was. I think it might have been in the freezer when I bought this place."

Pyrrhus relayed the news to the cowboys. They looked at each other mournfully, then picked up their ten-gallon hats and stalked out.

After that, everyone just sat at the bar. Phylas and Pyrrhus drank their imported vodka with cranberry juice. Leo had plain seltzer and looked out at his desert dominion. The tablecloths and the napkin blossoms Leo himself had once folded so fussily had given way to paper placemats and napkins. This mightn't have been so bad if there had been, underneath them, actual tables instead of squares of fiberboard bolted to metal stands.

Leo spoke:

"I used to run a bar, you know. We had burgers and stuff, little check-ered tablecloths, but it was a bar mainly. I had a rule, the day we opened I told the staff, 'Anybody comes in here you treat 'em good.' All different colors, dark or light or whatever, at least five distinct genders, everybody was welcome. Nobody ever had that idea. God, this was so long ago, Egyptians had to go to their own places, gay people had their dives run by gangsters, nobody ever said, 'Hey, here we are in the daylight and everybody in the world can sit down and have a beer.' And, you know, the whole world came. We were jumping. Piano player in the corner, people singing, just every kind of person side by side and nobody hassling anybody. People still talk about the old Leo's. I'll tell you something, I was cleaning up. Like in the old joke, doing well by doing good.

"Nights off I'd go to a restaurant. It's funny, people in the food business do that—as if a surgeon would spend his day off watching an appendectomy. We do, though; everybody I know does. I'd sit there, thinking, You know, they ought to have this on the menu, or The walls would look better in kind of a peach, or This waiter, if he worked for me I'd fire the little bastard. If I just had a real restaurant I'd show them how things should run.

"Meanwhile my bar went gay. I mean, like I said, we always had all kinds of people, but the balance kind of tilted, I don't know why. Oh, I do know—it was like mayonnaise separating. But it wasn't what I'd hoped. One day the cops came. I don't mean raided me, just came in and looked around at my customers and gave me a look, like, What have we here? I could see the whole future of the place right then. The little payoffs every week, the big ones when the license came up. This was a long time ago— you ran a gay bar you had no end of silent partners. I sold out, to this guy named Archias. You know the Escapade?"

"You mean where the strippers are?" Pyrrhus said.

"That was the place."

Phylas asked, "Did you have strippers?"

Leo said, "I don't think you've followed this story. Anyway, I took the money and opened my real restaurant. You should have been here when we started. You don't know what it's like, opening a new place—it's like you composed an opera or something. You know, you write your own menu, and you decide where the tables are gonna go and what's going to go on them, what the waiters should wear, all that stuff, and it's like putting on a show. A work of art, and you've made it all happen out of your head. Finally the sign painter comes and puts up a sign with your name on it: Café Leo. Like you own this little patch of the world, you thought up everything in it, and it works just the way you always wanted it to.

"You know, you start out, the customers are your guests, you want them to be happy. Twenty years I ran this place, did okay. The world changed around it, maybe. The portions were too big, I didn't add all the trendy dishes when they came out. I kept dishing out the cholesterol and killed off my regulars. One day it just turned: I looked out at the room, at the people, and they were my enemy. I knew they came in by mistake and they were never going to be back and I wanted to give them as little as I could. I should have closed it that day, said, So, it was good while it lasted. I always wanted to run a nice restaurant and I did for a while, on to the next thing. Except at my age there is no next thing. This is my last adventure, nothing left now but soap operas and pills and doctor visits, maybe in the evening going to sit with my seltzer in someone else's bar."

"You mean it's over?" Pyrrhus said. "This is it?"

Leo looked at him as if he were crazy. "Tomorrow's Friday, we always do better Friday."

He looked out again over the empty room. "Boys, why don't you go home," he said. "I get a sudden rush, I'll deal with it."

After a couple of vodkas and that cheery story, Pyrrhus wasn't in any hurry to go back to the apartment. He thought he'd go over to the Lighthouse. Phylas said he would, too, but then his lover called just as they were on the way out and nagged him into going home. Maybe that's what Pyrrhus should have done. Except Leucon was probably still up, and Pyrrhus wasn't a penny closer to making the rent than he'd been that afternoon when he left for work. Anyway, he was in kind of a party mood. Well, not exactly, but jazzed up somehow. He wanted something to happen.

The guy at the door collected the cover—weeknight, three bucks, and with that you got a drink ticket. A relative bargain. But three bucks farther from the rent.

It was Thursday, usually a big night, but only ten o'clock. All the other waiters in town were still at work, and the civilians were home napping, wouldn't be there till eleven or so. The place was all but empty, a few of the hard core at the side bar, just one couple on the dance floor.

Pyrrhus got another vodka and cranberry, though he was feeling the ones from Leo's and his party mood was already fading. The bartender looked affronted as he took the little orange drink ticket. Pyrrhus ostentatiously left a quarter on the bar, in a puddle. He wasn't one of those waiters who displayed their collegiality by overtipping. Anyway, he couldn't; a quarter was more than he had made that evening.

The regulars at the bar gave him the merest glance and, mostly, turned away. Back to their routine of courting the professionally flirtatious bartender. Pyrrhus wasn't a new face any more. Just a few weeks in town, and they had all made up their minds about him: he was too hot, and knew it, thought he was some kind of god, not worth wasting time or pride on. One or two made a point of glowering at him, as if he had come just to torment them.

It is hard to summon up much compassion for the travails of the beautiful. Who could care if he felt cut off by people's expectations about him, as surely as if he lived in a plastic bubble? He would burst the bubble later; when he felt like it he would walk over and just pick out anybody he wanted, if there was anybody he wanted. For the moment, though, he was truly at a loss, could not find a way of standing, or of composing his face, that was neither off-putting nor excessively encouraging. He could only glower back at them, when he really wanted to make friends. No friends, in his weeks in town, unless he counted tiresome Leucon.

He moved away and leaned on the wall under the DJ's booth, looking out at the dance floor. When the Lighthouse was crowded, you saw people, nothing else. Tonight he could see the place itself, the peeling walls and naked pipes, the sordid carpeting around the edges and the scuffed wood on the dance floor, which seemed even tinier, all but unpopulated, than when it was full.

The two guys on the floor were doing elaborate ballroom dance routines, a fad that had come and gone a couple of years earlier. One looked grim; the other had the fixed smile of a Miss Cosmos contestant. They whirled around on the empty floor, their swooping curves turned angular by the strobe lights. Pyrrhus wondered if they had just been doing this same dance every night, back when it was popular and ever since. They had learned the steps so well, possibly had never in their lives mastered anything else, how could they stop doing it? Get a life, Pyrrhus thought, automatically. But he began to think, as he went on watching, nothing else in the place to watch: They have a life. Their intricate steps, endlessly repeated, were just like life. Scraping up the rent month after interminable month, finding some other waiting job, table after table, Hi-my-name's-Pyrrhus, then trick after trick until he had used up the last man in the world.

The last man—or at least the last Pyrrhus would ever think of tricking with—now interposed himself between Pyrrhus and the tableau of mindless perseverance on the dance floor. The guy had to be fifty, dressed in a suit but with a dusting of gray stubble on his face and whiskey on his breath; Pyrrhus could smell it even before he got close. He got very close, right in Pyrrhus's face, and said, "Hi there."

Pyrrhus felt like just running, but he didn't want to hurt the guy's feelings, not immediately. He said "Hi."

"My name's Lamus. What's yours?"

"Pyrrhus."

Lamus stuck out his hand, and Pyrrhus shook it without looking at him. He said, in a voice so low Pyrrhus could scarcely hear it, so it seemed more a confidence than a proposition: "I really want to suck you."

Too bad: Pyrrhus would have to hurt his feelings immediately. "No, thanks."

"Listen, I'll give you fifty bucks."

"What?"

Still in a soft, urgent voice: "Come on, you'd like it."

Mingled with Pyrrhus's indignation—What do you think I am?—was a vagrant little thought that, yeah, he might like it. Instead of waiting around half the night for someone passable, just go off somewhere with this guy and close his eyes, one way, nothing more expected. And fifty bucks.

"No way," Pyrrhus said. Without conviction: even as he said it he realized that the voice inside that was supposed to be telling him how degrading and immoral it would be was silent. Somehow he had made it to twenty-one without anyone making such an offer before. So he had never known before that his repertory of scruples had this gap in it. As if he were just missing the brain cell that was supposed to store the basic precept: Never peddle your body for fifty bucks. It was almost more interesting than the proposal itself, learning this.

"I suck real good," the guy said, as if that were the issue. And he probably did.

Pyrrhus couldn't think what was wrong with it. If he had been honestly desperate for the money, that very fact might have drawn him up short. He might have seen the moment as the starting point of some perilous downward journey. But he didn't really need the money; he could always have gone home to Scyros and lived like a prince. Well, no, he couldn't do that, because he had undertaken the adventure of leaving Scyros. All right: this was part of the adventure, wasn't it? An opportunity waiting to be seized, as one would take the treasure guarded by the monster encountered on the roadside. Lamus surely qualified for the monster part, except that he wasn't guarding the treasure; he was practically begging to give it away.

Part of the adventure. More, its very essence. What was an adventurer supposed to do—take a bunch of tests and land a job at the post office? No, he was supposed to make his way with what he had, his wits and now, suddenly, his body; he could use his body. It wasn't wrong, it was triumphantly right. For how, really, was it any different from what his father did? Using his body, except that Daddy made his way by slaughter in fields slippery with blood? While Pyrrhus was going to lie back in this man's warm apartment and get a blow job.

"Where do you live?" Pyrrhus said.

"Over near—" Then Lamus understood that the question was an answer. He almost stammered, "No, we can't go there. I'm—maybe we can just go to that hotel down the street. You know, what is it? The Palace."

Pyrrhus had passed the Palace once or twice. Whatever royalty it housed reigned over lesser branches of the animal kingdom. Fifty bucks was one thing, fleas another. He had an inspiration. "What's that cost, about twenty?"

"I guess."

"Why don't you give me the twenty, too, and we'll go back to my place?"

"Great, let's go." The hugeness of the guy's smile told Pyrrhus right away that he'd made a mistake. Of course: at the Palace he could just have walked away, possibly scratching, when they were through. Now he'd have to get the guy to leave; what would keep him from staying the night? What if he just passed out? Well, Pyrrhus would deal with that. Twenty extra bucks, Pyrrhus could sleep on the living-room couch if he had to.

"I'll meet you outside," Pyrrhus said.

The guy looked around the room. "What's the matter? You got a . . . boyfriend here or something?"

Of course Pyrrhus couldn't say that he didn't want to be seen leaving with a monster. "I've just got to talk to somebody for a minute. I'll be out in one minute."

"Don't be long. It's cold out there."

Pyrrhus watched him go. Lamus stopped to have his hand stamped, so he could get back in if Pyrrhus took too long.

Pyrrhus finished his drink, set it down on a table, and zipped up his jacket, ready to head out for his adventure, when he remembered Leucon. Shit, past ten o'clock, Leucon had to be home. Pyrrhus was going to bring this creature home and Leucon was going to see.

The brave adventurer, ready to stun the bourgeois, stick it in the face of his mother and grandfather and everybody in the world except his own queer roommate—and the grim chorus at the bar, people he didn't even know but whose opinion mattered so much he'd sent the poor guy out to wait in the cold before he'd take his money. A scruple after all. Not about taking the money, just about being seen leaving with someone so inappropriate. In place of ethics he had an aesthetic. It was unseemly to be witnessed with Lamus.

He almost didn't go. No, that isn't right: nothing almost happens. The fingers of Nemesis do not slip from the wheel. Say rather that, before he did what he was bound to do, he tried to think about it. Balance weightless eidolons like shame against the solid truths of cash and a guy who sucked real good, if he said so himself. Before he could work it out, Lamus was already back inside, looking around for Pyrrhus. If Pyrrhus didn't hustle on out with him he might make a scene. Pyrrhus hurried to the door. And still, in that little mental disputation of his, not a single speech about right or wrong, or how we should live, no voice anywhere in him to utter that speech.

In the car, Lamus sat bolt upright and kept his hands on the wheel, ten before two. He didn't look at Pyrrhus, just glanced over once or twice when he needed directions. His bravado had evaporated; he looked as though he were already sorry for what he had done. Pyrrhus knew—didn't calculate, this was just instinctive, suggesting that he was better suited for this adventure than he would have imagined—he knew that Lamus shouldn't feel sorry, not for one instant, until after Pyrrhus had his seventy bucks.

Pyrrhus thought: Should I touch him? Take one of Lamus's hands off the wheel and hold it, or grasp his knee? Maybe not; he seemed kind of like the director of the temple choir back on Scyros—that public convenience frequented not just by Pyrrhus but even by the butchest boys on the island. Who could visit him without fear of comment because he actually recoiled from any hint of reciprocation, wanted you just to stand and be sucked and not even look at him. Maybe Lamus was like that, and Pyrrhus should just keep his hands to himself.

No: the choir director wouldn't have gone hunting in the Lighthouse, amid the boys who danced under the strobe lights. Besides, there was something a little scary about the idea of just standing there and looking away and letting someone take your cock. As if he might actually take it from you, or steal something less definite, if you didn't keep your eyes on him.

"So, um . . . Lamus," Pyrrhus said. "You ever done this before?"

"What?"

"You seem kind of nervous."

"No. I mean, of course I've done this." He swallowed. "Not very much."

38

"It's no big deal, you know? We'll have fun."

Lamus looked at him with puzzlement or even consternation, as if fun hadn't been on his agenda. "I'm married," he blurted out.

"You said." Or he'd almost said.

"I did? I only . . . this only happens once in a long time."

Which explained his elegant come-on in the Lighthouse. And also why it wasn't fun: this was something he was doing against his better instincts, something that erupted every once in a while over a lifetime of trying to keep it in. It was no more fun than when, after a night of the whirlies, trying to make the room settle down, you finally stagger to the john and vomit: then you can wash your face with cold water and feel weak but clean, resolve never to get that blitzed again, then sleep.

Pyrrhus wanted to touch Lamus's knee and he did. Not just because it was good business, but because Pyrrhus was there in the moment and he needed to dissolve the sorrow that was hanging over them both, and the anger he suddenly felt radiating over from Lamus. Anger at himself, maybe: Why have I done this again? Or at Pyrrhus: You think you're worth seventy bucks. Someday you won't be worth shit—right now you aren't worth shit and I have seventy bucks.

Pyrrhus touched his knee, and he did recoil a little, maybe just from surprise. But Pyrrhus grasped the unexpectedly firm muscle of his thigh and he slowly relaxed. Pyrrhus closed his eyes, did not look at Lamus. He found that, without any of the visual cues that attract or repel, he was actually excited by the very feel of Lamus's thigh. As if, with his eyes closed, the other senses took over and he became simply flesh that longed for flesh. The unbidden warmth in his groin as he began to stroke Lamus's leg affirmed it. Then what is it we hunt for, half our lifetimes, with our eyes foolishly open? When the gods so mercifully furnished us with lids.

He felt the strangest mixture of arousal and detachment. As if his body were setting forth on a mission and he were just tagging along after it. As if he had left Pyrrhus behind at the Lighthouse, watching the dancers. He was a little alarmed at first, but then he settled into the new sensation. For a night he just wouldn't be Pyrrhus at all. In the morning he'd be a richer Pyrrhus.

They had got all the way to the apartment and Pyrrhus hadn't thought of what to say to Leucon. He waited until they were out of the car and heading for the front door before he said, "Listen, I got a roommate."

"Oh, Lord."

"He might be in bed already, he won't bother us."

"I don't want to run into anybody."

Pyrrhus thought, You were just in the Lighthouse and you're afraid to be seen by my roommate? Well, so was Pyrrhus, after all. "I'll make sure he gets out of the way," Pyrrhus said, though he didn't see how he was going to do that.

"I . . ." Lamus was shaking his head. But he had got this far, his wanting was up in his throat so he could hardly swallow; when would he ever work up the nerve to get this far again? "Okay, I'll wait down here."

No way, Pyrrhus thought: he would drive off while Pyrrhus negotiated with Leucon. "No, come upstairs, it'll only take a minute."

Pyrrhus was loping up the stairs, trying to think what he could possibly say to Leucon that would explain why he not only had to make himself scarce, but also couldn't have so much as a glimpse of Pyrrhus's companion. Pyrrhus was a whole flight ahead before he realized Lamus had fallen behind. When he turned to look down he saw a red-faced old man puffing away and looking up at him — more with reproach at the number of stairs than with desire. If he ever got that old, Pyrrhus thought, he would have something better to do with himself.

He made Lamus wait half a flight down, opened the door, and at once heard Leucon's snoring. Leucon was passed out, fully dressed — on his own bed, thank goodness, instead of on the couch in the living room. Pyrrhus closed Leucon's door and led Lamus into the apartment.

Lamus sat down right away. He was gasping, one hand to his chest, his face damp. Shit, what if he had a heart attack right there? But Lamus recovered soon enough. "You got anything to drink?"

"Shh." Pyrrhus whispered: "I can check, there might be a beer." Pyrrhus went through his bedroom to the kitchen, opened the refrigerator. Nothing. He turned around to find Lamus already in the bedroom. Pyrrhus was more than just startled: he felt an instant of near terror. What had he let into the place? The worry passed; Lamus didn't seem especially crazy or dangerous. More like a scared kid, hands thrust in his pockets, waiting for some instruction. Pyrrhus smiled with a little satisfaction at the thought that, if he had let something crazy and dangerous into the place, it was his own body. Which seemed now to be closing the bedroom door without Pyrrhus's intervention.

What would they do now? Lamus was still just standing there. Pyrrhus got onto the bed, fully dressed, and lay back, knees up, legs spread a little. Lamus stood another second and then was on him, fingers worrying at his belt.

40

Leucon had been out with a couple of guys from the office. Straight boys, but funny, and good-natured about Leucon's little quirk. You could be friends with straight people, he thought, the way you could be friends with other species, dogs or cats. They had uncountable pitchers of beer, and Leucon completely forgot to eat and went straight home to bed. Around eleven-thirty he woke up with that little pressure square in the middle of the forehead that says, You drank and didn't eat and in the morning you will be punished. He got up to take some aspirin and see if maybe the half a cheesesteak sub from two nights ago was still around, unless Pyrrhus had got hold of it.

Pyrrhus's door was shut, and Leucon could hear him talking softly to somebody. He'd brought home a trick. Well, he had a right to; Leucon had brought people home. More than Pyrrhus had, really, for some reason. Probably no one was good enough for him. Anyway, it wasn't his fault Leucon couldn't get to the kitchen. Who would expect Leucon would need to at that hour? So why was Leucon getting angry, his headache already starting? Because he could picture them, of course, Pyrrhus and . . . someone good enough for him, someone equally unattainable. One of those gorgeous and impenetrable couples who live on a different plane from the rest of us; when Leucon saw such a pair walk down the street together, he felt both envy and a curious contentment, that such perfection should exist.

He sat in the living room and turned on the TV with the volume as low as he could get it and still hear. There was some standup comic telling hate jokes in a nondiscriminatory fashion, everybody got theirs, but especially queers and women. Leucon felt righteously uneasy, laughing at that stuff. But the guy was funny; pussy farts and limp wrists might be funny in a world that could stop at laughter.

Lamus bit. Not painfully, but at every stroke his incisors lightly scraped, in the way Pyrrhus would come to associate with neophytes. He didn't allow it, after that first time. This one night, though, he lay back with his eyes closed and tried to focus, past the abrasive feeling, on the underlying pleasure.

When he opened his eyes Lamus was looking up at him. Lamus's expression was, as a practical matter, inscrutable: a face whose lower

41

half is fully occupied cannot provide a rich display of emotions. Perhaps Pyrrhus knew he was just reading things into those staring eyes. His first reading was crude and self-centered: He is worshiping me, I really am divine, he is scarcely fit to grovel at my crotch. This was exciting enough, in its simple way. While of course this wasn't the first time he'd had his cock sucked, it was almost alarmingly gratifying to have the act stripped down to its basic dynamic, without the distracting baggage of reciprocity.

As he went on looking into Lamus's unfathomable eyes, he was suddenly granted a vision of what Lamus must actually have been thinking, to wit: I am already bored with this, how could I have forgotten, I can hardly breathe, how could I have forgotten from the last time, this isn't what I wanted at all. Not the gateway to the ineffable. He hated Pyrrhus, hated what he was doing; he wanted to stop.

Pyrrhus clutched his grizzled head and began fucking his face, indolently thrilled at his resistance, at last coming when he saw the trace of a tear at the corner of Lamus's eye.

When Lamus pulled away, Pyrrhus lay back and closed his eyes. Ready to doze but fighting it off, trying to focus — with almost clinical disinterest — on the feeling he had had in the last seconds before he came. The sudden impulse to hurt and degrade that seemed to have come from nowhere — literally nowhere, down in that newly discovered void where he had found no barrier, no inhibition to prevent this transaction.

Lamus said, "What's the matter with you?"

"Huh? Nothing, I'm just . . . you know, worn out."

"I mean with your dick. Why is it . . . ?"

Pyrrhus looked down. He had taken a battering; in the morning it would be black and blue. "Shit," he said.

"I didn't do that," Lamus said.

"You must have." It looked terrible, shrunken and swollen at the same time.

"I — somebody else did that." As if he were talking, not about Pyrrhus's injury, but about everything that had gone on.

"You stupid sonofabitch, just pay me and get the fuck out of here." Pyrrhus was just tired, and a little scared about what Lamus had done to him, but it must have sounded threatening. Lamus stood up — he had never even undone his trousers, he had gotten nothing out of this — fished hurriedly through his wallet, and, near panic, dropped a few bills on the bed and scurried away. Pyrrhus could hear him fumbling at the lock. But

42

by the time Pyrrhus got his pants pulled up Lamus had apparently found his way out.

Pyrrhus picked the bills up off the cover. The poor clown had left him three hundred. It was wonderful, such a gift; he might have been an emissary from the gods.

He got up to lock the door behind Lamus, and there in the living room was Leucon. Lamus hadn't found his way out: Leucon had undone the lock for him. Leucon had seen him. In place of a scruple Pyrrhus had at least a moment's mortification.

Pyrrhus's door opened. Leucon felt like running and hiding in his room. But he had a right to stay up and watch TV in his own apartment. More his than Pyrrhus's, given Pyrrhus's nonchalance about the rent. He stayed put, but kept his eyes on the screen.

He couldn't keep them there. What stepped — tore — out of Pyrrhus's room was a man who had to be fifty or something, wild-eyed with alarm. The guy fiddled with growing desperation at the front lock until finally Leucon got up to let him out. He evidently hadn't noticed Leucon: as Leucon approached he turned and looked absolutely terrified. The man backed away from the door. Leucon opened it and he zoomed through it like a dog who has to go. Then Pyrrhus appeared, buttoning his fly.

Leucon didn't think right away: He's doing this for money. If he had seen a pair like Pyrrhus and Lamus on the street he would just have assumed that money was somehow involved. But his initial feeling wasn't, Hey, I'm living with a whore and he's going to turn the damn apartment into a bordello. That would have been a practical issue: subject to negotiation, or rather to unfulfilled ultimatums, as with the rent. As a matter of fact they would, once Leucon had grasped the situation, work out a few ground rules.

Instead Leucon's very first thought was that Pyrrhus was some sort of deranged saint. He could have had anyone and he was giving himself to the likes of that. Or maybe he didn't own himself at all, he wasn't giving but was merely taken, picked up as easily as a pebble. Which opened up possibilities Leucon had given up thinking about.

Pyrrhus closed the front door, then turned around and looked straight at Leucon, daring him to say something. Leucon said, "I need to get in the kitchen for a minute."

"That's okay, I'm wide awake."

43

Leucon went through the bedroom—they hadn't even messed up the sheets—to the kitchen and opened up the refrigerator. His half a cheese-steak was gone.

Pyrrhus must have known what he was after; there was nothing else in the refrigerator but some dead soda and a jar of mustard. Pyrrhus called out from the living room, "Hey, I'm real sorry, I had that this afternoon. It was the middle of my favorite soap, and I was just starving. Why don't we . . . I could call out for pizza or something."

Leucon said, trying not to voice his irritation, but slowly enough so Pyrrhus wouldn't miss his meaning, "Things are a little tight. I haven't been able to pay the rent yet."

"Oh, yeah," Pyrrhus said. "I forgot, I got my half. And why don't I pay for the pizza? I mean, I owe you."

Leucon stared into the empty refrigerator and understood.

4

Sometimes, if you wake up in a strange place—a hotel room, some trick's apartment, even on your own living-room couch instead of your bed—your heart stops for a second. Not even a second; you remember faster than that where you are, why you're there, that you're not in danger. The remembering is, in its way, more unsettling than the instant of confusion that precedes it. It should take longer—if you were really at home anywhere, it should take more than a split second to recover yourself in a strange place.

Pyrrhus woke up in his own bed—on it, rather, lying naked on top of the sheets because the landlord had the heat so very high—and everything was fine, he was home where he should be, except he happened to glance down and descry that his cock was bruised and swollen. His heart stopped, then everything came back. There was the proof, purple and reproachful. Also: on the nightstand, forty bucks. He had given Leucon the rent, he had paid for the pizza, and he still had forty bucks.

Midas never felt so rich: the rent behind him, the next crisis weeks away, he could go out, he could buy a new shirt. The money was real, and what he had done to earn it was already behind him. As though it had happened to somebody else; there was no connection between wealthy Pyrrhus and the distant body that had transgressed the night before.

No connection except the outraged thing that was now under the sheets. Pyrrhus couldn't look at it any more just now, though it was . . . interesting to look at; even under the sheets he was still touching it, testing the tender spots. Finding after a minute that it loyally got hard, as a dog with a lame foot will still, limping, chase the ball or the stick, its tail wagging. Pyrrhus conducted one more, definitive diagnostic test and then went to take a shower.

In the hot water his cock stung a little, as if demanding that he think about what he had done. Okay: just as soon as Leucon left for work, and he was alone, then he really would sit down and see if there was anything to be learned from this episode. But Leucon woke up with a majestic, fully deserved hangover and called in sick; he would be there, intermittently moaning, all morning long. Pyrrhus got dressed, looking just one more time at his polychromatic souvenir, and went out for a walk.

It was one of those deceptive mid-November mornings, when the sun comes up so bright it hurts, and everyone is hurrying along to work, and you can be pulled along by the crowd for some time before you realize that it's fucking cold out. Pyrrhus scurried along with the commuters for a while, and of course you can't think very hard when you're scurrying. He slowed to a stroll, cold as it was, and now he really was going to concentrate.

All he thought was one sentence, over and over, interrupted by the occasional distraction of an interesting store window or a hunky passerby. His sentence became a cadence accompanying his steps, hayfoot/strawfoot: *It was just the one time, it was just the one time.* It had nothing to do with me.

The reader will recall the old joke: *Would you sleep with me for a million bucks?* Sure. *How about ten bucks?* What do you think I am, a whore? *We've established what you are, now we're haggling over price.* We've established what you are: the species may be divided between people who will do anything for money except fuck and people who will fuck for money; and Pyrrhus was in the latter class. The answer, *it was just the one time*, is in this scheme perfectly irrelevant. A parricide might as well argue to the Furies, "This was the first time I ever killed my father, I won't do it again."

Pyrrhus's grandfather Lycomedes believed that if, just once, he made a face when a dinner guest asked for a third helping, then he might as well be dead. For everyone would see that he was inhospitable, and there would just never be any making up for that. You are what you have done, Lycomedes would have said. Those bills on the bedcover may have got you through your little cash-flow problem, but they have marked you forever. We have seen you for what you really are.

Of course, Lycomedes' generation is all but gone. People now are prone to think that every day is a new one, that you can walk into some temple and pay for the sacrifice of some expiatory livestock and just start over, no matter how many bodies are strewn in your wake. And aren't they right? How could it be that the boy who had sold himself the night before, after one too many vodka-and-cranberries, was the true, unalterable Pyrrhus? That boy was already history, and the real Pyrrhus was the freshly showered youth who was driven now into a coffee shop to escape the cold.

He sat in a corner, with his coffee and cigarette as equipped for meditation as he would ever get, but the only thought that came to him was the same one he'd had outside. It was just the one time; the whole thing was just a funny little episode. No big deal. It had nothing to do with who he really was.

Even if—his little chant was already tasting false—even if he did it more than one time. It could all be temporary, a sort of excursion. Any day he could go home to Scyros and become a pampered child again; or he could stay right where he was and wait on tables. Not at Leo's; Café Leo was going down the tubes. A real job—one of the restaurants at Waterside Place, maybe, where they said a good-looking waiter could work the parties of female convention-goers and make the rent in two nights.

Or he could see, one more time, if a man would pay him just to lie there. This was what Thetis had promised, that the city would open its arms to him and reward him just for being himself. Except it wasn't himself; he would be himself some other time. That was a pretty good joke, really: they were going to pay for Pyrrhus and get nobody at all. Because, after all those years of not-this, surely it wasn't *this*. He would know *this* when he got to it.

That night, Friday, Pyrrhus worked at Leo's, and two shifts Saturday, a pretty good brunch for a change and swamped at dinner—not the god-I-have-so-many-tables-and-I-can't-remember-what-they-all-want kind of swamped, but the lots-of-queens-in-a-good-mood kind: keep the booze coming and I don't care if you feed me tomorrow. By Sunday evening, two shifts again, brunch and dinner, he practically had the rent for next month. Already, on the fifteenth, from honest labor. As if something were trying to tell him that he didn't have to be a whore. Something other than his cock, which had left the violet end of the spectrum and was heading toward yellow.

Monday he was off; he just sat around the house all day watching the soaps, and in the evening he went out with Leucon for a burger. Without the rent over their heads, they got along fine. Until the check came and Leucon wouldn't let him pick it up, insisted on paying half. As if Pyrrhus's money were dirty. Even though, by now, most of the comforting wad in his pocket was tips. There was scarcely anything left of the money dropped on the bed by a stranger in a hurry.

Tuesday night he was supposed to work again. He had pretty much forgotten about his little adventure; he was actually ironing his white shirt and thinking, Well, Tuesday, the run had to be over, a night of sitting at the bar and listening to Leo's stories. Earning nothing. As he ran the iron over the already fraying collar of his shirt—cheap piece of shit, he hadn't washed it but three times—he just couldn't help thinking about money. About how he could skip Leo's—Leo could handle his own tables on a dead night, he'd said so himself—and make a little. Not three hundred, that was a fluke, but fifty; maybe that was the going rate if Lamus said so. Or maybe Pyrrhus was worth more than that.

He caught himself. This was crazy; of course he was going to Café Leo. Except, maybe, just this one time he'd call in sick. Really, it was the practical thing to do, even fifty was fifty more than he was going to get at Leo's. He'd call in sick just this once. And no biting this time, he'd see to that, he was only just starting to look like normal.

He put on a white T-shirt and jeans and headed out around ten. To Club 23, that had to be the spot. He'd stumbled into it one time, after work—it was the only place on the list of gay bars in the weekly paper he hadn't been to—and he'd stumbled out again after about thirty seconds. It had a U-shaped bar of red linoleum, anchored at one end by a television showing sporting events and at the other by a jar of pickled eggs. Around the bar sat men of Lamus's age—wearing, say, a short-sleeved dress shirt, with a sleeveless undershirt visible underneath, and a rayon tie—some alone, and some in intense conversation with . . . a punk. That was the only word for the boys at Club 23; if you saw them it would come automatically to your lips in the way that you might say, "Look, a robin."

This night, assorted unclaimed punks lined the wall nearest the jukebox, each with one foot on the floor and the other on the wall, their bent legs as uniform as in a chorus line, each upraised thigh used as a sort of cocktail table on which was balanced a can of beer, usually empty. Occasionally an older man would get up from the bar and diffidently waddle toward one of the chorines. He might say something to his quarry, or he might just wordlessly point at the empty beer can; in either case the boy would presently accompany him back to the bar and accept a beer. There, Pyrrhus supposed—the blaring television covered everything—detailed negotiations would occur.

Pyrrhus could have slipped into the chorus line; he was already in uniform. But, while he was quite certain he would have stood out—as, on the commercials during the soaps, they showed you something white and then they showed you something *really* white—it would only have been in that way, as the superlative punk. Whoever first waddled toward him would claim him. Perhaps gloating at having found the one real bargain on the clearance shelf, but still quite sure that there was something scratched or dented about Pyrrhus, despite his apparent virtues. Else he wouldn't have been on the shelf, marked down.

He scanned the bar and settled on a man who looked a little more classy than the rest; for example, the guy had managed to tie his tie so that the wide end was longer than the narrow one. Pyrrhus sat next to him, ordered a premium vodka, paid for it with a hundred-dollar bill peeled from his wad of tips, took out a cigarette, and then turned and asked for a light. The guy must have felt that a god had swooped down on him, or at least a quarter of one. Of course he understood at once that a boy who paid for drinks with hundred-dollar bills would not himself be purchased with any lesser denomination.

The man didn't use his teeth. In fact, he courteously removed his upper plate. But after he had worked on Pyrrhus for a while he pulled back and gummed the disheartening message that now it was time for some reciprocal attention.

Pyrrhus was indignant, about to blurt out something about the man's incredible audacity. Except he suddenly realized, from the matter-of-fact way the guy had said it and the way, now, he was lowering his trousers and sitting on the edge of the iron hotel bed at the Palace, legs spread: this was the deal, he wasn't asking anything out of the ordinary. Pyrrhus had been misled; Lamus was an anachronism. The days when a hustler could get paid for sneering at the client and letting himself be blown were gone — if they ever existed, if hustlers hadn't always, once the door was closed, given fuller value than that. People weren't going to pay him to bring tears to their eyes.

Pyrrhus sank to his knees and did the very best job he could. Which must have been pretty good, because the guy tipped him another twenty on top of the hundred.

While Pyrrhus was working, just a couple of minutes was all it took, he was granted three important insights. The first was that, if the customer came and he didn't, he might be able to go back to the bar and find another customer. The second was that, if he concentrated very hard on breathing through his nose, it didn't matter very much what he had in his mouth. And the third was that — if he concentrated just as hard on being exactly where he was, shed his past and future, shame and disgust, and just let himself be where he was — he didn't even have to close his eyes.

He was there, every sense awakened, with his pants around his ankles and his bare knees on the cool, gritty linoleum floor, one hand clutching the stranger's almost hairless thigh, the other circling the base of his cock. Pyrrhus breathed in the scent of urine and sweat; Pyrrhus listened to the faint, constricted moans and the metallic sighs of the iron bed and the voices in the hallway; Pyrrhus opened his eyes and saw that, despite the guy's sagging white belly and gravid tits, his hipbones were elegant and hard; Pyrrhus lapped the first salt drops of clear syrup oozing from the guy's cock and ran a free hand now over the satiny skin taut across his hip. Pyrrhus could hear his own moans now, and held hard to the man's hip, because if the guy didn't finish soon Pyrrhus was going to touch himself and throw away his chance at a second customer.

The man finished; Pyrrhus swallowed; the man pulled up his pants and dropped the money on the bed — not in a hurry, but carefully counting out five twenties and then the gratifying sixth. He was gone before Pyrrhus could even get up off his knees. Pyrrhus could feel, almost hear, the guy's progress, down the stairs to the lobby, through the door. Pyrrhus even thought he could hear the footsteps on the street.

He rested a couple of minutes, then went down to the lobby himself. He was almost to the door when the desk clerk said, "Hey, the key."

Pyrrhus turned. "I was coming back."

The clerk smiled a little, the way a priest smiles, with just the lower half of his face. "I bet you was," he said. "The registered guest has checked out."

"Oh." Pyrrhus gave him the key.

As if Pyrrhus hadn't gotten the point, the clerk said, "You make any more friends tonight you can rent another room." With a larger and self-satisfied smile now, as if it had taken great mental prowess to deduce Pyrrhus's new vocation. No, as if he were the resident deity of the place, watching with bemused detachment the humping and fatuity of mortals.

Pyrrhus was in this place, being treated like filth by some loser who thought he knew something. The taste of some old fat man's semen coating the roof of Pyrrhus's mouth. His money lining Pyrrhus's pocket. "Okay," Pyrrhus said, smiling back at the clerk, loving the dirty feeling. "I'll see you later." He would; it wasn't even midnight yet.

One night a month or so later, Leucon was out barhopping with a friend named Gelanor. Barely a friend; someone he'd met once in a bar, hadn't tricked with, ran into again a few times. As this night, coupled by unspoken

50

agreement, reciprocal crutches for a few hours, while they searched for their respective Messrs. Right. It was still early, and they weren't looking very hard, just having one beer per bar, surveying the menagerie, moving on. Leucon had especially urgent carnal intentions, which would require him to cut Gelanor loose sooner or later. But it was fun to pretend for a little while that cruising wasn't the most important thing in the world. Though of course it was. Making it with someone was serious business, your whole being on the line every time. Each night's hunt like one of the numberless tests posed for the heroes in the old stories.

Gelanor talked funny.

"Oh, look," Leucon would say. "I think this is the hottest guy."

"That?" Gelanor would answer. "I've done it." Even back then, this way of speaking was archaic, roughly equivalent to men calling each other *sister*. "Hung for days," Gelanor would go on, "a veritable banquet. I was just about to partake of the feast when I discovered that she had sprayed breath freshener on her cock. Can you imagine? Heaven knows what other flavor treats awaited me. But I was obliged to take my leave."

Leucon hoped no one could hear him. To revive this self-lacerating camp in a modern, liberated bar seemed deeply reactionary, almost seditious. Yet there was also something titillating about it, as if Gelanor were speaking from some farther shore of self-acknowledgment and freedom.

It seemed as though anyone Leucon could point out was a *number* Gelanor had *done*, an *it* he had *had*. How did he even keep them all straight? But he'd had them all, he swore, the reigning beauties of each bar, and he knew something deflating about every one of them. "That one has back hair so thick you want to mow it . . . Her? She not only gave me crabs, but when we had a rematch six weeks later she still had them. As if they were pets . . . This number has a weenie so tiny, trying to find it was like playing hide-the-thimble. Getting warmer . . . warmer . . . colder." By the time they left each bar, the bodies on the floor were as thick as on a field of battle.

They came to Club 23. Leucon wanted to go in, but Gelanor held back. "Ever been there, honey?"

"Nope."

"You wouldn't like it. It's like a flea market."

"Huh?"

"Love for sale, honey."

"Let me just peek," Leucon said, and he did. There was nothing to see—what did he expect, boys with price tags? Just a bunch of old men and a scattering of punks, not even mingling, a space between them that no one crossed, not in the minute or so that Leucon stared. Stared at the space, mostly, realizing that the one distinctive feature of Club 23 was the absence of an entire generation, no one between the kids and the fossils. A few old heads turned to give him the once-over, and he scurried out. As if afraid that, if he lingered, he would be captured somehow, find himself indentured in Pyrrhus's new line of work.

He had half expected to come across Pyrrhus himself. Oddly, they ran into him at the next place they stopped. Oddly, because the next place, the Mirage, didn't seem especially mercantile. It had a pianist doing show tunes, with a loyal cadre who must have been there every night, so smoothly did they segue from the ballad to the novelty song. Not Leucon's kind of stuff, and presumably not Pyrrhus's, but there he was, at the fringes of the chorus, his lips moving as if he knew the words.

Leucon sort of hid behind Gelanor, half afraid that Pyrrhus would think he had come to spy. But Pyrrhus spotted him, ambled over, and said "Hey." Leucon introduced Gelanor. Pyrrhus gave no sign of recognizing him, but Gelanor had the flustered look people get when they are presented to someone they've already met.

Pyrrhus wandered off after about a nanosecond. Gelanor said, "That's your roommate?"

"Um, yeah."

Leucon waited to hear something terrible Gelanor knew about him, something unknown even to a roommate. Gelanor just said, gently, "You know he's a hustler?"

"Huh?"

"He . . . you know, he goes for money."

"No kidding."

"No, I . . ." Gelanor hesitated. "I've seen him places, and I think that's what he does." Leucon shrugged. "You know about this."

"Yeah," Leucon said. "I don't think he was doing it when he moved in." Defensively, as if needing to explain that he didn't knowingly pick a hustler as a roommate.

Gelanor looked as though he were about to utter another of his antique put-downs, summing Pyrrhus up as terminally as an epitaph. Instead he said, almost diffidently, "Does he ever . . . you know, bring someone home?"

"Yeah. Look, I bring people home. You do, too."

"Don't remind me. But it's not like I'm . . . running a business."

"Well, it's not like that. I mean, he has a visitor and they close the door."

"You're awfully casual about it."

Well, of course Leucon had to pretend to be casual. He wasn't going to tell Gelanor that he was upset about it. Besides, he wasn't, not exactly. He surprised himself: he seemed to have accepted Pyrrhus's new vocation nearly as easily as Pyrrhus himself had.

Of course, Pyrrhus wasn't just paying his half of the rent now. He'd bought the sectional in the living room, and the video player; on his nights off sometimes he'd get beer and carry-out stuff from the gourmet store. Leucon wasn't inclined to think very hard about where this bounty came from.

Or if he did: if he thought about it, hardly anything people did to make money could stand up to much scrutiny. Here Leucon spent his days at the law firm, copying the pleadings that would deprive a widow of her mite or justify the desecration of a river. If what Pyrrhus was doing seemed even more degrading, this was only a convention Leucon had been taught. In that place where Pyrrhus couldn't find a scruple, Leucon really didn't have any, either. Maybe no one did back then.

Once, right around that time, Leucon tried a new position. The guy he was with cried out in pain and then said, still gasping but trying to be nice about it, "I don't bend that way." Silly Leucon, of course he didn't. There are only so many different ways our limbs can be arranged; the opportunities for innovation in this arena have long since been exhausted.

I don't bend that way. This elemental protest described the only limit in the world Leucon and Pyrrhus had crossed into, that short-lived city where the only boundaries were those of physical possibility, and not everyone was sure just where those were. Once you'd thrown off those tiresome rules made up by people who didn't even play the game, what *scruple* was supposed to keep you from sticking tab A into slot B, when the proprietor of B was begging for it? None; and there wasn't any reason, none that Leucon could think of, why Pyrrhus shouldn't have been a whore.

Leucon was, even, a little proud, vicariously transgressing just by being Pyrrhus's roommate. Able to say, so casually, "As long as he brings in the rent."

"My, I had no idea that mild-mannered Leucon was living in the fast lane."

"More the shoulder," Leucon said, though he was blushing with pleasure.

The dark-haired guy near the piano, the one who wasn't singing at all but just looking curiously at those who did, as if the lyrics were in some foreign language: he was, yes, definitely cruising Leucon. Not exactly Leucon's type—Leucon's type now had only one representative on earth—but presentable. Leucon looked back; when their eyes met they held long enough to confirm that the deal was done.

Leucon was pleased; here it was not even midnight, and he had already completed his mission. As, say, a pilot on a bombing run lets go his payload and heads for home, not much caring if he hit the chemical factory or the children's hospital. Not his type at all, really, now that the guy was pushing through the crowd to claim him. Still: a near miss was better than lingering around till closing time, waiting to be shot down.

Gelanor had missed it all, apparently, or he should have disappeared by now. "Tell me: you get a discount?" he said.

"What?"

"Your roommate."

Why was he still talking about Pyrrhus? "I haven't asked," Leucon said.

The dark-haired guy was approaching; the piano had hidden his best features. Leucon hardly heard Gelanor's answer. "Oh, I would. In fact, I would haggle, honey. I would definitely bargain him down."

Leucon scarcely heard it. But he was confused just for a second: his mind on the guy approaching, what they would say, whose place they'd go to. At the same time this odd voice, as if from inside him, seeming to say it was all a business deal. From which he would get the short end if he didn't stand up for himself.

Pyrrhus went on working the bars for a while, but of course this had its drawbacks. For one thing, it took too long—you had to socialize, while the trick got drunk and you didn't. Most nights you could only score once. If it got late you could even find yourself granting a discount. Besides, he had already, despite his obvious ornamental value, been thrown out of a couple of places. Including the piano bar, the Mirage, which was a shame, because he really didn't have any competition: he was indisputably the hottest man who knew all the lyrics.

It wasn't Pyrrhus's fault if some deluded countertenor could buy him drinks for an hour without figuring out that he was a working boy. He was embarrassed at first, having to break the news to a jerk who thought he'd won the lottery. Pyrrhus almost felt as though he really had done something wrong. He was even trying to think of some way of apologizing without apologizing, when the guy started calling him assorted names, mostly accurate, and opined that the management shouldn't let people like him in. The guy went on and on, in a distressingly audible treble: it used to be a nice bar, creeps like Pyrrhus were ruining it. Pyrrhus just smiled at him, and he ran down after a minute. Maybe Pyrrhus was garbage, but the asshole had . . . overvalued himself. If Pyrrhus had a price, established through the invisible hand of the agora, then he did, too, and it was the complement of Pyrrhus's own: a negative number.

Still, his complaint had reached the ears of the proprietors. Why should they have minded if someone as well-mannered as Pyrrhus operated a little side concession on their premises? But they did.

He put an ad in the gay weekly, under *Escorts*:

> *Pyrrhus, 21, archer's body, reliable,*
> *versatile, discreet. In or out. GC.*

And the number of the new line he had put in, with an answering machine, so Leucon wouldn't have to take the calls.

He just followed the standard wording of the other ads. Well, not exactly standard. He gave his actual age and his real name, not some columnar alias like Rod or Lance. The rest, though, was as formulaic as a prayer.

Archer's body. Nearly every ad said that, except for the overwrought ones that specified arm and chest measurements. Of course the obligatory phrase wasn't meant to imply that Pyrrhus had ever actually picked up a bow and arrow. Just that he had the body for it: narrow waist, wide shoulders, swelling arms. A body with the latent power to pull the bowstring taut.

Reliable meant you showed up when you said you would, ready to perform and, if the guy insisted that you come too, faithful as a geyser. *Discreet*: well, the ads always said *discreet*, or sometimes *discrete*. Meaning, perhaps, that you wouldn't stand outside the guy's door and holler, "Your male whore's here, lemme in." Or call him at work. *In or out*, that meant Leucon hadn't complained about visitors so far, not in words, and it was too late now. GC: that meant he'd gotten a GeoCredit account. People could just give him the card number and expiration date over the phone, and avoid the distasteful exchange of cash during the actual encounter.

Just the standard ad; you might see the very same thing today, except it would also say *safe*. That omission by itself tells you how very long ago this all was, back in the age of heroes.

Oh, *versatile*, I skipped *versatile*. Surely the key word. Perhaps it was, in most cases, something of an overstatement. Pyrrhus's competitors might have been willing to assume a variety of postures, but they were not limitlessly malleable. There were things they wouldn't do.

Pyrrhus would do anything he was asked for. Things he'd never heard of. Things that, until their possibility was broached to him, he would not have supposed to be anatomically feasible. Other things that were quite plainly feasible—infants could perform them—but that he had never imagined anyone might pay him for. Yet they would: the city was full of men who took one look at him and were practically ready to refinance their condos, just for the right to cast him for an hour in scenarios that he might once have thought were vile or degrading. Now he did not think. He formed no *opinion* about the men he tricked with or the scripts they wrote for him.

I do not mean that he was anesthetized, or sleepwalking. On the contrary: he had—every time—the sensation that he had never been so alive. As at the Palace Hotel, when he had knelt before a drooping and edentate stranger and found himself hurling into the present tense.

Here is the mystery, I think: living in the present tense. I myself have never done it. Thus I can only imagine what it was like for Pyrrhus.

Have you ever taken a new job, but with a starting date a few weeks ahead, you just need to finish a few things at your old job before moving on? The memos flow uninterrupted into your IN box, but now they have nothing to do with you: what do you care about the conference next fall, or whether Dascylus is taking over Logistics, or the new procedure for filling out the monthly activity report? You sit in a meeting and you might as well already be gone. They may still want your advice about some thing or other, or want to know where you keep the Thyestes file; but your destiny isn't theirs, this is their business and not yours. You are there, but already gone.

Or have you ever lived for a while in an apartment you didn't intend to stay in, just a year's lease until you find something more permanent? You arrange the furniture, hang your pictures; if you're compulsive like me you put your books on the shelves in alphabetical order. After a few nights you can find your way to the bathroom in the dark and you stop hearing the odd noises, the unfamiliar rhythm of different traffic. Still, you don't think of painting the walls a different color; if you see a table that

56

would just fit in the kitchen you don't buy it, because who knows if it will fit in your next kitchen? You even go to the grocery store and buy things in small sizes, though of course you're going to use more than that in a year.

This is as close as most of us come: when there is a change ahead, so certain that we refuse to make ourselves at home. Then we may, for a little while, be awake to everything. As Pyrrhus was, while he waited for his real life to begin. His days were endless and his nights hectic with the narrowest facts: parts of bodies; the pictures on people's walls; the code words in telephone calls; the different ways people swore; the various deities they called on when they came.

5

Pyrrhus had left a white shirt at Café Leo—he'd always kept a spare there, in case he spilled stuff on himself. The next time he was sorting his laundry he missed it: he kept track of his shirts, they all had little personalities, and he missed it. So he went to Leo's to pick it up, went at mid-afternoon, when Leo was usually home for his nap, in his apartment right above the restaurant.

When Pyrrhus got to the restaurant, the sign was in the front window, *Closed Temporarily for Renovations*, like a funeral wreath, and the place was dark. He almost walked away; it was only a shirt. But it was a nice shirt, a special favorite, and why should he be afraid to see Leo? Leo probably had no idea what he'd been doing since he'd given up waiting tables. He stepped into the vestibule leading to the upstairs apartment and rang the bell.

After a minute he heard "What? . . . Who?" from out in the street. He stepped out of the vestibule, looked up, and there was Leo, leaning out his upstairs window, with a week's growth of silvery stubble, looking like a bum. "You. We closed. I was so heartbroken you didn't show up, I just had to shut down."

"I'm sorry."

"I'm kidding."

"No, I mean I'm sorry you shut down."

"I'm not."

"I left something in there."

"What?"

"A shirt."

"A shirt. You want I should come down and open up, like breaking into somebody's tomb, so you can find some old rag?"

"I don't know. I'm real fond of the shirt."

"Wait there."

Leo came down. He was wearing a retirement costume: baggy plaid pants, baby-blue sneakers and black socks, and a cardigan. He carried a ring of what must have been a hundred keys, from which he unhesitatingly selected the key to the restaurant.

"I haven't been in here in a couple weeks," he said. "Bet it's freezing in here."

"I'm sorry."

"Stop being sorry," he said. "I know how you can get attached to things. I myself have a schnauzer. Of course, it's more loyal than a shirt. No smarter, but . . ."

It was freezing in there. "I would turn on the heat, but I'm in the middle of an unfortunate dispute with a certain public utility that has shown no gratitude for the many years I paid tribute to them. By the same token I am unable to offer you any illumination."

"I think it's back in the kitchen."

"Ah. I'd just as soon not go to the kitchen. You go ahead." He sat down at the table in the front window and folded his hands, as if waiting for service.

Pyrrhus made his way through the dark bar, pushed open the door to the kitchen, and found out why he was entering it unaccompanied. Of course, with the electricity off, the little hoard of unsold comestibles had been left unrefrigerated for several weeks. It was cold, but not cold enough to preserve that last unbought helping of stuffed flounder. He took a lungful of the comparatively salubrious air of the bar and plunged in. He was almost out of breath before he found, in the little ration of light doled out by the lozenge window in the kitchen door, his gleaming white shirt. Where he'd left it, in the open locker next to the employees' washroom. He grabbed it and rushed out, as pleased with himself as if he'd purloined the Golden Fleece.

Leo was still at the front table. Cold as the room was, Pyrrhus thought it would be rude to just walk out. He sat down with Leo, clutching the shirt, though it had a faint fishy smell.

"Tell me what you've been doing with yourself," Leo said.

"Not much. Looking for work."

"Yes, I noticed you placed an ad, seeking employment."

"You saw that?"

"It's a free paper, I read it loyally."

"Oh. I guess I wouldn't have thought you read those ads."

"No? It's true that I'm not actually a likely consumer. Though I was once — for my seventieth birthday some friends chipped in, and . . . such a doll he was. But no more. Still, I like to read them, the free ones, the escorts, it doesn't matter. I try to figure, are people lying deliberately or are they fooling themselves? Especially the free ones. Because you know in this entire city there are not so many straight-acting hunks with senses of humor and large members as declare themselves in a single issue of that paper. Most of all 'straight-acting.' Such a paradox: is it acting like a straight boy to place such an ad?"

"I don't know," Pyrrhus said. He could sort of tell that this dissertation was in lieu of talking about his employment. He wondered if he qualified as straight-acting.

"And I like considering, just mathematically, the enormous dispro-portion between hunters and quarry. Column after column of bottoms seeking tops, and about one top per page: why am I left thinking about poultry? Oh, and age: every blessed man in there demands someone younger than he, a puzzle that makes this old head go in circles. I wonder if maybe one corner of Hades will consist of the people in the ads, having to make do with one another."

"Uh-huh." Pyrrhus wondered if he could excuse himself soon. Except he found that he did, after all, want to hear what Leo thought of his recent career turn.

"Or maybe we're already in that corner." A couple, seeing Pyrrhus and Leo in the window, stepped up and started looking at the menu, not noticing that it was dated weeks earlier. "Oh, the twits, they think we're open. You know, since I closed, I have this notion traffic on the street is heavier. Like there's people driving by, wanting to come to Café Leo, and then they see it's closed." He tapped on the glass, held his nose, and made a thumbs-down sign. The couple moved on. "It's just a notion. Like a phantom limb, itching. The last night, everybody came by, all the old regulars — they all knew somehow. The place was packed. But I had noth-ing to give them." He looked around at the dark room, then said, "Anyway, yes, I saw your ad."

"And . . . ?"

"And? I'm sure it meets a higher standard of accuracy than most."

"That's all?"

"Look, I ran a bar twenty years, there's nothing I haven't seen. So don't worry I'm shocked. Or don't hope I am, that's more like it."

"I don't care what you think."

"No, you came by to rescue this shirt. What do you want me to tell you, that I think it's a splendid way for a young man to get started on his career?"

"It's better than waiting tables, so far."

"You pierce me. You mean if I had only paid you enough you would never have fallen into sin and degradation?"

61

Pyrrhus had to laugh. "Nah."

"You bet, nah. This is all just a little adventure for you. You could always go back to . . . where was it?"

"Scyros. No, I couldn't."

"You're a prince or something."

"What?"

"They fixed my cataracts; I'm not blind. You're a prince, they'll always take a prince back. It's like you've got a net."

He hadn't thought about Scyros in weeks, the place he could go back to. Back to furtive evenings with the same old handful of closet queens, year after year. Back to the palace, furnished with proscriptions, his mother's encircling arms. Back to the looming expectation that he replicate himself.

"I can't go back," he said. Still, there was a net; he could feel it. Even if he was in free fall, as he looked down he could almost see it, far below him. It just didn't seem to be Scyros any more.

Leo took Pyrrhus's hands. "I've known kids who sold themselves because they were hungry, and I've known them who sold themselves because they couldn't see any other way to get ahead. But I never knew anyone to do it just because he was bored. After you get through with this, what? Robbing banks? Setting fires? In which case I may possibly have a business opportunity for you."

Pyrrhus said, "I'm not doing anything wrong." That seemed to him objectively true; none of it was wrong. Yet he felt the oddest weariness, saying this, as if it were tiresome to have to explain himself. Or tiresome not doing anything wrong: he felt a little flicker of interest at the idea of burning something.

"You know, I'm such a confused old man, I don't know if you are or not. Let's get out of here. It's colder here than outside, even—we must be jerks sitting here."

Out on the street, Leo said, "I'm sure it would not discourage you if I were to tell you that what you're doing is dangerous."

"Dangerous? I can always get a shot."

"I meant you could be arrested, or . . . get involved in things you can't handle."

"I'm not getting involved with anybody."

"No, I'm sure you're not."

"I've got to get going."

"Yes indeed. Mustn't leave the phone unattended." He put his hands on Pyrrhus's shoulders. "Don't hurt these people, just because it's a game to you."

"Hurt who?"

"Your customers. Give good value. I should have closed this place the day I stopped giving good value."

"Uh-huh."

One evening Pyrrhus, deferential and seemingly abashed, said to Leucon, "I was wondering if you could . . . if you had anything to do tonight." This was the way he always asked. Meaning: could Leucon make himself scarce, so as not to spoil some dotard's fantasies?

Leucon had always complied. Clearing out of the apartment for an hour or so, it was a small enough inconvenience, something any decent roommate would have done willingly enough if Pyrrhus had been giving it away. And since Pyrrhus wasn't giving it away, since he required the privacy in order to pay the rent and supply the other small luxuries Leucon had begun to take for granted: all the more reason Leucon shouldn't have minded heading out to the movies once in a while.

Tonight, though, he was irritated. Not at the inconvenience; at something else he couldn't put his finger on right away. "When?" he said, with a sharpness that surprised even himself.

Pyrrhus was also taken aback. "Um . . . around ten."

"Ten? For heaven's sake, I have to work tomorrow."

"It should only be like an hour or so. You could catch a nine o'clock movie and by the time you're back—"

Leucon cut him off. "There isn't any movie I want to see." This was true: Pyrrhus was in one of the peaks on his sales chart, and Leucon had been to everything. But it came out sounding whiny, as when a child complains that there's nothing to do.

Pyrrhus tried to help. "Well, maybe you could go to the Barracks. Or get a bite to eat somewhere, I don't know."

"We've got food in. This is costing me money, all this going out."

"Oh," Pyrrhus said. Leucon was just ticking off grievances, he didn't mean for Pyrrhus to say: "You're right, I hadn't even thought about that. Why don't I—I mean it's only fair, I keep asking you to—why don't I give you, say, twenty?"

Of course Leucon's very first thought was, I could use twenty. But he said, "You mean, like a cut? A percentage?"

Pyrrhus's face turned as red as his hair. He reached for a cigarette, then remembered their rule, the only taboo Leucon had succeeded in imposing. Instead he shoved his hands in his rear pockets, in that sexy way he had. "I didn't mean that."

Leucon felt that he must be blushing too. It was the first time he'd ever said, outright, that Pyrrhus was trash, and he didn't even feel it. Only that he was supposed to feel it, supposed to object to his own complicity in all of it, which would scarcely have been much increased by his accepting a twenty. He was ashamed of his hypocrisy. And then, at once, angry that Pyrrhus could make him feel ashamed, that they were living so entirely by Pyrrhus's rules.

"I'm sorry," Pyrrhus said. "Maybe I should stop bringing people here. Or maybe, you know, maybe I should get another place."

A rush of panic came over Leucon. A huge No from deep inside, don't let him go. Give up anything to keep him here. Even if you're getting nothing from him. "No, listen, I'm just in a mood. I—maybe I will go to the Barracks. I'm kind of horny anyway."

Pyrrhus smiled. "Thanks. You know, I do feel bad that I'm costing you all this money. Couldn't you—I mean, it wouldn't really be a cut, it's more like I should pay extra rent because sometimes you don't get the use of the place."

This was fine, nicely legalistic and solicitous of Leucon's lingering principles. He was almost ready to grab the twenty. But something in him had an inspiration, and the words were out before he could think about them. "That's okay. Maybe I'll take it out in trade some time." A second or two passed before he managed to laugh.

Pyrrhus didn't laugh, just stared, his mouth open a little. What was he feeling: contempt, pity, anger? Who was he to feel any of these things toward Leucon? He was a whore. Everyone else could get a piece of him, just for money. Even silly Gelanor had had him; Leucon had finally figured that out. Leucon was the only one in the world who was supposed to hold back. Even help peddle it, and never get any for himself.

Pyrrhus murmured, "Maybe so," and closed his eyes.

Shutting out yet another claimant for the contents of his trousers. Leucon realized that he must have held a special office in Pyrrhus's world: the only man who wasn't pursuing him. Now he had given that up. Just as well: what had he ever gained from his singular self-denial? Except that, when Pyrrhus opened his eyes again, he wouldn't see Leucon at all. Only another faceless customer, and one who was trying to get a bargain.

"I was just kidding," Leucon said.

Pyrrhus opened his eyes. "I know." He gave Leucon a big smile. "Hey, it might be fun some time."

Leucon didn't think it would be fun. Last week maybe — when Pyrrhus had no calls and they sat around watching TV — maybe last week, if Pyrrhus had just reached for him. But now, if it ever happened, if Leucon were to get some night the piece of Pyrrhus he rented out to everyone else: it would just be some sort of transaction. Charitable or, more likely, commercial. He'd want something back. Leucon said, "You'd better save it for the paying customers."

There. Leucon had killed everything. He felt a sere triumph. Months earlier, he had sat awake in his windowless room wondering how he could hurt Pyrrhus. Perhaps he had found the way.

"Oh, there's plenty to go around," Pyrrhus said, expressionless. "Just now, though, I do have this appointment. Are you sure you didn't want that twenty?" He reached into his pants pocket and pulled out a roll about equal to Leucon's monthly earnings. He peeled off a bill, held it; Leucon took it. Pyrrhus went into the bathroom and shut the door.

The visitor that evening might have been the single least attractive man on earth. Well, maybe not, but certainly the least attractive with whom Pyrrhus had ever contemplated going to bed, and lately he'd been getting some real dogs.

He didn't mind that the guy was old. True, in the first few weeks of his career he had zeroed in on the younger customers. Neophytes who picked him up as a sort of inaugural ball, conflicted queens who still thought hustlers were somehow straight, happily coupled guys who just wanted to try a few moves that were out of the question at home. But the young guys, sometimes, treated him with contempt, would even physically hurt him, in some small way he couldn't protest, that had to be taken as part of the deal. Sometimes that's all they wanted, to be able to hurt somebody and then not face him at breakfast the next morning. Other times they seemed to do it just because they needed to even the scales somehow.

Old men, on the other hand, accepted Pyrrhus's services with wistful gratitude. They knew exactly how little they were buying, and were happily surprised by just how much they got. They respected him as you might an honest car mechanic. And they almost never struck out at him —

having, perhaps, lived long enough to learn that their afflictions would not be healed by raising a few matching welts on a stranger.

If the visitor tonight was repellent, it wasn't his age so much as his circumference, and something in the way he looked at Pyrrhus that hinted at appetites so enormous they could not be satisfied by a battalion of hustlers. The guy wrote cookbooks or something; he was a little affronted that Pyrrhus had never heard of him—as if Pyrrhus read cookbooks. He was certainly a monument to his art, built like an enormous snowman that was starting to topple. He wore, not a suit—there were not enough houndsteeth or herringbones in the world—but a sort of artist's smock and, in place of a necktie, a huge floppy bow. His outsized head perched atop this confection without benefit of a neck; it was punctuated by silver eyebrows that rose so flamelike he must have moussed them. The rest of his face had a sort of squashed look, like that of some huge and pugnacious lapdog.

The guy wanted to socialize first. He'd brought his own bottle, and they sat together on the living-room sofa and drank. The snowman ruffled, with his pudgy fingers, the hair on the back of Pyrrhus's neck. Pyrrhus tried not to shiver, but did. Maybe the guy would take that as a sign of excitement.

After the second or third drink, Pyrrhus had relaxed a little. He was as ready as he was going to be, but the guy wanted to go on talking.

"Tell me about yourself," he said.

"Um," Pyrrhus said. "Not much to tell. I grew up in a place called Scyros."

"Yes?"

"Then I came here."

The snowman waited a minute, then said, "That's quite a story. And now that you're here . . ."

"Now? I guess you know that story."

"I guess I do," he muttered, displeased by even so oblique a reference to Pyrrhus's profession. "I meant, what do you want to do, what do you want to be?"

"I don't know." This was the wrong answer. He was supposed to want to be something implausible—movie star, singer—supposed to have some ludicrous ambition that would make it easier to condescend to him. "I haven't thought about it," he said, as of course he hadn't.

"You could be a model."

"No, I checked that out once. They don't like redheads much."

"Really? I do."

Pyrrhus smiled and looked modestly down at his drink, which was nearly empty.

"Let me get you another of those," the guy said. He stumbled through Pyrrhus's bedroom to the kitchen, making himself entirely too much at home, refilled their glasses, and—he must have thought he was making a smooth transition—sat down on the bed, so that Pyrrhus had to join him.

He wasn't through talking about Pyrrhus's career. "There must be something you . . . Have you finished school?"

"School?"

"College. Have you got your degree?"

"I never went to college," Pyrrhus said.

"Ah," the guy said, smiling and shaking his head. Perfect, he must have thought, a real moron. He started to unbutton Pyrrhus's shirt.

Pyrrhus wanted to say, You don't know who I am. My grandmother was a goddess, and my father—He kept quiet. To recite all that: he might as well have boarded the return ferry to Scyros. He kept quiet and made himself smile as the man fumblingly undressed him.

The man buried his face in Pyrrhus's crotch and made low grunting noises, as if he were a pig sniffing for truffles. Usually Pyrrhus could get hard just looking down at a man from this angle, just from watching the hunger. But they'd had so many drinks, and the man was so prodigiously ugly, and—and Pyrrhus was afraid the guy was going to eat him up. Just set his stripped carcass out in the morning with the whiskey bottle they'd almost emptied. The man started nuzzling Pyrrhus's neck and squeezing his limp penis, squeezing it and jerking it around like a gearshift, as if that would make it hard. Finally he leaned back and breathed into Pyrrhus's face: "What's wrong?"

"I'm just drunk, I'm sorry."

"What?" It was as if it hadn't occurred to him that Pyrrhus wasn't a kitchen appliance, ready to be plugged in and turned on. He was as angry and frustrated as you get when you bring a new gadget home and it doesn't work. You know you'll have to go back to the store now, just when you'd got all excited, opening the box and pouring out the foam peanuts, and the damn thing doesn't work.

"I'm a little drunk," Pyrrhus said. "Listen, why don't I get you off?"

The man said, sharply, even a little haughtily: "You don't have to, if I don't interest you."

Good, let him go, let him keep his money. To hell with the adventure:

let the monster, this once, keep his treasure. Other hustlers had some limits. Only Pyrrhus would make it with just anybody at all. No wonder he got all the monsters.

"Why don't you just lie back?" Pyrrhus said. Because, after all, if he started picking and choosing, then . . . then it wouldn't be a business any more, would it?

And it was, just a job; only by thinking of it as a mindless chore could he kneel down and bury his face in the crease below the snowman's middle sphere. He thought he might, just this once, close his eyes and picture someone else. It didn't work. With his head clamped between the man's stupendous, melting thighs, he was irrefutably where he was. He just worked diligently away, noting with the antennae of a professional what made the snowman sigh or quiver. Finding the right spot, the right speed, so that the man would finish soon and would be gone.

"Oh, Lord, yes," the snowman said. "Tell me how much you like it."

Pyrrhus complied. He was in the business of complying; it cost him nothing to say the words. When he had done speaking, though, and returned his mouth to its former employment, he felt a wave of revulsion. Not at the odious object to which he was ministering and that was, he could feel it, just about ready. Rather at the sudden, awful idea that the man must believe him, that the man must actually suppose that the appliance kneeling before him was Pyrrhus himself.

The man finished. Pyrrhus didn't, as usual, swallow, part of the service. He spat, right onto the mainsail of a smock the snowman had decorously kept on throughout. "Sorry," Pyrrhus said. "Wow. It was just too much."

When the man had gone, Pyrrhus poured himself the last of the whiskey and thought: what was the big difference between using his mouth to suck the snowman off and using it to say those words? He didn't mean it, it was just his body talking, the way his body did everything else. But all those questions, and then making him say that he liked it, tell how much: it was as if the guy wanted his insides too. Didn't just want Pyrrhus's body, but wanted to turn him inside out and make sure that he wasn't withholding anything, that the charge on the GeoCredit card had bought every ounce of Pyrrhus, beyond even the flesh.

His glass was empty, just a few almost syrupy dregs at the bottom. He stuck his tongue far down into the glass to reach them, playing, not desperate for a few more drops of whiskey. Just exercising one of his most popular accessories.

He almost forgave the snowman. He could sort of understand that, if you were a monster, you might long to hear those words, from some spell-bound beauty trapped between your monstrous thighs. Pyrrhus wasn't a toaster: he was supposed to talk. Declare, if he had to, that kneeling with some ogre's smelly dick stuffed in his mouth was the high point of his day. The snowman was entitled to hear the words, he had paid for them.

But he wasn't entitled to believe them, to thunder down the staircase and out of the building carrying in his head a phantom Pyrrhus who meant those words. A second Pyrrhus who would live forever enthralled in that enormous skull, testifying to the snowman's beauty and prowess.

Pyrrhus shrugged. So he had said a few things he didn't mean; who hadn't? Still, he couldn't shake the feeling that the snowman had stolen something from him. Leaving him as bereft as that sleeping huntress whose virginity was purloined by a god.

6

He'd had no callers for three nights. For one thing, he'd lost his GeoCredit account—the snowman had inexplicably repaid his ungrudging service by ratting on him to the bank people. So he had lost most of his impulse shoppers, in a trade very much dependent on impulse. Customers had to plan ahead now, go to the machine and get the cash. And people who planned ahead never planned on him. He had no repeats.

Imagine opening your door and seeing Pyrrhus, a virtual blank slate on which you could inscribe your most cherished dreams. An hour later, having done everything you always wanted, he would kiss you or not— your choice—and you would close the door behind him. You could call him again, over and over, until the screen at the bank machine read TILT. But then you would only learn, over and over, that you could do everything you always wanted in an hour.

There had been no callers; he'd seen every movie at the video store except *Seven Against Thebes* and *Seven More Against Thebes*. Maybe he could hit the bars. It had been a couple of months, maybe the Mirage would let him back in again. Or—where hadn't he tried? The Escapade maybe, the place with the strippers. If guys would pay all that money just to look at a naked boy, what wouldn't they pay to . . .

He paid his six bucks, made his way to the bar. Gratified that half the customers turned away from the dancers and stared, awestruck, at his fully clothed self. Before he'd even ordered a drink, he felt a tap at his shoulder. A voice like a buzzsaw rasped out, "Pardon me."

Pyrrhus waited a beat, put on his hundred-dollar smile, and turned around. The man who stood before him looked like the infant Eros: he was tiny, round, and pink, on his forehead a golden spitcurl. "Pardon me, my name is Archias."

"Hi." Where had Pyrrhus heard this name? "I'm Pyrrhus."

"You're hustling."

"Uh . . . maybe."

Archias turned to the bartender. "Erginus, give me six bucks."

The bartender did, and Archias offered the money to Pyrrhus. "I'm going to assume that you didn't know our policy and give you an opportunity to depart."

"Oh." Pyrrhus glanced up at one of the dancers. "These guys are just doing interpretive ballet?"

"My Golden Boys may occasionally, between sets, socialize with the customers. If they should happen to continue their conversation away from the premises, that's their business. Although they do occasionally show me their appreciation."

Pyrrhus wondered what percentage appreciation came to. "I get it. You mean, if I'm not a Golden Boy . . ."

"It is all, do you see, a matter of supply and demand." Archias stepped back. "My, my. How old are you?"

"Twenty-one."

"No, really."

"Really. You want to see my ID?"

"Not just now. I'd rather see—Why don't we go into my office?"

"What for?" Pyrrhus was a little nervous, suddenly. He had trespassed on the boy cartel. He pictured kneecapping, or some more pertinent threat to his professional capacities.

"I thought you might consent to an interview."

"An—What, you think I'm going to be a stripper?"

"Oh, pardon me. Is it beneath your dignity?"

In the office, Archias said, "You dance?"

"I guess."

"Here, why don't you step up on the desk. Come on, I'm the only one here."

Pyrrhus climbed up and began, hesitantly, a few little steps. He strained to hear the music from the bar.

Archias giggled. "I don't need the Dance of the Water Lilies. Why don't you take your clothes off."

Pyrrhus did, then stood fidgeting, wondering what to do with his hands.

"Uh-huh," Archias said. "Well, that's acceptable."

"Acceptable?"

"It's okay, well within the range of the normal. Not something that evokes spontaneous allusions to stallions or bulls."

"I guess not," Pyrrhus said.

"I think one of the first rules of marketing is to know your product. Turn around."

There was a draft from out in the bar; the wind seemed to be seeking Pyrrhus out like a spotlight.

"That's really very nice. Perhaps you might shake it a little."

Pyrrhus shook it a little. "I mean, shake it." Pyrrhus shook it a lot. "Okay, turn around again." Pyrrhus did, glowering; all these orders, as if he were a show dog. And cold, he hadn't thought it would be so cold.

He tensed, all over, to keep from shivering. He felt the cold air over every inch of his surface, as if it were wrapping itself around him like a bath of light.

He remembered his father, the night they came for him, his father naked in the moonlight.

The claim that the Greeks went to Scyros specifically in order to recruit Achilles is probably wrong. True, Achilles was an astonishing creature. But even back home at his father's, before he'd gone into hiding on Scyros, he had been no more than a local celebrity, and that more as a jock than as a soldier. Quite possibly Odysseus and the other officers had never even heard of him. Scyros was just on the way to Troy; they stopped for a few last provisions, odds and ends that had been forgotten.

Achilles, like everyone else, went down to the harbor to look at the great fleet, then up to Lycomedes' palace to catch a glimpse of the famous generals as they arrived for a courtesy call. He was, in fact, at the front of the throng that gathered beneath the porte cochere and that parted reluctantly to make way for Odysseus's rented limo.

Achilles had on his coveralls, and he remembered to slouch and even let his mouth hang open a little, so he looked about as unheroic as he could. Enough to fool the generals' driver into thinking that he was the valet parker. The man threw Achilles the keys. Achilles caught them deftly enough, then just stood looking at them, bewildered, until the real valet parker, a lithe dark youth, snatched them from his hands. Only Odysseus saw the flush of red that crossed Achilles' face, his anger and shame that he had so successfully disguised himself and was being treated like a servant. As the crowd broke up, Odysseus had a man follow Achilles home, to the bungalow in which Thetis had sequestered him.

That night Odysseus and Ajax came to the bungalow, rang the doorbell. Deidameia answered, in her bathrobe. Pyrrhus, half hidden behind her robe, looked out at these astonishing men in uniforms gaudy with medals and braid, and, past them, at the car, around which a curious band of neighbors was already forming. The driver shooed away a couple of kids who just wanted to touch the car; under the street lamps it glowed like a white opal.

Achilles had been watching football. He came out into the hall, beer in hand, and looked out at the visitors. He was almost as amazed as Pyrrhus. He stammered, "Wh-what can I do for you gentlemen?"

Odysseus said, "Come with us."

"What?"

"To Troy." The great persuader, Odysseus of unmatched eloquence, and all he said was, "Come with us."

Thetis had never said—when she had made her son hide on Scyros, she had never said just exactly what it was he was supposed to be hiding from. Yet he understood at once, even slow-witted Achilles, that this was it. Because he wanted, right away, to go with them. He could feel that this was his chance to escape the tedium of life with Deidameia and the little faggot, to do great things, to use every divine muscle. Of course, this is what she'd been afraid of. She wanted him just to stay here, in this situation comedy without a laugh track, until he died. Or until he got old and scrawny as his father-in-law. She wanted him to stay, instead of going with these splendid figures and . . .

Dying young. He didn't know anything about any prophecies, but that had to be it. Why else would his mother have gone to such lengths to keep him from this? From the heroic destiny that was now so unmistakably revealed to him—as he stood there in the hall his hand clenched, on its own, around the hilt of an unseen sword. He would die young, hundreds of miles from there and farther yet from his real home. He would fall down in the muck and die fighting for some cause he knew nothing about. He couldn't even follow the news stories on TV, it was all too confusing.

He hesitated. Deidameia watched him in suspense, though whether she wanted him to go or to stay is uncertain. Pyrrhus was not at all ambivalent; voicelessly he mouthed the word Go.

Ajax spoke up. "Forget this, I'm going back to the hotel. Find some broad in the bar, maybe. I don't know what comes over you—you see some big goon in the street and drag me out in the middle of the night on a recruiting party. Let's beat it."

He headed back to the car and stood waiting for Odysseus. Odysseus looked closely at Achilles. Maybe he was trying to compose some little oration that would bring Achilles along. But it looked as though Achilles wouldn't even hear whatever he had to say. The lummox was just standing there paralyzed. Achilles deep in thought was not an impressive sight. He had so little practice at it he didn't know how to compose his face; his eyes crossed a little.

Odysseus turned and was halfway to the car when Achilles growled to his wife, "Get my stuff."

He was an instrument honed for one purpose. Fine enough to look at, but in peacetime like a sword hung useless over the fireplace. He could only become himself when unsheathed; only then would the world see the awful beauty of him, mired in blood but gleaming through it like a silver blade tipped with the red-iron of his hair. He would be himself for a little while, for as long as he got. "Get my armor," he said.

Deidameia looked at him for a second, then headed to the basement without a word. Achilles stepped out onto the porch and started to un-button his grimy coveralls. Heedless of the crowd, he slowly stripped. Just then a cloud slipped away from the moon and it shone down on him. Pyrrhus saw it and was exultant; he felt as though a cloud was slipping away from his own life.

Ajax was the greatest man in the army, the most heroic, the most loved, and—though of course no one used the word—the most beautiful. Until now. He looked at Achilles the way, at a pageant, the first runner-up looks at the new Miss Cosmos. If for any reason Miss Cosmos should be unable to complete her reign then you, Ajax, will. . . . He saw at once how everything would be about Achilles, only the occasional stanza end-ing, Also present was Ajax. He knelt, right there on the sidewalk, out of some mixture of obeisance and defeat. Odysseus did not kneel. He un-derstood that he had uncovered something extraordinary, more than he could have imagined when he'd seen the guy in the street. But Odysseus didn't kneel for anything.

The moon bathed Achilles in light as if it had had no other purpose in rising.

Deidameia returned; Achilles put on the armor. Not the legendary suit forged by Hephaestus and bestowed on Achilles by his mother; that was years later, in the middle of the war. Just an ordinary suit of armor, picked up at a sporting goods store, the price tag still hanging from the breastplate. Deidameia snipped it off, and Achilles strode forward, squeak-ing a little.

The skirt of Achilles' tunic fell only halfway down his thighs. Under the bronze fortress of his upper body his bare legs, the slender and sinewy legs of a long-distance runner somehow conscripted to carry the enormous bulk of metal above them, seemed especially vulnerable. One might almost have guessed where his weak spot was. But that night the comparative frailty of the legs only magnified the astounding chest and the corded arms. The crowd of onlookers fled as he came down off the porch; even Odysseus involuntarily stepped back.

This is how the world pictures Achilles, in his armor. Pyrrhus always remembered, instead, those moments when he stood naked, waiting. The sight was so burned into Pyrrhus's vision that, even though it wasn't his earliest memory—he was ten, after all, when they came for his father—it was his organizing memory, the earth around which everything else revolved. The mixture of terror and desire never left him: even the simple word *man* could conjure it up, the fearsome torso and the hairy loins.

Pyrrhus stayed in the front hall, looking out through the screen door at his father, just inches away on the porch. He wanted to be his father, surely, to stand as silent and self-contained as Achilles did in the moonlight. Yet at the same time, he wanted to bury his face in those loins and gaze up at the heroic figure that he was quite sure he wasn't ever going to be.

He was that figure now. Under Archias's silent gaze, the draft from the bar interrogating every inch of him, he was a man without armor. If there is such a thing, if we can even imagine a man who isn't poised for battle, a man standing still, his fingers not itching for a weapon.

Archias said softly, "My, will you look at that. It very nearly has a mind of its own."

Pyrrhus looked down at the guilty member; it was true. He was furious, he was freezing his ass off, and he was spontaneously, helplessly erect.

Archias smiled. "I think you are what they call a natural."

Pyrrhus looked down at himself once again, then back at Archias. He smiled, too, surrendering to the hard fact of it. He and Archias grinned at each other like proud parents over their one-eyed baby. Yes, he was a natural. He gave a couple of bumps, to make Archias laugh.

"My dear, you're going to break hearts. I suppose I really should see some identification." Pyrrhus showed him. "You're honestly twenty-one—are you sure this is authentic? Scyros, I've been to Scyros." Pyrrhus flinched, wondering if he was about to lose his anonymity. "A veritable graveyard; I would have run away, too. I thought your name was Pyrrhus."

76

"That's . . . I don't know, a nickname."

"It's a stage name now. You can start tomorrow night. It's always kind of slow Wednesdays, you can learn on the job."

"Great," Pyrrhus said.

As he dressed, Archias went on. "You know, if things work out I think I can let you stay through the end of the month."

"That's all?"

"They get tired of you, you know? I mean, you'd think if you'd seen one you'd seen one, but they always want fresh . . . faces. Three, four weeks, everyone's seen you, then I need to rotate you out."

"For how long?"

"Few months. Then you can come back. If you've got fans, I can put it in the ad. 'Back! Limited time only! Pyrrhus!' "

"What do people do in between?"

"Well, whatever you did before."

"I guess you know what I did before."

"Oh." Archias frowned. "I had rather the impression you were a neo-phyte."

"No, I've got an ad and all."

"Have you?"

"Under *Escorts.*"

"An appropriate category, for once."

"Huh?"

"I mean that you're presentable. You could literally escort someone."

"You mean like to the opera?"

"I mean like you could be kept. A room of your own, meals in nice restaurants, clothes, money for the powder room."

"No thanks. I keep myself just fine."

Archias shrugged. "It's hardly in my interest to suggest it. But you need to think ahead. A clever boy like you could have any number of splendid futures, if someone were to take you under his wing. Why, you should see my friend Enceladus. Twenty years ago he was turning tricks, just like you, then he hooked up with the right man and now he's the most sought-after interior designer in town."

"I'm sure that'd be a good idea."

"You're not going to look this way very long. You should be investing. Every night you go out you're spending principal."

"Do you tell this to all the Golden Boys?"

"Most of the Golden Boys are cast from baser metals. Half of them have drug habits and the other half are mentally defective. I suspect you could single-handedly raise the average IQ of my stable by ten points. So by all means join us, let me use you up."

"Fine."

"You're making some point, aren't you? What are you doing, getting back at someone? Why don't you just send them a nasty letter?"

"Why don't we just finish the interview?"

"Why don't we?" Archias said, not sharply. "I didn't notice — any tattoos?"

The next night Pyrrhus came out of the bathroom after an unusually protracted toilet and stood before Leucon in the living room, his hands clasped behind him. Wearing for the first time his carefully selected uniform of khakis and white shirt.

"How do I look?" he said.

He looked . . . innocent. Somehow he had contrived to scrub away everything that had happened to him, those last months. He looked like the guy on the football team who doesn't drink or smoke because the coach said not to, or like the kid who comes to your door with religious pamphlets, the one with the holy smile and the guileless throat above his gleaming white shirt. You wanted, not to steal his innocence from him, but to give him a wonderful surprise.

How did he look? Leucon summed it up in a word: "Expensive."

Pyrrhus shook his head; not one hair stirred. "I'm going to be dancing tonight."

"You mean you're just . . . going out dancing? Like for fun? Where, the Lighthouse? Maybe I'll —"

"No, I mean — I'm going to be dancing at the Escapade. I'm starting there tonight."

The shock wore off so quickly Leucon was pretty sure he didn't even show it. Because, after a moment's thought, it made perfect sense. This was back before everybody and his sister started working out; people pretty much had whatever the gods had given them. With what the gods had given Pyrrhus it made sense.

"You ought to come," Pyrrhus said.

"I've got to get to work real early," Leucon lied. He had never, in all those months, seen Pyrrhus entirely naked. Now the whole city would. He didn't want to share it with the whole city.

78

We are here already, singer, where we came in. Pyrrhus on the bar; the emissary from the Fates already arrived. I am sorry. But if we could live in a flashback I'd be in the back room at the Barracks this minute.

It was near the end of the month. Pyrrhus was squatting in front of this old fart named Amyclas. Amyclas clutched Pyrrhus's penis in his right hand and a five-dollar bill in his left. He was just holding Pyrrhus's cock, as you might a flashlight, and Pyrrhus let him. It was a slow night, one more set to go and he hadn't made thirty bucks. He even ran his fingers through Amyclas's residual hair.

He danced twenty minutes at a time five times a night five nights a week, Wednesday through Sunday, and he usually made about a buck a minute. Not steadily all night long, but overall, less the first couple sets, most the last, so he took home about a hundred a night just from the dancing. Five hundred a week, all tax-free. If he could have gone on forever it would have been a nice middle-class living. But the month was almost up.

Over in the corner Archias was talking to the strange little guy with the white hair and the perfect suit, the one who knew Pyrrhus from some place. The man was asking about Pyrrhus, probably, maybe trying to get his phone number, or his price. Archias didn't usually give up anything; he accepted gratuities from his boys, but he didn't pimp for them. Tonight, though, Pyrrhus could see the stranger passing something to Archias, possibly a bill.

Maybe Pyrrhus would let it happen. He should have made more when he had the chance. Some of the other guys didn't do so well on tips, but they made up for it when they—as Archias put it—socialized. Pyrrhus hadn't been socializing much. After the high of feeling a whole room looking at him, he didn't feel like giving himself up to just one of them. Besides, they acted even worse than most tricks. Here they'd picked you out, like a puppy in a store window; they'd picked you out from the rest of the litter and taken you home and they thought they could train you. Still, he should have let them, should have made every penny he could, because he was near the end of his run. Almost for the first time since he'd arrived in the city, he was actually looking a day or two ahead. Wondering what he could do next.

The song had changed, the next shift was already climbing onto the bar, and Amyclas had a death grip on his five-dollar bill. Pyrrhus said,

"Hey, I've gotta get off," and kissed Amyclas on the top of his head. That did it. The bill slid into Pyrrhus's sock. Pyrrhus grabbed his clothes from the hook above the cash register, got just his shorts on, and scurried to the back room.

He had a break, and he felt like just sitting in the back room by himself. Except that he was still a little claustrophobic, hated sitting sealed in there with the music going on outside. Besides, he thought he really ought to score with the little white-haired man.

When he dressed and went back out the man was gone. He stood at the bar and ordered a soda. Archias insisted, no liquor: "We had a Golden Boy who used to get absolutely plastered. One night he fell backwards into the glass sink. By the time they finished picking glass out of him, he was no longer a hot attraction. Then he had the temerity to try to get workers' comp, the little cocksucker."

It was almost closing time. He had just one more set before they turned the lights up and herded everybody out: he really needed to socialize during this break. With whom? Amyclas was a big tipper, but he never took anyone home. As if, though he loved the Golden Boys, he had somewhere along the line forgotten how to play with one. The guy a few seats down looked kind of prosperous—nice suit, hair arranged in a fantastically intricate comb-over. But, though he held himself erect, he had the glazed composure of someone who is way past drunk, focusing on a cosmos somewhere in his forehead. You could take a guy like that home and he might pay you a fortune for the privilege of passing out next to you. Or he might, abruptly, sober up—and then panic: Where am I? Who are you? There was the kid who'd groped him earlier, before he'd moved on to the white-haired guy, and who was still timidly cruising him. Could the kid actually have any money? Or did he suffer from the surprisingly common delusion that, when a Golden Boy dressed, stepped off the bar, and mingled with the crowd, he was no longer working?

Seated right next to Pyrrhus was a matched pair of guys in leather. Not exactly matched: one was older, plump and heavily accessorized— collar, wristbands, harness, various other gewgaws—the way some kids used to overdecorate their bikes with streamers, lights, horn, mirror, mud flaps. The other was younger, sleeker, with a careful beard and a gym-honed but slender body under the leather. The two had handkerchiefs of the same color waving from their right buttock pockets. This was supposed to signify something, though Pyrrhus had no idea just what. Anyway, it must have meant that they both preferred to be the subjects of the same

80

verb, and in the same voice, whether active or passive. They weren't a couple, then, just out cruising together.

Pyrrhus had always regarded leatherettes, as Archias called them, with an odd mixture of disdain and awe. Of course he knew that all they did was dress up in costumes and pair off to act out their complementary dysfunctions: daddies and bad boys, masters and slaves. What were these two? Slaves, probably: he could picture either of them crawling around, licking boots or suffering whatever other indignities were visited on them in the name of discipline. Yet—this was the part Pyrrhus couldn't easily shake, contemptuous as he was—they were proud of it. The silly games, compounded of grainy 8-millimeter film clips and the spontaneous rituals of real boys' secret clubs, made them feel part of something. Something they took into the everyday world, with their bits of leather, like a widow wearing an amulet, carrying the temple around with her. Or like an initiate of one of the mystery cults. Just as silly, secret handshakes and the like, but they too knew they were part of something.

The senior leatherette was intent on the dancer who had replaced Pyrrhus on the bar. A slightly superannuated Golden Boy—still in pretty good shape, but looking somehow as if he held that shape only through an act of will. A moment's lapse in concentration and his flesh might sag down around his ankles. The older guy was feeding him bills with sufficient regularity to keep him from moving down the bar. The younger guy was looking steadily at Pyrrhus.

Pyrrhus was a little flustered. He was used to being looked at. Except the guy wasn't admiring him, just gazing straight into Pyrrhus's eyes. His brow furrowed, as if he too, like the little white-haired man, knew Pyrrhus from someplace. Pyrrhus thought: You don't know me from shit, not if you think I'm going to join your little club. But he didn't turn away, found himself standing perfectly still in the negative spotlight of the guy's staring black eyes.

Pyrrhus wanted to hit the guy. He wasn't angry, exactly; at most a little bit annoyed. Yet he had a sudden, clear vision of himself clenching his fist, driving it into that cocky, knowing face. He had never hit anyone, what would it feel like? To maybe break the guy's nose? It was as if the guy were asking for it, as if he had brought injury into the room with him and had settled on Pyrrhus as his instrument.

The impulse passed. It was just a guy staring, one more in a roomful of men who stared and made plans for Pyrrhus's body. Besides, Pyrrhus had a sudden insight that the guy might very well hit him back. He went

81

on looking into the stranger's eyes; defiantly now, as if to say, I am not here to fulfill your intentions.

The Golden Boy on the bar had at last moved on. The older leatherette turned to find his friend still staring at Pyrrhus. "Come on, Deucalion, let's get out of here," he said.

"In a minute," Deucalion said.

"I want to get to the Barracks before last call."

"You go ahead, then."

The older guy glanced at Pyrrhus, then turned back toward Deucalion, smirking. "I don't think you can afford him, sweetie." He headed, jingling and clanking, toward the exit.

When he had gone, Deucalion said, "Can I?"

"Can you what?" Pyrrhus said.

"Afford you?"

"I don't know. Look, my break's almost over, I gotta go." Deucalion said nothing. "Why don't you stick around? I might be having a sale."

Once in a while, through the last set, Pyrrhus glanced over and found Deucalion still staring at him speculatively. He thought: Yes, I am having a sale. We will do . . . whatever it is you people do. As he danced down the bar, he felt his usual, vocational erection grow, spontaneously, a little firmer. Although, confusingly, the image before his eyes was once again that of his fist, and of Deucalion's face, crumpling.

They must have looked mismatched, Pyrrhus thought, walking together through the lobby of Deucalion's building and into the elevator, Pyrrhus in his high-school letterman outfit, Deucalion in his fussy costume of denim and leather and metal. Of course Pyrrhus and his tricks were always mismatched. But in this case, for the first time in so many months, there would be no exchange of currency to ease the fit.

The apartment, way out in the suburbs, was a white box with a view of the beltway. It was sparely furnished with cheap knockoffs of stern modernist furniture. A baby grand piano sat before the picture window; on it was sheet music for songs from musical comedies. Something in common, though Pyrrhus suspected Deucalion wouldn't be in the mood for a sing-along just then. Deucalion got a couple of beers—longnecks, of course—and they wordlessly watched the traffic on the beltway, until finally Deucalion led the way down the hall. Past his bedroom, which was all ruffles and shams, in contrast to the stark living room. On to the second bedroom, its white hollow-core door closed. Deucalion stepped back so that Pyrrhus would open it.

The room was fully outfitted, as Pyrrhus had expected, with a *batterie d'amour*, including a remarkable chair whose occupant could be made to assume any feasible human posture. Pyrrhus tried to deduce, from its current alignment, what posture had last been assumed in it. The legs would have been here, and the head . . . The question, which Pyrrhus's ignorance of the language of kerchiefs had left unanswered, was whether it had been Deucalion or his partner in that unseemly and vulnerable pose. And what Pyrrhus was supposed to be. Of course, many of the objects in the room awaited scenarios of insult and pain. How had Pyrrhus been cast?

The question was settled abruptly. Deucalion knelt, expectantly. Pyrrhus just stood there for a second. It was like the actor's nightmare, thrust onto the stage without your script. Deucalion whispered, as if he were the offstage prompter: "The neighbors don't like noise." Pyrrhus stepped forward, wrenched the indecipherable handkerchief from Deucalion's rear pocket, and gagged him. While this might have deprived Pyrrhus of any opportunity for further instruction, Deucalion communicated perfectly well. Pyrrhus knew exactly what to do.

7

Long before the plague, if one had wished to predict how the authorities would respond to that nearly unforeseeable event, one would have needed to consider only one fact: poppers were legal. A mind-altering and some-what addictive drug with uncertain side effects—a substance that would surely have been banned at once if straight people had been using it—was bottled as "liquid aroma" or even "room odorizer" and openly sold to gay people in stores and through the mail. Because it didn't matter what happened to them or what they did to themselves.

Poppers are gone: there are some even more toxic facsimiles available, but those will surely be suppressed soon enough. People will wonder, not very long from now, what poppers felt like, just as I wonder what absinthe could have been like. I have never encountered a text that could explain the mysterious hold of that outlawed liqueur, green with wormwood, sacred herb of Artemis. Just so, I cannot hope to describe the evanescent rush provided by the fumes escaping from a little brown vial.

Poppers didn't do anything, exactly. They didn't bring you up or down, you didn't see patterns or colors, they just left you where you were. But you were there and nowhere else, instead of being a hundred places at once, as we usually are. The square inch of some stranger's flesh on which you were conferring your attentions was the universe, and you yourself were stripped of history and future. You were perched, until the rush dropped away, on the saddleback of time, not falling off one way or the other. The instant lasted as long as it lasted. And while you were there you almost became one of those creatures who live entirely in the present, without guilt or forethought or anything standing between them and the world.

Almost. Only for Pyrrhus did it happen utterly. Perhaps he was so close already, had so entirely stripped himself of titles and raiment and inhibition, that the vial Deucalion proffered was enough to carry him over. He was for a few minutes what he had striven to be all these months: nobody at all, just a body doing things to Deucalion's body. What things, exactly? I hear you asking. But you don't really need an answer; the details would only repel you or, worse, fail to. Pyrrhus did things to Deucalion, a stranger, that you or I might, in our most childish moments, imagine doing to someone we had hated all our lives.

Except that Pyrrhus—though he was nominally the *active* member of the pair—didn't feel as though he was deciding what would happen next. Rather it seemed that Deucalion was entirely in charge, choosing the indignities Pyrrhus would visit upon him. Deucalion was practically inflicting them on himself; he was the only actor in the room—bound to his versatile chair, gagged so tightly that no scream could disturb the peace of the ignorant neighbors. Pyrrhus his acolyte equally silent.

I forgot to mention one other thing about poppers. They could give you a headache, the kind that could make you look at the headsman's axe as a potential miracle cure. Sometimes not until the next morning. Sometimes right away, or, as this night, in the cab going home.

Pyrrhus was so relieved to be home, in such a hurry for his own bed, that he let the driver keep the change from a ten. He ran upstairs, foolishly exacerbating the headache, and queasily let himself in.

Leucon was awake, sitting in the living room. He jumped up as Pyrrhus came in. "Hey," Pyrrhus said. No sudden moves please. "It's four in the morning. Don't you have work tomorrow?"

"Yeah, but—keep your voice down. Listen, there's this guy in your room."

"What?"

"I mean, I told him you weren't here and I didn't know when you'd be back and you'd call him or something, but he just wouldn't go away."

"Why did you even let him in?"

"I don't know. He said it was important, and . . . I don't know, he *seemed* important."

"What's he look like?"

"Old guy."

"Shit. Since when are they following me home?" He crept over to his bedroom door, half afraid that whatever old fart had had the nerve to barge into his apartment wouldn't have stopped short of jumping in his bed.

No, the visitor was standing up, facing the doorway. It was the strange guy from earlier in the evening, the one Pyrrhus hadn't been able to place, who had looked up with an interest untinged with desire. He had evidently been sitting on the bed; he had just clambered up on hearing Pyrrhus arrive, and was leaning rather heavily on an oak walking stick with a brass handle in the form of a bird's head.

"Neoptolemus," he said.

Of course there were people in town who knew Pyrrhus's real name. Leucon had seen it on the lease, and his various employers, because they had to verify his age. Still, it wasn't something he just gave out. The stranger wasn't, as he had thought, some half-remembered trick. The man had something to do with home.

Or no: he had got the name from Archias, as he had evidently got the address. Pyrrhus was pissed: Archias would hear about this. Except the man didn't say "Neoptolemus" like a name he had just learned.

Now Pyrrhus could ask outright the question that had seemed too rude in the bar. "Do I know you?"

"Perhaps not. But you are unmistakable: the very image of your father, when he was young." He got a distant look. "You should have seen him, running with the wild horses." The little flick of his tongue that accompanied this reminiscence smacked less of prurience than of connoisseurship, as if he were a man who admired but never tasted.

"You know my father," Pyrrhus said.

"I even saw you once. Before the war. I am Phoenix, don't you remember me? Your father's friend? Well, you were tiny, maybe you don't."

"You're right, I don't." Pyrrhus had always hated being told about things that happened when he was tiny — the bulk of his mother's conversation, as she wasn't very pleased with his nontiny being. Perhaps some people are fascinated with such stories, like to hear about the self they don't remember just as we might like to hear about our predecessor selves in the Golden or Silver Age. For Pyrrhus, though, it was bad enough that people should know anything at all about him; he was unnerved at the idea that they might know things that he didn't. (Even though, that very evening, one customer at the Escapade had committed to memory the pattern of hairs around Pyrrhus's anus, which Pyrrhus himself had never beheld.)

Pyrrhus sat on the edge of his bed, in the little concavity Phoenix must just have vacated. Pyrrhus knew this was rude, but his headache had returned with new vivacity, and they couldn't both sit down. He left Phoenix standing before him, leaning on the walking stick. Phoenix didn't seem annoyed or uncomfortable, just stood patiently. Pyrrhus realized he was some kind of servant, no matter how nicely he was dressed.

"I'm sorry," Pyrrhus said. "I just can't remember. Shit, I hardly remember Dad. How's he doing, killing a lot of Trojans?"

Phoenix was quiet for a second, as if trying to remember just how Dad was doing. Then he said, "He's dead." With so little drama that it didn't sink in right away. Even when it did, Pyrrhus thought it wasn't true.

Not that Phoenix was lying, just that he was inexplicably mistaken, as if he had said it was raining when it was sunny out. Pyrrhus had not realized how much a part of the weather of his life his father had been, through his lifelong absence: what Phoenix was saying was as implausible and—surprisingly—unwelcome as a sudden shower from a cloudless sky.

"He can't be dead," Pyrrhus said, as if this were something you could reason about. Then he remembered that it was: "He can't be. My mother said there was this spell or something. Nobody could kill him."

"There was a loophole."

"What?"

"I'm sorry, I don't mean to be facetious. But there was. He was shot in the foot and—well, maybe it was poisoned, or maybe he was just astonished—but his heart stopped. You didn't know? It was in all the papers, on the news . . ."

"I don't keep up real well."

After a minute, Phoenix said, "Would you like to be alone?" For no reason: Pyrrhus wasn't even feigning grief. On the contrary, the picture was almost comical: the wayward arrow, his father outraged by the impertinence, keeling over.

"No, I . . ." It was going to be a long talk; he couldn't just leave Phoenix standing there. "Why don't we go out to the living room?"

Leucon was still there—days past his bedtime, he had to have been eavesdropping. Leucon started to get up, and Pyrrhus shook his head, no, stick around. As if he and Leucon, the present, could outnumber Pyrrhus's resurgent past, two to one.

"When did this happen?" Pyrrhus said.

"About a year ago."

"A year? You wait all that time, and then you come tell me?"

"I wasn't . . . sure where you were. I only just located your mother last week. I gather you haven't been in touch."

"You've spoken to her."

"A week ago. We had luncheon."

"How's she doing?"

"Surprisingly well. She seems to be entirely recovered—not altogether flattering to your father."

"She didn't . . . she kind of knew she wasn't going to see him again. I guess she was sort of a widow already the day he sailed away." And didn't give a damn, was grateful to be released from the bungalow-prison and restored to the palace. Almost as grateful as Pyrrhus was.

"I suppose so. Anyway, she told us where to find you."

"She knew where I was?"

"She knew you'd taken the ferry here. And once I'd got here: well, you weren't very difficult to track. I had only to show your picture once or twice, and—"

Leucon said, "Yeah, people have seen a lot of him."

Phoenix smiled slightly. "A great deal, yes."

Pyrrhus interrupted this annoying burst of camaraderie. "Well, so—what? You just came to tell me this news?"

"I had thought it would be of more than passing interest."

"I—" Pyrrhus knew he must seem like a monster; maybe he was, he felt so little about the news. Not grieving but tired, with the scene in Deucalion's playroom still in the back of his head. And the insistent headache from the poppers at the front of it. "Of course, but all this time . . . you haven't spent a year looking for me."

"No, I've been at the front, rather uselessly. Quite at loose ends, since your father died. It was only lately that I realized I . . . I felt that I could be of service to you."

"What?"

"I don't mean that there is any particular service I can render. Only that I belong with you. You understand, I was with your father so long, and with his father, Peleus, before that, you Peleids are more or less my life's work."

Pyrrhus almost laughed in his face. "You mean you're out of a job?"

"Essentially."

"Well, I hate to break this family tradition, but—look around, you can see I'm not exactly loaded. I'm not ready to take on a . . . valet, or whatever you are."

"Counselor," Phoenix said, not indignant, just getting it straight.

"I don't need a counselor." Unless maybe he had a good headache remedy.

"Evidently not," Phoenix said. "You're making such a splendid life on your own."

Pyrrhus said, as automatically as you answer *Fine* to *How-are-you:* "It's my life." Even as he said it, he felt it wasn't so. This wasn't his life. It was all temporary, a detour. Obviously this couldn't be his life; any fool could see where such a life would end. He added, lamely, "At least I'm doing it on my own."

"Indeed. Your father would be so proud."

"Like he knew how to live."

"He was a great man."

"Terrific, so he's dead. No one ever dies from sex."

"I suppose not." Phoenix sat back. "Do you mind if I smoke?"

"Please don't," Leucon said.

Phoenix looked over at Pyrrhus as if he would overrule Leucon. He didn't.

"Very well," Phoenix said. He stared at the bird's head on his walking stick.

After a while, Leucon said, "So: you've been with the family a long time." Pyrrhus glared—here he wanted the guy out of there so he could take his headache to bed, and Leucon was making chitchat. Leucon ignored him.

"Since I was very young. Peleus, you might say, adopted me."

"Peleus?"

"Neoptolemus's paternal grandfather."

Leucon looked over at Pyrrhus, grinning at hearing the name that he had only seen once, on the lease. No, twice: on the late rent notice, too. He turned back to Phoenix. "What, he just picked you up somewhere?"

"It's late, it's rather a long story."

"No, go ahead."

"Yeah, tell him your story," Pyrrhus said. "I'm going to bed."

Phoenix said, "I hadn't finished—"

"I don't have any business with you. I'm going to bed."

Pyrrhus practically slammed the door. He started to undress and found himself, as if he were still at work, stripping slowly in front of the mirror.

I have never said what Pyrrhus looked like. I just realized, I've called him divine and perfect and assorted other nice things, but I have never exactly described him. Maybe because I was afraid he wasn't your type. Now I have caught him in front of a mirror, here is my obvious chance, his face was—

The problem with this venerable literary device is that he did not see what you or I would have seen, if we could have been in the room. He saw an outside that was congruent with his inside. A face that was intelligent, spiritual, decent—a face that you might wish to see across the circle in your reading group, not in bed, not hovering above yours in your playroom as you lie strapped to your chair. He saw the body of a little boy, clumsy and defenseless.

If we could have been in the room—well, we could have if, so long ago, we had had the money. Not together, we couldn't have been there together with him; he was at least wise enough not to do couples. But *you* could have been there. Then you would have seen the astonishing object that hovered above the drinkers at the Escapade, that went on hovering above them after they drove home, put out the cat, lay down with their favorite masturbatory aids. The grave eyes and the faint, dissolute smile; the archer's body like a pale, silver frame for the cock that rose up, spontaneously, like a wicked idea in the mind of a schoolboy. You would have seen that creature who seemed to have been placed here specially to act out your most cherished and secret intentions.

You would have seen that creature, but he could not. He tried, he looked in the mirror as faithfully as you look into yours. He could, if he concentrated, see himself part by part. Each part fine; he had no complaint with any of his parts. Only the aggregate eluded him. What you or I would have seen seemed to him a delusion, and our hasty assumption that it had something to do with his insides an affront.

Except this night, his head pounding, fresh from his strange, half-involuntary encounter with Deucalion, the news about his father somewhere in the room: this night he caught himself by surprise and saw the stranger everyone else saw. The body that was a part of the landscape of other people's lives and about which they made up the most preposterous stories.

He saw, more particularly, what Deucalion must have, the pale body looming over Deucalion in the dramatically lit playroom. Deucalion would have looked up at him and seen . . . something unspeakable. He must have seen it even at the Escapade; that's why he had stared so hard that Pyrrhus had finally come along with him. He had looked straight into Pyrrhus and seen the creature who would act out his rituals with him.

Pyrrhus was a little scared, and his heart was pounding as if the poppers hadn't worn off. Partly because he had ventured to the bottom of the cavern in which no scruple was to be found, and had uncovered the evidence—just the monitory traces, the droppings, a gnawed bone or two—that there was some creature, deeper still, with which he was not sure he wished to become acquainted. But maybe we all have that creature, even if it's just a little tiny one, safely chained up. Okay, he wanted to hurt a guy a little, just once. That didn't mean that he had joined the party of hurting.

Perhaps he was more dismayed that Deucalion had known something about him that he hadn't. Out in the living room was an old man who knew still more things and who called him by a name he had discarded. In the mirror was a perfect stranger about whom he knew nothing. He had thought he was the world's authority on himself, that he could get every question right in the category Pyrrhus. But the experts were outside him. They knew his past and his present better than he did. For all he could tell, they knew his future.

He tried to sleep. They were still talking out there; Pyrrhus's past was droning on to Leucon. Pyrrhus couldn't make out what he was saying, probably telling Leucon things about someone named Neoptolemus. He didn't want to know those things. It was too late for the past to come knocking, importunate, calling him by his real name. That was just his given name, an unwanted gift from his father. Neoptolemus: *the new war.* Whatever could Achilles have meant by calling an infant that?

He wasn't any kind of war. He was just Pyrrhus, the redhead. He would never be Neoptolemus again: his father was gone, across the river that surrounds the world.

Still, Pyrrhus thought about Deucalion, and he could feel, somewhere indefinable down below his waist, somewhere between gut and genitals, the awakened monster who was hungry to visit that playroom again. Or to do battle in some larger arena.

In the living room, Phoenix told his story.

"When I was very young, your age or not even that, my father's girl-friend . . . had a crush on me, I suppose you'd say. She was forever trying to catch me alone, and one night she succeeded. Father was out of town somewhere, Mamma was already in bed, and Father's girlfriend—we were all by ourselves, and she said I shouldn't be afraid. Father would never find out, why didn't I come closer? Well, I wasn't altogether certain Father would never find out, and in any event I wasn't the least bit attracted to her. She was an enormous, blowzy thing—that's what Father preferred, something he could sink into like a tepid bath. At any rate, nothing happened; I eluded her as fast as I decently could.

"Father returned home a few days later, and she went straight to him and told him *I* had made advances toward *her.* Not an unprecedented event, I have learned since, though I can't say I've learned how anyone manages it. I surely didn't know then. Father called me in, and of course I said her story was absurd, I didn't even like her. Father couldn't grasp that idea.

"Father was—not self-centered exactly, he could be generous, maybe even loving—but he was incapable of seeing anyone else's point of view. I mean, incapable of seeing that another point of view even existed. If you disagreed with him, he couldn't believe you were serious. You had to be toying with him. When I protested that his girlfriend was not to my taste, this was incomprehensible to him. I think if I had got down on my knees and said yes, I did try to seduce her, lord, please forgive me, he would have. But no: I insisted, the very notion of my caring for her left me with a sour taste, I had never looked twice at her. He was sure I was lying. Lying and also somehow mocking him, though he couldn't get the joke.

"He grew more and more furious, and I finally brought out the best alibi I had, the truth: that I wasn't interested in his girlfriend because I wasn't interested in women, period. I can't imagine why I thought that this would mollify him. Again, if I'd said I really was after her, he would have been angry but also proud—chip off the old block and all that. I'd only made him angrier, and stung particularly because he imagined that my . . . condition was somehow a reflection on his manhood, as if his very sperm swam to the left.

"I think he considered killing me, simply erasing me like an unfortunate first draft. I'm sure he did. Have you ever looked in someone's eyes and seen that he was thinking of your death? Not just wishing you dead, but positively contemplating bringing it about? I tell you, nothing brings home to you so clearly that the planets would go on circling the earth if you weren't on it, that the world might even be happier without you.

"At any rate, Father was, not religious, but at least superstitious. He dimly recalled that something not so nice ensued if a father killed his son. Oh, yes, the Furies, that was it. Instead he sent me off to the court physician to be cured.

"Which was fine with me. I wanted to be cured. This was a long time ago; who wanted to be an . . . invert? Living upside down? It was long ago, and the last time the court quack had opened a book was even longer ago than that, so he cheerily expounded a theory that had probably been discredited before my father was born. My problem stemmed from excessive sexual energy. There was only one cure.

"I can't even remember it hurting—I mean, it hurt later, abominably,

93

but at the instant all I felt was astonishment. And, as I recuperated, a faint amusement—of a distant and ironical kind—when I looked up one day and realized that the orderly who brought my lunch was . . . comely. They had mutilated my body, but I was intact, and as inverted as ever.

"Do you know, I have never really missed them, those overvalued little objects. Scant enough good they did me, or would ever have done. Without them, however, I was extraneous. As if I had never been anything but a vehicle for toting my testicles about. Of course my father wasn't going to leave me the estate, as I was no longer equipped to pass it on. The other way to keep myself in the style to which I was accustomed, a good marriage, was similarly closed to me. My father let me stay at the palace; I believe he was genuinely contrite over what he had done. Still, I felt rather like a wing-clipped peacock, strutting around on the terrace until someone notices that its plumage is getting a little tired and pops it into a casserole. So I left home—I didn't steal away, my father saw me off—and hired myself out as a tutor.

"I wasn't especially good at it. Geometry in particular has always eluded me, and my employers for some reason were especially eager that their little brats acquire that useless and impenetrable discipline. But I was entertaining enough at the dinner table. Usually they would keep me on for a while just for that, and when the welcome wore off there was always another place. Until I came at last to Peleus. You have heard of Peleus?"

"No," Leucon said.

"No reason you should have, his only distinction was that he had, through an odd set of circumstances, married a goddess. Thetis, of course you've heard of Thetis?"

"I guess." Leucon tried to think back to temple school. "I'm not sure. What is she the goddess of?"

"Well, nothing, actually, nothing in particular. Maybe some river. Just a miscellaneous goddess, but very well connected. At any rate, she was long gone by the time I showed up. There was just Peleus and his boy, Achilles, and—"

"Wait, Achilles?" Leucon said. "The guy in the war?"

"Yes."

"Pyrrhus is related to him?"

"Neoptolemus is Achilles' son."

"No shit." Leucon shook his head. "I'm sorry. Anyway, you got there and . . ."

94

"And there were Peleus and Achilles and a manservant who spoke in monosyllables and did what passed for cookery—mostly large, underdone roasts and frozen fries. A house of overabundant, even rampant masculinity; I cannot describe to you how it smelled. Peleus took me on, despite my inability to square the circle, because he thought the place needed a eunuch's touch.

"He entrusted the boy to me. You cannot imagine what Achilles looked like, when he was young, before the awful muscles just arrived, like a curse, and spoiled him. Your roommate, comely though he is, is like an imperfect memory of young Achilles. His father put this extraordinary object in my charge. As if testing me: was it true what they said about eunuchs? Well, it *is* true: we are capable of passion, though for the most part we'd rather have a second dessert. Yet he trusted me, you see, even though he must have known I would be tempted. While my father couldn't trust me even when I *wasn't* tempted. I was flattered or touched or—I don't know, but I understood I couldn't ever lay a hand on the boy.

"I just . . . watched him. I couldn't teach him very much: he was always running somewhere, or showing me how far he could throw the rhetoric text. I never really taught him even to read, though he would occasionally, on a rainy day, spell out a line or two of verse I gave him, if it was short enough and someone got disemboweled in it. Mostly I just watched him, all the years of his life except those few when he hid out on Scyros."

"Scyros," Leucon said. "Where Pyrrhus is from."

"Yes, Achilles' mother appeared one day when Peleus was out of town and told me she was taking her son on a little trip. I was overawed; she might have been a lesser deity, but still—I didn't argue. And Achilles: he scarcely remembered her, but he went unhesitatingly. He was just eighteen, he thought it was an adventure; little did he know she was going to sequester him in a suburban bungalow for ten years and make him dress as some sort of laborer. He went, and I stayed behind. Nothing to do at all—not that I had done so very much when Achilles was there. Peleus kept me on. We were quite a household, he and I and the grunting manservant. I needn't tell you who had to keep the talk going at dinner. Years on end of hearing nothing but my voice, I'm surprised we didn't all go mad.

"At last Achilles sent for me. I got a note—dictated to someone, I suppose—begging me to come. He was lonesome and trapped and hadn't the slightest idea of why he had been consigned to Scyros. We hadn't even known where he was. I was thrilled, I was going to go and fetch him home. Even Peleus, who never showed anything, seemed excited; he paid for my ticket and off I went. To find—

"A man. I was, am, an eternal boy. We had really been boys together, he and I—I a bit smarter and a good deal older, he much swifter. Boys, dwelling together all those years in Peleus's house. We had not been servant and master, nor even tutor and student: even when I tried to teach him, it was as one boy teaches another. Can you understand, the friendship we had?"

Leucon could understand: his old dream of playing catch. Maybe that was the only way he could have had it, the pregenital communion with another boy he had always longed for: if he had been a eunuch.

Phoenix went on. "But he was a man now. With a shrewish, acquisitive consort and a son, frail and timorous. Neoptolemus."

"Was he frail?"

"Very. And he—I can scarcely recall, but it seems to me that he hid much of the time. I mean literally hid: under the sofa, behind curtains, whenever his father and I would enter a room."

Leucon laughed. "I guess he got over hiding."

"He seems to have done. At any rate: his father was a man. Quite an awesome figure, enormous and forbidding. Not what I had come to fetch. The idea of bringing him home left me the minute I laid eyes on him. It would have been impossible, seeing him every day in all those places where once we had been boys together—the woods, the fields, the den on a rainy morning. After a few days I went home without him—I told Peleus he'd refused to come along, though really we'd never even talked about it. And all those places were still mine. To walk through alone, seeing him as he had been."

"But you wound up with him after all?" Leucon said.

"I beg your pardon?"

"In the war, I mean."

"Oh, yes. As soon as he had joined the army, he sent for me again. This time, however, it was quite plainly a summons to a servant. I went as a servant."

Leucon glanced at the window and realized that the sun was coming up. He hadn't had any sleep at all, and he would have to go to work; he'd used up all his sick leave. He got up to make coffee, but he didn't want to go through Pyrrhus's room. Not with this stranger around; he might think there was something between Leucon and Pyrrhus. That would be intolerable. "Listen," he said. "I've got to get ready for work." Phoenix said nothing, so he added, "I mean, you've got to go."

"Of course." Phoenix got up, slowly, with the aid of his walking stick. "I'm sure I've bored you."

"No," Leucon said.

"Do tell Neoptolemus I shall be seeing him again."

"You want to be his servant."

Phoenix looked down at the bird on the handle of his walking stick. "Do you know," he said, softly. "His mother lent me a picture, so that I could find him here. It must be a few years old; he is fifteen or sixteen. I had, up until the very minute I walked into that establishment—what is it?—the Escapade, I had the most foolish notion that he was still the boy in that picture and that I might be . . . something other than a servant. But . . ." He shook his head, went to the door, and let himself out.

Leucon locked the door behind him. He could finish Phoenix's thought. But he's a man now. It had never occurred to Leucon that Pyrrhus was a man, or he himself. He who had longed to be a boy, with another boy: it had never occurred to him that time had foreclosed this possibility forever. Even now some part of him didn't believe it. The word *man*, so casually dropped, could not dispel a vision that was the closest thing he had to a religion, stronger than anything he felt about the gods.

He was not alone. One would have needed only to peer over Leo's shoulder at the personal ads to discover that it was a vision many men took to their graves.

8

Anyone's origins are fabulous. As a child Leucon used to listen, rapt, to the tale of how his parents met at college, courted, married. This homely story was magical, partly because the picture of his parents as lovers was as difficult to conjure as, say, Europa and the bull; but mostly because the story ended with Leucon. His mother might have met somebody else, Leucon might have been entirely different: handsome, rich. Straight. Yet here he was, the culmination of some frantically busy weaving at the fringes of the web of Destiny.

No less magical—but no more, either, only just as much—was the myth of Pyrrhus's beginnings, the story from Phoenix, the few additional details Leucon was able to elicit from Pyrrhus himself until he clammed up. How his grandmother was a goddess who married a mortal and bore a son. How that son dodged the draft by hiding out on Scyros. How he met Pyrrhus's mother there and, in due course though without ceremony, produced Pyrrhus. To Leucon, the goddess bit might have been the wondrous part of the story, but of course to Pyrrhus the wondrous part was that he had come to exist. The rest he seemed to take more or less for granted.

We are accustomed to thinking of history as having some main events and a great many sideshows. Achilles and Pyrrhus and a few others are in the center ring: everything that happened from the birth of the world led inexorably to the war, everything that has happened since the war is, simply, the postwar. The great heroes are at the heart of the tapestry, the place where every thread comes together in one impossibly intricate knot and the gods themselves condescend to join in the weaving. While Leucon, and you and I, are off at the periphery somewhere.

Of course there is no periphery. If I had titled this volume *Leucon*, I might have shown you how every heavenly power conspired to bring Leucon into being, how every time he belched or broke something he set off a chain of events that built empires and then leveled them. He was just as important as Pyrrhus.

Except he didn't think so. He might have conceived, at one point in his sophomore year, the smashing idea every sophomore sooner or later stumbles on: that the world came into being the day he opened his eyes, that it was all created to baffle or amuse him. He got over it, as most of us do. He exiled himself to the edge of history, where nothing he did mattered very much. So he was excited by the news from Phoenix, pleased to find himself a minor character in the epic of Pyrrhus.

And aggravated that Pyrrhus wouldn't let him play even his supporting part. He wanted to know everything: how it felt to be sort of divine, what it was like to grow up as a prince, with a heroic father and all. Pyrrhus answered only in monosyllables. As if Leucon's interest in the astonishing news of his identity were somehow . . . vulgar. It was vulgar for Leucon to throw himself so eagerly into the role of history's roommate. It was vulgar for Leucon, even jokingly, to call Pyrrhus Neoptolemus. It would have been supremely vulgar for Leucon to remark — as he very nearly did — that Pyrrhus had a famous father and a wealthy family and had evidently been playing some sort of protracted game. That, for example, his ostentatious casualness about the rent last fall had been well founded; how it must have amused him to watch Leucon worrying about money.

A few withering looks from Pyrrhus were all it took to make Leucon's position plain. He was so trivial, so minor a figure in the hero's story, that he could not participate even vicariously. He was not to speak of it; he had to pretend that he had learned nothing. Above all, he was not to mention Achilles. If he dared to utter the name, Pyrrhus seemed to shut down. As, when you turn off the television, the image shrinks to a faint blue point, then vanishes: so Pyrrhus's face when Achilles' name came up. After one or two times of that, the name just seemed to hover in the air between them. Leucon and Pyrrhus were so doggedly silent about Achilles that he might as well have been sitting in the living room with them.

He was. Pyrrhus had been ten when Achilles left, old enough positively to revel in his departure. Though Achilles had seldom bothered to strike him or even speak to him, Pyrrhus had already lived for years under the cloud of his father's contempt. Every room in the house was filled with it; even the backyard was strewn, in place of crabgrass, with markers of the sites where Pyrrhus had let his father down, declining to catch the ball, falling off the bicycle, refusing to run when he was It. That especially, refusing to run because you couldn't outrun Achilles, and there was that awful feeling as he got closer and closer. Even if you knew all he was going to do was tag you (too roughly), you felt the way some hapless Trojan boy would have. Running, the sun at your back, seeing on the ground before you your own shadow and Achilles', his shadow growing until it swallowed yours up: you turned and knew you had seen the last of the sun.

He had lived in that shadow every day for the first ten years of his life. Every moment of pleasure or self-esteem, every hour in the company of his mother or alone, reading or playing, eclipsed by the possibility that his father would appear to destroy it. His life could be lived only when he was out of his father's sight. How could he not have felt—when Achilles got into the limo with Odysseus and Ajax, not even saying goodbye to the mock family that was, to him, just part of the disguise he had worn on Scyros—how could Pyrrhus not have felt that a cloud had passed from his world? He had been discharged from the eternal boot camp of the bungalow to a palace where he was at last free to be himself.

His negligible, despicable self. It was too late, probably, even ten was too late. He must already have acquired the habit of invisibility, keeping himself out of anybody's sight, not just his father's. As if anybody at all who looked into Pyrrhus would see what his father had seen. Or hadn't seen: the vacancy, the hole where Achilles might have said valor should have been, where I have said scruples were lacking—both a little off the point.

I can't see far enough into him. I feel . . . vulgar even guessing. But maybe what was missing was the sense that there was anything worth trying, suffering, resisting for, so that he wouldn't wrestle with his father or with his conscience. Nothing good would come to him because his father's power would take it from him. Or everything good would come to him through fate or luck or magic. Maybe he felt both those things, learning one from Achilles and the other from Thetis. Or maybe Thetis never visited him, her message just grew up in him, his vague and grandiose sense of entitlement just a child's invented light to dispel his father's shadow. I am guessing. Maybe the way we usually guess about other people, by turning them into ourselves.

I don't suppose Pyrrhus actually thought of Achilles much, all those years when he was out of sight. It didn't matter: Achilles was alive somewhere, those many years. There had always been, somewhere, one man who had seen straight into Pyrrhus and found him . . . insufficient. There had never been anywhere he was out of his father's sight.

And now, with his father safely in Hell? The shadow gone and unmourned, now surely he could begin to live, come out of hiding? Except now he would never hear his father say . . .

Somewhere he must always have harbored the wan hope that he would hear — maybe this is what the hole was after all: the place in him waiting for those words — that he was all right. That his father had seen him, seen into him, and had assented to his existence. Now that hole would never be filled. Nothing he could do, or refuse to do, would ever make a difference. Achilles would never stride naked and radiant into the room, lift up the infant Pyrrhus, and whisper to him: I have seen you, and you are good.

Is it any wonder that — ten years into the war and no end in sight — the Greeks had sent Phoenix to fetch him? Isn't it just such a man who burns cities?

A day or two went by before Pyrrhus, stopping at a fast-food joint on his way to the Escapade down the street, came upon Phoenix again. Phoenix was in the front part, the smoking section in those days, just in the act of pouring cream-substance into his coffee from the tiny plastic container when Pyrrhus came in. An incongruous figure, Phoenix, sitting on the little swively chair in his elegant suit, his walking stick leaning precariously against the table. He scarcely looked up, seemed to be absorbed in stirring his coffee, as if he had known Pyrrhus was going to walk in.

Pyrrhus strode by without greeting him and ordered a bacon cheese-burger, small fries. While he waited he looked around for some place to sit. He wanted to be in smoking, but there was only one table, two down from Phoenix's; in between, a bunch of high-school kids. They looked about ready to leave, exposing Pyrrhus to an assault by his incarnate past. He thought of just taking his food to the Escapade. But he wasn't going to be forced out by Phoenix; the man wasn't going to make him change his life. He asked for water, which the woman behind the counter supplied in a tiny, grudging cup.

The kids who sat between Pyrrhus and Phoenix had something greasy about them, as if they not merely subsisted on but were somehow made of the tallow-fried output of the kitchen. Their long hair fell in oily, apathetic waves across their faces. They wore, all three of them, tattered denim jackets and begrimed T-shirts with the names of rock groups whose members, now deceased, burned their instruments or ate vermin on stage. The largest of the boys, just old enough to have a proto-mustache and so the apparent leader, cradled a boom box, which he presently turned on.

Even Pyrrhus was startled by the sudden racket of it. He spilled a little of his water, then looked over to the food counter, expecting someone to come forward and make the kid turn it down. The staff, as is usual in

102

such places, appeared to be living in a different dimension from the customers; if the sound reached them they gave no sign of it. Pyrrhus thought of saying something himself. Except he was intimidated: these were real boys. He peeked around them at Phoenix, who was eyeing the boom box as if it were a live bomb. Good, let them drive him out.

Phoenix leaned toward the proprietor of the boom box and murmured, "Could you turn that down, please." Not asking, but in the tone, confident of fulfillment, with which one might say, "I'll take the check."

The kid looked at him with exaggerated amazement, as if he had just noticed this astonishing figure who had materialized in a burger joint. "What?"

"I find it disturbing. In fact I'm surprised that the management permits—"

The smallest of the kids, with stringy copper hair and a rodent face, tossed a bit of shaved ice from his drink at Phoenix. "I'm surprised the management lets me do this," he said, in a wickedly perfect imitation of Phoenix's gelded alto.

"Yeah, or this," the third kid said, tossing a fry, missing, then scoring with a second, a minute spot of ketchup appearing on Phoenix's perfectly rolled lapel. He looked down at it with bewilderment, picked up a paper napkin, and paused. He was so absorbed in trying to decide whether it would be better to dab at it or leave it alone that he ignored for a minute what had become a sporadic hail of ice shards from the rat-faced kid.

Pyrrhus watched with mixed feelings. He was young enough to be half in sympathy with the kids, could have joined in mocking Phoenix's fruity arrogance. But he wasn't, either, especially thrilled about the boom box. And they were the kind of kids who might as easily have turned on Pyrrhus if he had been a little less . . . straight-acting.

The fry warrior reached over and grabbed the walking stick. "Look at this fucker. What's this supposed to be, some kind of bird?"

"It is a phoenix."

"A phoenix, what's that? It looks like a chicken to me. Yeah, a chicken on a stick."

"If you would," Phoenix said, gesturing for the stick in the absurd confidence that he would get it back. The confidence that came, perhaps, from having spent so many years knowing that the meanest demigod on the block was just a whistle away. If Phoenix could have whistled.

The lead boy took custody of the stick and inspected it with the air of an appraiser. "This looks kind of dangerous to me. I don't know that old guys should walk around with something like this. I think we're going to have to confiscate it."

Pyrrhus suddenly reached for the stick and said, "I think you're going to have to give it back." Before he could get a grip on it the boy handed it off to rat-face.

"Why don't you mind your own business?" the leader said.

A good question. What did Pyrrhus care about Phoenix's self-referential walking stick? Besides: Pyrrhus had never been in a fight. There was no good reason to suppose he could outfight even the little rodent, much less the leader with his vague mustache. He heard himself saying, "This is a friend of mine." That wasn't what he meant; of course they weren't friends. Still, they were on the same side, if there had to be sides.

"Yeah? What do you do, play with his stick? Hey, Malis, give it back here. Okay, dude, you want it, why don't you take it from me?"

"All right," Pyrrhus said. He stood, and the boy was up, too, holding the stick with both hands as he must have seen men do in the martial-arts movies. They were of a height, he and Pyrrhus, but the boy was just a boy, all head and legs. And there was something lax about his grip on the stick, as if he were having second thoughts about the whole scene. Pyrrhus felt for a second that he could, yes, overpower the little brat. Just grab the stick and—

Break the kid's head wide open. Yes. The desire rose in him like an aura, deeper and warmer than sex. Had his father felt this, up in his throat, this savage mixture of exultation and contempt? It had come so fast, the feeling: he wanted to vomit, almost, yet at the same time he was joyous and whole, poised to smash some stranger's skull in. This had to have come from his father.

It only lasted a second: he was already coming to his senses, recalling that he hit like a girl and had no idea how to block a punch. But of course the boy had no way of knowing that: all he could see was that he was head to head with a hemidemigod. Whose face had accidentally taken on an expression that might have been interpreted as warlike.

Before Pyrrhus could back off, the kid retreated to the far side of the table. His army, more impressed by their leader's surrender than by Pyrrhus himself, made for the door. The kid dropped the stick, saying, "Who wants this piece of shit," grabbed his boom box, and followed them. Pyrrhus just stood for a minute, listening to the diminishing sound of the boom box as the kids headed down the street and out of sight.

Phoenix retrieved the stick, then gave Pyrrhus a little bow. "I am beholden to you," he said. "The little hooligans."

104

"I didn't do anything."

"Nonsense," Phoenix said, already returning his attention to the ketchup spot on his lapel. "I don't suppose this establishment would have club soda. Nonsense, I believe you have saved me from considerable harm. I feel as though . . . as though I had a protector again."

"Look, I don't even know why I bothered." Pyrrhus sat down and contemplated his congealing cheeseburger. He had lost his appetite. Or his appetite had been cheated: he still felt the strangest longing to run down the street and finish something with that ugly kid.

"It's just what your father would have done. That is why I followed him all his life."

"Lived off him, you mean."

"I suppose."

"Well, the gravy train's over. It's all I can do to take care of me."

"I'm afraid you've more or less inherited me. Along with some bequests of more tangible value."

"I don't want anything he left," Pyrrhus said. His burst of obligatory scorn at once, of course, overtaken by curiosity about just what he might be spurning.

"You should. The armor, if nothing else—quite spectacular."

Oh, was that all? "I don't have much call to wear armor."

"Or anything else. I'm rather glad your father didn't live to see that."

"I wouldn't care if he had. I wouldn't care if my mother hopped the ferry from Scyros and caught my act." This defiant little utterance had the unhappy side effect of compelling him to picture his mother at the Escapade, looking up at him as he stroked himself. Her expression, as he pictured it, was less reproachful than anxious. Was he warm enough? Was that other boy getting better tips? He was trying to think of some way of escaping her gaze when Phoenix interrupted.

"It's probably worth something, the armor. The shield, especially."

"Fine. Maybe you could have it sent. Or just pawn it yourself and we'll split the proceeds."

"You need to come and claim it on your own."

"Come where?"

"To the front."

"Troy?" Pyrrhus said. "You expect me to go to Troy?"

"You need to claim everything that belongs to you. You could be rich. Not just the armor, but the ships. And the men."

"Men?"

105

"The Myrmidons."

"The who?"

"Your father's army."

Pyrrhus snickered. "I inherited an army?"

"In a manner of speaking. They are headless now. Waiting to be wielded, like your father's sword."

"So I'm General Neoptolemus, huh?"

"Exactly," Phoenix said.

Pyrrhus laughed again. Although he did see, just for an instant, an army looking up at him, awaiting his commands. And felt a tiny stirring of something, rising from somewhere near the spot in him that had wanted to hit the boy just now. He overcame it. "Look, this is the most bizarre discussion I've ever had. I don't have anything to do with this shit, armor and armies and all that."

"Your father left it, all of it, just for you."

"My father didn't even know I was alive."

"Oh, come."

"Oh, come yourself. Did he ever mention me? All those years you hung out with him, did he ever say my name?"

"Of course," Phoenix said, looking Pyrrhus straight in the eye. Not as if he were telling the truth; as if the question were so silly it didn't call for the truth. "He wanted you to have everything."

"I don't have to take it. Listen, I could practically be running Scyros if I were interested. But I'm not, I'm here. I don't need anything people have to give me."

"They need you. They are waiting for you to lead them."

"You think I'm going to come back with you to Troy and become some kind of soldier? I swear, this is the craziest thing I ever . . ."

"I think it's your . . . destiny—is that too big a word?"

That was much too big a word. "My destiny right now is to head down the street and take my clothes off."

"Very well, I shall finish my coffee."

"Yeah, you do that. Then you can come see my act."

"I've seen it, thank you. And I am rather exhausted after our contretemps with that band of ruffians. Here." He took out a little notebook and began scribbling with a tiny gold pencil. "I am staying at the Park Court if you should wish to speak further. Room 208. I do hope you'll call."

. . .

If the Escapade was his destiny, it was a short-term one. This was positively his final night. Phoenix had merely distracted him from the — now rather pressing — task of deciding what he would do next.

He could put his ad in the paper again, but things had been so slow, if he hadn't found this gig he would practically have been giving it away by now. He could move on to some other city: there was a whole circuit, Archias said, he could dance a month here and a month there until —

He sat with his soda in the little back room, waiting for his first set, trying to think things through. The unfamiliar act of thinking ahead led him to think much farther ahead than he had meant to. Moving to one city after another entailed adding one month to another, year upon year until his youth was gone and he became, in some city, one of those men you saw on the park benches, still handsome but wan and filthy. They had sold their time, in hours or, for a bonus, whole nights; now they had endless time and no takers. Their lives over at thirty, or sooner, nothing ahead but the drugs or some last customer who would descend on them and take everything.

Maybe his vision wasn't quite so clear as that. Maybe he just glanced over at the other kid waiting to go on — not Tydeus tonight, but a new kid, Pyrrhus hadn't even caught his name. He was skinny enough that his ribs showed, and his face was the before picture in an ad for acne medication, but the bulge in his elastic shorts was about the size of his forearm. The kid was looking at a comic book — not reading it, his lips weren't moving — just staring at it, whatever drug he was on making him focus on some single panel. Maybe Pyrrhus looked at him and understood, however dimly, that anyone bursting in on them would have seen . . . a pair of something. Not one empty-headed kid already well into a downward spiral and one Pyrrhus, magically exempt. Two of the same thing.

What burst into the room was Archias, crying out, "Golden Boys! Are you on strike? The world is clamoring for you."

Well, he could have been on strike. For the first time, he really didn't feel like going up there, in tandem with some little brain-dead whore. What if the crowd couldn't tell one Golden Boy from another? What if they looked up at him and saw, not a hemidemigod, but a boy in free fall? If you waited long enough he would fall into your bed; if you waited longer you wouldn't want him any more.

With nothing ahead past tonight, what did it matter if he went on this one last time? Well, a hundred bucks, give or take. He chose to go on. Yet even this was a new sensation, *choosing*. As if he had choices. Doing this, or taking Phoenix up on his ridiculous job offer. He chose to climb up onto the bar and started to unbutton his shirt.

He hung up his shirt on the hook over the cash register in the usual way, undid the top button of his trousers, turned and looked down at the faces lining the bar like so many footlights. All the regulars, looking up at him—as, when you are flipping the channels and you find nothing to watch but an episode of a situation comedy you've already seen, you watch it anyway. Knowing each punch line as it's being set up, you listen wearily to the phony, digressive dialogue that wanders away from the plot in search of the fifty-dollar joke. How could they come, night after night, to watch him slowly peel away the layers of clothing and reveal what they had already seen a hundred times? What punch could still be left in the punch line for them?

He looked over to his right, at the other dancer. He was already displaying his prodigious cock, and the customers at his end were showing their appreciation. Pyrrhus thought, Why do they care about his cock? Not envious, Pyrrhus didn't mind that the kid's cock was bigger; over-endowment bears its own curse. But it was just a gob of flesh dangling from his body. Everyone in the room had one, had one of every other part this boy had, or Pyrrhus. All over the world men were walking around with penises and ankles, livers and earlobes, all pretty much the same. The differences among them measurable in mere inches, here and there. And in years, of course.

No wonder Phoenix hadn't come; he had seen this episode once already. The wonder was that anyone at all showed up. What Pyrrhus was doing wasn't shameful. It was inconsequential. He had chosen to be inconsequential, just a body. How could people care so much about a body?

He took off his pants and his briefs much faster than usual, as if he were too weary to build to the punch line—as the actors in the situation comedy might have felt at the twentieth take, let's just do the goddamn joke and go to lunch.

He wasn't hard. Always before he had been, effortlessly, excited by the waves of desire that rose up to him on the bar. Tonight he felt as though they didn't want him at all. Didn't want Pyrrhus in particular, that is: any old penis would have done. And he had better get his erect if he expected to make any money.

How did people do that? He had seen the other boys work themselves up to it, stroking, their eyes getting a distant look—picturing something, obviously, the way some actors force tears by remembering when their collie died. He looked away from the crowd and no picture came. Not the chauffeur's son, not any trick paid or free thereafter, no image he could conjure up excited him. He couldn't remember a time when he had been excited by someone else. It was as if he had always been excited by the fact of himself. Every memory of sex was of himself, the other shadowy, a mere backdrop to the theater of his own hard-on. With that calling in sick, there was no show.

Nobody tipped him. At the end of his set he got dressed, found Archias, and said he had the flu or something, he couldn't do the rest of the sets.

"You mustn't be upset at a little attack of stage fright, it happens all the time."

"I'm not sure. It wasn't like stage fright."

"You have to go back up. Otherwise you'll get some sort of complex, and then you'll always have trouble." As if Pyrrhus were a trapeze artist.

"It doesn't matter. I mean, this was my last night anyway."

"No, I was going to talk to you. I was thinking of holding you over."

"You were?"

"Don't get a swelled head. There's only one part of you that needs to be distended. But you're the most popular Golden Boy ever."

"Really?" Pyrrhus couldn't help being gratified, even if the competition wasn't much.

"Yes indeed. I thought perhaps we might ride this horse until she drops."

"I don't know."

"Unless you have something better to do," Archias said, in a tone that suggested Pyrrhus would never have anything better to do.

Pyrrhus was annoyed enough to say, "I don't know, I might." Might what—go be a general?

"Fine. It was just an offer."

"I'm sorry. I probably should, I just need a few nights off."

"Oh, that's fine. Why don't you give me a call?"

"All right."

"Are you okay now? There isn't something I should know?"

Maybe he meant well; he seemed genuinely concerned. But only the way a swineherd on Scyros might be if a pig was off its feed. "I'm fine. I'll be back Friday, maybe."

"Wonderful. I assure you, next time you go up you'll be your old self. Every inch of it."

Everyone in the dining room at the Park Court must have assumed that Pyrrhus was a kept boy and Phoenix his sugar daddy. Well, this was nothing new, he'd been out to fancy places with tricks—he was the only Golden Boy who knew how to hold a fork. Except this time Pyrrhus was, absurdly, the prospective sugar daddy. Phoenix had talked about his impending wealth all through lunch—which in Phoenix's case consisted of no fewer than five courses; Pyrrhus had a burger. Phoenix must have thought that when Pyrrhus found out how rich he was, he would naturally pick up the tab.

Pyrrhus's wealth was far away. It apparently consisted of the more portable household goods of half the suburbs of Troy: flatware, VCRs, limited-edition commemorative objects. Jewelry. A few cars. A small congregation of women and children—though these tended, Phoenix said, to be more trouble than they were worth and were chiefly of symbolic value.

All of it seemed to be more trouble than it was worth. What was Pyrrhus supposed to do, go all the way to Troy and have some enormous tag sale?

"Well, as I believe I've intimated," Phoenix said, "there was some hope that you would take up your father's command."

"Who hopes this?"

"Actually, to be more precise, it is prophesied that you will take up your father's command."

"Prophesied?"

"Personally, I've never given much weight to these things. Or I didn't, until your father's case demonstrated how very accurate these predictions can be."

"What, that if he went off to war he might die? Pretty amazing."

"Actually, it was rather more detailed than that. It doesn't matter; I'm not soliciting your belief. I am merely reporting that there is a general expectation among the Greeks that you . . ." He waved a hand vaguely and dug into his white chocolate mousse.

"Will come and die too?" Pyrrhus said.

Phoenix looked startled, but his mouth was full and he didn't answer right away. Pyrrhus was a little startled himself. That is, he didn't believe any of this stuff, but the notion that there were people out there confidently discussing his future was scary. People a million miles away thought they knew when he was going to die, and how. He was young, in those days young men didn't think about their own death. But strangers were helpfully thinking about his for him. And had, perhaps, sent this man to hurry it along.

Phoenix swallowed and said, "I don't recall the subject of your death coming up. It won't be in the war, at any rate."

"You're damn right, because I'm not going."

"Because you will, personally, take Troy."

"Right. Me and my Myrmidons." He snickered, though it did sound better than dying. "Don't you feel silly even repeating this shit? I mean, can you see me dressed up in some uniform, in front of a bunch of grunts?"

"I can, as a matter of fact. I think you might be rather inspiring."

"Uh-huh. And then, knowing absolutely jack shit about battle or anything, I'm going to lead these guys right into Troy."

He shrugged. "Someone is going to."

"Says who? I don't see the papers much. How long has it been, ten years?"

"Longer."

"It's been dragging on all this time, this pointless war, maybe nobody's ever going to win it. Least of all me. I think your oracles just get a kick out of telling people the most incredible things and then watching them kill themselves trying to make it happen."

"I'm not an expert in these matters. Still, it doesn't seem entirely implausible to me. You need to understand the situation at the front. The Trojans are wearing down; one last assault and it will all be over. Yet here sits a major part of our forces, idle, when if they could be brought to bear . . ."

"Great, why don't *you* dress up in my father's armor and lead the damn Myrmidons?"

Phoenix chuckled. "Can you imagine? A eunuch . . ."

"I'm a card-carrying fairy. I doubt the Myrmidons could tell the difference."

"The Myrmidons aren't terribly quick on the uptake. There's no reason they would have to know about . . . your experiences before you arrived."

"You mean I could pass?"

"I mean that your history need not dictate your future."

How very un-Greek, almost subversive, this glib response was. Imagine Pyrrhus's grandfather Lycomedes uttering such a line, he who thought that some single misstep or omission, like denying a stranger a third bottle of wine, could shadow you forever.

"It's an option," Phoenix said. "At any rate, if nothing else interests you, there are still the goods. You could have the money."

"And then treat you in the style to which you are accustomed?"

"You are already treating me in the style to which I am accustomed."

Meaning, perhaps: with contempt. Pyrrhus took it more literally. "Not quite," he said, as he walked out on the check.

Phoenix looked at it with some dismay. How was he going to account to his employer for a lunch equal to his whole per diem? Well, you know how it is, sir, the boy is a very hearty eater. Like his father.

When Pyrrhus returned to the Escapade a few nights later, he was able to perform, if tumescence constitutes a performance. Being a body didn't seem as paltry as it had the other night; he was pleased to be a body once again. This night, though, it was different: he was playing with the idea that his was the body of Neoptolemus.

If, most nights, he had been in an ecstasy of anonymity up on the bar, reveling in the way men he would never know shamelessly gave up to him their whole soul: tonight he had a surge of identity. I am not just any body, an effigy through which you work out leftover confusions from high school, I am Neoptolemus, who is to take Troy. I could be looking down, not at your begging eyes, but at the princely sons of Priam. You thrust your dollars into my socks and long for my cock when they could be lying at my feet pleading for their lives.

Still just playing, savoring the joke. He had not chosen. I share the reader's impatience: we could move things right along. Let him cast off his anonymous Boydom and take on an identity which is specially destined for him and which will work itself out in unforgettable deeds of comic-book violence.

The *Neoptolemid*, starring the hero son of Achilles: watch as he burns the most beautiful city on earth, hurls the infant son of Hector from a tower. Stand with him at the altar as he cuts out the heart of Priam's daughter to appease his father's ghost. All these stories I will be able to tell if he will only just embrace his name, step off the bar and onto the larger stage. Of course they are awful stories: he will do terrible things, the more terrible because he is not the pure, cleaving animal his father was. Still, what would you rather hear: this, or the story of how he came to be a used-up whore on a park bench?

Well, you don't get a vote; no more do I. But what he was feeling, up there on the bar, was the novel sensation that he did get a vote, could simply choose a future. Or rather—maybe this is what choosing feels like—that he was already two people.

Somewhere beneath the walls of Troy, strangers were waiting for Neoptolemus. Dejected, the Myrmidons lay in their tents, dreaming of the arrival of Neoptolemus, the New War, resplendent in his father's armor. Hundreds of miles away, an alternate self lived in the minds of those men; he was already there with them. While a hustler nicknamed Pyrrhus for the redness of his hair stood on the bar, absently noting the accumulation of dollars in his socks, Neoptolemus stood before his army, a general. In place of the drunks at the Escapade, looking up at him with their various plans for his body, was an army of real men. Ready to give him, not their dollars, but their lives.

There was one little detail. He turned his back on the men at the bar, looked at himself in the mirror, and said half-aloud, solemnly: "I don't want to kill anybody."

If he had any such misgiving it was, I suspect, not a powerful one. A lot of young men in those years didn't go to the war, ran every deferment until they were safely past conscription, and told themselves they were acting on principle. Perhaps enough time has elapsed that we can now acknowledge that their conscientious objections to killing happily coincided with their understandable desire not to be killed. Of course every thinking person thought the war was silly and wrong. But everyone might not have been quite so vocal about it if he could have been assured, as Pyrrhus was, that he would emerge unscathed, standing at the war's conclusion on the ruins of the enemy's capital.

He said it again: "I don't want to kill anybody." He heard the lack of conviction in his own voice. What he really meant was that he didn't know how. Didn't have the requisite skills: couldn't aim a lance at that place between breastplate and helmet, or hold it firmly enough to pierce through a shield. Maybe he didn't want to, especially, but he didn't want *not* to. If he wasn't exactly bloodthirsty, he was at least curious. Indeed, as he turned to face the crowd again, he realized that there were a few people out there he wouldn't mind so much aiming a lance at.

9

Pyrrhus was lying in the bedroom; he had been all afternoon, smoking so many cigarettes that a blue cloud stretched all the way into the kitchen. They were supposed to be meditational aids, but the very act of lighting each one broke his chain of thought and left him . . . Oh, as if he had *had* a chain of thought: he couldn't think about this, any more than he could think, the morning after his first time with Lamus, about whether prostitution was a wise career move. If Destiny had to come knocking, she should have come the way she had for his father: the generals appearing suddenly one night and, seconds later, threatening to depart. Leaving no time to think. Destiny should not have come in the form of a tiresome little eunuch who just lurked about for days on end, wanting to talk and talk about it.

And what a destiny. The thrilling opportunity to go camp out on the muddy plains of Phrygia with a bunch of unwashed straight guys who probably spent their tedious days having spitting contests. The little rush of wanting to do it, as he had stood on stage the night before, had worn off. Not the longing for it; he just couldn't envision it as easily as he had last night.

In the day he could picture himself: running like a sissy, holding his sword like a girl—and not an Amazon. So nicely reared that he didn't even know how to spit. He could picture the Myrmidons, like a thousand rough facsimiles of his father, looking at him with amazement and contempt. Then turning their backs on him—like the boys who used to climb the tree behind the palace, who would tease him for a while and then just forget about him, boys together in a tree he'd never climb.

This was all much clearer in the daylight. How could he have been seduced, even for one evening, by Phoenix and his implausible oracles? Yet even now he could not talk himself out of it.

You have your palm read at the carnival. The fortuneteller solemnly declines to notice the smirk you keep on your face, because your friends are there. As you walk away, you laugh with them; only when you're by yourself do you hold your hand under the light and peer closely at the lines: this for things of the heart, this for wealth, this one here for long life. You may know the oracles are frauds, the augurs quacks, but you listen, because no one else can tell you what you want to hear.

But if what they foretell is ludicrous? The fortuneteller declares, say, that you will enter Troy next Thursday while roller-skating. You respond: I don't skate. The fortuneteller cackles: There's a whole week to learn.

Prophecies are not about accidents, or random caprices of the gods. They are about what *you* will do, in defiance of everything you thought you knew about yourself. And if all you know about yourself is that you deserve more than you have ever got, that you are manifestly superior to other men despite your history of underachievement? Then there's really no way the fortuneteller can lay it on too thick.

Leucon came home. Pyrrhus's first, official thought was: Shit, I was going to try to think this through, and now I can't. Leucon's glum presence will just hang over the whole place, as it always does, a cloud as thick as the blue cigarette smoke. About which he'll complain. But when Leucon appeared in the doorway, flailing his arms and making his tired remarks about the need for a gas mask, Pyrrhus was relieved. He wouldn't have to think for a while.

"Let's go out," Pyrrhus said.

"What?"

"I mean, let's go out for a pizza or something. We haven't done that in months."

"You've been busy."

"I'm free tonight." He saw the little smirk dawn on Leucon's face and amended this. "I mean, I'm through dancing."

"Oh yeah? Now what? You go back to—"

"Waiting on tables, maybe."

"Uh-oh. There goes the rent." Pyrrhus didn't answer. Leucon blushed satisfactorily and said, "Anyway, it's Friday. I was going to take a nap."

"So you can go out later and find that special someone?"

"Yeah, some of us actually have to look. It doesn't just come to us, waving money."

"I'm through with that," Pyrrhus said. He didn't mean it, he hadn't decided; he was just irked into saying it. Yet he found that he liked the sound of it. "Look, you're still dressed. I'll get a tie on and we'll go to the Golden Steer."

"I can't afford the Golden Steer."

"I'll pay," Pyrrhus said. Before Leucon could compose some further remarks about the sources of his money he added: "I've earned it. I've worked like a sonofabitch for my money, and you're not too good to eat with me."

Of course Leucon couldn't say anything. Except, faintly: "I was going to go out."

The poor guy, waiting all week for Friday, just so he could stand around at the Barracks waiting for anything at all. Pyrrhus was depriving him of that, half his weekend, one of just 104 opportunities per year to find ecstasy. Pyrrhus said, "You can still go out. We won't drink too much, you'll be fine."

But it was the Golden Steer, with the black walls and the pin-spotted portraits of semiclad women and the cocktail pianist and the leather-bound menus. They each had a couple of vodka martinis before they even ordered. By the time their food came, steaks so rare they might have been hacked off at the altar from the haunch of a sacrificial beast, Leucon was babbling away, his speech only a little slurred.

"I'm maybe gonna go to law school," he said.

"Yeah? Is that what you want to do?"

"I don't know. I don't know what else to do."

"Oh, that's a good reason," Pyrrhus said.

"I think it's kind of interesting. I mean, sometimes I read the stuff I copy and, I don't know, I kind of like the archaic language and all. And they make little jokes, in the footnotes."

"Neat."

"You want the rest of this sour cream?"

"No."

Pyrrhus watched Leucon spoon the stuff onto his potato and thought, No wonder he's getting a little pot. Even so, here in this soothing place — with the filtered downlights that could make a harpy look good, or a spouse, or a roommate — Leucon suddenly seemed kind of cute. But in a strangely distant, untouchable way. As if Pyrrhus were seeing him in memory. As if Pyrrhus were already on the ship to Troy, looking back. This premature nostalgia the clearest augury yet that he was, truly, going.

Leucon said, "I want some wine."

"You better not."

"Oh." He sat up a little straighter, as if to show he wasn't in such bad shape, then smiled, a little contented smile. Because Pyrrhus was paying attention to him.

They finished their steaks in silence, had coffee. Leucon said, "It's like a club."

Pyrrhus thought he meant the restaurant. "Yeah."

"I mean, there they are, they're all lawyers, and I'm the only guy there who isn't. Except the guys in the mailroom. It's just like they're all in this fraternity, and I can't help wanting to be, too."

"Then if you were running the copy machine in a hospital you'd want to be a doctor?"

"I guess." He put way too much cream in his coffee, then said, "I was in a fraternity once. In college. I mean, just for a few weeks — I pledged, but I never went through the initiation and all."

"What happened?"

"Well, I didn't . . . once I'd been to a few meetings and saw everybody, and what went on, it all seemed kind of stupid. But you know, during rush week, all you want is to get tapped, you don't even think about whether you really want to do it. Just so they won't ignore you, leave you all alone in your room on pledge night like Neleus."

"Who?"

"Oh, this screaming queen who was in my freshman dorm. Are you going to have dessert?"

"No." Pyrrhus saw a little flash of disappointment and said, "You go ahead, though."

"No, that's okay. Why don't you have a cigarette?"

"I thought you hated it."

"I do."

"I'll be all right. What if you got to law school and you didn't like that after a few weeks?"

"What?"

"I mean, if you're just doing it because you want to be part of the fraternity?"

"Then I could quit, I guess. I mean, it's not a life sentence." He looked startled at his own words, and then pleased. The guy who had practically had a stroke at one late rent notice, now he seemed to have picked up a little of Pyrrhus's insouciance.

While Pyrrhus, lately deeply souciant, chewed on the words. It's not a life sentence.

Because that is how he'd been thinking of his decision. As if his options had arrayed themselves into the multiple choices for question 37 of life's aptitude exam:

Select the passage that best completes the following sentence. At the age of twenty-one, Pyrrhus decided that he would spend the rest of his life as —

(A) a call boy
(B) a general
(C) a mama's boy back on Scyros

Usually in standardized tests, all the choices seem wrong. You read the different answers and say: None of these fit, what in the world could the test designer have been thinking of? You read through the answers again. Not looking for the right one; it's not going to jump out at you. Destiny isn't a beckoning light. It's just the answer that feels least wrong.

Anyway, there's always a next question. He could go and pick up his father's loot and then move on to the sentence after that one. There, decided: (B).

Possibly he hadn't read the passage in the instruction book that says there's a penalty for wrong answers, to discourage guessing.

"Let's get a brandy or something," he said.

"I like that stuff with hazelnut," Leucon said.

Leucon was sprawled out on the couch back at the apartment. Looking thoughtful, in kind of a dazed way. Probably thinking something abstruse like: If I stood up now, would I fall down before I got to the bathroom? Pyrrhus felt an odd little burst of affection for him. Timorous, irritating, sloppy Leucon, with steak sauce on his shirt and even a little spot on his glasses, and his hair like an indecisive mob. He wasn't much, but he was the closest thing to a human connection Pyrrhus had made in all his months in the city.

So little to leave behind: why was Pyrrhus suddenly scared, much more than the day he'd crept away from Scyros? He had stepped off the ferry into a city that hadn't known he was coming, that had no expectations for him, nothing for him to fail at. Now he would be entering a world that knew all about him and had large plans for him, all kinds of opportunities to prove his insufficiency.

He wanted a cigarette and, true to their only rule, headed for his bedroom. Leucon called out, "You can smoke in here. I don't care." Pyrrhus came back out and, instead of returning to his chair, joined Leucon on the couch—the sectional, each unit of which represented the earnings from three or four nights embodying the dreams of monsters. Leucon seemed a little startled, that Pyrrhus had sat down so close. He shifted an inch or two, then stared straight ahead, hands clasped modestly in his lap.

Pyrrhus loosened his tie, kicked off his clunky go-to-the-Golden-Steer wingtips, and put his feet up on the couch. He lit his cigarette, feeling more sinful than he had in months. A momentary look of annoyance crossed Leucon's face, as if he hadn't really meant to give his permission. Then he was expressionless again, still not looking at Pyrrhus. Even when Pyrrhus put a hand on his knee — placed it there, as deliberately as one moves a token in a board game — Leucon didn't look over right away. Pyrrhus was sure he was getting ready to say something nasty, something about how he couldn't afford Pyrrhus, any more than he could afford dinner at the Golden Steer; that was the kind of thing he'd say.

A mercy fuck, that's all Pyrrhus had in mind. He could have gone out right that minute and picked up anyone in the city; he didn't need this skinny little twit with the perpetual furrow in his brow and his lips clenched together in a straight, disapproving line. Pyrrhus's hand, still resting on Leucon's knee, felt huge to him, like a thoughtless remark he couldn't take back.

Leucon, finally, put his own hand on Pyrrhus's. Pyrrhus felt enormous relief, almost gratitude. As if he were the one who required mercy.

Gelanor, Leucon's campy bar buddy, once said to Leucon: "Sooner or later you get everything." Leucon had been mooning over an aloof beauty at the Lighthouse, a blond poured into faded denims who seemed to show up every week or so, drain a single beer, and leave without talking to anybody. "If it shows up again and again, sooner or later it will fall into your bed."

This was too neat; Leucon didn't believe him. And in fact it would be a couple of years before that particular blond arrived in Leucon's bed and un-veiled endowments rather more negligible than had been apparent through the denim. A couple of years beyond that, Leucon would look around the Lighthouse and realize that he had — with his shy approach and awkward, rehearsed opening lines — picked off one by one every gorgeous man he'd ever had a crush on. And it was true, what Gelanor went on to say: "You will get it, honey. And it will always, without fail, let you down."

"Why?"

"Honey, if you bump into something at ten minutes before closing and you stumble home with it, you might get a happy surprise or you might just get a humdrum fuck. But if you cruise the same number for years it stops being about him, it's about you, about how unworthy you are. When you finally catch him, you don't think, Huh, I must be better than I thought. Or at least the best he can do tonight. You think: He's doing this against his will. Something has blinded him, or made him mad. You hear him say, 'Okay, let's go,' those words you've always wanted to hear. You see his lips move, and you know you're not hearing his voice, you're hearing some mischievous goddess who is speaking through him as a joke. And after that, honey, you might just as well go to bed with an inflatable doll."

Leucon was kissing Pyrrhus's breastbone. Pyrrhus's hands were on Leucon's shoulders, but not holding him, just perched, as weightlessly as if a pair of birds had happened to light there. Leucon drew back and looked down on the extraordinary body that seemed to lie there defenseless, open to his every intention, the way a naked picture in a magazine offers itself unresistingly to anything you can imagine doing with it. Pyrrhus's eyes were closed; Leucon could look as long as he wanted to.

This was not very long. After he'd averted his eyes for so many months, you'd think he would have wanted to just drink it all in. Instead, after a few seconds he was, astonishingly, bored.

Yes indeed, this was Pyrrhus, all right. After all these months. The archer's body, as advertised. The genitals, as conjectured. Well, almost. There it all was. Leucon was beside himself. I don't mean excited, I mean standing next to himself, watching himself look at Pyrrhus, touch Pyrrhus here, then here.

Pyrrhus opened his eyes and said, "What do you like to do?"

Leucon wasn't sure anyone had ever asked him that before. No, once or twice, when he and some trick mysteriously didn't fit and it was necessary actually to negotiate just where the puzzle pieces might go. He was a little chilled: it was easy enough to imagine Pyrrhus posing this question to all his customers. This was different, Pyrrhus was here voluntarily. Except of course Pyrrhus was always in bed *voluntarily*, he just didn't happen to go to bed for the conventional reasons. And tonight? What was his reason?

They had staggered to Pyrrhus's room so quickly, there had scarcely been time to think about it. But now Pyrrhus was lying there like . . . a hustler. Even a man whose self-esteem was sturdier than Leucon's might have begun to wonder: Why are we here? He can't want you, why is he doing this?

There had been some other, more urgent question? Oh, right: what did Leucon *like* to do? What, more precisely, given only one chance

121

forever—this was it, however it happened it wasn't going to happen again—what did he want to do with Pyrrhus?

Well, clearly there was only one choice: Pyrrhus would have to fuck him. Not that this was what Leucon wanted, exactly. On the contrary, he hadn't been fucked much in his few months out, Pyrrhus was bigger than he was used to, he expected it would hurt. But it had to be: if there was only this one time, he had to have Pyrrhus inside him. It was as if he were choosing the contents of a time capsule. Some time in the future, when he broke the seal and opened his memories of this night, he would want to have a memory of Pyrrhus inside him.

"Why don't you fuck me," Leucon said. He found that just saying those words electrified him, the surrender and at the same time the aggression of saying aloud that harsh beautiful word *fuck*. He heard himself almost growl: "Fuck me."

Leucon was right: it hurt. And he was having trouble keeping his legs up—he wasn't much of a gymnast. Pyrrhus was visibly annoyed. Every time he pulled back a little, Leucon's legs would drop, forcing him out entirely. At last, exasperated, he grasped Leucon's ankles and held Leucon's legs straight up in the air, socks waving at the ceiling. Then he plunged in as mechanically as if he were drilling for oil.

Pyrrhus's face, hovering above Leucon's, was sightless and slack now. He had lost consciousness and become only his cock. Leucon was, helplessly, thrilled: once Pyrrhus had found home, each stroke was astounding; he might have been battering at Leucon's very soul. Except Pyrrhus's cock didn't know anything about souls. Leucon might have been anybody at all.

Poor Leucon: while he was nearly as unconscious as Pyrrhus was, while the deepest part of him knew only sensation and wanted it to go on forever, some flicker of self remained awake, watching. Narrating. Disapproving. He tried to silence it, slip as deeply into the moment as he could. But it was overpowering, a voice inside that could not stop in the present but insisted on telling the future: In the morning you will still be living together and he will have done this to you, you will have been this thing he fucked, he will have come inside you, just minutes from now you're going to be sitting on the john, looking down into the bowl, at his semen and your blood.

Merciful Aphrodite, drug him, distract him, drown him just this once in that sweet oblivion that you grant to the humblest of men, even to beasts. Let him be, for once in his life, a hole. Emptied of worry or self-consciousness or pride, just a hole grateful to be filled up.

This prayer answered by proxy, perhaps; perhaps it was she who inspired Pyrrhus, at that moment, to reach over to his nightstand and get the poppers.

When he was finished using the john, Leucon stood in the dark living room, naked, at the vortex of the two ribbons of light cast on the floor, one from his own half-opened door, the other from Pyrrhus's. After a minute he went, as reluctantly but conclusively as a man pays the oarsman and steps on the ferry to Hell, to his own bed.

10

Pyrrhus thought he would go see Leo one more time. He put it to himself that way, *one more time*: he had made his decision, hadn't he? Though he wasn't sure if he was going to Leo to be blessed or to be dissuaded.

He walked. It was one of those false spring days in February when some people, unable to trust their senses, are still wearing their overcoats and others are already in the parks, getting an early start on their tans. As always, Pyrrhus tried to think while he walked. But it was so nice out. The city seemed entirely populated with beautiful men. The streets were thick with them, in their hopeful outfits, shorts that displayed their winter-white thighs, even a scattering of tank tops, though it wasn't really that warm. As always, Pyrrhus was distracted, his plans to think things through once again stymied.

Yet he felt, looking at the men, not lust, but a strange, rising sadness. Another twinge of precocious regret: as if men were something he had left behind long ago.

The old façade at Café Leo was gone. The place was being renovated, but there wasn't any sign to say what it would be next. Pyrrhus rang Leo's bell and, as before, stepped back into the street so Leo could peer down at him. While he waited, though, there passed before him a workman so comely that he all but forgot where he was. Radiant curls above a snug white painter's outfit. The guy caught Pyrrhus looking, grinned, then bent down to stir some paint—didn't squat, but bent from the hips. Whether or not this was a deliberate provocation, it certainly prevented Pyrrhus from looking up at Leo's window. But again the sadness; the sight of the guy's friendly, welcoming butt filled Pyrrhus's throat with sorrow and loss.

When he had looked back on Scyros from the ferry, on the day of his escape, looked at all the familiar places of his childhood splayed out before him in a panorama flat as a postcard, he had felt nothing like this. As if the white cloth taut across that perfect ass were a screen on which he could see a vista of his true home. He had to smile: these grand thoughts about some guy's butt. Still, he couldn't turn away.

"Shut your mouth," Leo said, close beside him. "You'll catch something." Leo was, of course, wearing an overcoat.

"How do you like it?" Leo said. Pyrrhus thought at first he meant the painter, Pyrrhus's opinion of whom was obvious, but Leo gestured at the new storefront — sort of an aerodynamic design on which the painter was now slapping a coat of purple.

"This is yours? A new restaurant?"

"A bar. I must be crazy, I'm pushing eighty. But I was bored — in between your frequent visits, that is — so . . ."

"I thought you were, like, bankrupt."

"Café Leo was bankrupt. Leo isn't bankrupt. I managed to hold on to the building. And your current employer put up for the renovations."

"You mean Archias? You know I've been — "

"Of course I know. If you were trying to be inconspicuous you picked an odd line of work. Anyway, I needed a partner, and Archias was tired of the warehouse district."

"He didn't say anything. That mean you're going to have strippers?"

"Please. This is going to be a classy place. I hired the piano player away from the Mirage."

"Oh, a wrinkle bar."

"A wrinkle bar. With show tunes. No hustlers, I was very insistent with Archias. He can keep that garbage at the Escapade." He slapped his forehead. "Excuse me, present company excepted. You will always be welcome."

"I'm leaving town."

"Are you? Heading out on a ballet tour?"

"Heading for Troy."

Leo couldn't suppress a brief laugh, like a bark. "Ha. The one variety of degradation you haven't tried: a camp follower."

"Actually, I might be a general."

He didn't laugh at this, as if it were so preposterous he could tell Pyrrhus meant it. He steered Pyrrhus around the painter, who smiled again as Pyrrhus passed, and into the unfinished bar. The little bar at the back of the room was gone, replaced by an extraordinary confection of curving white laminate and blue mirrors that snaked the length of the room. Before it stood a few of the battered stools from the old Café Leo.

They sat, and Leo, still in his overcoat, listened seriously as Pyrrhus told him the story.

Pyrrhus finished: "I know this all sounds silly."

"It's the first thing you've ever told me that didn't sound silly."

"I — You know, mainly I'm just going to check out what he left. I mean, even I don't believe the part about being a general."

"Why not? What's so hard about being a general? At least your employees tend to show up on time. And then you say: See those guys over there? Go kill them. Piece of cake, anybody could do it. Not to mention they tend to find their own provisions. That's the nice thing about an army, minimal upkeep. They get hungry, they just go sack a convenience store. Milk shakes and microwave sandwiches."

"See, you do think it's a joke."

"I think it's a job opportunity. What you've been doing is a joke. Not a very funny one: like a suicide note with wisecracks."

"You think I've been killing myself?"

"I think it would not have required the services of any fancy oracle to figure out your future. You haven't said what you think of my bar."

"It's unusual."

"I hate it. The designer is some protégé of Archias, Archias insisted. It was his money." He chuckled. "They make a wonderful couple, he and Archias. They fly in here screeching, you'd think the harpies had descended."

"Archias is okay, I kind of like him."

"Archias is a vicious man who drags young boys down about as far as you can go without seeing road signs for Hades, and then sets them out with the trash when his customers get tired of them."

"He does what?"

"You take everything too literally. Maybe this prophecy thing, too."

"He always treated me okay," Pyrrhus said. "Anyway, you're taking his money."

"You're right, it's a shame. I should have borrowed my money from people who got it honestly. Like bankers." Leo looked around the unfinished bar. "We're going to have a white piano, too. I'm going to end my days as the proprietor of the nelliest spot in the universe."

"I don't think you're ever going to end your days," Pyrrhus said. Although, now that he thought about it, Leo looked older than before, if that was possible.

"No? Well, I might outlast you, now that you're going to be this hero."

"I won't die. I mean, that's what they say, I don't die in this thing."

"What a relief. So what will you do next?"

"Next?"

"Wherever it's written, that this is what you're going to do, it doesn't say what you do next?"

"Not that they told me about."

"Just as well, I wouldn't ask."

"I guess I'll just be a veteran."

"Ah, you will, won't you? In which case I withdraw my offer of perpetual welcome. Nothing can drive people out of a bar faster than a veteran."

"Yeah?"

"There used to be this guy, came into the old Leo's, where the Escapade is, it was that long ago. Every time he had one too many, he'd launch into his war story. I mean, you could see it: he'd knock back that one-too-many and it was like dropping a coin in a jukebox. A jukebox with one record, all about how he slew so-and-so and brought home this many cattle. I'd pretend to listen, so he wouldn't bother the paying customers. One night he said, 'You don't believe me.' Not mad, more like he was amazed. I said, 'You buy a drink, I listen. Believing, there's an extra charge.'"

"I promise not to be like that," Pyrrhus said.

"You must be promising never to get old. Look, why don't you save a step—don't even go to the army, just come in here and talk about it. I'll believe you for free."

Pyrrhus laughed. "It's a deal."

"No, you'd better go," Leo said, suddenly serious. "It's better than the trash bin."

"I wasn't headed for the trash bin."

"No? Let me tell you something. The first time you stepped in here, I said to myself: This is an exceptionally good-looking boy. This is a boy you could just look at forever and never get tired of. But, you know, there is no such boy."

"You mean you're tired of seeing me?"

"Oh, goodness no. Not yet. I just mean, if you're going to make a living being a face, you shouldn't show it in one place too long."

On his way out Pyrrhus ran into the painter again. The guy was through for the day, loading stuff onto his panel truck. He stopped and looked at Pyrrhus—not flirtatiously, but almost expectantly, as if they already had a date. Pyrrhus stopped, too, but only for a second; then he tore himself away and headed down the street. Halfway down the block he felt the guy still watching him, but he didn't let himself look back. The sun was already going down, taking with it the unseasonable warmth. Everyone on the street was dressed too lightly, they were all hurrying, and Pyrrhus hurried with them. Feeling again the soft pangs of regret and renunciation.

What was he renouncing, exactly, what did he have to give up if he went to Troy? Well, obviously, at least in the near term, sex. He supposed things went on in the army, if maybe not as routinely as the porno books suggested. But of course he couldn't participate, not if he had the slightest thought of leading the Myrmidons. Which he didn't expect to, it still seemed silly, but he hadn't ruled it out. Consequently he wasn't going to be getting anything for a while.

No, there was more to it than that; the decision to go seemed to involve more than just a brief period of enforced celibacy. He was planning not to want it any more. He was going to a world where men fought and bathed and slept side by side and never thought of one another that way. And he wouldn't either. It was like taking a vow.

Not the fantastic vow he had uttered once or twice as a boy, late at night, the frantic prayer that he might somehow stop wanting what he wanted, be cured. Pyrrhus can't have thought that his orientation, as we call it—his whole body *oriented* to men as the compass's needle to the pole—was mutable. Maybe just that it could be muted? That he could dwell for a time in a discipline, one that he could put on as readily as the uniform of a general.

Maybe that was all he wanted: a clean, pressed uniform. Not some storm-trooper, dress-as-your-own-oppressor drag, but something trim, chaste, with creases that could slice butter and discreet but gleaming ornaments. He wanted to be defined. Not the way the gym rats use the word, as they pound their bodies into little landscapes of carefully arrayed hillocks and valleys. But defined the way people are by titles and uniforms and, if they can manage them, beliefs, even loyalties. He wanted to be a member of something, clothed in ordinariness.

Do you remember, so long ago, when the boys' department of a big downtown store had a scouting section? There were all the official outfits, summer and winter, kerchiefs and caps and the approved paraphernalia for making a fire or digging a latrine or marching in a parade. Their insignia and badges offering a painless escalator to manhood in carefully ordered steps, from mewling and puking wolf cub to stolid and mature eagle. All so easy and clear, even if something died at every step.

He couldn't be two people. If one of them was going to have a future, the other one would have to die.

On his way home he practiced. If some man's eyes met his, he would stare back with the what-are-you-looking-at? menace he had so often seen in straight boys' eyes. It felt funny the first couple of times, as if he were just playacting. Before he had gone many blocks, though, he found that he actually was a little bit angry at being cruised. As if they were trying to sabotage him, as if just by looking at him they could weaken his resolve. Until pretty soon the menacing look was genuine. And I wonder if this isn't how straight boys acquire it.

"I feel bad just skipping out," Pyrrhus said. "I don't know what Leucon is going to do, he can't make the rent by himself."

"I'm sure he'll find somebody," Phoenix said. He sat on Pyrrhus's bed and watched as Pyrrhus picked through an enormous assortment of white socks, rejecting some, depositing others in his duffel bag. Phoenix wondered what principle of selection was involved.

"Yeah, but my stuff—what's he supposed to do, just leave it all here?"

"He'll do something with it."

"But I mean, it's my stuff. All my furniture and my tapes and . . . my shirts. How long am I going to be gone?"

"How long? Do you mean you think you're coming back?"

Pyrrhus stopped sorting socks. "I don't know. I'm not, then?"

"Oh, I have no idea. I didn't mean the prophecy says anything about it. I suppose after it's over everybody goes home. Is this home?"

"I don't guess."

"Is Scyros?"

"No. God."

"Well, you'll have to go somewhere. I can't imagine there's going to be much of Troy worth lingering over."

"I thought we were going to *take* it," Pyrrhus said. The *we*, perhaps, worth remarking on. Except that at this point he might still have meant nothing more than *we Greeks*, my countrymen, instead of *me-and-my-army*.

"That is the usual word, yes. However, our soldiers—after all these years they've built up certain appetites. You should see what they've done to the suburbs. And those were just an hors d'oeuvre."

Pyrrhus tried to picture the sack of Troy, but could only conjure up an image of rowdy boys stomping out somebody else's sand castle. How could anybody stomp out something as big as Troy?

"I've always wanted to go there," Pyrrhus said. "Ever since I was a kid."

"You shall."

"I mean as a tourist. Not to tear the place down."

"You mean, you thought we were going to storm through the gates and then sit about at the sidewalk cafés."

"I hadn't thought about what *you're* going to do," Pyrrhus said, re-

130

tracting his casual *we*. "But maybe I don't think what I'm going to do is all spelled out by some voice in a jar."

"I told you, I scarcely credit these things myself. Still, I should find that voice at least as persuasive as the interior one that has impelled you to dance naked on a bar." Phoenix smiled, whether to soften that remark or just because he was pleased with its shapeliness.

"I think maybe I'm just going to pick up my father's stuff and come back."

Phoenix sighed. "Then you needn't pack so very much hosiery."

Leucon came home and found Pyrrhus's new friend, Phoenix, in the living room, smoking a cigarette.

It had been a terrible day. The copier had broken down three times, and Leucon had been harried all day by lawyers about to miss deadlines. They were like college kids, the lawyers, always putting off their term papers until the night before they were due. Screaming at him as if he, and not the machine, had broken, or as if he and the machine were indistinguishable.

He thought he was being pretty restrained when he said, mildly, "Would you mind taking that outside?"

"Do you know, I'm awfully sorry, but I rather do mind. This damp weather . . ."

"Hey, Pyrrhus," Leucon called. "Could you ask your friend not to smoke in—"

"Leucon, can't you just give it a rest?" Pyrrhus came out of his room carrying a pile of clothing. "Phoenix, I hate to ask, but maybe you could step outside a second."

"I swear," Phoenix said. "Of all the ways life has deteriorated since I was young, none is more irksome to me than this relentless badgering of the practitioners of harmless petty vices."

"No, I just meant I wanted to talk to Leucon."

"Oh. By all means." He went out into the hallway, leaving the door open. Pyrrhus went to the door and looked at him, and he headed on down the stairs. That is, Pyrrhus didn't have to say anything; it was as though Phoenix really were his servant. Leucon was not so much impressed as alarmed. As if he had some inkling of why Pyrrhus might require a servant.

When they could hear the street door open and close, Phoenix well out of earshot, Pyrrhus came back and sat down, the pile of clothing in his lap.

"He thought I ought to just go. Maybe I should have, I don't really need any of this shit. But I didn't think I should just leave without saying anything."

"You're leaving? I mean, moving out?"

"Yeah. I'm sorry."

"You prick, you were just going to disappear."

"I was going to leave the rent. Look, I got it here. You'll get someone else. I—maybe I can do two months. I mean, Phoenix must have some money."

"I don't want his money. What's he doing, whisking you off to the tropics? Finally scored big, huh?"

"We're going to Troy."

"What?"

"They want me to lead my father's army. I don't know if I'm going to do that, but . . . he left stuff, I ought to take care of it."

All Leucon could say was, "We had a lease."

He took it out and looked at it from time to time, the solemn covenant on long paper, filled with the same archaic phrases as the documents he copied at work. Everything said twice, in the demotic and in formal speech—*agree and covenant, keep and maintain*—so that no one could claim to have misunderstood its essential message, that the tenant was obligated, in a hundred ways, and the landlord not at all. At the end, the two signatures, his own and Neoptolemus's. How could anyone walk away from something as weighty as a lease, stronger than any other bond between them, their two signatures there? It was as if Leucon had been plunged into the war zone itself, where no covenants held.

Nothing else between them as strong. Not their months together; surely not their brief convergence, or collision, the other night. Which already seemed awfully trivial, like one of those encounters whose only residue is the sensation, on seeing a faintly familiar guy in a bar, that you might once have tricked with him. Nothing binding them but the lease and its promise that Pyrrhus would be there the next day and the next. A promise of persistence, of ongoing presence in Leucon's world.

Pyrrhus was going to go, and Leucon's world was going to consist of the copy center and an empty apartment and the Barracks on Friday nights. No, not an empty apartment; he couldn't pay for it by himself, he'd have to find some replacement roommate who would probably be not even one-quarter divine.

He heard himself say, "Take me."

"What? Look, I don't know how long I'm going to be gone. I mean, this isn't just a business trip, I might never come back."

"That's okay, I . . . I want an adventure." This wasn't exactly so, of course: he didn't want a real adventure, with its privations and perils, canned rations and no hot water. He just wanted a future with some surprises in it, something less linear than law school, lawing, lying down to die. "I could—I don't know—I could help you out."

Pyrrhus looked away for a minute. Leucon thought he was actually considering it. Which made it as good as done: if Pyrrhus was actually forming the image of himself and Leucon, marching side by side into the future, it was as good as done. Leucon was already composing his list of things to pack when Pyrrhus turned to face him again.

With a look of utter weariness and sorrow, maybe even a little anger. That he was once again being forced to play a scene that he hadn't initiated and that was no fun at all. He composed himself and said, "I'm sorry, but . . ."

Leucon finished the sentence for him. I'm sorry, but I only need one eunuch.

Leucon insisted on riding with them in the taxi to the marina at Waterside Place.

It was ten at night, and Waterside Place was shutting down. The shops had already closed—the one that sold nothing but hats, the one where everything was white. The theme restaurants were withdrawing their mechanical welcome from the last stragglers. On the terrace at the cantina, small undocumented persons were furling the umbrellas and stacking the plastic chairs. At the old seafood palace the last table of conventioneers was just being served: their hearts rose as the waitress shuffled across the sawdust with an enormous and festive salver.

But the stuffed shrimp special was niggardly and dry; the fisherman's sampler did not resemble the picture in the menu; ricotta oozed listlessly from the cadaver of the seafood lasagna. The waitresses dealt these indignities out to the diners like platters of bad news. Just minutes before, the menu had promised triumph, as an orator by the ships at sunrise might foretell a day of victory; now all was undone. The customers received what the Fates dished out to them as hopelessly as the vanquished in battle.

Above the restaurants, across Harbor Boulevard, the towers of the financial district were dark. The restaurants were an isthmus of gaiety between the towers and the equally dark marina. Docked there were the cabin cruisers kept for business entertaining—here and there the houseboats in which a few mildly heterodox commuters from the towers made their homes; as they lay in bed the faint jostle of the tides afforded them a sort of adventure, however firmly moored. Farther out, in the channel, the gray blot on the gleaming, oily water might have been a warship at anchor. From it, a tiny launch headed for the docks.

Leucon followed Phoenix and Pyrrhus through the marina. They picked their way past the sailboats and the houseboats, coming to the very end of the dock just as the launch arrived to meet them. In it sat a sailor, windburned and battered. How had he been summoned? Leucon wondered.

The sailor wore grimy white trousers and a rumpled blue shirt: a hint, maybe, that Pyrrhus wasn't entering the starched world he'd dreamt of. The shirt unbuttoned to display a profound belly and a silver-haired chest across which was blazoned a tattoo so ancient and blurred that it was nearly past deciphering. Leucon allowed himself to stare—people who acquire tattoos having given up some degree of modesty, made themselves public as billboards—until he could make out the name *Alcestis*.

Phoenix stepped down into the launch with the easy footing of a perpetual voyager. Pyrrhus handed down his little bit of stuff, duffel bag and boom box, then turned toward Leucon. "I'm sorry," he said again. He stepped closer, and Leucon thought maybe they might at least hug. But there, right behind them, looking up, was a burly sailor with a woman's name pricked into his chest. Pyrrhus just shook Leucon's hand, gripped it pretty loosely and let it go fast, promptly jumped down into the launch, where Phoenix and the sailor waited. Leucon was still feeling the disappointed tingle in his hand as the launch pulled away and he watched it slice through the greasy water, toward the cloudlike ship.

At the cantina, the scowling little men were chaining the stacks of chairs to the terrace rail. Leucon strode by them in the dark, toward Harbor Boulevard. The defeated diners at the seafood joint paid their check and staggered, belching without satisfaction, into the Gay Nineties saloon. The piano player, somber in his red-and-white striped shirt and foam boater, was just finishing up. But he nodded as the conventioneer with the beribboned nametag stuck a bill in the brandy snifter and asked for one more number.

Leucon was already too far away to hear as the pianist closed his eyes and, softly, improvised the opening bars of a brand-new song: the *Neoptolemid*.

ARES' SPARE PARTS

1

The Sea Lord was on the bridge of the *Penelope*, watching as the lieutenant at the helm brought the great ship about and teased her through the channel toward the open river, skating between the shoals as deftly as you or I might slip into a parking space.

If you drive the same car long enough, its boundaries become your own; you are no more likely to scrape a fender than you are to lose track of an elbow. Just so, the lieutenant had become a subcontinent, his body a million pounds of steel that he steered with such light fingers the Sea Lord, watching, almost wanted to laugh, the way you do at any sleight of hand—the astounding card trick, the moment when the juggler has everything in the air at once. The little exultation one feels at such moments is nearly self-gratulatory. Look, a human is doing this, and I am a human too; aren't we one hell of a species?

Of course the Sea Lord could not laugh. It would have been undignified, for one thing. Besides, there was always the voice in him saying: I could have done that. It isn't so marvelous. He's just practiced, any fool could do it. As, in the midst of battle, he would glance over at some godlike comrade, a human mountain wielding a lance the size of a middle-aged tree, and think: You soulless untenanted piece of meat, when you are in Hell and your feats of arms are just another couplet in the catalogue of slaughter, men will remember my sagacity and cunning. The very armor you strip away from the corpse today I will win from you with oratory tomorrow. This was true: the world didn't belong to the Agamemnons and Ajaxes, enormous infants who sulked, artlessly blurted out their childlike thoughts, lived lives that resembled continuous tantrums. The world belonged to the Sea Lord, patient, articulate, wakeful. Why did he have to remind himself of this, so often? Why was he left, always, with this faint bitter taste at seeing other men who had mastered some trivial skill or other?

He mightn't have minded so much if the lieutenant had been an old salt. But he was just a kid, mid-twenties at most, not even visibly weathered. A technician, sleek and expressionless. No, not really expressionless: he was frowning, his eyes darting about with a grim omniattentiveness. Registering everything—including the Sea Lord, a supernumerary at this moment; it was a wonder the lieutenant didn't shoo him away from the bridge.

Of course the Sea Lord had never been much of a sailor, despite all the nautical artifacts in his office back home. Many lawyers' offices — in Ithaca, at any rate — were filled with allusions to the maritime life: charts, antique navigational instruments, pictures of the lawyers themselves in their sloops, their doleful life-jacketed children peering down into the dark water. Why does sailing appeal so to lawyers? They rush from their offices to the docks on a Friday evening and cruise out into a harbor that is a veritable gridlock of ill-piloted vessels, each with a lawyer at the helm and some shanghaied offspring trying to raise the jib. Perhaps it is like the law, sailing, with its special language and antique rituals and its fittings of wood and brass. And lawyers, too, cruise on the surface of the ineffable in their little manmade vessels; if the craft are tightly made, wet reality does not seep in.

The lieutenant lit a cigarette, offered one to his commander. Who took it, though it was unfiltered and nasty-looking, because it seemed like a gesture of acceptance, as if he really did belong here on the bridge, they were mates.

They smoked together, one calmly piloting a hunk of metal the size of a city block, the other grudgingly awestruck. Into this clubhouse of gray steel and manly puffing suddenly burst Phoenix, like a bouquet of flowers delivered to the wrong address, with his perfect little suit and dandified walking stick.

"My lord Odysseus," he piped.

Odysseus just nodded and went on looking out at the black water. The lieutenant was threading carefully between moored pleasure boats and, on the starboard, an abandoned hulk on which a solitary heron roosted, auguring something or other. The river banks were as dark as the water, punctuated by the occasional light from a riverfront estate. That one to port, the sprawling house that perched on a hilltop like a bad toupee, was not unlike Odysseus's place in Ithaca. But not enough like it to make him truly heartsick.

Phoenix coughed, and his lord finally turned to face him. "The boy is on board," he announced, with a melodramatic fruitiness.

Well, of course the boy was on board; why else were they sailing? But he expected to be praised. "You've done very well," Odysseus said.

"Thank you."

"Where have you got him?"

"I didn't know what to do. He's just sitting around in the officers' mess. Did you want to see him?"

"Not tonight. Not till we're on the open sea." That was just arbitrary; there wasn't any reason. Except Odysseus really didn't want to see the kid just then.

"Where should he go?"

"I don't know. Lieutenant, anybody on the officers' deck got an empty berth?"

"Well . . . I do, sir."

"There you go. Stick the kid in there."

Phoenix said, "That would hardly accord with his social st—"

"Then give him your cabin." Why must he worry about accommodations, like a hostess planning a country weekend? "You bunk with the lieutenant . . . er . . . "

"Nereus, sir."

"I—" Phoenix began. "Very well."

Odysseus put a hand on Phoenix's shoulder, a little repentant. The little gelding must have had a higher estimate, however deluded, of his own social standing. "It's only for a couple of nights, if the weather holds up."

"A couple of nights? We were almost a week coming from Arisbe."

"We're not going straight back to Arisbe. We're stopping at Lemnos."

"Lemnos? Whatever for?"

"Think about it. Now get the boy packed away and meet me in the mess. I want to hear about him. Half an hour."

Phoenix departed with a little satirical bow. Odysseus turned toward the lieutenant, wanting to revive the moment of comradeship the intruder had shattered. "Will the weather hold up?" he said.

"No, sir. We're heading straight into a squall."

"How do you know?" Odysseus squinted into the night sky.

"It was on the radio. To the northeast. Nothing we can't handle."

"I should hope not."

"We might lose a day."

"What's one more? It took that old fart a week to get the boy on board."

"You would have done better," the lieutenant said, with no insubordinate question mark.

"Who can say? You know, some people think I'm pretty persuasive." The most celebrated advocate of his day relished his own modesty. "But

I don't know how to talk to these kids. The new recruits lately—they line up in front of the ships, you try to inspire them, and they just seem to stare at you till you run out of words." He had meant to be confiding, but he sounded like a crotchety old man. It seemed to widen the space between him and the lieutenant. Who was, after all, more nearly of the staring generation than of his own. "I'm sorry to have stuck you with Phoenix."

"No big deal, sir."

"He's homosexual." The lieutenant visibly stiffened. "In the abstract, that is. I don't think you need to be concerned about praxis."

"Sir?"

"I mean, I don't think he's going to molest you. Let me know."

"He better not try anything," the lieutenant said, a little overemphatically. Odysseus was amused, at the way younger men seemed to feel so vehemently about harmless fairies, or affected to.

"I'm sure you can fend him off, Lieutenant. Your larger worry is that he'll talk your head off."

"Yes, sir."

They were at the mouth of the river now, nothing ahead of them but open sea. Odysseus found this unnerving. As if the city and the river behind them were the past and the green vacancy ahead were the pathless future. Yet the lieutenant stared into, steered into the void with perfect calm. There was nothing to do but trust him. Not something that came easily to Odysseus. He watched only a minute longer, then went below.

Phoenix found Pyrrhus where he had left him, seated at the long table in the officers' mess. The boy had got hold of a beer; enterprising lad.

"I'm to give you my cabin," Phoenix said. He waited for Pyrrhus to protest: No, I can't put you out like that. Pyrrhus didn't.

"How long does it take to get to Troy?" Pyrrhus said.

"We're . . . a few days."

"What do I do? I mean, until then?"

"My dear boy, do you think the oracles have spelled out what you're going to have for breakfast tomorrow?"

"No, no, I mean—what am I supposed to do with myself?"

"I have no idea. I myself have never found a shuffleboard court. Look at the sea. Meet people. I suspect you'll be meeting Odysseus."

"Who's that?"

"You've never heard of Odysseus?"

"Oh." Pyrrhus looked down at the table. "I guess."

Astounding: the boy must have lived in a world where the great doings of Odysseus, Ajax, his own father, were just the stuff that filled one of those all-news channels that the clicker was programmed to skip. Phoenix felt a moment's remorse, that he had dragged the poor child onto that tiresome channel, as if forcing him through the screen.

"So this guy Odysseus is on board?" Pyrrhus said.

"This is his ship."

"You didn't tell me that." He looked at Phoenix thoughtfully. Perhaps generalizing: his ship, his eunuch . . .

"Didn't I? An oversight. Anyway, I'm sure you'll be meeting."

"Why not right now?"

"He's busy. Just setting off, you know, he has things to do."

"You haven't . . . told people anything about me?"

"You mean about your recent activities? I thought you weren't the least bit embarrassed about them. What was your remark? That you wouldn't care if your mother hopped the ferry from Scyros and caught your act. I believe that's what you said."

"I just—I don't see any reason anybody has to know."

"Well, I'm not at all certain I can withhold from Odysseus . . ."

"I thought you worked for me."

Phoenix didn't answer for a minute. He hadn't—an extraordinary lapse for a eunuch—actually thought about just who his employer might be. To whom did he owe his loyalty?

The boy was trash. Even if the silly prophecies were true and he was going to conquer everything, he was . . . the sort of boy who would walk out on a lease, leaving that annoying roommate of his to pick up behind him. He might just as easily abandon Phoenix, leave him standing there in the smoldering ruins of Troy and just walk away. Odysseus wouldn't do such a thing. He'd find Phoenix a place somewhere, or pull some strings and get him a pension, whatever. No matter if he despised Phoenix, as he evidently did; he was the sort of man who recognized his obligations. Old-fashioned, that way, one of the last of a generation that found responsibility a surer beacon in life than desire.

Yes, Odysseus was far the more promising master. Why should Phoenix have felt bound to this boy, negligent and perhaps not incapable of cruelty? Because he was the last of the Peleids, Phoenix's lifetime meal ticket? Or just because he was pretty, and—if one had to spend one's life following someone — one would be better off looking at Pyrrhus's backside than at Odysseus's?

"Of course I work for you," he said. "And you're right, I can't imagine any reason that Odysseus needs to know."

"Good," the boy said. "It can just kind of be our secret."

"Absolutely."

"I guess I might as well go to my cabin."

"I need to remove my belongings," Phoenix said, stung by the casual commandeering of *his* cabin. As if the boy were entitled. Well, it was Phoenix's fault: after he had inflated Pyrrhus's head with notions of his destiny, it was a wonder the child didn't go straight to the bridge and take over the ship.

"Would you mind?"

"Very well . . . sir."

"What's he like?"

"Odysseus? He's . . . very much respected."

"Uh-huh. But what's he like?"

It didn't matter what Phoenix answered; the boy wasn't going to repeat it. He decided to risk the truth. "He's like a lizard."

Let us suppose that he was referring only to Odysseus's heavy-lidded eyes, which made him look indolent and mournful when, some minutes later, he joined Phoenix at the same table.

Odysseus had never really paid much attention to Phoenix. He was just another of Achilles' overpriced accessories, like the white roadster and the two-hundred-dollar sunglasses and the silk shirts. Achilles surrounded his excessive body with these noisy, self-proclaiming objects, as if the in-animate world were a triumphal parade whose climax was Achilles himself. Phoenix was, perhaps, a more refined accouterment, but still an extravagance — couldn't cook, wouldn't iron. He just followed Achilles around, less a footman than a superfluous footnote, thus: Achilles strode forth from his tent.[1] Now, if I were to block that sentence and delete it, the footnote too would perish. But Phoenix had, uncannily, lingered, a gloss on an obliterated text, in the year since Achilles' death. Treated by the feral Myrmidons as a sort of exotic mascot, spending his days settling

[1] Phoenix.

Achilles' complicated estate, which involved no fewer than three common-law wives, and trying to keep the eternal mud of the campground off his elegant, tiny suits.

No one had paid any attention to him, not until a Trojan captive had spilled the vital news: that the Greeks would take Troy when they came with Neoptolemus. That was just about all the oracle said about the boy. Like most prophecies, it seemed to offer little practical guidance; vital details, such as the kid's current location, were omitted. And the little it did say was rather vexing to the commander, Agamemnon, king of kings—who had assumed that, with Achilles out of the picture, he himself would be starring in the final scenes of the epic. The outcome of a ten-year struggle could not possibly depend on the last-minute arrival of some provincial adolescent. Agamemnon insisted that they should simply ignore the prophecy and go on pursuing the same grand strategy they had followed for a decade. Just send out wave after wave of men to meet wave after wave of Trojans. Until Troy didn't have any more to send.

The steadily dwindling number of officers at the war councils—while they all of course thought that a war of attrition was a splendid notion, the sort that could only have been hit on by a genius like Agamemnon—looked around and realized that the candidates for any further attrition were in the room. Besides, who knew when Troy would run out of soldiers? Of all the arts for which Troy was famous, none had been more assiduously practiced than procreation. Even King Priam, nearing dotage, still seemed bent on populating the world with little facsimiles of himself. What if it took a century before the last wave of Trojans broke against a gap-toothed line of Achaians? It was agreed: they would fast-forward to the end of the story, help history along by—first—fetching Neoptolemus.

Once word of the plan had got around, Odysseus seemed to run into Phoenix everywhere. Always wanting some bit of legal advice or other on settling Achilles' estate, and the conversation always turning to Neoptolemus, how Phoenix was the only man for the job. He had been in touch with the family, he had an idea where the boy was. He only wanted to be of service; there was nothing in it for him. Neoptolemus would naturally trust him, the old family retainer.

Odysseus thought that, if Neoptolemus would trust this no-balled parasite, he had to be even stupider than his father. Still, Phoenix had done the job: he had procured the essential boy. Odysseus wondered what he would want now.

Phoenix dragged himself up from his chair, promptly but with no effort to disguise his weariness. The man had spent his life standing up and sitting down when and where important people told him to. Well, Odysseus thought, which of us has not? Odysseus himself stood up for Agamemnon. But Phoenix had made a career of it; he should have learned to disguise his weariness.

"Where's the boy?"

"In my cabin. As you instructed."

Odysseus poured two whiskeys and they sat down.

"Tell me about him."

"What do you want to hear?"

"Is he like his father?"

Phoenix shook his head. "No. Striking enough in appearance, but otherwise rather ordinary. Not especially bright. A bit petulant."

"So far he sounds just like his father." Odysseus half-regretted this indiscretion. Whatever he and the other lords said among themselves, it was usual to feign admiration for Achilles. Phoenix was expressionless. Perhaps no one had any illusions about Achilles. "How much did you tell him?"

"About the prophecies? Everything. Or, rather, the little you confided in me."

"That's all I know. It's about as specific as oracles get. He's with us when we take Troy. Oh, and I think maybe he kills Priam."

"Does he?"

"I don't suppose, if everything works out, that it will be much of a feat. What is Priam, seventy?"

"At least." Phoenix raised his empty glass. "May I? I must say that having encountered the boy has rather reinforced my skepticism about oracles. It's hard to see, even though I've got him here, how he's supposed to carry out his grand destiny."

"Does he believe it?"

"I can't tell."

"This is important."

"Perhaps a little. He is ostensibly interested chiefly in the estate."

"The estate?"

"The armor and things."

"I own the armor," Odysseus said, quietly and with no evident indignation.

"Yes, well, I had to promise him something a little more tangible than prophecies."

"I suppose. But if he's so interested in his father's things, why didn't he show up a year ago?"

"He didn't know about Achilles."

"Didn't know? You mean, that he was dead? It was in the news for days, how could the boy not have known?"

"He's the sort of boy who doesn't watch the news."

"Surely someone would have told him."

"No one knew who he was," Phoenix said.

"I see." Odysseus cocked his head like a pigeon. Phoenix hadn't been around him enough to recognize this mannerism, which was Odysseus's way of signaling that he was granting you his entire attention, a favor most people might happily have forgone. Phoenix elaborated: "He's been living anonymously. Out of touch with his family, using the nickname Pyrrhus. Nobody knew."

Odysseus said, innocently, "How ever did you track him down?"

"I showed his picture about. No great detection—I just showed his picture. In bars, and the like."

"How long did this take?"

"Not at all long. I actually found him the first night."

"Did you?" Odysseus spoke slowly, the way he used to when he had to get a point across to the thickest of jurors. "Finding him so quickly, an anonymous youth in such a big city, that's really quite miraculous."

"Oh." Phoenix stammered: "It—it is, rather. But he's a . . . memorable-looking boy." Odysseus just stared at him, and he surrendered. "And happily I knew where to start."

"Where would that have been?"

"There is one detail I might possibly have omitted to bring to your attention. Neoptolemus is gay."

"Who told you this, the family?"

"No one told me, I deduced it. Pampered little prince scampers off to the big city: what else could he have been?"

"So you *deduced* that the boy was queer and felt no need to disclose this to me?"

"What difference did it make? What would you have done, sailed away without him?"

What difference did it make, why was Odysseus upset about it? For he was, a little, even if just minutes ago he had mocked the young lieutenant for feeling the same way about Phoenix. Not that he thought very much about queers one way or the other; what had they to do with

145

Odysseus? He supposed he just didn't know how to talk to one. It was very important that he know how to talk to Neoptolemus.

"So," he said. "You found him in some bar?"

"*On* a bar, actually."

"On it?"

"The boy, when I found him, was dancing naked on a bar."

"You're kidding."

"He is a stripper. And also, as I understand it, a prostitute. Or has been."

"For men."

"For men. A sort of call boy, I gather."

Odysseus couldn't help it, he broke out laughing. At first because it was such a splendid joke on Achilles—he wished Achilles could have known. Well, he must have known by now. He must have been the only shade in Hell who was actually blushing. But of course it was a larger joke than that: that their great enterprise should rest on the rounded shoulders of some mincing little whore. The Fates were cards.

Phoenix didn't laugh.

Odysseus said, "The boy isn't what you were hoping for, is he?"

"Hoping?"

"Here you were going to latch on to the next generation of Peleids, another big strong man to tote you about like luggage. And you get a call boy."

"Oh. I suppose I can understand your merriment." Phoenix went on, not merrily, "I do sometimes wish there were just one strong man in the world."

"Do you? I've never encountered him," Odysseus said, just to tease. But he hadn't, really. Maybe the generation before theirs was different, the heroes: Theseus, Jason, Heracles. Among his contemporaries, though, he could not think of a single man whose strength was not sabotaged by vanity, superstition, hopeless longing. Only he himself bore the terrible burden of moving through life without self-deception. "At any rate, I suppose the line stops here. You'd better not outlive this one."

"I—I was rather thinking of changing lines."

"Hm?"

"I've already been of considerable use to you. I shouldn't wish to suggest that you owe me anything."

"Uh-huh. You understand, it may be that the late meathead required a counselor. I don't."

146

"I have the boy's confidence. You require that."

Odysseus cocked his head again. Phoenix was a rapid enough learner; he must have seen that he was again on dangerous ground. Yet he continued. "After all, I'm the one who persuaded him to come this far. I'm the one he trusts. You can't be certain of getting him any farther without me."

"I am certain. Unless he's planning to jump overboard, he will be coming some distance with us. As will you." Odysseus stood up. "I can understand the temporary euphoria that may have come over you at finding yourself, for once in your life, between engagements. But you're an old man, you'll never learn to be your own master now. You need to pick a side."

It didn't matter which one. This weightless old fart couldn't tip the balance one way or the other. Except it was odd, wasn't it, that he should already have had Odysseus thinking of *sides*, as if there were some sort of struggle impending? Eunuchs seemed to do that; intrigue seemed to enter the room with them. If you saw a eunuch muttering to himself, you were witnessing the birth of a conspiracy.

Odysseus considered it as he went back to his cabin. Phoenix had spent a whole week in the Park Court Hotel—at Odysseus's expense— never reporting back, all that time. Plenty of time for Phoenix and the boy to have reached some understanding. But what could it possibly consist of? How could a eunuch and a faggot conspire to frustrate Destiny?

If Odysseus was left with any small misgivings, they were soon overtaken by a little euphoria of his own. He had that jazzy feeling he used to get when someone accidentally spilled the key fact in a deposition, or when a clerk who'd been up all night strode into his office first thing in the morning and showed him the decisive precedent. There was always more to do, maybe a lot, before the matter would be wrapped up. Now at least he could see his way to it: the end of the beginning, the light at the end of the tunnel—all those phrases for the instant when you could visualize the end of a lawsuit, or a war, that seemed endless.

Things were clicking into place: they were going to finish, any day now. In a few weeks he would be home.

2

In the morning Pyrrhus was queasy. Not seasick, exactly—they were moving through calm waters, and the pitching of the ship was almost imperceptible unless he focused on it—but on the edge of seasick: the nagging little feeling of wrongness in the world one sometimes gets, which might be physical or might have to do with a forgotten appointment or unfinished task. He made himself sit up and looked around the tiny cabin.

Phoenix hadn't, after all, taken everything away. There was a dressing gown hanging on a hook on the door—moiré silk, he can't have worn it out in the passageway, in front of the sailors. He must just have sat here in it, feeling elegant. Under the desk was a pair of shoe inserts; he must have been even tinier than he looked. On the desk, a little leather photograph frame, the kind you take traveling and that opens like a book. Pyrrhus wasn't really ready to stand up, but he had to see. Of course, when he opened it, he found a picture of his father. Younger than Pyrrhus remembered, younger even than in the picture his mother kept dutifully in the TV room and never glanced at.

He looked a lot like Pyrrhus. Not enough that anyone could have confused them. His eyes were closer together than Pyrrhus's. And already, at whatever age he was—sixteen maybe—his neck was like a marble pedestal on which his cranium perched like a little *objet de vertu*. But enough like Pyrrhus: if the boy in the picture had grown into Achilles, so might Pyrrhus.

Pyrrhus got dressed, went out and found the bathroom, oddly labeled *head*, then—not knowing where else to go—made his way back to where Phoenix had left him sitting the night before, the officers' mess. A couple of guys—young officers, Pyrrhus's age or a little more, scrubbed and looking as though even their souls had creases—were having breakfast, huge portions that declared they were not in the least seasick. They glanced up but did not acknowledge Pyrrhus as he came in. When he got coffee and sat at the far end of the table, they looked only at each other and did not speak. Maybe they had been talking about Pyrrhus.

Pyrrhus said good morning, and they nodded, still not looking at him. He insisted. "My name's Neoptolemus." It felt funny, saying that. Still, he would have to start being Neoptolemus sooner or later.

"Yes, sir," one said.

"Yours?"

"Lieutenant Nereus."

Nereus at least managed to face Pyrrhus. His mate stared at the wall and mumbled, "Hyperenor."

Pyrrhus said, "I thought maybe Odysseus might be here."

Lieutenant Nereus looked at Pyrrhus as if it were presumptuous of him even to utter this name. "The commander doesn't chow with us."

"Oh." It hadn't, oddly, occurred to Pyrrhus that there was a commander and that he himself was somewhere else in the hierarchy. He had thought he answered only to Destiny.

There was a long silence. Pyrrhus sipped his coffee, trying to think of something else to say and wondering if it might not be a good time to go hunt for the shuffleboard court.

Hyperenor spoke. "Man, I cannot wait till we put in at Arisbe." Nereus grunted neutrally and he went on. "I got this babe waiting there . . ." He glanced toward Pyrrhus as he said this. Pyrrhus forced a one-sided smile. Cool, a babe. Hyperenor looked a little perplexed and didn't return the smile; nor did he have anything further to offer about his babe.

Pyrrhus hadn't responded just right; Hyperenor had sensed something odd about him. As he took another drink of his coffee, he felt that somehow he wasn't doing that right, either. How would a straight boy hold his cup, and what would he do with his other hand? Or would he use both hands to hold a cup? Would he have his elbows on the table?

He had forgotten—a few months away from home, living in the gay neighborhood of a great city, and he had forgotten what it felt like to be irregular. How he used to walk the streets of Scyros wondering: Can they see? How he would never smile, because he had that delusion gay people have, that nobody can tell if they are serious enough. When just the opposite is true: we are most obvious when we are grave. He had forgotten, how he used to try to compose himself to meet the world.

"We should be at Arisbe—when? Friday, right?" Hyperenor said.

"Um," Nereus said. "I don't think so."

"What do you mean?"

"We . . . we kind of changed course."

"Shit." As if Hyperenor couldn't hold it another minute, had to get to his babe before he exploded. "Where are we headed, then?"

Nereus wiped his mouth with his napkin, not prissily but with mechanical precision, and said, lowering his voice about half an octave,

"Odysseus ordered a little correction, that's all. Maybe because of the storm."

"But we're heading straight into it."

Pyrrhus thought Nereus glanced at him before turning to Hyperenor. "We're skirting it. Don't worry about it."

Hyperenor said, "I got watch," and scuttled out. Lieutenant Nereus looked a little panicky for a second, left alone with the stranger. He must have thought of following his buddy, then decided he wasn't going to be scared away from a second cup of coffee. He got one and then, in a gesture that touched Pyrrhus disproportionately, held up the pot to ask if Pyrrhus wanted a refill too.

He didn't, just then, but he let Nereus top off his cup. When Nereus sat down again, Pyrrhus said, "Arisbe, where's that? I thought we were going to Troy."

"That is Troy, sir. I mean, the harbor nearest the Greek camp."

"Oh."

"A manmade harbor, it's kind of cool."

"Oh, uh . . . pontoons and things?"

"Yeah. And things." Nereus smiled for the first time, perhaps at how very civilian Pyrrhus was. "We should be there in a week or so."

"That long? That's a pretty big detour."

"Tell me about it. And after we just spent a fucking week anchored at the capital. Pardon me. They wouldn't give anybody shore leave, not even officers. You know what that's like? Stuck on board, and you could practically reach out and touch the city, the lights."

If Pyrrhus didn't know about pontoons, he knew about the city. "It's not that hot when you're there," he said, trying to sound impressively jaded.

Nereus was only Pyrrhus's age, or a couple of years older, though his light hair was already receding. He had an acolyte look about him, round cheeks and bright eyes, only the uniform and a forced, grown-up frown giving him the tautness that had intimidated Pyrrhus at first. Pyrrhus tried to picture him on shore leave, with his buddies, roaming the bars, arriving at last at some strip joint. With women, that is.

Nereus and his buddies, throwing back the watered drinks, hooting. Challenging one another to approach the babe in the corner, who would talk to you if you bought the fifty-dollar split of pink champagne. Who would, for some further gratuity, take you to the booth at the back of the bar and give you a hand job. Who was Pyrrhus to find this picture disgusting? But it was: Nereus's face slack, some whore with a beehive reaching into his pants, Nereus clutching her boobs. Could that be the destination he imagined when he spoke so wistfully of the city and the lights? Sometimes Pyrrhus thought straight boys were the greatest mystery in the world.

Pyrrhus said, "So . . . you got a girl at Arisbe, too?"

"Sir?" Nereus was startled; he had been staring at Pyrrhus as hard as Pyrrhus at him. "No, I . . . I got a girlfriend back home."

"Oh, yeah? What's her name?"

"Um . . . Pleione."

She was an invention, Pyrrhus could feel it. Someone he had summoned up because he was too shy to approach the hangers-on at Arisbe. Pyrrhus wondered if Nereus was a virgin. He was sorry to have made Nereus speak of Pleione. Her made-up name was a curtain Nereus drew over himself.

But he had been, until then, friendly enough—with no one around to monitor him. Pyrrhus hazarded, "Where are we really headed?"

"Beg pardon?" Nereus stiffened. "Like I said, just a little correction. Nothing to be concerned about, won't hold us up very much." He wasn't looking at Pyrrhus any more. He stood up. "Been away from the bridge too long. I hope you have a pleasant voyage." Then, as an afterthought: "Sir."

Pyrrhus sat alone for a while in the officers' mess, thinking about the change of course. Not that he had the least idea how to get to Arisbe, nor that a day or two could matter. But it made him feel that there were a million miles between him and the prophecies. And that the lieutenant— he and Odysseus, not Pyrrhus—knew how they were going to get from here to there, and how fast.

Pyrrhus felt completely surrounded by the ship, encased in it like a particle of dust that has found its way into the works of a pocket watch. He was hungry for a little light and air, and he left the mess and made his way upwards. After he'd climbed a couple of ladders he was sure he was at the level of the main deck. But he couldn't find a way out; there were just a lot of metal doors with inscrutable stenciled labels. He wandered the passageways, looking for a hatch that said WORLD.

Once or twice he ran into a knot of sailors. They would step aside deferentially, as Pyrrhus was a sort of officer. Except that in one narrow

152

passage a sailor smiled faintly as Pyrrhus approached, reached into his trouser pocket, and rearranged himself before letting Pyrrhus by. Pyrrhus pretended not to notice and maintained his quasi-official dignity as he squeezed past.

Another guy stood stock-still as Pyrrhus approached, like a squirrel hoping not to be noticed. Pyrrhus wanted to ask him: How do you get outside? As Pyrrhus got closer, though, the sailor maintained a glassy stare, didn't so much as glance at Pyrrhus, as if he had willed himself into a different dimension. Pyrrhus walked by, then stopped a few feet beyond him. Pyrrhus thought the sailor would have to turn around then, that anyone would just naturally turn around, hearing Pyrrhus's footsteps stop. Instead he kept his back turned, stayed absolutely rigid, like the guards at the palace. Only when Pyrrhus walked on and got near the end of the corridor did he hear the poor guy, behind him, scurrying away.

Pyrrhus must have made the circuit of the ship two or three times before, just ahead of him, a door was flung open and a sailor stepped into the passage, his green deck jacket lightly spotted with rain. Here at last was the way, but it was evidently lousy out. Pyrrhus went anyway.

No one was on deck. A steady drizzle was falling almost straight down: no wind, they weren't in a real storm, but nothing you wanted to stand around in. Still, he'd hunted for the door so long, he couldn't just go right back inside. Instead he went to the railing—not all the way, he was afraid of falling in, and his years of avoiding the pool where the real boys splashed him had left him a splendid candidate for immediate drowning. Anyway, he didn't have to get right up to the railing to see that there was nothing out there, just dark water all the way to the horizon and the silvery featureless sky above it.

He turned and looked around the deserted deck. There were gun batteries, which he—the future general—hadn't the slightest desire to inspect. Lifeboats, which gave him the willies. Various mysterious lockers and hatchways and boxes, everything as gray and unfriendly as the sky. The superstructure of the ship towering over him like a ziggurat. He felt even more enclosed than he had below deck. Because now he was outdoors, and the whole world around him was still monochromatically alien.

Pyrrhus was being taken someplace in a vessel of which he was not the master. Nor, come to think of it, was Odysseus—not Odysseus or his hired helmsman. All passengers on a cruise whose itinerary had been laid out on the day the world was made.

He felt, for the first time since leaving Scyros, that hollow place growing in him, squeezing the breath out of him. He made himself ignore it. And suppressed the momentary thought that he had made a truly stupendous error.

Pyrrhus looked up at the bridge. He thought he could make out, through the glass, two indistinct figures. He wondered if they were watching him. He wondered if one of them was Odysseus. His commander. He shivered, just from the cold and wet.

There was the boy. Out on the deck in this weather, and not even a jacket on. Probably thinking grand poetic thoughts about the sea. He was bigger than Odysseus had expected: you said "fairy" and you naturally pictured a little wispy thing, though of course they must have come in all shapes and sizes. The boy's shape, gradually revealed as his shirt drank in the rain, was more or less perfect.

Not that Odysseus was aroused, not the tiniest bit. He was entirely heterosexual; he could honestly say that he couldn't recall ever having felt the smallest contrary twinge. Still, he could not fail to register that the boy's body was, in every dimension, not just normal but normative, not a temple but a template. Well, what did he expect from Achilles' son? Except that Achilles' body, while overpowering, wasn't . . . inspiring. The boy's perfection was what poetry required; men like the Myrmidons would follow such a figure, give up their lives for it.

Why, because they were all secretly queer? Not exactly. Rather that each would think that he, among the company of ordinary men, was the most like the general. Each would want some sign from him that he had seen it too. You can't be perfect, but you can be perfection's deputy, the title conferred by the least nod, the slightest prolongation of a glance. Yes, you're the one; I know you're different from the others. In the hope of such approval a man would even try to die gracefully, not crying out or shitting himself like the rest of the crowd.

Odysseus should have been satisfied, that the boy turned out, at least in his surface aspects, to fit the job description. Another piece falling into place, a step closer to finishing and going home. Yet there was also something disturbing about it, seeing him out there alone in the rain.

Odysseus felt the way you do when you can't get the last couple of words on the crossword puzzle and you're just about ready to peek at the solution. You want to see it, but you don't. The boy's very arrival was a sign that the last act had begun. They were just days or weeks short of the climax of history, the summary event for which every event since the creation had been mere preparation. When it was over they would go home.

Of course, Odysseus was, famously, eager to get home. Back to Penelope and Telemachus, back to house and office and the drive in between he could probably still do in his sleep. For ten years, he had thought of nothing but finishing. Not of sacking Troy or restoring to Menelaus his kidnapped or escaped wife, certainly not of killing, though he had done some killing. Just of finishing, closing this episode and returning to his life. As if it were all a protracted business trip.

You take your evening flight, arrive in the darkness in a strange city, sit up late in your hotel room preparing for the meeting or the deposition the next day. In the morning you go down to the coffee shop and have a big breakfast, read every filler in the paper, because ten is still hours away and you can't walk the dog or start the sprinklers or do any of the things you would have done at home. Then you do your business, and at four o'clock it doesn't matter if there are a few unsettled items on the agenda, a few questions you haven't asked, because you are in a hurry to get your flight and get home. You just want to wrap things up.

The plane lands, you get the shuttle to the parking lot, get in your car and start to drive home. All you have thought of all day long, this drive. But, as your exit comes into view, you are filled with a strange dread. Because Penelope is still a little angry about the joke you told at the party on Saturday, and Telemachus is failing geometry and also has kind of a sneaky air about him lately, and you haven't done anything about the leaky ceiling in the spare bedroom. You don't want to be anywhere else; you couldn't have stayed in that hotel room another night. This is the only place on earth for you. You think about taking the long way home.

Here the boy was, already; it was practically over. What had been Odysseus's hurry to see him?

Pyrrhus went back below and promptly got lost again. He wandered the passageways for a while. At last he came to a cul-de-sac, probably near the bow. The passage just ended, and he turned around to go back the way he'd come. At the far end there appeared from around a corner a sailor with a mop. He didn't look at Pyrrhus, just started mopping listlessly in Pyrrhus's direction as Pyrrhus continued toward him. When Pyrrhus got to the boundary of his slosh, he saw Pyrrhus's feet and looked up. He drew himself into a sort of attention, a present-mop posture, and said, "Sir."

Pyrrhus found himself almost saluting, then said, "Um, hi. I'm not an officer or anything."

"What are you, then?"

"I don't know. Just along for the ride."

"I thought you were the new general."

"Whatever. Right now I think I'm a little seasick."

The sailor smiled a little, his upper lip drawn down in a futile effort to conceal a pair of buckteeth. "You'll get over it."

He was a kid, not a day over eighteen, with hair as red as Pyrrhus's own and skin of the same color against the white of his T-shirt, fair skin brutally exposed to the sun and protesting with an angry red glower. Under the T-shirt, Pyrrhus knew, would be skin as pale as the page you are reading.

"I got lost," Pyrrhus said. "Ship's bigger than it looks."

"Not when you been on it a while." He leaned his mop against the wall. "You want I should show you how to get where you're going?"

"I'm not going anywhere. Just out for a stroll."

The sailor smiled again, still covering his teeth, at the notion of a promenade through the gray labyrinth of the *Penelope*'s hold. "Sightseeing."

"Yeah." Pyrrhus let his eyes do a standard scan, up-down-middle, to intimate that the sailor was the only sight worth writing home about so far.

The sailor looked down at the deck, with its inscrutable hieroglyph of drying mop strokes. "My name's Corythus," he said.

"I'm Pyrrhus."

"Oh. I thought you were —"

"My friends call me Pyrrhus."

Corythus looked up, startled to be friends with an officer. "I could show you around."

Pyrrhus dimly recalled some half-formed resolution about keeping his trousers buttoned, so the Myrmidons would respect him.

The Myrmidons were far away. "Aren't you supposed to be . . . don't you have to stay here?"

"Nobody gives a shit. Anyway, if I'm with an officer, who's going to ask?"

"I'm not an officer," Pyrrhus said again.

. . .

Although this pickup had been enacted with an effortless fluency on both sides, things slowed down considerably once they got to a closet, undressed, and lay on a metal floor whose startling coldness might have distracted the most ardent of lovers. Corythus shivered as Pyrrhus ran his hand over young skin, stretched taut across a body so slender that Pyrrhus could intuit the skeleton beneath the flesh. This feeling he had almost forgotten in just a few months. But Pyrrhus didn't know what to do next, exactly, and Corythus was so eager to please he was practically limp.

Pyrrhus was used to being handed a script. Not a script, exactly, but the *sides* that actors used to receive, with their own lines and no one else's, just abbreviated cues to let them see where they fit in; thus:

> . . . *someone's coming.*
> [YOU enter.]
> YOU: Hello, everybody.
> . . . *are you?*
> YOU: I'm fine, thanks, how have you been doing?
> . . . *a seat?*
> YOU: Thanks. [YOU sit.]

And so on, except that for a hustler perhaps it was rather the reverse. As though he had been handed the other player's sides by mistake and had to reconstruct his own part from the elliptical fragments. Corythus was supplying no cues at all, just inviting Pyrrhus to do whatever he wanted.

It wouldn't be quite right to say that Pyrrhus, professionally versatile, had ceased to have preferences. Everyone has preferences. What he had lost—after, say, three hundred encounters, his career really was quite brief, three hundred occasions of doing what other people wanted, trying to read their signals if they were reticent, overlooking their rudeness if they were not—what he had lost was any sense of a causal connection between his desires and what he did with his body. Pyrrhus had been, perhaps, the converse of a quadriplegic: the latter wished to do things but could not make his limbs move, while Pyrrhus made his limbs move without wishing to.

Now he might as well have been paralyzed. Already Corythus, puzzled, was shifting away from him. Well, if Pyrrhus didn't want anything in particular, he certainly didn't want Corythus getting away. He tightened his grip, found himself, almost unintentionally, squeezing so hard it must

157

have hurt. He could feel the instinctive refusal; Corythus started to squirm out of his arms; he held on even tighter. Corythus relented, with a tiny groan of resignation, a little rodent sound: he didn't want to be hurt, but he didn't want to be left alone.

Pyrrhus himself could not have said if he was just playacting, moving with professional ease into what had been one of his most frequently requested impersonations: rough. Or if he was actually aroused by Corythus's sadness and smothered resistance.

Was this, then, his preference? I don't mean being on top: that is not a preference but a location. Rather something about the resistance, about taking what Corythus did not wish to give up? Might we then say there are two types of men: those who seize what the other would withhold, those who are happier surrendering?

Yet the happy surrender is itself a contradiction. He who capitulates can say: I didn't want this, you made me, I am not really this. Giving up his cake and having it, too. Being punished for his desires at the same time that he fulfills them.

And the one who takes, who compels, the rough one? This is harder; we are so accustomed to supposing that this is just how male animals are, driven by some immemorial instinct to seize what is not willingly given. But there is no such instinct. Perhaps there is rape in nature, but rams or bulls are merely heedless of resistance; they are not inflamed by it. Why should a man, and not a ram, need to force his way in? Pushing all the harder because Corythus was audibly whimpering now?

Maybe this: maybe there is no difference between the one who forces and the one who gives up. As in the room with Deucalion, that night, when Pyrrhus wasn't sure who was conjuring up the next hurtful thing he would do to that body stretched out under him, wasn't sure whether he or Deucalion was in charge. It didn't matter, so long as someone was getting hurt.

Because desire is vile, pleasure is vile. And *someone* in the room must be punished for it.

They lay together in the storeroom to which Corythus had led them. Pyrrhus was right about Corythus's skin; his burned arms were like a pair of red sleeves crossed against his pale chest. Pyrrhus reached for his shirt to get a cigarette. The pack was soaked through, from the rain earlier. "Shit," Pyrrhus said.

"Can't smoke in here anyhow."

"How come?"

Corythus gestured behind them. Pyrrhus sat up and looked. He hadn't seen the stenciling on the wooden crates around them. Depth charges, shells. He was a little pleased at first, at the thought that they had made love in this storeroom of Ares' spare parts. Except that they hadn't made love. What he'd done to Corythus was perfectly consonant with the death in the room. He was afraid he had broken Corythus already, like a toy you get for your birthday and smash that very day.

Corythus stretched and brought his face up close to Pyrrhus's. He wanted to be kissed. He had forgiven Pyrrhus, or didn't even know there was something to forgive, thought that what Pyrrhus had done was . . . natural, just the way Pyrrhus made love. He closed his eyes, as if it were inconceivable that Pyrrhus could fail to kiss him. Pyrrhus did. For some time, his tongue loitering over Corythus's buckteeth. Then he lay back.

Corythus told a little of his story. Pyrrhus might almost have told it for him. The small town, working in his father's hardware store, knowing he was funny but not exactly how. Joining the navy to get away from a life sentence of varnish and nails. Getting to basic and learning—the tuition free if brutal—just how he was funny. He finished: "And then you came along." As if Pyrrhus were, not the most recent event in his colorless history, but its logical culmination. Or maybe he just didn't know how to finish a story. Pyrrhus didn't tell his own story. He wanted a cigarette.

"You want to go back to my room?" Pyrrhus said. There was a fresh pack there.

"Cabin. I better not. Maybe later."

"Okay."

Pyrrhus thought they'd get up then, but instead Corythus, rather abruptly, began sucking Pyrrhus's nipple, then wandered gently down to the groin. Pyrrhus was afraid about his teeth, but he had evidently learned a lot since leaving the hardware store. Pyrrhus still sort of wanted a cigarette. In fact, it was a toss-up, which he wanted more. But Corythus was doing pretty well. When he had Pyrrhus hard again he lay on his belly and closed his eyes, tightly. As if he were planning, during the act, to picture someone else.

When Pyrrhus was finished Corythus lay splayed out beneath him like a pithed frog. Corythus hadn't come, and Pyrrhus thought of maybe doing something about that. Corythus didn't turn over, though, evidently didn't

159

expect even that simple courtesy. Pyrrhus didn't, after the replay, have the energy to give him anything he didn't expect. They got up and dressed in silence.

Corythus cracked the door, peered out, gave Pyrrhus an all-clear nod. As they emerged from the storeroom—Pyrrhus feeling the sort of movement between realms he used to when he was a kid and went straight from masturbation to the dinner table—Pyrrhus looked at the door and saw the MUNITIONS sign he hadn't noticed going in.

After their confinement Pyrrhus wanted to go back up on deck, drizzle or no. Corythus led the way, and whispered without turning around, "I could come to your cabin at sixteen hundred." While Pyrrhus struggled with his arithmetic, Corythus went on: "I mean . . . maybe you got things to do."

"No," Pyrrhus said, a little surprised at his own eagerness. "Four o'clock."

Corythus turned and grinned, this time not bothering to hide his prodigious teeth.

They passed a couple of sailors. Corythus said, gruffly, "This way, sir." He wouldn't come out on deck with Pyrrhus, had to get back to his mop. As he walked away, Pyrrhus regarded his butt with a certain proprietary feeling.

Pyrrhus felt wicked. Not bad, but smutty and defiantly happy, the way he had felt so long ago after lying with the chauffeur's son. He had snuck into a storeroom with a cute enlisted man and screwed around. Possibly he hadn't treated Corythus quite as well as he might have. But Corythus was all set for a rematch: he must have been content enough. Maybe this was how people treated people; Pyrrhus couldn't quite remember how people acted with their bodies as their only currency.

Even if they hadn't had an especially good time, he was exhilarated: he had forgotten what it was to be wicked. In the city, where everything goes (or went, then), where—as Thetis promised—nobody knew who he was or cared what he did, he had felt nothing at all. Here, in the floating citadel of masculinity, he and Corythus had deviated, transgressed. Their boyish humping an undiscovered mutiny against the gray oppression of the war machine.

Or against the Fates themselves. Here they had tried to conscript him, and he had proved that he answered to no commander. Except maybe the one between his legs. Just an hour ago he had felt so tiny, lost on the ship. When he was the only free man aboard.

He stepped toward the bow, looking forward as fearlessly as he had that morning on the ferry, when he had left Scyros behind him. At first he hardly noticed that it wasn't just drizzling any more: they were headed into a genuine storm. Even when he did notice, it seemed somehow of a piece with his new autonomy to stand for a minute in the pelting rain. As if this, too, were a subversive act.

But now the waves they breached came sloshing over the deck, and he had a vision of himself swept overboard, no one even missing him. He was just thinking he'd better go below when Phoenix appeared, in a green slicker that made him look like a debonair toad. "My dear boy, I've been hunting everywhere for you. You'll catch your death."

"I'm okay." Pyrrhus had meant to go in, but now he felt like staying on for a minute, just so Phoenix wouldn't rescue him.

"Odysseus sent me to fetch you."

"Oh, the great man's ready to see me now?" Pyrrhus said. This orneriness a way of resisting the actual rush of trepidation that came over him. He didn't, all of a sudden, want to see Odysseus very much. The same way he hadn't wanted to pass through a room containing his father.

"He's been very busy. He is eager to see you." A gust of wind came that nearly knocked Phoenix over, like a green duckpin. "Please, won't you come down?"

3

When they got to the officers' mess, there he was, the Sea Lord, smoking a cigarette and looking meditatively at a tumbler of whiskey.

He was not Achilles. You could tell he was a commander, because no one less exalted could have been so slovenly: tunic unbuttoned, graying hair drooping over his forehead. But nothing like Achilles. Of course it was the eyes Pyrrhus noticed, as Odysseus raised his head, the eyes shining with wonder. As if there were a child in him, for whom everything was still new. Above them, the heavy lids, ready to descend at the inevitable disappointment.

"I'm Neoptolemus," Pyrrhus said. Odysseus just looked. "Achilles' son." As if he didn't know that, but Pyrrhus thought it would put them more nearly at a level. No one was his commander yet. He made himself go on looking into those dark eyes, even if he expected to see in them, any second, the amazed disgust with which his father had always looked down at him.

Odysseus gestured toward the sideboard, which held his whiskey bottle and various others. Pyrrhus shook his head. Odysseus said, "Oh, drink something," in a sharp coastal twang.

It wasn't even lunchtime yet. "I haven't been feeling too good," Pyrrhus said. "Maybe a beer."

"Try the icebox."

"I know." Pyrrhus fetched one and sat across from Odysseus.

"Been seasick?" Odysseus said.

"Just took a little getting used to."

"I always get sick."

"Really? You'd think sailing would be in your blood, being from . . ." Phoenix had told him. "Where is it, Cephalonia?"

"Ithaca. I don't think it would matter if you were born under water. It's just damned unnatural. I won't feel right till we get to dry land."

This was just like an ordinary conversation. "Yeah, how much longer is that going to be? Till we get to Arisbe? I hear we're not headed straight there."

Odysseus was alarmed. "From whom—Phoenix?" He should never have confided in Phoenix, not for an instant. The whole ship must have known they were bound for Lemnos, and why.

The boy said, "No, some officer. Says we changed course."

Good, he didn't know anything. Odysseus didn't want to tell him, not yet, that his future was a contingent one. Hard enough nudging him on his predestined course without letting him know there was an obstacle in the way, one ten times more recalcitrant than Neoptolemus himself.

Odysseus was casual. "We're making a little stop at a place called Lemnos. For something we left behind. Then on to Arisbe, only another few days." He shrugged, as though a little delay wouldn't concern Pyrrhus very much. "Though it's gratifying to find you so impatient to get into the thick of things."

The ordinary conversation was over: it was as if Pyrrhus had been conscripted in a single sentence. He, just automatically, refused induction. "I haven't made up my mind about that."

"What?" Odysseus looked at Pyrrhus with those terribly curious eyes and cocked his head a little.

"I mean, I'm not sure I want to fight or anything."

"What are you doing here?"

"Phoenix said there was . . . you know, an estate. Stuff."

"Ah. You're just here for the *stuff*," he said. Not sarcastically, just pinning things down.

"I'm not sure."

Odysseus shrugged. "It shouldn't surprise me. Your family has never been in any hurry for battle. Your own father hid out on Scyros until we happened on him."

"I was there," Pyrrhus said. "When you came for Daddy. I saw you."

"You can't have been, I would remember."

"I was just a little kid, hiding behind my mother's skirt. You were—" Pyrrhus couldn't connect the memory with the rather dumpy figure before him. How very small Pyrrhus must have been. "You were the scariest thing I had ever seen."

"I think you're confusing me with Ajax. I have never been especially scary."

Looking at him, Pyrrhus didn't think he had been. It must have been the other guy. Odysseus seemed like an ordinary man. If he could be a commander, maybe anybody could.

"You were there," Odysseus said, looking off into space as if still trying to remember. "Then you'll recall that we had to shame your father into coming along."

"Uh-huh. Well, you can't shame me."

"That's right, you're just coming for the stuff."

"Phoenix said . . . the armor and everything, Phoenix thinks it's worth something. Maybe—once we get to Arisbe and I can check things out, maybe we can talk then."

"If that's all you came for, you needn't wait. I've brought the armor."

"You have?"

"As it happens. In my cabin."

"Oh. Do you mind . . . ?"

"No, go ahead. Down there, second door to the left."

No, of course the boy couldn't be shamed, how absurd. The little faggot can't have had any shame at all. How in the world would anyone ever make a soldier out of him? That was the only way soldiers were made, even Achilles: shame, fear of being thought a sissy.

Well, no, not Achilles. Odysseus couldn't really say that it was shame alone that had made Achilles come along. When he stood there naked, waiting for his consort to bring out the armor, he was like a dumb horse, waiting to be saddled, champing for his early death. Something in him wanted it, so impatient for immortality. For what—to spend an eternity with the other old shades, emitting ghostly belches and bragging of what they did on earth?

Maybe the boy was feeling the same thing now. Even if he evidently didn't mind being thought a sissy, maybe it ran in the blood, whatever it was that had driven Achilles. He certainly was taking his time looking over the armor; maybe he was like his father. No, that was too much to hope for. Probably he was just captivated by the confounded shield. And why not? Even the Myrmidons, who were no connoisseurs of the decorative arts, had been entranced by that incredibly ostentatious shield.

Odysseus crept halfway down the hall to find out what was taking so long. He could see, through the crack of the door, that the boy wasn't admiring the shield at all. He was trying on the breastplate, in the shape of his father, the way his father had looked in the moonlight the night they had come to get him. Could he remember, the boy? The heroic body he would never possess and that he was now supposed to strap on.

The breastplate fit him, sort of. From where Odysseus stood he couldn't be sure that the boy's chest actually filled out the sculpted pectorals. But then who knew if even Achilles really filled that breastplate? The boy didn't, at any rate, look silly, as Odysseus did the night he won the stuff, brought it back to his billet and, the doors locked, put it on. Feeling like a child playing dress-up, and also like a graverobber.

Odysseus went back to the mess and poured himself another whiskey. He'd had the first just to impress the boy, to make himself seem a little more hard-boiled. He had never been much for drinking at midday. It was still common when he joined his first firm—you'd go out to lunch with a partner and you'd have to have a couple of drinks, lest your abstinence be taken as a comment. He was always stupid the rest of the day. Partners could afford to be stupid; clerks couldn't.

Still, he poured another. Because he was uncomfortable with the boy? Or just because once you've had one it's easy to pour another? Anyway, Phoenix was right; the boy wasn't especially sharp. Odysseus didn't need to worry about diminishing his faculties.

Odysseus wasn't so very much smaller than the boy. It wasn't as though, the night he'd tried the armor on, he'd gotten lost in it the way Penelope used to in his dress shirts. But he had looked like a lawyer wearing armor. The boy, at least, could imagine he might grow into it. Possibly he even would. The very idea made Odysseus tired. Maybe you became an old man when you no longer imagined you could grow into things.

What was taking him? Odysseus stepped back to the cabin, knocked, pushed the door wide open. There the boy was, every piece of the armor in place, as if he just knew exactly how it went, every strap tied and catch done up.

Why wasn't this boy laughable? He had never seen battle at all, he was a beardless little tart, and he looked like a warrior. And why should Odysseus have begrudged him this, Achilles' whelp? Odysseus was so fond of saying that the mission was everything, the point was to finish—no sacrifice too great, no stratagem beneath them, no scruple to be maintained—finish and get home. Why should he have minded, more even than Agamemnon might, that it should be through this boy? Through another Peleid like a splendid animal?

The boy evidently saw it himself. He was trying not to preen, but he was stealing looks in the mirror.

"It might have been made for you," Odysseus said, sounding to himself like some haberdasher.

"You think?"

"It makes me—you know, I'm not a credulous man, I don't put too much stock in oracles. But it makes me think there's something to it all."

166

"Uh-huh," the boy said, with deliberate flatness. Though by then he was standing squarely before the mirror, staring at himself, lips parted in something like awe. As if he had never seen himself before, maybe never existed before.

This was what the name meant. Neoptolemus, the New War. That is how the boy looked—new, clean, born that very moment. This was what it meant, this was the fresh start that would finish it all. Odysseus, almost involuntarily, said the name aloud.

"Huh?" Neoptolemus said.

Odysseus repeated the prophecy. Lightly, making himself smile, so the boy wouldn't think he was so silly as to credit any random oracle. But Neoptolemus was interested—you could see that, even if he forced a little one-sided smile to show he wasn't so easily seduced. He was taken by it, if not taken in: who wouldn't be?

The kid was going for it. Odysseus thought he might even improvise a few details, flesh out the story a bit to make it more convincing. He stopped himself; excessively specific prophecies could be proved wrong. Neoptolemus was quite caught up enough.

Even if he still affected skepticism. "Okay: I put on this armor and head over to Troy and then what? They're so knocked out they just throw open the gates and surrender?"

"I don't know then what. The oracles don't always give you a complete blow-by-blow. Anyway, I've been working on another scheme for getting through the gates."

The boy smirked. "You're this famous brilliant guy and all, and you believe in oracles."

"I don't believe it just because it was an oracle. I believe it because it makes perfect sense. The Myrmidons have just been sulking for a year now. If you were to return to lead them, then . . ."

Then no matter what you are, what you've done: if I get you into battle we'll have Achilles' men. You're just a sort of flag, something for them to rally around. It doesn't matter if you're struck down in the first five minutes—you probably will be, you poor little cocksucker, I'd bet you've never so much as lifted a sword—they'll fight all the harder then.

"It just makes sense," Odysseus said. "I'm not sure I believe it, any more than I believe if I step on a crack I'll break my mother's back. But I don't step on cracks, do you?"

"I do, sometimes."

Neoptolemus returned to the mirror. Odysseus wondered if the boy could see what he saw now: however much the armor gleamed, it also looked a little ridiculous. Because who, really, could be the mythic figure for whom that armor was forged? Not even Achilles, though it might have fit him like skin. The divine smith who hammered out Achilles' final suit could not steep his heart in bronze. No man was *man enough*, the armor said. Underneath the shining, ridged belly with its incised navel—as if the armor itself had been born of a bronze mother—were human, reluctant guts.

The boy said, "This stuff's heavy."

"Uh-huh. It even slowed down your father a little."

"And it didn't protect him much."

Odysseus shrugged. "That's not what armor's for, really."

"No? What's it for?"

"I don't know. It's . . . circular. You put on the armor and you're a warrior."

The boy surveyed himself one more time in the mirror. "I'd better take it off."

He turned to face Odysseus and then just stood a minute, until Odysseus realized that the boy wanted him to leave. Imagine this shameless child unwilling to undress in front of Odysseus. But Odysseus did step out, and Neoptolemus shut the door as firmly as if it were his cabin and not Odysseus's.

Alone in Odysseus's cabin, Neoptolemus took off the armor, piece by piece, slowly as he used to strip at the Escapade. Until he was just Pyrrhus again, naked and white. He scrambled into his mufti, but he had not forgotten the vision of himself, what he had seen in the mirror. Before his qualms set in, how very right he had looked in his father's armor.

He had had for a minute that settled feeling any of us might have if we were just what we were *supposed* to be, if we could have stuck to the road laid out for us and simply put on the costumes when the stage manager said it was time for the next scene. Or, more to the point, just stepped into our fathers' clothes. Maybe it wasn't ever easy being a man, but it was surely easier when what you were to wear, whether armor or the loincloth of a slave, was handed to you off the rack at birth, along with what you were supposed to feel and do.

Here was Neoptolemus, just born and his armor handed to him. Or rather, there was Neoptolemus, the heap of steel and leather on the floor.

Maybe Pyrrhus could be what it betokened, slip into it as easily as he had figured out how to do up all the straps and buckles; maybe it would all come as naturally as that. Perhaps he had a nature that he had never learned about.

Maybe if he were to take the armor back to his cabin and just . . . practice, pose in the mirror, see himself in it long enough, he could be the Neoptolemus it was supposed to fit. Except he had for some reason a feeling that Odysseus would object. The armor was Pyrrhus's; why shouldn't he take it? Still, he left it where it was, as if it didn't really belong to him yet. As if taking it would mean—not so much embracing a future as letting it encase him.

Pyrrhus was right: Odysseus would have objected. He knew he would have to turn over the armor pretty soon, because it was the only way to finish things. But he hated it.

For one thing, Odysseus had earned the armor. The Greeks had awarded it to him, after Achilles' funeral, in tribute to his extraordinary *utility*. They didn't give it to beauty or valor, to Ajax, the first runner-up: beauty and valor had been dismembering each other for a decade. They had given the armor to Odysseus, with resignation and maybe a little contempt. As if, though they counted on his trickery to win the war at last, that very fact took some of the savor out of winning.

He could give the armor up, the clanking hand-me-downs that he'd never even worn, never planned to. Perhaps what he really hated was that the armor fit itself to the boy so effortlessly. As if it had been waiting for him, had never for one instant belonged to Odysseus. Was this just envy? That a garden-variety faggot was going to swish his way to triumph? That he even had to be cajoled into accepting, until he might condescend to stoop and pick up his unmerited laurels?

Odysseus had, too, planned to wear the armor. Just once, on the final day. He had hoped that when, by virtue of his cunning, he stood on the ruins of Troy, the real winner of the war, some poet would happen by and be dazzled by the armor. And so paint him for eternity as the champion he never was. But no: all eyes would turn to Neoptolemus. Resplendent as he administered the final coup to a doddering and defenseless king.

Perhaps the most painful part of all—painful but also entertaining, Odysseus got the joke—was that he would have to help the boy along.

Beg him, drag him if necessary. He would have to see Neoptolemus realize his destiny to complete his own.

Sometimes you have to give the Fates a little hand, Odysseus thought. He would nurse this boy along every inch of the way to Troy, if he had to. Let the boy have the glory, even. All that mattered was that they finish. Even so—he couldn't help it, he knew it was childish, but there it was and couldn't be gainsaid—he knew he wanted the boy to march through shit before his triumph. Of course this was the whiskey talking. Odysseus needed to restrain these thoughts, lest what he wanted interfere with what he intended. But he did want it: if it did not require too great a detour he would, somehow, shame this newborn hero.

Pyrrhus had lunch, sitting in the mess with . . . his fellow officers; he was maybe a step closer to calling them that. Lieutenant Nereus was there, and his buddy Hyperenor, with the babe at Arisbe, and a few equally crisp-looking nonentities. Plus a little plump guy, kind of sloppy and looking sufficiently at sea (or at-sea squared, given their situation) that Pyrrhus guessed his profession before anybody called him Doc.

The waiter—a cute dark sailor who quite outshone Corythus, but who wouldn't meet Pyrrhus's eyes, ruling out any further complications on this voyage—said, "We got liver." Pyrrhus would as soon have had them throw the liver to the sharks, but the kid had a no-substitutions tone, so Pyrrhus just nodded.

There was, unlike at breakfast, a little conversation. No one spoke to Pyrrhus, of course, but the table was crowded enough that he was a little less conspicuous. The officers talked shop, or ship; Pyrrhus didn't even try to follow it. Just tried to look pleasant and interested while he waited for his lunch.

It arrived. The cook at the palace, on Deidameia's instructions, had over the years presented Pyrrhus with liver in any number of unappetizing forms, from half-raw (temple-style, he thought of that as) to shrunken and leathery. But he had never before had it visibly singed.

Nor had the surgeon. "Will you look at that?" he said. The first words anyone at the table had addressed to Pyrrhus.

"I didn't think you could do that to liver," Pyrrhus said.

"No indeed. You know what it reminds me of? Back when I was an intern . . ."

There was some clattering of silverware and at least one audible sigh:

another intern story. Pyrrhus wasn't sure he was up for an intern story himself, but no one else was talking to him. "Yeah?" he said. A little pleased to annoy the other officers by egging the surgeon on.

"Where I interned, at Laconian General, there was a drunk proctologist. Oh . . . what was his name? . . . Alcyoneus. Used to come right into the OR just sozzled. Everybody knew it, chief of staff on down, but in those days physicians stood up for one another. Not like when I—Anyway, we had a long rotation in proctology. I mean, it's not exactly one of the core specialities; anywhere else interns spent a week or two and moved on. But at Laconian you had to spend a goddamn month with old Alcyoneus. Because they couldn't leave him unattended, see—he'd stagger into surgery and at least there'd be an intern to . . . assist.

"He was one of those elegant old guys, still wore striped pants and a frock coat. I mean, not in surgery, of course he wore a gown, but—"

"Fuck, look at the time," one officer said. He jumped up from the table, abandoning his half-eaten cobbler, and scurried off. Hyperenor didn't bother to feign urgency, just pushed himself away from the table and slouched out of the room.

The surgeon was unperturbed. "Anyhow, this one time during my turn there, we had some guy scheduled for surgery at . . . it must have been eight in the morning. Hemorrhoids. Alcyoneus and I scrubbed together and—eight in the morning, mind you—he smelled like a distillery. We get in there and . . . I don't know if you ever saw a hemorrhoid job. We used to use a cautery iron, red-hot thing, and you'd just burn the suckers." Another couple of officers departed, and Pyrrhus must have looked a little distressed himself. "The patient was under general, it wasn't that big a deal. This one morning I was supposed to burn a couple vessels and, I don't know, I must have hesitated and Alcyoneus got impatient." He started to laugh. "Just grabbed the iron out of my hands and went at it himself. Before I could stop him—" He laughed louder. "I'll be damned if he hadn't burned the poor bastard a second asshole. The room was just filled with the smell of seared flesh."

He was all but guffawing, looking around at his diminished audience. Pyrrhus was the only one who even tried to smile. The surgeon subsided.

"What happened to him?" Pyrrhus said. Nereus looked at Pyrrhus with open annoyance.

"Alcyoneus? Well, nothing. I was an intern; I certainly wasn't going to say anything about it. This was before there were lawyers practically hanging their shingles in the recovery room."

"No, I mean the patient. With the second asshole."

"The patient? Damned if I know."

The remaining officers, all but Nereus, shuffled out. The surgeon followed them, shaking his head. The patient, imagine.

Pyrrhus expected Nereus to leave, too, but he sat looking at Pyrrhus. Steadily, just inspecting, until Pyrrhus was uncomfortable and spoke. "I guess you people have heard all his stories."

"Doc? Not that one, I hadn't heard that one."

"Well, he sure cleared the room."

"Does it every time. First time he ever told a malpractice story, though. He's kind of touchy about that."

"Yeah?"

"He used to practice years ago. I mean, in civilian life, he had an office and all. He was a surgeon, a—what do you call it?—abdominal surgeon. But he had this funny habit of forgetting things. I mean, they'd have a patient all sewed up and they'd be missing a sponge or a clamp or whatever. So he wound up in the navy."

"The navy's not too picky, huh?"

"Well, you don't exactly have to be Asclepius or somebody to be a ship's surgeon. Anyway, I hope you already had your appendix out. He likes to stay in practice."

They chuckled together. Pyrrhus felt that they were almost pals, after talking at two successive meals. He said, "So how did you wind up in the navy?"

"Huh?" Nereus said.

"Like, do you believe in the war, or what?"

"Believe in it?"

"It all seems kind of silly to me. Guy runs off with some woman, and a couple hundred thousand Greeks rush off to get her back. What do you care about Helen?"

"Oh." Nereus scratched his incipient bald spot. "I don't think about that much. You know, this is a job."

"That's all?"

"Everybody's got some job, right? I mean, most of the guys are here because they couldn't think of anything else to do, or maybe they thought they could pick up a little plunder. And some guys get into the spit-and-polish crap, and some guys maybe really want to kill somebody. They show us movies sometimes. *Why We Must Fight*, that kind of shit. But nobody pays any attention. It's just—you know, you got to do something."

"I guess," Pyrrhus said. "I was kind of drafted."

"I heard."

"So it's different."

"Is it?" Nereus scratched his head again. "I think everybody was kind of drafted. Even Odysseus."

Pyrrhus went back on deck. He had thought it might still be raining, that he could be by himself a little longer. But the storm had broken. There was a lingering drizzle, but the sun was out, behind them, and the air was warmer. Sailors were everywhere, doing sailory things; cleaning up, mostly, the odds and ends Aeolus had strewn about like a child who forgets to put away his toys.

No matter where he stood he was in the way. Finally he found himself forward. Sitting on a hatchway, looking at the sea ahead, was the old sailor who had piloted the launch, the one with the tattoo on his chest. How had the artist ever etched a name beneath the clumps of silver hair? Of course: it must have been done when he was very young, his chest smooth. The hair had come later, half obscuring the name, like moss on a gravestone.

The old man caught Pyrrhus staring and looked back. "Hey," Pyrrhus said.

He wearily stood up. "Sir."

"You don't have to do that."

He sat down again. "No, sir."

"I mean calling me 'sir,' either."

He shrugged.

"Everybody's busy," Pyrrhus said.

"Aye."

"I guess there must be a lot to do, after a storm."

"Not so much. They make up jobs, just to get everybody up and about."

"What's your job?" Pyrrhus said. The sailor looked up and squinted at him. "I'm sorry, I didn't mean—"

"I'm supposed to keep you occupied."

Pyrrhus laughed. "You are? I haven't even run into you."

"You seemed well enough occupied."

Could he mean Corythus? No one had seen them, only that couple of sailors they had passed just before they parted. "Yeah, I had to meet with Odysseus and all. And then—"

"This ain't a big ship, as ships go, and the crew packed tight as hogs in a pen. A body can pretty much smell what his mates have been up to."

Pyrrhus realized, suddenly, that this was literally so; the scent of this morning's sedition was on him. He wondered if Odysseus's nose was as sharp as his curious gaze.

Perhaps Pyrrhus blushed; at any rate, the old sailor said, "It's nothing to me, mate."

"No?"

"Not my cup of tea, but why should I give a fuck?"

Cheering though it was to encounter some ancient eccentric who actually recused himself from voting on other people's lives, Pyrrhus had to ask: "You think other people know?"

"By now? Half the crew maybe. By sundown . . ."

"Shit."

"Oh. You were . . . what do you call it?"

"Passing? I thought I was."

The old man shrugged. "You wouldn't be the first officer to hop an enlisted man."

Pyrrhus started to protest once again that he wasn't an officer. Except maybe you *were* an officer if everyone treated you like one. "I didn't—" Well, he did, technically, hop Corythus. But he wasn't an officer doing it to an enlisted man; there was none of that hierarchical dimension about it. Unless everybody thought so, maybe including the enlisted man.

"What do people . . . think about them?"

"Think? People don't think too hard about what officers do. Except if you're off in some closet with a yeoman second-class, you ain't on their backs for a while."

Pyrrhus sat down. The old man slid over a bit, then reached in his shirt pocket for cigarette papers and tobacco. "I just kind of wanted to . . . keep it a secret for a while," Pyrrhus said.

"How long, say?"

"What? Just until . . ." He hadn't thought about *until*. The old man finished rolling a cigarette, one-handed, as if he'd practiced for a century; then he offered it to Pyrrhus. Pyrrhus shook his head and took out one of his own. "Just so I haven't gotten Corythus into any trouble."

"Him? He's been in trouble. You probably helped him."

"I have?"

"Now he's friends with an officer, they may lay off him."

Pyrrhus found himself staring at the old man's chest. When the guy looked in the mirror, there—backward—was the name of a woman he had probably forgotten years ago. Pyrrhus turned away; both of them looked for a while at the featureless sea.

"The sun is behind us," the old man said.

"So?"

"We ain't bound for Arisbe."

"Oh. No, we're going to Lemnos."

"Says who?"

"Odysseus." Pyrrhus felt a little important, that he had hobnobbed with Odysseus.

Admetus was evidently unimpressed. "Did he happen to say why?"

"No, just a little stopover, he said. For something he forgot."

"I see. You reckon Odysseus forgets much?"

Pyrrhus laughed. "I guess not. What's your name?"

"Admetus."

"Pyrrhus." They shook hands.

"Neoptolemus, you mean," Admetus said.

"I don't use that name much."

"Here, you know, everyone knows who you are. You can't just be Pyrrhus here."

"Everyone doesn't know who I am. They just know who my father was."

"That's a long way to knowing who you are."

"Not with me, it isn't. I'm nothing like him."

"No?" Admetus drew back and looked at him. "You know, when you stepped into the launch, I thought you was . . . I thought we'd put in at Hades and I was picking up your father's shade."

"I may look like him, but that's all."

"Oh. That's a shame. He was a hero, your dad."

"Good for him," Pyrrhus said. Too bad; he had just started to like this old guy, and now he turned out to be president of the Achilles fan club.

Admetus seemed to ruminate a minute before saying, "An asshole, too."

"What?"

"Your father. Dumb as a post, and selfish."

"Was he?"

"Never thought about nobody but himself."

175

How wonderful: Pyrrhus felt taller just hearing those words. He offered corroboration. "You know, I never got . . . not so much as a postcard." Well, of course not, the poor lunk couldn't write. At least he could have had Phoenix send one.

"No, I'm sure. He thought he was the only person in the whole world."

"Damn right."

"But you wouldn't be nothing like that."

If there was some spin in this remark, Pyrrhus missed it. "Of course, if I'm not like him, I can't be much of a general."

"I don't know. Maybe there's more than one kind of general."

"You think?"

"I guess there must be. Though from where I stand there's just one kind of officer. It wears the insignia, you salute it."

Three bells rang. "What time is that?" Pyrrhus said.

"Thirteen-thirty."

"Oh, is that all. It's funny how slow the day is going."

"This is how fast they go. It'll be sixteen hundred soon enough."

"What—How do you know about sixteen hundred?"

"Your mate'll be getting off then."

"I was . . . maybe if everybody knows I shouldn't see him again."

"Ah. You ought to."

"What's it to you?"

Admetus grinned, the first smile Pyrrhus had seen on him. "I'm supposed to see you're occupied."

Phoenix was on Admetus almost as soon as the boy walked away. "What did he say?"

"Sir?"

"About his plans?"

"Oh. I forgot to ask. We talked about his dad, mostly."

"That's all?"

"That's what we talked about. I guess I don't make a real good spy. Oh, there's one thing he told me. We're headed for Lemnos."

"That is correct," Phoenix said.

"You knew. How come?"

"We—" Phoenix had no idea. "I am unable to discuss this with you."

"Is Philoctetes still there?"

176

Philoctetes! Phoenix had forgotten Philoctetes. "Er . . . possibly."

"That's why we're going? Odysseus suddenly felt bad about Philoctetes?"

"I don't know," Phoenix said. Preferring to expose his ignorance than to sign on to the implausible notion that Odysseus might feel bad about something. "I suppose."

"Well, he should. That was awful, what we did."

"I'm surprised anyone even remembers. Were you a friend of his?"

"I knew him. I wasn't too friendly, I guess. I was . . . when I was younger, I was kind of skittish around homos."

"Philoctetes? He was gay?" A remarkable piece of intelligence. Phoenix wondered if Odysseus knew.

"Yeah. I thought everybody knew that."

"I had forgotten," Phoenix lied. He raised an eyebrow. "When you were younger. What were you ten years ago—eighty, ninety?"

"It's funny, but I'm . . . I'm still growing up. You know, I've never been so quick. It'll be a long time before I'm as wise as you and Odysseus are." This said without apparent irony, though Phoenix couldn't be sure. "I've spent ten years watching guys carve each other up. It don't seem so bad if they should want to fuck instead."

"My, that is very wise," Phoenix said. "I myself am unacquainted with either impulse."

"No?" Admetus chuckled. "I don't guess my equipment's any more ready for duty than yours, these many years. But I still get the *impulse*." He looked at Phoenix wonderingly. "You never did?"

"Perhaps," Phoenix said coldly. "I strive not to have desires that cannot be satisfied."

"Ah. No matter how old I get, I don't think I'll ever be so wise as that."

177

4

Five bells woke Pyrrhus up. He had dozed for an hour on top of the sheets in just his underwear; when he woke he was cold and something else. Hungry, partly—he hadn't eaten anything in two visits to the mess. Something else, though; maybe just irritable, the way you can be if you sleep in the middle of the day.

He still smelled of Corythus, and he wanted a shower. It was right down the passageway, one of the few stenciled doors he could decipher. Phoenix had left him a tidy stack of towels, like a matron with a houseguest. He took one, swathed himself as one used to at the baths, and padded down the hall.

He could hear the water before he opened the door. He wouldn't be alone. He felt for an instant the scalding modesty of his schooldays. As if he'd been thrown back into the world of boys, where he couldn't look at them or be looked on. He had to make himself go in, a man who just a week before had been boogying naked on a bar.

Beyond a tiny anteroom with a hook for Pyrrhus's towel, there was a cramped gloomy space with three showers, close together. Under one of them stood . . . a man: officer, sailor, passenger, how could one know? Except that he had the same coloring as Corythus, the arms dark to mid-biceps, and the face. A sailor.

The sailor looked startled when Pyrrhus stepped in to join him. Well, that was natural enough; anybody would be startled for a second if an intruder broke into a solitary shower. He had picked the middle shower, so Pyrrhus had to stand just to his right, very close. The sailor turned his back, shivered, turned to face Pyrrhus, turned his back again. As if uncertain which of his aspects was least vulnerable to Pyrrhus's gaze.

He needn't have worried. None of his aspects would have inspired lengthy scrutiny, even if Pyrrhus hadn't been just a few hours past Corythus. Pyrrhus looked at his adequate butt, just a butt. The guy shivered again, as if he could feel Pyrrhus looking. Perhaps he imagined that Pyrrhus was thinking about screwing him.

Yes, the sailor was clenching now, defending his permanent cherry. Except that, even in imagining the trespass, he had made it happen. Just by barring entry to the ghostly violator, he had become a man who could be entered. The sailor could feel it, down there, must have imagined it would feel like a cautery iron, that his conjectured surrender would be accompanied by the smell of seared flesh.

He turned around, his blank face telling Pyrrhus that he hadn't thought any of these things. Maybe hadn't even heard about Pyrrhus, one of the half that didn't know yet. The guy left, on his way to learn, some time before sundown, just what he had shared the shower with.

Pyrrhus stood under the shower for a long time, the scent of Corythus whirling down the drain. But he had been crazy to think he could just shed it all, wash off his past the way he used to scrub the scent of a trick off in the shower, and then step into a new life as into a clean, pressed uniform. Sooner or later everybody would know.

He was surprised to find that he was relieved, almost grateful, as if a burden had been lifted. So much effortful dissimulation forgone; no more worrying about how to hold his cup.

Maybe he could at least be sort of neuter? Just a regular guy with this one peculiarity they might suspect but to which their attention would never be too emphatically drawn. Maybe if they didn't think about it too much, and if he didn't say anything and never let his eyes rest where they shouldn't, maybe they could kind of overlook it after a while. See only his insignia.

It was Pyrrhus's turn to feel someone behind him, in the little ante-room. Whoever it was wouldn't come in, must have been waiting for Pyrrhus to finish. Pyrrhus turned to face him. *Boo.* The newcomer looked at Pyrrhus impassively, but clutched the towel a little more tightly about his middle. They went on staring at each other for some time before the guy got up the nerve to say, "Sir? There's only so much hot water."

Matter-of-fact, as if Pyrrhus were supposed to understand, as if it were just in the order of things that he couldn't join Pyrrhus in the shower. Pyrrhus was furious for a second, thought of standing there till the water turned cold. Just stand there looking into the eyes of some vicious little straight boy who thought Pyrrhus was contagious somehow. The city was already far away. He was here now, here with this—pretty cute, he couldn't help noticing—stranger who already despised him. But who also called him "sir."

When had he ever been so lonely? He felt for a second that he would give anything—give up anything—to fit for a while in this world. Just because he was here, for a while.

Pyrrhus got out of the shower. The guy pressed so close to the wall, to let Pyrrhus by, that he might have been a bas-relief.

Pyrrhus got dressed and went back up on deck, hoping to run into Admetus. The ship was fully out of the storm now, the clouds behind them, the sun breaking through it. The sun to the stern and a little to port: they were still sailing due north, their course taking them ever farther from Troy.

Pyrrhus couldn't find Admetus anywhere, but he did bump into Corythus, part of a crew that was pointlessly scrubbing a deck that had just been pretty well scoured by the storm. Corythus glanced at Pyrrhus and turned away, went on scrubbing. Pyrrhus wished he could warn the kid that his discretion had come too late; everybody knew about them. He supposed Corythus would find that out soon enough.

He went aft to look at the painterly vista of sun, clouds, and sea. It was, in the abstract, gorgeous. But coldly, forbiddingly so; it had nothing to do with Pyrrhus. A composition of three of the elements, no earth. Odysseus was right: it was unnatural to be here, Pyrrhus would be happy to step on the ground again. Arisbe or Lemnos, it hardly mattered.

Someone materialized to Pyrrhus's right. He turned, and it was Phoenix, depressingly jaunty in blazer and ascot. "Good afternoon, good afternoon, what a splendid day it has turned out to be! Will you take a turn with me about the deck?"

"I guess." He added, "Actually, I was looking for Admetus." Just to make clear that he wasn't an idle object for Phoenix to attach himself to.

"Ah," Phoenix said. They began walking along the perimeter of the deck, Phoenix to the outside; Pyrrhus was still a little leery of getting too close to the edge. "I trust you have been amusing yourself."

"I guess," Pyrrhus said. Wondering if Phoenix, too, knew about Corythus. "I haven't seen you, at lunch or anything."

"I take my meals in my cabin. To tell you the truth, I feel rather out of place at the officers' mess. The grim, unrelieved maleness of it. It reminds me of your grandfather's table. Except that there I constituted a sort of . . . leavening, if you will, an element that had been missing. I felt welcome and necessary. While here I feel that I am a threat of some sort, as if being a eunuch were contagious." He giggled. "I'm sure you have no idea what I'm talking about."

Pyrrhus shook his head, though of course he knew exactly what Phoenix was talking about. Still, he had the lingering sense that, here on the *Penelope*, you had to pick a team: men or eunuchs.

Phoenix went on: "At any rate, I've been spending my time quite alone. I am grateful for this bit of company. Even if you evidently prefer that of Admetus."

Pyrrhus didn't disagree. "There's something . . . calm about him. He takes everything easy."

"As well he should. Am I walking too fast?"

He was; Pyrrhus hadn't realized just how quickly he was gliding along, as Pyrrhus unconsciously strained to keep up. They slowed down. "Why should he?" Pyrrhus said.

"Why should who do what?"

"Why *should* Admetus take everything easy?"

"Oh. I only mean that I myself would take it easy in his peculiar position."

"Position?"

"Condition, if you'd rather. Although I'm not sure, in the long run, that I should really like to live forever."

"What?"

"Didn't you know? Admetus can't die. I thought everyone knew this story."

"Oh, right, sure, I remember," Pyrrhus said, wanting to fend off some endless narrative. Of course curiosity overcame him. "Well, no. What's the story?"

Phoenix stopped walking and gazed up at the sky for a moment, composing a mental outline of a tale that would probably stretch into the following morning. Then he started walking again, cleared his throat, and said:

"Apollo once owed Admetus a favor. That is, he didn't owe it, the gods owe us nothing, but he felt a certain degree of obligation towards him, because Admetus had . . ." He glanced at Pyrrhus and apparently read his mind. "Well, I shall spare you that; it is sufficient to understand that Apollo felt a miscellaneous benevolence towards him. A sentiment that the gods rarely display towards mortals without some underlying intention of getting them to bed. Which intention was, I believe, entirely absent in this case, as Admetus was little more prepossessing in his youth than he is today at—well, I suppose he's a centenarian."

"He's a hundred?"

"At least. All this happened very long ago, before I was born, if you can imagine that there was a time before I was born. Admetus would have been, say, thirty. Married, with the assistance of Apollo, to a woman named Alcestis."

"That's the name on his chest," Pyrrhus said, feeling foolish right away.

"That is correct. An expression, I suppose, of youthful exuberance at having carried off one of the most sought-after women of her day. I wonder how she must have felt, looking up at him and seeing her own name blazoned across his pectorals in an expression of crude proprietorship. At any rate, he was thirty, rich, well-married, very possibly the happiest soul on earth. Then his number came up. It was time for him to die.

"Apollo intervened again. You understand, I'm not saying that Admetus was in some specific peril and Apollo saved him; that would just have meant it wasn't really his time. But it was his time, he was on Death's week-at-a-glance engagement calendar. Apollo struck a deal. Admetus could live if, on the appointed day, someone took his place. Voluntarily.

"That was the key word—more or less the fine print in the contract. *Voluntarily.* Of course he couldn't kill anybody. Nor could he find someone on life support and ask the family if they'd mind having the plug pulled a few minutes early. Nor someone suicidal, nor someone so poor he'd take the plunge if Admetus would care for his widow and orphans. That is, the very people who might seriously consider Admetus's impossible request were ruled out precisely because of the circumstances that made them plausible candidates. Because those circumstances had themselves been established by the Fates. Do you see?"

"No."

"You must see. This was to be the one time in all history when Destiny was frustrated, and it couldn't be because Destiny had laid herself a booby trap into which she then stepped. It had to be because someone, for once, did something he or she had not been prepared for, not by birth or upbringing or chance. Voluntarily, freely. Someone who had something to lose.

"He asked around. Most of his acquaintances, of course, greeted him with disbelieving laughter. A few got angry. What was he saying—that his life was more important than theirs? Oh, no, no, of course not; just thought it couldn't hurt to ask. After a while, he saw the point: he needed to find someone who valued Admetus's life above his or her own.

"Naturally he went to his mother. She wasn't exactly on her deathbed, but she was obviously on her way there: more bad days than good, and the good shadowed with anticipation of the next thing going wrong. It didn't seem wholly impossible that she would accept the bargain—she had so little to lose, and a chance to make her child immortal. Look how your own grandmother worked so hard to do that for your father, and couldn't. While Admetus's mother could do it just by departing a little early.

"She wouldn't. Grim as her life was, she wouldn't give up a minute of it. Perhaps there comes a day for everyone when his mother looks straight at him and says, or doesn't have to say beyond the look: You have got all you're going to get. Even mother love is finite. Somewhere inside there is still room for a kernel of the self-love that keeps us breathing. You may have taken up, love for you may have taken up, all the other space inside her. Still, there is that kernel. You look her in the eye and see that she, too, is a being, that you exist because she did first, not the other way round. She is not merely an inexhaustible breast.

"Admetus's mother pointed out—gently, she was of course still fond of him—that everyone has his time and it wasn't hers. He probably wanted to smother her. I often wished to smother my mother for much less, haven't you? But it wouldn't have counted, as she hadn't volunteered.

"He had found no one, and the last day dawned. He was blind with frustration and terror. I have seen it, once or twice, once was too often: the face of a man kneeling before your father, already mortally wounded, your father getting ready, calm as a surgeon, to administer the merciful final incision, the shriek of victory already gathering in his gut. I have seen the faces of men in that instant. While this: this was no instant, it was a whole day, his every motion and utterance the equivalent of one protracted scream. It was nearly time; he had found no one; he screamed.

"Do you know how, in the night, someone's car alarm goes off—not one of those new ones, that at least shuts itself off after a minute or two, but the kind that just shrieks on endlessly? You know the miscreant owner is sound asleep a block away, he'll never come turn it off, you lie there counting all the tortures you would inflict on him. Or at least on his vehicle: you ought to get up right now and smash his windows or slash his tires, so the alarm won't have been for naught. Yes, you sit up, you're going to get dressed and you're going to, yes, this time you're going to— Then of course it stops. But you still can't sleep: you know it will come again, a pigeon will light on the car and set it off, or a breeze, a tiny zephyr sent by some malevolent minor god.

"Just so, that day when Admetus lived a scream. The sun was setting, it would be any time now, the oarsman would appear at the threshold any time. Suddenly he was calm. Alcestis watched him in the same relieved but untrusting way you wait for the alarm to sound again. Better the oarsman should come right now and take him, better now than that she should have to endure the scream another minute. Or if he would not come, better that she —

"Do you know, he's told me about it a dozen times. If there's anything worse than an old bore like me, it's an old man with only *one* story. And as many times as he repeats it I still cannot picture that moment when she offered herself and he accepted. I can picture her offering, out of great love, as he always tells it, or out of tedium. But his agreeing to it, imagine: loving life so much that he would want to live it endlessly even at the price of remembering endlessly, every morning and night, what had bought it for him.

"I cannot imagine myself in his place. Or I won't. I should prefer to think that I would, in those impossible circumstances, have refused. That I would have had — not the decency to act rightly, but the foresight to know how guilt would poison the endless life she bought for me. I can't think myself into extremity; I don't want to know about the part of me that would — stopped dead in the middle of my scream by her sudden astonishing offer — have said, Yes, let it be you. And then would have sat on the sofa, looking on, as the oarsman came to collect her. Not getting up, surely not going to kiss her goodbye, having at least enough foresight to know that the taste of that kiss would never go away. I don't want to know about that part of me, the deepest animal part, that knows only one imperative: save yourself. The part that would kick away a drowning man, your own son or brother, lest he take you down with him.

"As for Alcestis, though: I can think myself into her. Her thoughtless offer, the words out of her lips before she fully understands them, and his near-instantaneous assent. Their interchange briefer than their marriage vows. Just as at a wedding the couple must, however happy they are, be struck for a second by the awful eternity of the words they've just uttered, must think, What have I done, how can I have promised to do this forever?, before their lips part for the obligatory kiss — so she must have thought a near-comical *what have I done*. And: as the newlyweds sink awkwardly into their too-public kiss and are restored, I have done the right thing, so she recovered and almost at once felt the rightness of it. Having uttered the vows that would dissolve their marriage, she wondered chiefly how she would get through the remaining seconds or minutes of it. Seeing, now, that she had been married all along to death. The knock could not come too quickly now; she was breathless to leave the earth and not have to look at her bridegroom for one more instant.

"She went, more than voluntarily, the impossible clause of Apollo's contract with the Fates amply fulfilled. She practically rushed into the arms of the oarsman, as if he had come to take her dancing.

"It was some days before she returned. During her sojourn in Hell Admetus was busy, the way we keep survivors busy: getting the notice in the papers, reserving the temple, haggling with the caterers and the florists. All these activities that don't just distract you from grief but positively affirm the central fact of your situation: you're not the one who died, you're still here doing all these things. I've seen mourners who were practically giddy, watching themselves with wonder and near-glee as they went through their humdrum duties. The way some potions, they say, can make you stare, astonished as a baby, at the way your own fingers wiggle.

"Admetus went through the funeral that was not his own—perhaps not even noticing the looks he got from his mother and his friends, who were trying not to believe that Alcestis's sudden departure could have anything to do with the preposterous proposition he had put to them just a few days before.

"The funeral guests departed; he was alone in his house with the dirty dishes and the leftover food, the caterer's platters that looked as though a tornado had hit them. He started to put the stuff away before it spoiled: the smoked salmon into this plastic bag, the ham and roast beef into that, hadn't there been a lid for the potato salad? Busy, busy, as he stood in the kitchen he heard the front door open. He didn't have to go out into the hall, he recognized the footsteps at once. And must have thought that he had indeed gone to Hell on the appointed day.

"As with everything else, there are differing accounts of how Alcestis was restored to him. That Persephone spontaneously returned her, or that Heracles went into Hell to fetch her—some people want to thrust Heracles into every story; he would have had to be a million places at once. At any rate, she came back. Came straight from Hell to the house. Not to taunt or reproach him, probably, but just because she couldn't think of any place else to go. She was as if jet-lagged, perhaps, able to look only straight ahead, to perform only the most automatic moves; else she might have gone to her parents', or anywhere. Instead she came straight home.

"What could he say? 'Thanks, hon,' or 'Glad to have you back'? He just looked at her, stood there with a ravaged platter of cold cuts in his hands. There she stood before him—her clothes in tatters, her face be-

186

wildered—born again, scarcely more able to focus than at her first birth. This woman who had been such a desirable commodity, a hundred more prepossessing men than Admetus had sought her, and she had spent herself on him, entirely, like some creature we burn on an altar. She stood before him the embodiment of all we have to push aside to make room for ourselves to breathe, everything that must perish so that we can stumble forward. He saw what a futile and vacuous thing it was he had asked for, life.

"Nothing but a platter of cold cuts, ourselves nothing but organisms that swim about, swallowing up other organisms to get some essential nutrient or other, everything reduced to that. She had turned herself into a platter of meat, like the charred tidbits we offer to the gods, and he had eaten. Have you ever been to a banquet where they tastelessly bring out the pièce de résistance with its head still on? Looking up at you with an expression of dazed reproach? Of course he wished her back in Hell.

"She had left the front door open. He stepped past her—still carrying his platter—and went out."

"He just left her," Pyrrhus said.

"Left her and ran off to sea. There was some sort of settlement. She got the house, and so on. Rather a messy proceeding, as I understand it; her temporary death had triggered conditional clauses in a number of other estates, a trust terminating here, an entailment kicking in over there. The litigation was still going on when . . . oh, two or three years later, she died for real."

"She died?"

"Oh, yes. When *her* day came, it came. None too soon for her, I suppose. He's the only poor chap who has to live forever."

"What's it like, I wonder."

"I think it is . . . as if all the iron has gone out of him. He never needs to hurry, because time is his; he doesn't look both ways when crossing the street, because it is never his day to be run over; he makes no plans, because everything will sooner or later happen to him. All the tension of living has been drained from him. He might as well have died when he was supposed to.

"You know, the gods never give anything away. Every promise they make, every oracle they let you hear, is the setup for one of their grisly practical jokes. There is always a catch, some little payoff, like your father's heel. They share it, the gods—'Oh, look over here at what Hermes got this fellow to do'—and everyone on Olympus chuckles for a moment before returning to their eternal divine tedium. The butt of the joke is forgotten at once; they are soon busy hatching some new one. But he goes on among us, living out forever the consequences of their little prank. The older I get, the more I see around me nothing but walking punch lines, the battered veterans of a vaudeville routine."

Pyrrhus wasn't sure he believed this story. That is to say, he did not entirely disbelieve it; just by stepping aboard this ship he seemed to have crossed over into a world where such a story was merely unlikely and not absurd. If he was not persuaded, he was far enough along to bracket his disbelief. To ask, just for the sake of argument: "What joke is being played on me?"

"Whatever can you mean?"

"The gods have all these plans for me, what happens when they're through with me?"

"How should I know?" Phoenix said. He chuckled. "Perhaps when it's all over, you could simply return to your former employment. Indeed, I am sure your value as a spectacle could only be enhanced. 'Live, tonight, the conqueror of Troy. Every inch of him.' "

Of course he was joking, but he didn't know how big a joke it was. How impossible that the patrons of the Escapade should wish to see someone with so implastic an identity, someone who had a history instead of being a vessel into which they could pour their dreams.

"Will I be somebody else then?" Pyrrhus said.

"Somebody else?"

"I mean, I'd have to be, wouldn't I? I'll have to change somehow."

"I suppose. Perhaps you might begin by displaying a touch more self-restraint."

"Oh. You heard, too."

"It doesn't matter a great deal. Generals are permitted their idiosyncrasies."

"That's what Admetus said. But I—I'm going to have to change more than that. Turn into this . . . Neoptolemus everybody's waiting for. I don't even see how I get there from here."

Phoenix shrugged. "I don't, either, to tell the truth."

"Maybe there's some kind of misunderstanding."

"Possibly. We'll find out soon enough."

"I need to know." Pyrrhus stepped away from Phoenix and leaned for a moment on the railing. Fearlessly; he was for some reason no longer especially worried about falling in. Maybe because he had started to believe, just a little, in his destiny. If he was going to take Troy next week, he couldn't drown today, could he? Any more than the big star gets killed off in the first reel of the movie. "I'm ready to be somebody else, whoever I'm going to be."

"Are you? Then I think you are already the most daring man who ever lived." Seven bells sounded. "Three-thirty," Phoenix said. "Aren't I becoming the old salt? I'm going to take a nap. If my new roommate is absent."

"I guess I'm going to bed, too."

"Yes, I had heard you had an assignation."

Pyrrhus shook his head. "This ship gets smaller every minute. I don't think the old ladies on Scyros gossiped this much."

"The sailors must tire of discussing the lovely seascape. In any event, I suppose you shall be postponing your transformation."

"I've got a while. We're taking a detour."

"Yes."

"You know why?"

"Who knows?" Phoenix smiled. "Perhaps we're not meant to get to Troy until we have Neoptolemus on board."

Eight bells. Pyrrhus hurried back to his cabin, half-expecting to find Cory-thus waiting in the passageway, tapping his foot, like any date you're late meeting. But of course he couldn't just loiter outside Pyrrhus's door. Maybe he hadn't come yet. Or maybe he'd found Pyrrhus not at home and given up. Pyrrhus went inside and waited, just sat facing the door for a few minutes. If he came, Pyrrhus was going to tell him that they had to knock it off; he was nice, but Pyrrhus wasn't going to play any more this trip. Why? Corythus would say. And how would Pyrrhus answer? Mutter something incoherent about transforming himself? He wasn't even sure exactly what that meant. Maybe he would just point out the risks, how everyone had already noticed.

Pyrrhus didn't want to have this conversation; he should have been pleased when the minutes passed and Corythus didn't appear. Still, no one likes to be stood up. All of us have, one time or another, made a date with some flighty little creature who didn't show. There's no reason to take it personally. But of course you do. You can't help thinking that, no matter how scatterbrained the guy is, if you'd really been special he would have shown up. It was especially insulting, given the paucity of competition, that Corythus could have forgotten this engagement, or decided against it, in the space of a few hours.

Pretty soon Pyrrhus was positively fuming, and it was only when he had entirely given up on Corythus that he realized how much he had wanted Corythus to come, that if Corythus had shown up he would have postponed his metamorphosis for another hour or two.

A bell rang, once. Four-thirty, that must have meant. Pyrrhus had been sitting there a long time, but there was a longer time yet to dinner, and nothing to do. He wished he had taken the armor. He felt like trying it on again, trying on the new self that could do without Corythus.

There was a knock at the door—a loud one; Corythus could have been a little more discreet. Pyrrhus stood behind the door as he opened it and whispered, "Get in, quick."

But it was Admetus who stepped in, grinning. "Sorry to let you down, mate."

"Oh, I was expecting—"

"I know what you were expecting. Not much of a substitute, am I? The kid pulled galley duty. Said to tell you he'll try to get here after dinner."

"Okay. Did you want to come in?"

"I am in. And I've found out why we're stopping on Lemnos."

"Oh yeah?"

"You'd better close the door."

Pyrrhus did, and gestured for Admetus to sit on his bed. But Admetus wouldn't sit on an officer's bed, and Pyrrhus couldn't sit down while a centenarian stood.

"Did you ever hear of Philoctetes?" Admetus said.

"No."

"Well, you wouldn't; they hushed it up. The press never caught wind of it. He was a guy who sailed with us to Troy. I mean he started out with us, he never got there. He wasn't a famous hero or anything, just a reserve officer, I think, who got called up. Anyway, him and me were both on the *Penelope* here."

"You know, I've been wondering," Pyrrhus said. "Why did you join up, at . . ."

"At my age? Just a notion. I had time on my hands." He grinned mournfully. "Anyway, we set off for Troy. On the way we stopped at this little island called Chryse. I don't know why; it seemed we were always stopping for some reason or other. Pick up your father, refuel, sacrifice to some local god. I swear, we never got far enough to lose sight of Greece for the first six months. We got pretty impatient, even me a little, and I'm never in a hurry. But everybody else was, wanted to get to Troy, get it done with. We all thought it would be done with so quick. I guess if we'd known, how long it would last, we wouldn't have minded so much stopping off and looking at the scenery.

"So we were all on this godforsaken island, Chryse, and Philoctetes got bit by a snake. That's all—he just stumbled on it or something, but he got bit. And it wouldn't get any better. We picked him up and we took him along to the next place, and the next one, but he wasn't getting any better, it wouldn't heal. People started to get scared. Like maybe it was a curse or something, Philoctetes had offended the gods somehow and was being punished. And if we didn't get rid of him something terrible would happen to all of us."

"Wow, that's so stupid," Pyrrhus said.

"I don't know. He was—well, he was . . . like you, you understand?"

"Like me? Oh, you mean . . ."

"Some people thought that was it, that he was being punished for that. Anyhow, the morale got pretty lousy. I mean, it's lousy now, but that's 'cause we been at it for ten years. The officers got kind of worried that everybody was in such a bad mood just starting out. They got rid of him."

"They killed him?"

"No. People talked about it, just chucking him overboard. Except, you know, they couldn't have covered that up, somebody might have blew the whistle. Instead they dropped him off at Lemnos."

"That's why we're going?"

"I think so. I mean, it's the only reason I can think of—to bring him back. But it's hard to see why. I mean, I can't picture Odysseus feeling guilty all of a sudden."

Pyrrhus said, "Why is it all such a big secret?"

"Search me. Unless—I don't know, maybe they're afraid folks'll get scared again. Most of the guys on this ship weren't even around when it happened. Just me, Odysseus, a few others. The surgeon, I guess, he was here. Maybe they're afraid word will get around, if they bring him back on board it will all start again."

Pyrrhus yawned. He couldn't see what all of this had to do with him. "This was ten years ago?" he said.

191

"More than that."

"How do they even know he's still there?"

"You're right. He was pretty sick, chances are he's dead by now. I don't know, maybe Odysseus really did start feeling guilty. Or maybe he just has to know for sure."

5

Pyrrhus went to dinner. It was crowded, with much the same cast as at lunch: surgeon, Nereus, a scattering of junior officers.

They were served chicken. Underdone, about the color of Corythus's pale chest. Still, Pyrrhus hadn't really eaten since the day before, back in the capital. He had seconds.

He was, for some reason, a little less uncomfortable than before. Not that he didn't think everybody despised him. But they despised him casually: he wasn't a big deal to them. They might even be getting used to him. He began to feel again, however tentatively, that he could somehow fit in. Have a place at this table. It was funny how strong that desire could be, so that you didn't even think about whether you'd *want* to fit in with these starched nonentities. It must take a finely developed sense of yourself not to wish, every time you encounter a closed circle, that it would open for you.

The surgeon actually greeted Pyrrhus with some show of pleasure. Just because Pyrrhus was someone who hadn't heard all his stories. It occurred to Pyrrhus that the surgeon might have one story that was actually worth hearing. He waited politely while the surgeon concluded a thoracic anecdote that had been suggested by the chicken carcass on his plate. Then Pyrrhus asked innocently, "Did you ever hear of somebody named Philoctetes?"

The surgeon looked at Pyrrhus the way you might look at a process server who has just handed you a subpoena. As if Pyrrhus had boarded the *Penelope* just to track him down and ask that question. No one else paid any attention; as Admetus had guessed, they were all too young to have heard of him. Except maybe Nereus was a little too ostentatiously occupied with his chicken, fastidiously separating iotas of meat from bone.

"Where did you hear that name?" the surgeon said.

"Just a story someone was telling."

"And he mentioned me."

Pyrrhus might have said, He just thought you'd been around long enough to remember him. The surgeon's excessive reaction made Pyrrhus shut up. He was rewarded.

"If Asclepius had been on board, or Chiron, I don't believe there's a damn thing they could have done for him. I ran every goddamn test I knew how, I read all the books—I happen to have an excellent medical library on board, all the classics in the field—and I happen to be well up on toxicology anyway, almost thought of going into that line before I took up surgery. I can tell you this: no practitioner ever encountered what he had. It was entirely unprecedented, and any suggestion that there was some further measure I might have taken is simply frivolous."

"Oh."

"Odysseus wondered why I didn't just amputate. I could have, there was no reason to suppose it had spread, we could have saved most of the leg—hell, there are people dancing jigs with less than he would have had. But I just couldn't recommend it. Anyone who tells you I'm not a conscientious physician ought to know this. It wasn't getting any better, but it wasn't getting any worse. You know the old joke about dermatologists— never kill 'em, never cure 'em—it looked to be that kind of problem. I just couldn't justify a radical procedure, even to please Odysseus. So he . . . I suppose you could say he did his own surgery, amputated the patient from the ship.

"I couldn't blame him. I mean, it looked like some kind of snakebite, but it behaved so oddly, I couldn't swear there wasn't any danger to anyone else. It seemed like a reasonable prophylactic measure to—"

"Leave him to die," Pyrrhus put in.

"Oh, we did nothing of the kind. Everyone talks as though Lemnos were some sort of desert island. There was no reason to suppose he'd fare any worse there than on board this ship."

Pyrrhus persisted. "You abandoned a patient."

"Sometimes a physician is obliged to consider the general welfare. The health of the ship outweighed my obligation to a specific patient."

"Because Odysseus said so."

The surgeon looked around the table. "Has anyone ever refused an order from Odysseus?"

No one answered. Until Nereus put down his knife and fork and said, hesitantly, "I . . . Maybe I would if it were wrong."

"Who's even to say it was wrong? They . . . you understand, some people said he was being punished. By the goddess who ruled Chryse, or whoever."

"Uh-huh," Pyrrhus said. "Is there a chapter on that in your classic medical texts?"

"It's common enough for young men to be skeptical. You and the lieutenant here." (Though Nereus was staring at his plate.) "Any experienced practitioner will tell you that there are manifestations, things that can't be explained any other way. It's so easy to offend the gods. The whole world is booby-trapped, trellised with invisible lines you mustn't cross. You step off the sidewalk to avoid some dog shit and you've wandered into some consecrated vacant lot. Next thing you know somebody's threatening to turn you into some unknown species of wildflower if you don't say you're sorry and by the way roast a couple of sheep in expiation.

"You can try to avoid it maybe, go through life assuming that anything unexpected is a snare and try to sidestep it, but they'll get you when they're ready."

"You mean he brought it on himself?" Pyrrhus said. "That's why you couldn't do anything about it?"

"I'm saying it wasn't any ordinary snakebite. He broke some kind of rule."

"Uh-huh."

"And we all know what it was," the surgeon said, darkly.

Pyrrhus thought he had better drop the subject. Even if by now 100 percent of the crew knew about him, he shouldn't have gone any further. But he had to. "Doc, if everybody who broke that rule got the same punishment, you sure would have seen a lot of snakebites."

"I don't mean just that he was a fairy." Yes, everyone looked straight at Pyrrhus when the surgeon said this. Everyone but Nereus: was it possible he was the only guy on board who didn't know? Isolated on the bridge, cut off from the gossip? The surgeon went on: "The gods themselves occasionally diddle a boy. Nonetheless . . . I heard about his life, in the city, before he was called up. You can't imagine the way he lived, the things these guys did with one another. I know my anatomy, and let me tell you, the things I heard about: they just weren't meant to be."

"You're saying they crossed some boundary," Pyrrhus said. "Broke some natural law."

"That's just what I'm saying. And I'll tell you this: whoever he offended, whoever afflicted him, was a lot more powerful than Chryse."

The younger officers did not take their eyes off Pyrrhus. As if wondering what sort of snakebite he had brought on board with him. He felt an odd solidarity with this man he'd never seen, who had done unimaginable things with his anatomy. Pyrrhus wanted to jar them, break their easy assurance that the way they lived did not offend the gods. It just popped out: "Well, I guess if he were so dangerous we wouldn't be stopping to pick him up, would we?"

Everybody was gratifyingly alarmed. Even Nereus, though of course he had known where they were going. He pushed away from the table, visibly upset, and left the room. What was his problem? That Pyrrhus had spilled a military secret?

Pyrrhus got up, too, wanting to go after him and try to explain. But explain what? It wasn't Pyrrhus's secret, he had no obligation to Nereus or to Nereus's master. And he rather liked the idea of all these breeders terrified of the dangerous queer guy, like elephants scared of a mouse.

Everyone looked up at Pyrrhus, as if he had some further intelligence to offer. He felt for the first time—having had this tidbit that was news to them—that he was something other than a passenger. He was, sort of, part of the inner circle. Distanced from the lesser officers, as Neoptolemus would have to be. Except of course he didn't have the slightest idea why they were going after this Philoctetes guy.

Any second and somebody would ask, exposing just how little Pyrrhus knew, how peripheral he was. He left and headed back to his cabin. When he got there he found Nereus at the door. Nereus hustled him inside.

"What the fuck is the matter with you?" Nereus hissed. "First screwing around with that kid, and now—"

"Look, everybody on this boat knew I was queer the minute I stepped on it."

"Yeah, but you don't rub it in people's faces. It just makes it harder for the rest of us."

"Us?"

"What did you think, three hundred hands on this vessel and you and Corythus were the homosexual contingent?"

Out of uniform Pyrrhus would have known him right away. In uniform he blended right in; everybody in uniform looks gay. Maybe because only the military groom themselves as carefully as gay men do, their whole vocation to be a body.

"Well, you may have to explain to me how what I do or don't do affects you."

"Because it raises everybody's radar. You, like, brought everything to the surface. Everybody's on full alert."

"So."

"So you get to have fun and the rest of us are pushed further in the closet than we ever were."

Hm. Pyrrhus understood that he was supposed to feel bad, but he said, "Hey, I didn't stuff you in that closet."

196

"Huh?"

"Like I asked you this afternoon. What are you doing in the military anyway?"

"I don't—Oh. You mean why didn't I go to beauty school?"

"Realistically, yeah."

"I was eighteen, I didn't know what the fuck I was. Just a kid. Like Corythus probably, but not even that far out. I'd never even touched anybody. Later—I mean, when I'd touched enough people and looked in the mirror enough that I was ready to say the words for what I was—by then I was twenty-three, just getting my first commission. What was I supposed to do?"

Quit anyway, Pyrrhus thought, cut your losses, start your life. As if he had some idea how you did that. What could Pyrrhus tell anybody about starting a life? You go to the big city, some pathetic drunk pays you for a blow job, and that's a career track? Or a eunuch comes along and says you have a destiny, follow me. Really the same event, in each case, like sitting having a malted at the drugstore counter, until the film mogul happens by and says he'll make you a star. How did people without a destiny live?

Nereus said, "Not everybody gets to just walk in and be a general. The rest of us have to make some choices."

"I don't?"

"Well, maybe you do. And maybe if I were you I . . . I mean, if I were outside the recruiting station right now and I knew all about myself, maybe I'd take a hike. But I don't have that option, not any more."

Pyrrhus looked at him. Two years older than Pyrrhus and speaking as if he had a whole life behind him, instead of ahead. Because what was ahead? More striving, more concealment. That's how people without a destiny lived. If he did well enough he would be promoted one tiny step at a time; if he stumbled he would be hurled out into a civilian world that was scary, not least because there would no longer be any excuse for the refusal to be himself.

Pyrrhus had an inspiration. "You know, when I get to Troy I might need some help. I don't know what you'd call it, an adjutant or something."

"What?"

"I mean, you could come with me."

"I'm not a soldier, I'm a sailor."

"Well, I'm none of the above. But I'm going to need help. I mean,

I guess I can pick anybody I want. You could be a colonel, or what-ever."

"No, thanks." Nereus said this so sharply that Pyrrhus understood he must have thought Pyrrhus was propositioning him.

"I wasn't talking about anything funny," Pyrrhus said. "I just might need somebody who understands how the military works. It could be a big opportunity for you."

Nereus was quiet, didn't look at him. He realized how patronizing he must have sounded: Look, I can raise you up. But he could; he just hap-pened to be in this position, it wasn't his fault. And it was a big chance for Nereus. Pyrrhus could see him thinking that: he could jump about ten promotions.

"I'm sorry," Nereus said. "I've got a career here."

Pyrrhus was as annoyed as if he had been propositioning Nereus after all, and had been turned down because he wasn't pretty enough. "What kind of career? Sweating your way up rung by rung and waiting to be found out?"

"Better than spending the rest of my life known as Pyrrhus's little hand-picked assistant."

Which he would, of course. Still: how could that be worse than the life ahead of him? What pointless pride kept him from accepting Pyrrhus's intervention, just as Pyrrhus was on the verge of accepting the divine intervention that put him in the position of making the offer? Why shouldn't the guy ride with him to the top, as the Fates and not Pyrrhus were paying the fare?

Because he had a self. Real people weren't waiting for—weren't even gratified by—divine intervention. They knew who they were, and didn't expect to be anybody else next week.

"Don't you see?" Nereus said. "It'd be like . . . like being gay was the most important thing about me. But I—just being here, I decided it wasn't the most important thing about me." As he headed for the door he added, "Why don't you make Corythus your assistant?" He smiled. "Your aide-de-camp." The joke suggesting that he had been around a bit more than he had let on.

When Nereus had gone, Pyrrhus lay on the bed. Intending, once again, to think about who he was supposed to be next week, and how he would possibly get there from here. Instead he found himself wondering about Philoctetes. He who had offended the gods, or at least Odysseus, and who hadn't had the protection of oracles proclaiming his indispensability. From what the surgeon said, he must have had a life like Pyrrhus's, or close enough, and had then inexplicably joined the service. Not like Corythus or Nereus, just falling into it and one day discovering his . . . unfitness, incompatibility. But joining up in full awareness, he must have been crazy. Or as crazy as Pyrrhus was, imagining that he could just become someone else. It wasn't going to happen.

He sat up. None of it was going to happen, they had misheard the oracle or something, it was all a mistake. He wasn't going to change into anything; he was a fairy, it was the most important thing about him. Sooner or later they would have to dump him on some island.

The rap at his door was so faint he ignored it at first; only after a minute did he realize it was Corythus. He had a strange, heavy feeling as he got up. He was eager enough: he was already half-hard as he opened the door. Yet also bitter, as if Corythus were a habit he couldn't give up. Or a sphinx he couldn't get past, preventing him from his adventure, foreclosing the possibility of any other life.

Almost sunset. Odysseus returned to the bridge for the first time since the storm: captain only during calm seas. He didn't know but what the view this evening was worse than a storm. There was nothing at all, in any direction, as far as the eye could see. Or as far as Odysseus could see, at any rate. He knew intellectually that they could not be very far from land, would reach Lemnos before morning. But the existence of Lemnos, straight ahead, was something in which one could only have faith, as in the gods' existence, and in the face of persuasive evidence of their absence. He looked over at the pilot. Not what's-his-name, Nereus, but some nearly interchangeable young officer whose name Odysseus also had difficulty recalling.

The pilot was looking directly ahead, into the vacancy, with a sort of bland confidence, the same Odysseus's mother used to display in what was, to Odysseus, an empty temple. What was this guy's name? Odysseus's memory was going so quickly. Or atrophying, nothing to remember all these years but the equally interchangeable names of the dead.

Phoenix appeared, as if he had been summoned so that Odysseus could talk to someone. Uncanny. Odysseus was beginning to see why the

Peleids kept Phoenix around all those years. They went down to the map room, just below the bridge.

Phoenix stared out at the the sea as vacantly as Odysseus had. He couldn't see anything ahead, either. What use was he, after all?

Odysseus said, "It looks like we'll be at Lemnos by sunrise."

"Then what? Are we looking for Philoctetes?"

"I knew you'd figure it out."

Phoenix didn't say he had required assistance. "Why ever are you going back for him?"

"The same reason we went for Pyrrhus."

"Ah, another prophecy?"

"The same one, actually." He recited: " 'When Philoctetes' bow is brought to Troy, then shall the hero son of Achilles take up the sword of his father, and Priam's children raise loud their lamentations.' "

"Oh. I never heard that first part."

"It was classified," Odysseus said. "You didn't have what they call a need to know. Unless you can talk Philoctetes onto the ship as easily as you did the boy."

"I?"

"It would be a considerable service."

Phoenix had a fleeting vision of an annuity before he sighed, "I am afraid you overestimate my persuasive powers. I suppose he must harbor no inconsiderable resentment."

"I suppose."

"Perhaps your own unmatched eloquence is required," Phoenix said. Fawning, but also just repeating what every Greek acknowledged.

"As I am the principal object of his resentment, I don't expect he'd sit still for much of my unmatched eloquence."

"Perhaps not. But what else? Just send out a shore patrol and shanghai the poor chap?"

"Damned if I know. I really didn't plan past getting the boy. If we've even got the boy. I'm a little bit concerned about creating an incident."

"You'll do that the instant you pull into the harbor."

"Yes, we can't do that. I thought we might anchor on the other side of the island. And then you and, say, Admetus could go ashore and—I don't know, get into town somehow. Rent bicycles."

"Oh, dear," Phoenix said. "I . . . an ancient injury prevents me from riding a bicycle. Not to mention that Admetus and I are scarcely equipped to overpower the fellow."

"He was pretty sick, the last we saw him—he shouldn't take much over-powering. Maybe Admetus and some young officer. That Nereus guy."

"Perhaps. Anyway, the two of them are supposed to bundle Philoctetes into a sack and bring him back hanging from the handlebars?"

"Well, that's where I'm rather stymied. He has to want to come, don't you think? I mean, it wouldn't do to just drag him kicking and screaming."

"I don't see why," Phoenix said. "If all your precious prophecy says is that he has to be there."

"It doesn't even say that exactly. Just that the bow has to come to Troy. So is the requisite item the bow or Philoctetes-wielding-the-bow? How would you read that?"

"I'm sure it will sustain any reading so skilled an interpreter of oracles chooses to put on it."

Odysseus shrugged. "Oh, it will—they all do. I just can't settle on a reading. I suppose it's easier to spirit away the bow than the man."

"There you have it. Except—wasn't there a story that no one but Philoctetes can use the thing?"

"Now who's the superstitious one? Philoctetes and his magic bow. The bow's not actually going to do anything. It's a symbol or something. Maybe Philoctetes is superfluous. I don't know why we should bother with him."

After a moment, Phoenix said, "Maybe you need to right a wrong."

Odysseus was involuntarily impressed that Phoenix should have come so close to guessing his thoughts. This was probably a necessary skill for a career lackey, but not one Phoenix would have had much opportunity to practice, working for Achilles. Achilles didn't have very many thoughts to guess: I want to eat, I want to sleep, I want to kill somebody.

"I didn't commit a wrong. I did what any practical captain would have done. He was destroying morale, I would practically have had a mutiny on my hands if I'd left him on board."

"You don't have to persuade me."

"No," Odysseus said. "Do you know, I had forgotten him? In the heat of everything else, those first years, before we settled down into this eternal stalemate. Since then I've had altogether too much time to think."

"And you think about Philoctetes."

"Understand: it's not that I think some god or other is literally pun-ishing us, keeping us from victory until we bring him back. It's that I can't go on. It—I don't know—it breaks my concentration." He had begun pacing. "Do you know, I've never won a case without believing that my side was right?"

"You've never defended a guilty client?"

"Oh, of course I have. Innocent people don't need to pay my rates. Anyone who hires me is guilty almost by definition. But they are *procedurally* innocent. I don't get nearly so outraged by someone embezzling or taking a bribe or even killing somebody as I do by the state proceeding improperly."

"So now that you're the state, you think you've proceeded improperly and that's why we can't win?"

"Something like that."

Phoenix smiled. "I hate it when people say 'something like that,' as if I were a bit dense and we'd all better settle for a near miss."

"I've never thought you were dense," Odysseus said. Though he had, really, until lately. "Why not just say it's about symmetry, closing circles, something like that? Achilles started, his boy finishes. Philoctetes was gone, now he's back."

"Except he isn't."

"No. He must be . . . seduced, I think. Maybe a woman."

"But—"

"Damn, we should have brought a woman. I hear Lemnos is filled with nothing but lesbians. I bet Philoctetes would—"

Phoenix disguised his enjoyment at springing the news. "Philoctetes is gay."

"What are you talking about?"

"Admetus told me."

"He's gay," Odysseus repeated tonelessly.

"I had no idea. Admetus said practically everybody knew."

Odysseus closed his eyes. "Lord, is that how we're supposed to win this war? Round up every goddamn faggot between here and . . ."

His voice trailed off, and he turned to look out over the water. Phoenix peered with him—having, for once, the sense not to speak. There was still nothing to see: water, clouds. Except that the line between them, straight ahead, seemed to thicken almost imperceptibly. As if Eurynome, she who drew the horizon, had borne down just a little on her pencil. Could that be Lemnos?

"Well, then," Odysseus said briskly. "A woman won't exactly fit the bill, will she?"

Phoenix wondered why he sounded so cheerful. "Evidently not."

202

"Luckily, we have a more suitable candidate on board."

"Do you mean Neoptolemus?"

"I believe he's eminently qualified."

"You would send him to see Philoctetes."

"Exactly."

"You think Philoctetes will—what? Fall in love with Neoptolemus and follow him swooning back to the ship?"

"I take it from your tone that I'm missing something. That didn't seem to me entirely implausible."

Phoenix said, patiently, "Neoptolemus may not be his type."

"Type?"

"Even homosexuals do have their preferences."

"Neoptolemus is young and good-looking."

"I mean more specific preferences than that. Do you fall in love with every woman you see?"

"That's a different matter. Obviously feelings between men and women are rather more complex."

"How is this obvious?"

"Well, all right, maybe it isn't. I haven't spent much time studying the mating habits of faggots."

"Evidently."

"Anyway," Odysseus said. "He's been stuck on an island with nothing but women. I can't imagine he's going to be very picky."

"Lemnos isn't just for women any more. Mostly lesbians, still, but gay men come there too."

"Really?"

"Really. Accordingly, I'm not certain that Philoctetes has been living a life of uninterrupted celibacy."

"It doesn't matter. The boy is remarkable looking."

"You've noticed?"

"Yes, even I couldn't help but notice. And if I think so, then a fairy must—" He added, pounding the map table for emphasis, "It will work." His sudden certainty was not feigned; Odysseus knew when he had had a positively Odyssean idea. "What's he doing now?"

"Neoptolemus? I believe he's with a friend."

"Friend?"

"A young sailor he . . . encountered this morning. I had rather the impression he intended to be more discreet, now that he was joining us," Phoenix said. "But—"

"But he couldn't keep it in his pants for a single day? I don't believe I was ever that young. Who's the sailor?"

"His name is Corythus. Just a child."

"We'll need to see that he's discharged when we land at Arisbe. Pay him off and send him home."

"To what purpose? I doubt that it would take Neoptolemus very long to replace him."

"I guess not. Still, we can't just leave the kid on board when we disembark; the men will eat him alive." Or, more probably, do whatever Neoptolemus was doing, but more rudely. "I suppose it would be impolite to interrupt them."

"Rather."

"Well, I've done without for ten years," Odysseus said. This was hyperbole; he had had his share of the spoils of the Trojan suburbs, if not as big a share as he deserved. Hapless women who lay in his tent and who watched him, as he undressed and approached them, with a prescient mixture of apprehension and ennui. "I don't guess it will kill him if he can't get it twice in one day. Why don't you go talk to him?"

"About your stratagem? I think perhaps you are better equipped to explicate it than—"

"You're the one he trusts, you told me so yourself. You have the boy's confidence, you said."

Phoenix was quiet a minute. At last he said, wearily, as if it were too obvious to waste his breath on: "What if Neoptolemus doesn't want to play?"

Guessing Odysseus's thoughts again. Odysseus didn't have an answer, but said with feigned certainty, "He has played for pocket change. He'll do it to realize his destiny."

"He came because I persuaded him that his destiny might be something other than being a whore."

Odysseus smiled. "Then you have badly misled him. We all have." He looked out at the sea, the waves tipped with red by the setting sun, red-iron like the tip of Achilles' divinely forged sword. He smiled again, at the thought that Achilles' son was destined to prevail with a rather more prosaic weapon. Perhaps he had found the way to shame the boy before his victory.

6

There is—somebody has to say this, and the muse has apparently elected
me—such a thing as lousy sex. I read book after book in which there are
no middle grades between celibacy and shooting stars. When all over the
world at this very moment people are thinking (cannot say aloud): not so
fast, not quite there, harder, over an inch, please don't use your teeth.
Other people are closing their eyes or keeping their hands away from the
flabby parts or avoiding kissing that fetid mouth. Others are doing things
they didn't want to do, they are rolling over, they are opening their
mouths, they are trying to get hard enough, they are—with infinite weariness and resentment—relenting, doing another's will. Because it is better
than nothing.

Surely Corythus must have felt this, after months of nothing at all
(life on the *Penelope*, at least, was not a pornographic paperback).
Maybe Pyrrhus was a little rough, maybe he didn't—once again—worry
very much that Corythus hadn't, well, finished. Corythus could finish
himself at leisure, thinking back on this; it was enough just now to be
lying there with Pyrrhus in Pyrrhus's cabin, sticky, the sex smell on
them.

It was better than nothing. That's all. Why should he have taken great
risks for it? Because you can invest all you have in something that is almost
indiscernibly better than nothing?

Seven bells sounded. Pyrrhus calculated—only seven-thirty. Foreplay,
the act, the cigarette after: all had consumed a mere half hour. Corythus
sat up. "I gotta go."

"No, stay here a while."

"I can't, people are gonna figure it out."

Pyrrhus didn't say they already had. "Then you shouldn't. I mean, we
shouldn't."

Corythus was pulling on his T-shirt, it was over his face. "What?"

"You shouldn't get in trouble over me. We should stop."

Corythus's face, now uncovered, was baffled and pained. "What are
you talking about?"

"I just mean—"

"I thought you . . . that we . . ."

Pyrrhus thought: one fucking day, or rather one day fucking, and the kid thought they were married. Why should he have been surprised? Pyrrhus had sometimes had a trick who had convinced himself—with the money all but lying on the dresser—that he and Pyrrhus were an item. Pyrrhus had had plenty of rehearsal and knew just how to pitch his voice: "I like you a whole lot, Corythus. But in a few more days I'll be off this ship."

Corythus sat down on the bed. "I know."

"And then, you understand, we'd probably be finished anyway. I mean, you know that."

There were, for pity's sake, tears in Corythus's eyes. Pyrrhus held his arm, and he didn't pull away. He swallowed and said, "Uh-huh."

"So it wouldn't be worth it. I mean, just for a couple more days, it wouldn't be worth your getting in trouble."

Corythus got up and reached for his trousers. He didn't put them on, just stood there a second. Then, tears running now down his sun-red face, he said, "I thought it was worth it. For an hour I would have."

He turned away, ashamed of crying. The poor little shit. But it was better than leading him on. Pyrrhus was surprised to hear himself say, "Wait."

"What."

"You're right. It's worth it." Corythus turned around, and Pyrrhus went on, not meaning a word of it. "Even if it's just for a couple of days." What the hell, a couple days, a tear-filled parting—better to hurt him that way. That way it wouldn't be Pyrrhus's fault, just the Fates'. "I just didn't want you to get in any trouble."

Corythus looked at Pyrrhus uncertainly. Soon he smiled and ran a finger across his upper lip, where his nose had dripped a little. "I don't give a fuck about them," he said.

Pyrrhus got up and went to him; they kissed. Corythus closed his eyes and wrapped his skinny arms around Pyrrhus, so tightly. Smothering him, or rather smothering that other self, the Neoptolemus who wasn't ever going to be born now. Yet Pyrrhus squeezed back just as hard. Their tongues met, Corythus was running his hands up and down Pyrrhus's body as if making sure he was all there, and Pyrrhus thought: What if, when we land, I can't get rid of him?

Phoenix stood outside Pyrrhus's door. He couldn't hear anything.

While I am too squeamish to rehearse the specifics of Phoenix's curtailment, it may be sufficient to remark that he encountered the surgeon at the age of twenty and was left mechanically equipped for any number of gratifying activities. If he had never performed any of them, it wasn't that he was unable, or had taken some vow. Nor even, exactly, that he didn't want to. He felt about sex the way you might feel if you were standing in the checkout line at the supermarket and suddenly remembered that the recipe you were planning to prepare called for fresh ginger. You could go back to the produce section and lose your place in line, or you could stay where you were and accept the prospect that the entree might be missing a little something.

Phoenix was eternally conscious of a small deficit in his life, but had never felt the lack sharply enough to step out of line and remedy it. Indeed, he had never much wanted to know what he was forgoing. Once or twice he had stood outside Achilles' tent, listening to the muffled squeaks and grunts as his master disappointed some semi-acquiescent captive. He could have peeked; he did not. The sounds had been enough to tell him that he didn't want to see. He didn't buy shrink-wrapped picture magazines; at the video store he never stepped through the curtain that sequesters the hard-core stuff from the mayhem meant for children.

Yet he was for some reason eager to see Pyrrhus and his little sailor — hesitated at the door, not because he was afraid he would interrupt them, but because the silence suggested there might be nothing to interrupt.

He tried the knob; the door was unlocked. He opened it as quietly as he could. And found Pyrrhus and the sailor locked in a kiss so deep they didn't even notice him at first. No: Pyrrhus noticed. His eyes met Phoenix's, yet he did not break the kiss.

The sailor must have felt the lapse in Pyrrhus's attention. He pulled away, turned, saw Phoenix, and confusedly saluted. Phoenix, even more startled — the sailor was wearing only a T-shirt — saluted back and heard himself saying, "At ease." He couldn't suppress a nervous giggle.

He hadn't expected to interrupt a kiss. If he had imagined them at all, he had not imagined a kiss.

The little sailor was rummaging for his clothes. Pyrrhus said, "To hell with it, come back to bed. He'll be gone in a minute." But the child dressed as fast as he could and scurried out to the passageway.

Pyrrhus stood brazenly before Phoenix, as if they were back at the Escapade. "You didn't knock," Pyrrhus said.

Phoenix looked at the floor. "I'm so sorry, I thought you were still at dinner."

"Nope."

"It just occurred to me that I might have left a few things here. Do you mind . . . ?" Phoenix, without raising his eyes, gathered up his shoe lifts, retrieved his moiré silk dressing gown from the hook on the door. He held it out. "Perhaps you would like to borrow this," he said.

"I'm fine."

Phoenix came upon his framed picture of Achilles. He was a little peeved that Pyrrhus had opened it, or perhaps embarrassed that Pyrrhus should know he carried that picture everywhere. "This, maybe you wanted this," he said.

"No. I can picture my father well enough." Pyrrhus sat on the bed.

"Of course." Phoenix stood for a second, letting Pyrrhus hope that he had only come for his things and was about to scram. "As long as I'm here, do you mind if I sit down as well?"

He glanced at the highly incriminating towel on the guest chair; he was too fastidious to remove it.

"For a minute. I'm getting kind of sleepy."

"I imagine you are. I shan't detain you long." Phoenix lifted the towel between thumb and forefinger as if it were an afterbirth and deposited it on the floor. He made himself look at Pyrrhus; he wished the boy had accepted the dressing gown. "As I believe you have been informed, we are not sailing directly for Troy. We thought perhaps you might be interested in learning the purpose of our little excursion."

"Not especially," Pyrrhus said. He was more interested in the *we*, which must have meant Phoenix and Odysseus. He had thought Phoenix was his own retainer. He didn't mention this; it was just good to know. "You got all your stuff?"

Phoenix sighed. "I truly intend to be brief. We are proceeding to Lemnos in the hopes of reattracting to our cause an officer named Philoctetes, who was some time ago detached from our force under certain regrettable circumstances that—"

"I've heard all about this."

"You have?"

"He was a queer, he got hurt, Odysseus got rid of him."

"A bit oversimplified, but: in essence."

"So now Odysseus feels guilty or something and we're going to go get him back."

"Well, no, I hope it will not disillusion you to learn that remorse is not high on the list of Odysseus's typical motives. He is pursuing Philoctetes for the same reason that he sought you: it has been made clear that he is indispensable."

"You mean by . . ."

"By the oracle, yes."

"That's great," Pyrrhus crowed. "Odysseus dumped him, and then it turns out that—"

"Exactly. You are correct that there is a certain irony in this, which is not altogether lost even on Odysseus."

"Irony? It's like you practically need a lavender brigade to win your war."

"This, too, Odysseus has remarked upon. Although he is not in fact certain that we require Philoctetes himself, as opposed to a miraculous weapon that he may possibly still possess, a bow bestowed on him by Heracles that—"

"A magic bow?"

"A bow, at least, of some metaphorical importance. Heracles used it, or toted it around, when he captured Troy many years ago. Thus it is— for those who believe these things, I think I have made it clear that I am at best agnostic on these points—it is symbolically appropriate that we have it, and perhaps its current proprietor, with us as we repeat its original owner's exploit."

"How did its current proprietor come by it?"

"I'm not sure. That is, Heracles evidently gave it to him, but I don't know why. This—the whole incident, the wound, the deposition on Lemnos—actually antedated my joining Achilles at Troy. It wasn't, as no one knew anything about the prophecy, it wasn't a matter much spoken of, and I'm afraid I haven't all the details. Except that there is a bow, which evidently only Philoctetes can use."

"Whatever," Pyrrhus said. If they had hoped to make him believe their silly prophecies, they might have avoided throwing in details like magic bows. "Anyway, you pick this guy up, and then we finally head for Troy?"

"Ah, I wish it were so simple. As you may imagine, it is not inconceivable that Philoctetes is somewhat aggrieved over his earlier treatment."

"No shit."

"While there is a faint possibility that he will be gratified at our returning for him, it is at least as likely that he will tell us to—"

"Go fuck yourselves."

"Something of the kind."

209

"Well, I wouldn't blame him. If he has any brains, he won't join you either."

"Either?"

"I made up my mind. I'm just going to get the stuff and go home."

"Oh. We're back to that."

"I decided I'm not going to be anybody but who I am. I'm sorry. You and the generalissimo are just going to have to find some other sucker."

"I'm sorry, too," Phoenix said. And realized that he was. Not because he had ever believed the silly oracle—or even cared if the Greeks took Troy or not. Rather because some part of him had been hoping to witness the boy's transformation. The idea of Pyrrhus at the head of an army, this boy whom he had just captured in the midst of a seditious kiss: it would have proved something. Redeemed things somehow. "Of course, the longer it takes to prevail upon Philoctetes, the greater the delay in going to get your stuff."

"What?"

"Odysseus is an obstinate man. He will not sail without Philoctetes. And if he has fought a war for a decade, who knows how long he might sojourn at Lemnos? Weeks, months. . . ."

"While I stay on this goddamn boat? One day and I'm bored out of my mind."

"After your many diversions? You *are* difficult to entertain," Phoenix said. "As it happens, Odysseus has had something of an inspiration. As you remarked, Philoctetes happens to be gay."

"So?"

"This is . . . I told Odysseus he might be presuming too much. However, he thought possibly . . . he thought Philoctetes might be interested in you."

He sat still, one eyebrow raised. He was waiting for Pyrrhus to puzzle this out, and it really did take a minute. Then Pyrrhus understood why Phoenix hadn't been more explicit. "You want me to go seduce him."

"In a word. As I say, I told Odysseus that—"

"Because I'm a pro, that's what you mean."

"Well, you are, rather."

Pyrrhus stood up. He thought at first he was going to hit Phoenix. After days of wanting to hit someone, he had found the perfect candidate—who had insulted him so deeply and who, conveniently, wouldn't even hit back. Perhaps some vestige of his father's sportsmanship kept him from beating up a defenseless eunuch. Who had not, after all, insulted him, simply told the obvious truth.

He sat down again and mumbled, "This is what you guys planned all along. All that other stuff, me and my destiny, you made all that up. Because you needed a whore to get at some poor faggot who—"

"Nonsense, this idea only just came to us; all the rest, about you, that was all entirely true. It is merely a lucky coincidence that you should have proved to be in possession of certain skills that . . ."

"That I don't plan to use anymore."

"I suppose I can understand that you might have some reservations. Nevertheless, if you were prepared to make yourself available for small financial rewards, it doesn't seem unsuitable that, in pursuit of the very much larger treasure that awaits you, you might—"

"You don't understand at all. I didn't come here to just go on being a whore. I was going to be . . ."

Pyrrhus couldn't complete the sentence.

"I thought you were going to be exactly who you were," Phoenix said. He rose from the chair, gathered up his belongings—including his precious picture of Pyrrhus's father; he closed up the frame and held it to his chest as if it were the last thing he had in the world. Well, the last thing of the Peleids, anyway, now that he had turned out to be just some lackey of Odysseus.

Pyrrhus wanted to make this clear. "My father would have been disgusted, that you would even come in here and suggest . . . that you and Odysseus could think . . ."

"I am sure your father would have been rather more distressed— wherever he is, I am sure he is appalled to know that our suggestion was by no means an implausible one."

Which served Pyrrhus right. Not because he was a whore, but because he had thought to use his father as a weapon, to score a cheap shot through him.

Phoenix left, looking rather smug.

Pyrrhus got dressed and went to hunt for Corythus. A whole day on board, and he still didn't have the slightest idea where the crew hung out. But Corythus had been right: the ship got smaller every minute, he shouldn't be so hard to find. After just a few minutes of wandering the passageways, Pyrrhus heard a rough chorus of men's voices; it had to be that way, just around that corner. Before he had turned the corner, he had a sudden picture of himself bursting in on the crowd of able seamen and beckoning to Corythus. He turned around and made his way back toward his cabin, then thought better of it and headed up to the main deck.

There was no one around, and no light—just the stars overhead, constellations who had once been overambitious hemidemigods. Even the bridge was dark, as if the ship were pilotless; except he could, when he squinted up at it, make out a tiny glow, maybe from the instruments.

He went to the railing, clutched it tightly, and made himself look down into the black water. He could hear, somewhere below him, the men's voices. What could it have been like for Corythus, trapped in some hole with those men, month after month? Well, he was about to find out, wasn't he? Stuck on this stinking boat for who knew how long, while they tried to suck in poor Philoctetes. Too bad their very best strategy hadn't worked out.

How could they have mistaken him for a whore? It was just a game he'd been playing, after all, not something inside him. Unless maybe, if you played this game too long, people would get mixed up. Just smile at you, smugly as Phoenix, when you tried to explain. Until finally you couldn't be anything but a whore, because you'd played at it too long, there wasn't any other way to end the sentence.

It was time to stop looking at the water. He thought he might stroll a little more before returning to his tiny cabin and its empty bed. He had only got halfway round the ship when he came upon Admetus. Leaning against the rail, as if he had just been waiting to see Pyrrhus.

Pyrrhus wanted to talk about Philoctetes, and Phoenix's insultingly sensible proposal, all of that. But he didn't know how to begin—seeing that he would have had to start by explaining his previous career. Unexpectedly, Admetus said, "I saw Corythus. He's looking all calf-eyed."

"I guess."

"You ain't."

Pyrrhus should have said it was none of the old man's business, but he just shrugged and shook his head. Admetus looked at him, expressionless, and he said, "I can't help it. I mean, I haven't done anything to lead him on. He knows, once I get off this boat, that's it."

"Ah. He shouldn't have fallen for you, you mean."

"That's right. It was stupid."

"I guess so. I'm pretty stupid myself, everybody says. I don't know how smart people do things. What, you kind of plan ahead before you fall for

212

anybody?" Pyrrhus didn't have an answer, and Admetus said, "Or ain't you ever fell for anybody?"

"I don't want to talk with you about this."

"I'm sorry, sir. I guess I'm insubordinate."

He was as old as . . . a Leo and a half, at least. Pyrrhus felt like a fool when he said "sir." "No, I just . . . it feels funny. I mean, you're straight, aren't you?"

"Yeah. You know, all the time I got, I think sometimes, hell, maybe I should spend a century trying the other way. I never done it, though." Pyrrhus just looked at him, and suddenly he laughed. "You thought that was a come-on."

"No."

"You did. You think everybody's trying to put the make on you."

"Lots of people are."

"Don't knock it. Wait till you look like me and the broads won't look twice at you." He turned and looked out at the water. Perhaps, for him, no more tedious a vista than any other. "I don't mean to butt in. I don't give a shit that you're queer, you gotta believe that."

"Okay."

"But you're gonna hurt that kid."

"What the fuck am I supposed to do about it? He's hurting himself. Anything I do, he's going to get hurt."

Admetus shook his head. "You know, your dad, I said he was kind of a hero."

"You also said he was an asshole."

"He was. But he was an honest asshole. He never pretended nothing, or told nobody a lie. He just said whatever he felt, right then."

Now there was no chance of bringing up Philoctetes. Admetus would simply draw the unhelpful moral: your father wouldn't have done it. As if the example of Achilles offered a path through life.

"So what's the moral? I go to Corythus and say, 'Hey, I don't give a damn about you, you're just a mercy fuck, I can't wait to get off the damn boat'?"

"Ship," Admetus said. "Is that what you feel?"

"Yeah, I . . . No, I don't know."

"You don't know."

"It doesn't matter. That's the point. I mean, a few more days, why would I tell him something like that?"

"Right. A few more days. And then you get to act out the prophecies."

213

"Nah, none of that's going to happen."

"No? What'd you do, find some other oracle down the street?"

"I just know it. They got it wrong or something, I'd have to—I can't change that much, I'm not some hero."

Admetus shrugged. "What's a hero? He's just the guy who shows up when he's supposed to. If you're it, you're it. You don't got to change nothing."

Pyrrhus didn't listen. "I just want to get to Arisbe and get done with everything."

"Meanwhile, you're just going to string the kid along for a bit."

"I guess."

"If that's what you're doing, if that's what you really feel."

"It doesn't matter," Pyrrhus said. "That's it, anyway, it doesn't matter what I feel."

Admetus grabbed him suddenly, held Pyrrhus close to his chest. Pyrrhus tried to pull away, but he was awfully strong for an old man. He whispered, "God, you poor little shit. If *you* don't even care what you feel, who the fuck will?"

Pyrrhus could smell the whiskey on him, and the sweat; it was sickening. He wanted so much to pull away, and instead he found himself burying his face in Admetus's shoulder.

After a minute, Admetus muttered, "Maybe you're right, about Corythus. Maybe some folks don't want to know any further ahead than they ought to."

Admetus left him. Pyrrhus went up to the bow, sat on the hatchway where he had first talked with Admetus, and looked ahead into the darkness. He wanted to try, one more time, to think. He wasn't stupid, he wasn't his father; why should it have been such a challenge just to sit down and think a few things through?

Maybe if he couldn't work out his destiny, he could at least figure out what he felt about Corythus. Except that he already knew the answer: nothing. Odysseus and his eunuch were right, he was a whore all the way through. Nothing else inside him, there hadn't ever been. He wasn't going to change.

Far ahead, on the even line where the black sea met the black sky, there was a little patch of something else. Not light, still blackness, but a different shade: as if light had tried to invade the dark and been swallowed up. Maybe that was Lemnos, maybe they were almost there.

He stood up.

I suppose only a few men are ever really granted a vision of their fate. We all may have our fortune told, or we may guess it on our own. But we are not forced up from our seats, we do not stand transfixed by a sudden apprehension of the whole web of the world and how we fit in it. How our nature and our destiny have contrived together—as they must—to make a place for us, a place we've been marching toward all our lives. Sailing toward—what was now, unmistakably, the light of Lemnos.

He finally understood how oracles worked. If you're it, you're it: he didn't have to make choices, didn't have to transform himself into some alien Neoptolemus. The casting call was for a whore, and one had shown up just in time. History turned on him; the world was waiting.

THE BOW

1

Lemnos. The town was all of one fabric, at least when you first looked at it, all gray shingle and white woodwork. Here and there a deviant, attention-craving door of yellow or blue. The post office alone was of red brick, as everywhere in the distant kingdom to which Lemnos paid tribute. As if the kingdom itself were nothing but a gridwork of red cubes, stelae left behind in towns of gray or white by a band of raiders that had long since sailed away.

All gray when you first looked at it. Only gradually did you begin to make out the rich spectrum underlying the monochrome: from new shingle, reddish gold, to the weathered ash just before rot. As if some buildings were children and adolescents, others graybeards. Except the graybeard could become young again: several were in the midst of this amazing rejuvenation, their wise silver striped with courses of fresh-hewn tawny.

It all looked gray to Odysseus in the predawn light. He put down the binoculars and said, "I don't like coming this close."

Nereus didn't look at him. "I don't decide where the shoals are. There's no other way around the island."

"We need to be out of here before the town's up and about."

"You've said, sir."

Odysseus picked up the binoculars again. As far as he could see, the place hadn't changed an iota. Not one building was different; even the gulls were roosting on the very same pilings they had occupied ten years earlier. Maybe it was a town ordinance, forced through by all the watercolorists who made a living slapping out scenes of the picturesque village. Nothing could change. That way they wouldn't even have to step outside their studios to check on things; they could paint the same vista from memory for years on end and the reality would dutifully conform.

Lemnos, ten years and they were back at Lemnos. They might have sailed away yesterday. As if everything they'd gone through had never happened. The battles, the burning suburbs, the homesickness that, at length, burned itself out, so that you almost stopped believing you'd ever been home, couldn't tell your particular exile from the general exile from Arcadia. They might just as well have dropped anchor a mile offshore and sat for ten years. And all the deaths were pointless. Well, no; Odysseus had to believe they were necessary, but only in the sense that they had to be numbered, like the days, lives peeled off one by one like the sheets of a calendar in the movies. That was all: they had to tick off the months and the deaths appointed for each month, and no one counted for more than any other. Achilles and some luckless nonentity who never saw anything after Achilles: each was one digit in the reckoning.

So many days behind them and so few ahead, Odysseus didn't know how he could just keep counting them off one by one. He wanted to race ahead, tear off the last sheets of the calendar in one great fistful. "Show me again, once we get around the island—"

Nereus drew in his breath. "We're in a difficult passage, sir, I can't show you just now."

"Then tell me."

"Just north of the island is another one, tiny, Sidheritis. Uninhabited. We anchor to the north of Sidheritis and we can't be seen from the main island. But a launch can reach town in an hour, easy."

"Is there a harbor?" Odysseus said.

"Huh?" Obviously there was a harbor; they were passing it right now. Oh, he meant at Sidheritis. "No. We can anchor, but I'm not real happy putting in there."

Odysseus swallowed, and Nereus went on, concealing his glee, "We may be nudged a bit, if there's weather."

The memory of the last time they were nudged a bit—more nearly flung around by Poseidon as if the *Penelope* were a bathtub toy—gave Odysseus a sort of premonitory queasiness. He sat down and looked at his own feet, just to avoid for a minute the rocking vista of Lemnos. Then he was afraid to look up. As if he might see that they had never been away at all, the ten years were only starting.

"I never saw so many dykes in one place," Pyrrhus said.

"It is rather daunting, isn't it?" Phoenix said. "There's a story behind it."

"Isn't there always?"

They were walking down Port Street, Pyrrhus and Phoenix and, some steps behind them, Admetus. He had fallen behind when he'd stopped to roll a cigarette, and he had never spent the little bit of energy it would have taken to catch up. He was just strolling, smoking and ignoring the consequent indignant looks from what was, indeed, a formidable procession of lesbians.

220

Phoenix had come along in the launch just to show them around, because he had been to Lemnos once or twice. "Just to see the galleries, you know. I've never cared for the beach, and the other attractions of the place are . . . beyond me." He would be going back; it wouldn't do for all three of them to prowl the town like a press gang. Just now, with a story coming on, he took a seat on one of the long benches in front of Town Hall.

He waited for Admetus, unsuspecting, to catch up. Then he began:

"There was a time when Lemnos had the ordinary preponderance of heterosexuals. Extraordinary, really: it was stupefying how exactly coupled the populace was, not an odd man or woman out, spinster or invert. Just row after row of proper families, each in its quaint cottage. The gods themselves could not look down on the place without yawning. Which is, I suppose, why one of them decided to stir things up a bit.

"One day the women started to stink. I mean, to high heaven — they say it was beyond imagining. The whole town was suffused with an intolerable fetor; it was like living in a bouillabaisse."

"Oh, come on," Pyrrhus said.

"I beg your pardon?"

"Some guy made this up. Some breeder who can't really stand women."

"Possibly," Phoenix said. "Though it is repeated in all the authorities, and there must be some bit of truth in it. At any rate, the women said Aphrodite had done it, because they had neglected some obligation or other. Agnostics have suggested something more mundane, like a yeast infection — the universal transmission of which would suggest a certain amount of shuffling and recombination of the constituents of those oh-so-perfect couples.

"Wherever the affliction came from, it wouldn't go away. In consequence the men of Lemnos began to neglect their marital duties, dwelling for a time in a state of fastidious celibacy and at last straying — eyes and noses wandering — finding release with women of other islands or, in the not exceptional case, with one another.

"Understandable as their husbands' errancy may have been, the forsaken women of Lemnos were aggrieved, and one day they killed every last man on the island."

"How?" Pyrrhus said.

"Oh, any number of ways. The improperly identified wild mushroom in the evening stew, the well-hurled cooking utensil, the ignited bed. In one monitory instance the chainsaw, directed first to the erring member and then . . . At any rate, by sunset the town had taken on its current homogeneity of gender."

"There isn't . . . I don't think I smell anything."

"No, that went away soon enough. In fact, just a year or so later, Jason and his crew landed here on their way to some adventure or other, and they took it into their heads that it might be a good deed to repopulate the place. The women demurred. In their solitude they had begun to take some comfort in one another's company; the visitors were superfluous. Not to mention that, after so long at sea, the Argonauts had acquired a certain aroma of their own.

"One or two of the sailors failed to take the Lemnites at their word and afforded the women a fresh opportunity to practice their deadly skills. The rest got, as they say, the message and pulled anchor. Taking with them only one Hypsipyle, who had begun to find the place a touch monotonous and who had mistakenly surmised that Jason was as masterful in bed as at the helm. When she discovered that this analogy was ill founded, she began vocally and unceasingly demanding to be returned to Lemnos. As this was out of the question, and her complaints had become ever more tedious, they sold her to the king of Nemea at the next port of call. What happened to her next is itself a story of not inconsiderable—"

Admetus growled, "No, no, stick with Lemnos."

"Well, there's nothing more of that story. There they were, the women, and here they are. Welcoming, as you can see, only those varieties of men who can be counted upon to make no unwelcome advances. It's become quite a popular resort."

"Yeah, I've known guys who came here," Pyrrhus said. "There don't seem to be many now."

"It's the middle of the afternoon: beauty naps. Not quite high season, besides. Wait a few weeks."

"I don't think Odysseus is quite that patient."

"No, indeed. I'm sure he'll be annoyed if you don't have Philoctetes aboard by nightfall."

"We'll be lucky to find him by nightfall."

Admetus said, "I don't expect we'll even look till then."

"No?" Phoenix said. "Well, I suppose not. It's easier to track people down at night." He smiled at Pyrrhus. "I'm sure you can entertain yourselves. The food is dispiriting—rather too much tofu and sprouts for my taste—and the beach is so rocky that lying on it could serve as a penance. Still, the shopping isn't bad: a little surplus of clever things done with seashells, but some pretty good galleries up at the west end, and—"

"T-shirt shops," Pyrrhus said.

"Yes. I don't think there were so many, last time I was here. Perhaps they metastasize somehow. At any rate, as I myself never wear undergarments with literary content, I believe I shall take my leave. When should the launch come back for you?"

"I don't know," Pyrrhus said. "I mean—"

"Midnight," Admetus said. "And not here at the harbor. Better have 'em wait at that inlet we passed, just east of here."

Pyrrhus was surprised at this sudden authoritative tone. Phoenix smirked. "If I recall, from my last visit, that particular stretch of shore can be surprisingly populous at midnight."

"All right, at the harbor. But they'll have to wait. I don't know how long we'll be."

For most visitors, Lemnos was a single street, Port Street—a lane, really, so narrow that two women on motorcycles could not pass each other— which ran east-west, parallel to the water's edge. At the western terminus of Port Street there was allegedly a beach, though many visitors never confirmed this rumor. To the east was a heart-sinking realm of marshes and, in the dry places, trailer parks. Just to the north of Port Street, the actual town, with its permanent residents doing permanent things, and past that a little stretch of scrubby woods, then the dunes. The whole north end of the island, rolling hillocks of sand, here and there a shanty. Overlooking, across the channel, the little island of Sidheritis. To the north of that, just now, the *Penelope*. Pretty well masked from view by the sporadic vegetation of Sidheritis. Yet actually visible. Anyone on the dunes might have seen it, but only if he looked for it.

Again, most people never got very far from Port Street. On either side were shops and guesthouses and restaurants and bars. It was then, as now, but of course much more then, a boulevard of the body. By day there were the straight tourists from the cruise ships. But on a summer evening, on Port Street, you might have thought the whole world was gay. The restaurants, the kitsch shops, the ice-cream stands overflowed with gay people. Every clothing store sold five-hundred-dollar sweaters and underwear in little tubes. In the bookstore, the usual bestsellers about spies, or twelve lessons entrepreneurs might learn from the labors of Heracles, languished on a single shelf, while the aisles were full of movie stars' memoirs and quarto albums of oiled, artistically lit nudes. And people cruised unceasingly—not in any predatory way, it was in the rhythm of the place. There was no difference, as one strolled along, between looking in a window at a witty T-shirt and glancing up at a cute man. A transaction might or might not follow in either case.

Pyrrhus, of course, had his share of glances, and returned a few. Admetus was oblivious and just hurried Pyrrhus along from bar to bar. Those on the south side of Port Street overlooked the picturesque harbor and tended to have strings of lights and piano players. Those on the north side were gloomier, closed in on themselves: their patrons dressed not to dazzle but to dismay. That evening, Pyrrhus and Admetus went through every one of them, looking for Philoctetes.

Have you ever been dragged along by someone who's looking for someone else, a stranger to you? You stumble with him from place to place; at each stop the two of you scan the room together. He knows who he's looking for, while you try to muster a sort of objectless alertness. You know you could be staring right at your quarry and not recognizing him. After a while you feel like an inverted amnesiac. While the amnesiac sees a familiar face and cannot place it, you see nothing but unfamiliar faces and give them all the same name.

Every bar was a throng of potential castaways. It was Pyrrhus, finally, who spotted the man. Not what Pyrrhus had been looking for. He had pictured some sort of hermit, loins wrapped in fur, licking ants off a stick. But he knew Philoctetes at once: that one there, tucked away in the far corner of the U-shaped bar, next to the blender.

Pyrrhus gave a tiny jerk of his head toward the shadowed figure. Admetus glanced for just an instant and looked back at the crowd. "Aye, that's him. Dear heaven, that's all of him now."

There was none of him to spare. He was at that eerie point in the downward glide when every redundant ounce has been pared away, as by a carver, but just before the carver has done that one stroke too many, here and then here, leaving at last bright eyes peering from a cranium all but stripped of flesh. One of death's passing jokes, this moment: to Pyrrhus, Philoctetes looked perfect, taut as a panther. To Admetus, who recalled him strutting with the other overfed officers ten years earlier, he looked like an admonition.

He wore jeans in a waist size that was probably in single digits and a flannel shirt washed so often that its plaid had become a ghostly memory, the one soft touch on a body as austere as bone.

They found seats at the base of the U, just where it turned toward the leg at whose terminus sat Philoctetes. Pyrrhus got a beer, but Admetus ordered a frozen daiquiri. Pyrrhus looked at him with momentary amazement, then understood. The bartender would have to use the blender, and Admetus would have an excuse to stare in that direction. The stratagem worked: after a minute Pyrrhus could see the puzzlement cross Philoctetes' face, then the recognition. Admetus aped him, made as if he had suddenly noticed Philoctetes. They looked at each other, separated by ten feet and as many years, and did not move.

Philoctetes, astonishingly, smiled. The skin that had already seemed so taut pulled even tighter across his skull. "I know you. Goodness, it was a long time ago. Where do I know you from?" He had one of those country drawls that, in a city boy, would sound effeminate, too liquid and musical.

Admetus said, "Um . . . ," not sure how much to say.

"No, don't tell me. It was back in the city—lord, before the war. You used to hang out at—"

"No." Admetus went over to him. "No, it was since the war, Philoctetes."

"Since . . . ?" Philoctetes peered at him, shook his head. "No, I can't—"

"On the *Penelope*."

"Oh." Philoctetes' smile vanished for an instant, then he forced it back into place. "The *Penelope*. You—what did they used to say in the movies?—you have the advantage of me."

"Admetus. We, you know, we didn't know each other real well. I mean, we didn't pal around together or nothing, you and me."

"No, no one hung around with me very much on the *Penelope*."

"I just meant 'cause you were an officer."

"Oh."

"I always wondered what happened to you."

"This is what happened to me." Philoctetes made a broad gesture that took in his own wasted body, the bar, the whole island.

"I was in the launch," Admetus said.

"The what?"

"When we dropped you off."

Philoctetes shrugged. "Well, that's all she wrote. You dropped me off and here I am."

"I thought you might've . . ."

"Died? No, I didn't yet." He turned away and stared into his drink, clear as water, with a tattered lime buffeted by tonic bubbles.

"I didn't mean died," Admetus said. "I meant left, got home somehow. I'm sorry."

Philoctetes pulled himself up and managed a very narrow smile indeed. "No, I guess I'm the one who's being rude. I mean, it's almost good to see you. I think about it every day, the *Penelope* and all; I hardly ever think about anything else. I guess it's good to finally see someone from back then. It shows I didn't make it all up."

"Uh-huh."

"But I didn't ever get home."

Admetus took a sip from his frozen daiquiri, swished it around in his mouth a little. "You know, I ain't never had one of these. That's life, something new every day."

"For you, maybe," Philoctetes said.

Admetus chuckled, though Philoctetes apparently didn't get the joke; maybe he didn't remember who Admetus was.

There was a little silence, and Admetus looked over at Pyrrhus, scowling, as if to say: You're supposed to be the enchanting one, come and do your stuff.

Philoctetes followed his eyes, noticed Pyrrhus for the first time. "Lord, you've brought—"

Pyrrhus stood up. Philoctetes squinted over at him. "Oh, no. I'm sorry, I thought . . ."

Admetus said, "You thought he was Achilles."

"Well, I did, but of course not." Philoctetes stuck out his hand, gravely. "How do you do. I am Philoctetes."

"Pyrrhus."

As they shook hands—Philoctetes' grip hard, but also damp and surprisingly warm—Admetus said, "You know, I thought the same thing, first time I clapped eyes on him. I mean the face, don't you think the—"

Pyrrhus had had enough of being examined. "I'm his son."

Admetus looked at him aghast. He hadn't thought this was part of the script. He drew back: it was Pyrrhus's play from here on.

"Are you?" Philoctetes said. "Imagine Achilles having a son your age. Shit, how old does that make me? You do look a lot like him."

Pyrrhus shrugged. "A lot smaller, I guess."

226

"But very nicely built, I'd say. Your father is a bit overblown. I've never much cared for these pneumatic men."

Pyrrhus was, in front of Admetus, a little embarrassed by this bit of camp. "He's dead."

"Achilles? You're kidding." Then, perhaps recalling that the bereaved tended not to kid about it: "Oh, I'm awfully sorry. I mean, I just wouldn't have thought that was possible."

"That was all . . . it was just a story, about his being invulnerable and all."

"I never even heard that story. Did they say that about him? How silly. I watched him run once, did you ever see him run? It was something: big as a ten-wheeler, and going just as fast. Like some kind of machine, that's what he looked like, in a ton of sheet metal, just barreling along. He wouldn't have been, like you say, invulnerable—I mean, a truck can crack up. But it doesn't die, dying's different."

"Well, he did."

"It's been a long time, I guess a lot of them are dead. Have they been fighting all this time?"

"Off and on," Admetus said. "A lot of them are dead."

"Who all?"

"Who ain't? Ajax, Patroclus . . ."

"Odysseus?" Philoctetes said, hopefully.

"No."

"No. He's the machine, the invulnerable one."

"Just smart."

"You bet." Philoctetes bit his lower lip and left them. That is, he was still sitting there, but he was obviously transported, in a sort of melancholy trance, to the events of ten years earlier. Pyrrhus wondered if it was just their arrival, bringing back the memories too potently, or if he was always on the edge of it, ready to be set off by any glancing reminder of what had happened. The latter, probably; he snapped out of it in an instant and restored the smile to his face.

"What's your story? Don't tell me you're going to Troy." The tone suggested that the destination of a whole generation of men was an outlandish one—making it easier for Pyrrhus to recite the tale Odysseus had drilled into him.

"No, I'm headed home. I only went to claim what belonged to me."

"What belonged to you, how grand. You mean, you went to take your father's place? Or just his stuff?"

227

"Who could take his place?" Pyrrhus said; he hoped he sounded sincere. Philoctetes gave him an oh-please look, eyes heavenward. "Just his stuff."

"What, armor and things?"

"More than that," Admetus put in. "Half the shit in the suburbs."

"Oh, plunder. I knew everybody didn't go just because they took some oath."

"Why did you go?" Pyrrhus said. He did wonder: how a queen, a relatively unflaming one but still patently a queen, had been dragged into it all. Well, it was prophesied, just as it had been for Pyrrhus. But no one had known that, when they started out; Philoctetes couldn't have known that.

"I was expecting an enormous boy-scout camp, skinny-dipping and circle jerks. Only it was just jerks. As you must have noticed." This was not the fiery outrage Pyrrhus had been prepared for; he hadn't expected mere rue. "Anyway, you've got your . . . booty, and you're headed for home."

"I didn't get anything."

"You mean they—"

"That bastard Odysseus had already claimed it all."

"Nobody stood up to him? Not Ajax, or Patroclus?"

"Like I was telling you," Admetus said. "They're all dead."

"Oh, you did say that. Short-term memory loss, one of the warning signs of something or other. Whatever it is I have. So: the best are gone, and there's just Odysseus?"

"The sonofabitch," Pyrrhus said, perfunctorily. He didn't want to lay it on too thick.

"Don't tell me about Odysseus. If it weren't for him I wouldn't be here."

"What do you mean?" Pyrrhus said.

Philoctetes looked at him a little oddly, as if maybe he hadn't gotten the tone of ignorance just right. "Never mind. Everybody's heard this story. Right, Pterelas?"

The bartender looked over. "What?"

"Everybody's heard my story. Haven't they, Pterelas?"

Pterelas said, gently, "Everybody's heard everybody's story, honey." Pterelas was a man of indeterminate age who had, a decade or two earlier, been cute. One of those men who are never told, not by their closest friends, that they can't be cute any more. And who therefore remain chemically blond into their fifties, who wear open tropical shirts over pastel tank tops that disclose too much. He ambled over to Pyrrhus in a nimbus of cologne. "You should see this place in winter. Down to a skeleton crew, all the tourists gone, just Philoctetes and me and a couple hundred dykes with cabin fever. How long you in town for?"

"I don't know," Pyrrhus said. "We—"

Admetus corrected him. "Just a couple days. Then we're headed home."

"Home is . . . Phthia, isn't it?" Philoctetes said. Looking pleased with himself, that at least his long-term memory was holding up.

"Um . . . ," Pyrrhus said. Phthia was his father's home, and Peleus's. His home was—where? Leucon's apartment?

Admetus jumped in again. "That's right."

"I grew up right near there," Philoctetes said. "In Thessaly."

"I remember," Admetus said.

"I think about going back. I mean I could have, any time, if I'd just gotten a little ahead."

Pterelas said, "Honey, with your tab, you're going to be here till the day you die."

"I think more and more about it. Just so I don't end my days here."

"We should talk," Admetus said, pretty casually.

Philoctetes said, just as nonchalantly, "Okay. Hey, Pterelas, why don't you bring us all another round?"

"No, we gotta go," Admetus said.

"Already?"

Admetus gestured at Pyrrhus. "We gotta get some food in this one before he passes out."

Pyrrhus hadn't felt especially drunk. But he was—all the places they'd stopped, having a quick one at each stop so they wouldn't be quite so obvious a search party.

"Any place good around here?" Admetus said.

Philoctetes said, "Um . . . I don't eat out much."

"He drinks his dinner," Pterelas said. "You like seafood?"

"Sure."

"You better in this town, it's that or tofu. Try the Red Shack, couple blocks east. You can't miss it, it's gray."

While Admetus paid the tab—he'd been paying all night, Pyrrhus just wasn't in the habit of picking up tabs—Pyrrhus smiled inanely at Philoctetes.

He seemed a little flustered by the attention, but managed to say, "Do stop in again. I'm curious, you know, about what happened to everybody."

"Sure. Maybe tomorrow. I like this place, we'll be back."

"Great," Philoctetes said, but tonelessly, and he was already staring again into his drink.

As they went out into the street, Pyrrhus said to Admetus, "This is going to be easier than we thought."

"You reckon?"

"I mean, we just tell him we'll take him back to Thessaly, get him on the ship, and *whoosh.*"

Admetus shrugged. "You don't look like you're ready to do surgery on a lobster. You wanna just get a burger or something?"

"Okay." They stood back to back and squinted, searching in opposite directions for the familiar logos of burger chains in the undifferentiated gray.

"That was bar talk," Admetus said. "He ain't a man who's going no-where."

Philoctetes didn't go anywhere, didn't move a muscle, for a good five minutes. Just sat at his corner of the bar—really his, a little principality; Pterelas wouldn't let anyone else sit there even if it didn't look like Philoctetes was coming in. Then his trance lifted and he moved his glass, almost imperceptibly, just a quarter-inch or so closer to the bartender's well. Pterelas—who you wouldn't have thought was even looking—came and poured a hit of vodka, no more tonic. "Thinking about the war?" Pterelas said.

"No, it's funny. I was thinking about the city."

"The city."

"Back in the city, before the war. I never think about that." Philoctetes grinned. "I almost feel horny. I think this is what horny felt like."

"I shouldn't wonder."

"No? Oh, you mean that kid."

"He was something," Pterelas said.

"Wasn't he?"

"And he was looking at you."

"Don't tease me. Nobody's looked at me in ten years."

"I watched."

"Then he was just staring at the freak show."

"I don't think so." Pterelas started to rinse some glasses, lazily, just to have a reason to stay at Philoctetes' end of the bar.

Could it be true, that Philoctetes never thought about the city? The city, before the war—to listen to the scattered survivors of those days, you might suppose they think about nothing else. Kids who come along now are sick of hearing about it. Why should I add to the overburdened shelves of hymns to that time and that place? Yet I must: it will truly be gone the day we leave off singing about it.

They were the heroes, the very Eronauts, of love. And first among them Philoctetes.

They had done everything that can be done with two or three or four bodies—the number of possible permutations proving distinctly finite, if you weren't careful you could run through them in a night. They had worn every possible costume, had fucked in every possible venue: trailers and piers and baths and tearooms and beaches and bushes and back rooms and video booths and saunas at the gym. The Mile High Club had done it in the john of a jetliner, the Mile Down Club in the motorman's booth of a subway car. Also: in squash courts and choir lofts, in the stacks at the library, and once, famously, in a box at the opera during the twilight of the gods.

They had crossed every frontier, circumvented every inhibition, acted out their deepest wishes and their shallowest fancies. When pleasure grew humdrum, they turned to pain; when freedom palled, they looked for masters; when the masters made them giggle, they turned to asceticism or designer drugs. Through it all they danced, night after night, shirts tucked into their belts, their sweating bodies gleaming in the strobe lights; they held amyl-soaked kerchiefs to their noses, like dandies, and they screamed and laughed and worshiped. And at the center of every party, Philoctetes.

They were lawless. Of course they obeyed most rules: they never jumped a turnstile or ran a red light or spat on the sidewalk; they seldom shoplifted and then only as a lark, never anything of value; they showed up for jury duty. But they were lawless in the manner of heroes. They sailed west without a chart, beneath night skies with unnamed constellations. They plummeted off the edge or found safe harbors that they claimed for all of us. They did it for everyone who had come before them. The Eronauts lived out their freedom for all the generations that

231

had been caged, so that every impulse was a holy obligation. They did it for everyone who came after. And, a league ahead of the pathfinders, Philoctetes.

Now the sea lanes they charted have closed behind them. All they discovered, that had waited since the dawn of time to be found, swallowed up. No one will ever go that way again, not even if the cure is found. Partly because we will never own our bodies again, as they did. We are vectors now, or vessels, sources of transmission; our bodies belong to the unseen. Well, it has always been so, we have always belonged to the Fates. We just never thought the Fates were so tiny.

"Has it been that long?" Pterelas said.

"What?"

"I mean, since you . . ."

"Oh. I don't know. I kind of screwed around when I first got here. Except . . . I don't know, it wasn't the same. After a while I kind of stopped looking for it. Or people stopped looking for me, whichever."

"Well, you could have had me, any time."

Philoctetes smiled. "You were hot, I remember."

"I need to get a sign put up: No Past-Tense Compliments to the Bartender."

"Okay, you're still hot. I just got tired."

He remembered, as he had a few minutes earlier, as he did a hundred times a day, standing on the dock and watching the launch pull away. With, apparently, Admetus in it, though he didn't remember that, just a couple of sailors' backs, growing smaller.

Lemnos had been the nearest harbor; he was lucky they hadn't just left him on some desert island. With his magic bow, right, as if he were supposed to hunt for his dinner. And how would he ever have shot down any vodka? Instead they happened to leave him on Lemnos. Even as he stood watching the launch until he couldn't see it any more, he thought: if he weren't so angry, angry and humiliated, this would be a pretty good joke. He turned finally and faced the island of his exile.

The hero of love stepped off the dock and into the village. Even though he limped a little, plenty of guys looked him over. Sick as he was, his face was tan and deceptively healthy, his hair bleached gold; he had on his officer's whites. He could have had the whole island on its knees, those people who weren't already. He knew it, felt even a glimmer of excitement, a memory of the nights in the city before the war.

He might have plunged right in, but for his anger and his weariness and his aching leg. Here on an island consecrated to beauty he wanted to hide in some room with the blinds pulled, hide in the dark like a sick animal.

He found the room, with a shared bath, in one of the tackier guest-houses. He slept during the day, when it was quiet, went out for a little carry-out, and sat up alone in the room at night, listening to the endless party he was too weary to attend and nursing his grievances. Imploring every god whose name he could remember to pour down pestilences upon the Greeks. Contemplating the purchase of Trojan war bonds. Except that his savings were running a little low.

He had a little, was able to live some months on the money wired from his old accounts in the city. He had never spent money in the city. He had worn cheap clothes, he had lived in the tiniest walk-up studio, and he had been taken places. Not kept—he never offered himself as exchange—but taken; people just brought him along. At the end of an expensive meal, a check for six might be divided five ways; after a while he didn't add to the awkwardness by thanking anyone. They all had so much money: some of them snorted in a weekend what he earned in a month, and he didn't ask to go to the River Room or Parnassus, people just insisted he come.

Thus he had managed to save a little before the war, and now he scraped by in that dark room in the guesthouse that was cheap because it had somehow contrived to be the very longest walk both from the beach and from tea dance. Until his first remission, his first and longest and most deceptive, when his strength so nearly came back that he felt, each morning, not much worse, say, than you do at the end of a truly catastrophic day at the office. He felt that good, and he left his burrow and started to work at the T-shirt shop and started to get a little sun and at last was ready for the healing jubilee of Lemnos. To live once again as he had done back in the city, to rejoin the eternal party that had just gone on without interruption. Punctuated, never stopped, by transient annoyances like crabs, clap, amoebas, hepatitis.

233

It was all still going on, and Philoctetes was ready to dive in, when his strength came back, as if the war had never happened. He left his room and walked, scarcely limping at all, to tea dance. When he stepped into the disco, with its glittering ball, he felt—oh, perhaps the way Pyrrhus expected to feel that day, soon now, when he would stand before the Myrmidons. Philoctetes strode onto the dance floor like a hero saluting his waiting army.

Philoctetes said, "Pterelas, I don't think I can walk home."

"You didn't take your painkiller, did you?"

"If I do, I can't drink. I'd rather my leg ached than . . ."

"It's almost closing. You stay right there and drink coffee. I'll drive you."

"I'm a lot of trouble."

"You sure are. It's no wonder they threw you off that tub."

Actually, by the time Pterelas closed up and they headed for his car—four-wheel drive, nothing else could have made it to Philoctetes' shack—Philoctetes was over it. It was that way sometimes: sometimes the pain was just for a minute or two, but so intense Philoctetes saw white light, or became the light, as if someone had fixed wires to the twin wounds just above his ankle and then closed the circuit. Or it could go on for a week, never sharper than the gentlest toothache, but insistent, so that if it let up for an instant it was as though Philoctetes' heart had skipped a beat.

It even had a sense of humor, the pain, flaring up just before a dinner party and receding when it was too late to go. Or—that first night at the disco, when he'd been chatting with a stranger, just when they were clicking, right when Philoctetes was about to suggest . . . The twinge hadn't even been so very strong, just enough to pull Philoctetes into himself for a moment. The stranger had looked into his suddenly unreadable face and thought he had simply lost interest. Before Philoctetes could explain, the guy was gone.

If he had been egotistical, Philoctetes might have said that these pranks were evidence of the ongoing intervention of whatever malicious deity had afflicted him. The gods surely had bigger fish to fry; they couldn't have taken time out from their bloody board game at Troy to screw up Philoctetes' infrequent attempts at a pickup. Still he couldn't help, some-

234

times, feeling that all the wheels of Heaven were turning to grant him a morning of respite or a night of agony. Solemn councils on Olympus deliberated: Shall it burn today? Shall it be more like an arrow?

Evadne, the lesbian who ran the frozen-yogurt shop, said it all came from inside. Couldn't he see, the way it would hit right when he was about to connect? It had to be that he didn't really want it; the pain was a wall he put up.

Well, bullshit, he thought. I didn't bite myself. Anyway, it wasn't just the pain that screwed up every trick. Sometimes he would look into an apparently sympathetic face and, foolishly, tell his story. Of course no one wanted to trick with him after hearing his story. Other times, when he managed to shut up about it and just be charming, the withheld story would hang there nonetheless. He would be smiling just as broadly as he knew how, would feel from inside the muscles pulling across his face, and then he would glance in the mirror over the bar and see that he was offering the stranger not a grin but a mask of grief.

Until at last nobody saw him. He had become one of those people who sits in a bar and whom nobody sees at all: a gray space, a lacuna in the corner of the room.

The twinge had passed; he was quite over it by the time he and Pterelas left the bar. But he was also a little tipsy and a lot tired, so he limped out, not too persuasively, and let Pterelas drive him home. They parked at the foot of the dune that wore Philoctetes' shack like a toque. Pterelas, perhaps noticing that Philoctetes had recovered considerably, stayed in his seat and let Philoctetes get out unassisted. He waited, though, didn't pull away until Philoctetes had staggered all the way up to the shack.

When Philoctetes got into bed he jerked off thinking about Pyrrhus. I don't mean he started jerking off and Pyrrhus happened to come to mind, or that he thought about Pyrrhus and happened to start jerking off. I mean that he got a towel and the grease and turned off his kerosene lamp and lay down planning to picture Pyrrhus. As if it were a way of meditating about him, the way somebody else might sit and write in his diary about it.

Pyrrhus wasn't the prettiest thing Philoctetes had ever seen. If hemi-demigods didn't show up every night—still, in those days, the gods sometimes dropped from the skies and randomly sowed glints of divinity. And it was not so uncommon for their offspring to pop up in a bar on Lemnos. Pyrrhus wasn't even precisely Philoctetes' type—if Philoctetes could be said to have a type any more, it had been so long. So many years of magazine love, boys on paper who had gradually merged into one generic impossibility.

Surely he didn't believe Pterelas's nonsense about Pyrrhus cruising him back; he wasn't even sure Pyrrhus was gay. Although perhaps no one visited Lemnos who wasn't at least curious. In the daytime at high season, when Port Street was clogged with straight couples from the cruise ships and their sticky infants in strollers, you could see it in the husbands' eyes. Wandering, speculative—they hadn't picked the only cruise in the brochure that stopped at Lemnos for nothing. Even the wives could sense it, would hold tightly to their husbands' arms, as if lashing them to the mast. No, if Pyrrhus had stopped off in Lemnos on his way home, he was probably at least open to a little experiment. Though most likely not with Philoctetes.

What had caught him, why had Philoctetes hurried home for a little friction and fantasy about this boy he had glimpsed for a few minutes and who had hardly said two words to him, just another one of the thousands of pretty boys who passed through Pterelas's bar every season? Why did he have the peculiar—and not entirely welcome—sense that he was being called back to life? A feeling that persisted even when he had finished and was glumly wiping himself off, alone in his dark shack.

2

The next evening, on board the *Penelope*, Pyrrhus found Admetus at his usual perch, on the forward hatchway, and said they'd better start down toward the launch. Admetus just shook his head and stayed where he was.

"What, aren't you coming?" Pyrrhus said.

"No, you best be on your own tonight. Somebody else'll pilot you in."

"How come?"

"So you can do your *job.*"

Perhaps Pyrrhus was only imagining that Admetus put some special emphasis on the word. He was a little stung. His job was necessary; what did Admetus know about necessity? Still, he heard himself nearly pleading: "Look, you can leave us alone if you have to. It's just, I'd feel better if you were at least . . . on the island, you know? You could catch a movie or something."

"What are you scared of?"

A good question; what could possibly happen that Pyrrhus couldn't handle? He would search out Philoctetes, they'd talk, another step or two on the way to—

To making the poor sucker fall in love with him. He hadn't really thought about, had more or less accepted, Odysseus's assumption that this had been his occupation, back in the capital. Making men fall in love. But of course it hadn't: men falling in love with him, or at least wanting him, had been the condition, the prerequisite for his work, but he had never done anything to bring it about. He had allowed men to love him; he had never induced it.

Really, never at all? Not the way he had dressed, or the attitudes he had struck when he had sensed that an attitude was desired? All right, he was practiced in making himself lovable. Men didn't just happen upon him in a state of nature and fall head over heels. Still, it was one thing to put forth your little generic flower of masculinity and wait for some bee to come suck it, and quite another to set your sights on one particular bee. What if Philoctetes—as Phoenix put it—had his preferences? If anything could be more discreditable than setting out on this mission, it would be failing at it.

No, that wasn't it, he wasn't afraid of failing; he was afraid of success. Usually if a guy was deluded enough actually to fall in love with Pyrrhus, that was his problem. Pyrrhus was no more responsible, just because of his profession, than if he hadn't been hustling, just living, and some fool had developed a crush on him. He wasn't responsible for the ludicrous stories people draped on the armature of his body.

Except this time he was going to tell the story himself. Not just mouth a few unmeant words on command, *tell me how much you like it.* He would have to spin forth an elaborate fiction about innocent Pyrrhus, who shared Philoctetes' grudge against the Greeks, who was captivated by Philoctetes, who was ready to go anywhere with him just as soon as he felt up to it.

Was it that he hated being cruel, already dreaded the moment when the fiction would be exploded, when the launch rounded Sidheritis and Philoctetes saw the *Penelope* and his heart broke? No. Maybe Pyrrhus had never hurt anyone with such cold deliberateness. But hey: that was war. No worse breaking Philoctetes' heart than running it through with a spear.

Perhaps he just wanted Admetus along for the same reason any warrior wants company. He was off to fight what was, in effect, the decisive skirmish of the war. And it is easier to do the ugly chores Ares sets for you if you have a comrade by your side. Together, you and your comrade are human, and the one whom you must kill or capture or enthrall is . . . something else. Harder, maybe, to think of him as something else when you face him alone.

Admetus was immovable, and Pyrrhus headed into town by himself.

Pyrrhus was perhaps unduly surprised to find Philoctetes exactly where they'd left him, in the most shaded corner of Pterelas's bar.

"Hey," Philoctetes said, with effortful exuberance. "Still in town. Where's your friend?"

Pyrrhus couldn't say, Back on the *Penelope.* He tried: "Looking for some pussy," though the words felt funny.

Pterelas overheard. "Boy, has he got the wrong island."

"I thought maybe you two were an item," Philoctetes said.

"Shit, no," Pyrrhus said. "He's straight."

"I thought so. I couldn't remember, but—"

"Not to mention old as the seas."

"And you?"

"Me? I'm twenty-one."

"No, I mean, are you straight?"

"Are you kidding?"

"Oh." Philoctetes shook his head. "I used to be able to tell. You know, the way some guy's eyes would meet mine. It's been so long since anybody looked at me that way."

"What are you talking about? I think you're hot."

"I think you lie like a Greek. But it's sweet to hear it." This last said rather dismissively, Pyrrhus thought, like: Save it for the rubes. "Hey, Pterelas, give this boy a drink on me."

"On me, you mean," Pterelas said. "Still drinking draft?"

Pyrrhus said, "Sure. Or . . . no." Not beer, as if he were a punk posing at the Club 23. Something more festive, sissier. "You know how to make a Kneebend?"

"You mean with cognac? And, what, melon liqueur?"

"Is that what it is? Yuck."

"I got something that'll get you bent," Pterelas said.

When he got Pterelas's concoction, with ice cream and some unknown spirit that made it mauve, Pyrrhus clutched the glass with two hands as if holding himself up by it. What now? Usually the trick kind of kept the conversation going. He pretended to look around the room, scanning the sparse midweek crowd. There was nothing to see, but he kept miming absorption, turning his head back and forth in a slow, fixed arc, like that of a table fan. The range of his oscillation never brought him face-to-face with Philoctetes, but he could see in his peripheral vision that Philoctetes wasn't looking at him, either. Just staring straight ahead, in the classic posture of the smitten but tongue-tied. Pyrrhus had learned that the best thing to do in this situation was wait; sooner or later the guy would come up with something to say.

Philoctetes did, finally. "Tell me about . . . what happened with Odysseus."

Great: Pyrrhus could recite his little story. "What's to tell? I mean, Dad died, they knew perfectly well he had a family, but they just said, 'Hey, we're a million miles from nowhere, let's just divvy everything up.' "

"Then they did."

"They did. Including even his clothes and stuff. Odysseus is sitting there with my father's armor, doesn't even fit him."

"You mean he wouldn't even let you have that?"

"He claims they had a contest or something and he won it. I mean, not that I need armor or anything. It's just kind of the principle."

"Uh-huh," Philoctetes said, flatly, as if uncertain what principle might be involved in desiring goods for which you had no use. "You know, I never got to Troy."

"No?" Pyrrhus said, as if he didn't know the story.

"No, I . . . only got this far. What's it like?"

Someone, during the little briefing Odysseus and Phoenix gave him before he set forth in the launch, someone ought to have anticipated this question. "Um . . . I, you know, didn't see very much. I just had this one meeting with Odysseus and it's . . . it's just a big sort of camp. Nothing was going on, just a lot of guys hanging around."

"You mean, there wasn't any fighting."

"No, I think they only do it once in a while." He returned to his grievance story. "Meanwhile they've got all the stuff. I mean, I guess I could sue, but—"

"Sue Odysseus? That'd be like me arm-wrestling with your father." Pyrrhus must have showed something, because Philoctetes said, "You don't like me mentioning your father."

"I don't care."

"No, I saw it last night."

Pyrrhus was annoyed, his usual annoyance at people who presumed to know him. "I hardly remember him. It doesn't matter. Anyway, what's your story? How come you never got to Troy?"

"I got sick."

"Yeah?"

"You don't want to hear this," Philoctetes said. Not the way people usually say that, wanting encouragement to go on, but with flat certainty.

"No, I do," Pyrrhus said. And he sort of did.

"Okay." Philoctetes looked down at the bar, cleared his throat, and, still not looking at Pyrrhus, began.

"We were on our way to Troy, and we stopped at this island, Chryse—just to refuel, and a few of us got off to stretch our legs. There wasn't much to see, just one of those little islands that barely seems to break free of the water, a few scraggly plants that blew in from somewhere, and more bugs than you could believe—I guess there wasn't anything there to eat them, except a few little grass snakes. I don't know what ate the snakes. Except the guys at the refueling station looked like they might have eaten snakes.

"Anyway, we wandered toward the center of the island, there was some

240

kind of shrine. To the goddess Chryse, the island was named for her or maybe vice versa."

"I've never heard of a goddess Chryse," Pyrrhus said.

"All she rules over is this little piece of rock, that's it. But the Atreid boys — you know, Agamemnon and his dumb brother — always insisted on stopping at every goddamn shrine on the way, no matter whose it was. As if they could line up minor deities on our side the way a candidate for something lines up votes. Promising every one of them something: I think Agamemnon must have mortgaged the treasury of Troy about five times over, and we weren't halfway there. So we had to go sacrifice to Chryse. She couldn't do anything for us, or to us; she doesn't even have friends in high places. She just has this rock.

"Agamemnon led the way to this temple, if you can call it that. It was really just a kind of hut, out of driftwood and whatever kind of sticks you could pick up on the island. Agamemnon had to crouch down to go inside, and nobody followed him: you could see there was nothing there, not a statue, not an altar. It was like seeing our whole stupid religion for what it was, without the priests and the statues and the unlucky livestock, just a pile of sticks with nothing inside. Agamemnon knelt; he was muttering something, making promises and begging favors from a patch of bare ground. The rest of us just stood around in various reverent postures, some looking up toward the sky, others down at their feet. I was looking up, half-expecting to see a skywriter come along and spell out WHAT A CROCK.

"Something bit me on the ankle, right through my sock. A snake, I guess, though the flies were just about as big. I barely noticed it. I mean, I went Ouch, which pissed Agamemnon off, breaking his solemn moment. But it didn't even hurt after a second or two. Just a little bite.

"Except it didn't heal. It's never healed — see?"

He raised his left leg, just a little. Pyrrhus had to lean way over to look. There, on Philoctetes' ankle, bare above his ratty sneakers, was a grimy little adhesive bandage; it looked as though he must have changed it about once a week. Philoctetes slowly peeled it back, just what you wanted somebody to do in a bar, and Pyrrhus saw:

A pair of tiny sores, like a dieresis: · · No bigger than pinpricks, each oozing the merest droplet of something yellow. So tiny, yet something baleful about them. Like the eyes of the snake itself, but sightless. Or like golden, delicate beads of poison.

"That's it," Philoctetes continued. "It's been just like that for ten years.

It's hard to believe something so little could hurt so much. After a couple days I went to the ship's surgeon. He looked at it and backed away, like you're doing—a surgeon. Of course he was a drunk—I think it's in their job description—and I could hardly make sense out of what he was saying."

Pyrrhus was about to say he'd met him, but caught himself.

"He said he couldn't do anything, he'd never seen anything like it before. People didn't usually ooze little yellow drops. Maybe I ought to keep it covered—who knew, it might be catching. Then he reached for some gauze and adhesive; I thought he was going to bandage it. But he just handed the stuff to me and staggered out of the sick bay, leaving me alone to dress my own wound. Maybe he went to tell everybody right away, or maybe it just slipped out of him during one of his monologues a day or two later. However it happened, pretty soon everybody on board knew that I had a mysterious wound that would not heal. And that it might be catching.

"You could see it in their faces, this kind of weird mix of terror and disgust, pity and contempt. People didn't visibly retreat from me, they just happened, so casually, to stroll over to the other end of the ward room, or if I stood by the starboard railing, they had something that needed tying down over on the port side. Or if someone found himself near me and couldn't think right away of any good reason to sneak off, he'd be balled up like a hedgehog. Maybe with a little tight smile on his face, like if he didn't offend me I wouldn't infect him."

Pyrrhus could picture it, it was so much like his own few days on the *Penelope*. But this was different, after all. Pyrrhus didn't have some kind of weird disease.

"No one asked me how I was doing, and I learned after a while not to bring it up myself, but there was nothing else to talk about. On my bad days I was my pain and on my good days I was so conscious that this was a good day and I mustn't waste it that I couldn't throw myself into anything. Not that there was anything to do; they'd pretty much taken all my jobs away from me. My job was just to be the guy with the wound.

"I wasn't, after all, the only guy on ship with a disabling injury. Guys fall, something backfires, you just cut yourself on KP: there were plenty of guys limping around with worse problems than mine. No one treated them like some kind of leper—just the opposite. People would bring them coffee, go out of their way to invite them to play poker or whatever, so they wouldn't mope. Even guys with really scary wounds—lost fingers, whatever, the kind of thing that makes you queasy to look at because you think of losing your own—people would swallow and make themselves deal with it. Crowds practically gathered around these guys. No one whispered about how they had somehow offended the gods: accidents happened, that was all.

"My wound, though, my tiny wound that people couldn't even see unless I rolled up my trousers—which I didn't do after the first day, and even then because guys were curious—my wound made me some kind of untouchable. Even before the doctor started spreading it around that it was a freak thing and maybe catching. Because of course it was a neon sign saying the gods were pissed at me for something. It didn't take any oracle to figure out just what it was.

"Here we had started to make our way, even in the navy most guys didn't think it was any big deal, and the gods had stamped me with this reminder notice. Which didn't just signal open season for intolerance, but brought back that feeling that was drummed into them when they were kids and that a few of them had just started to get over: that if you tolerated faggots you were one. That was the infection people were afraid of, not two little gold drops, but that if you treated me like a human being you had . . . a soft spot in you that was a beachhead of disease and had to be wiped out.

"They hated me so much, pretty soon I started to hate myself. All those years, out, in the city, we thought we had gotten over it. Even on the ship, before it happened, when—not very often; I was an officer, after all—I encountered some open bigot, I could still think, You fucking moronic cracker, and not feel that it had anything to do with me. But the way everybody treated me now—as if my wound literally gave off a bad smell, that's what some people said, can you believe it?—it all got to me. Not just because it was kind of unanimous. But because it seemed like such a gut thing. Like it wasn't something they all had to learn but just came up naturally from deep inside.

"Until I started to feel it. Feel it again, like they were waking up some part of me that I hadn't killed but just buried. I didn't believe at first that I had gotten the wound because I had—what was the word?—transgressed. But I started to believe it, that I must have, that all those years of freedom were one long crime, the whole great party one huge sin against the gods. Because deep inside we had felt it all along, half the fun of the party was shoving it in people's faces, breaking rules. Not just the stupid laws of the city, about what you could wear and where you could stick what, but any rule we could find. I swear, if we could have broken the law of gravity there would have been levitation parties. Now I was a million miles from the party, and it all seemed wrong and sick, else everyone wouldn't feel that way. I deserved my wound, every twinge I got I felt that.

"After a few weeks, Odysseus called me into his cabin. It was one of the bad days, and I was a little sick to my stomach. Even so, I couldn't help noticing how nicely done up his quarters were. He had this—stateroom, really, with the most spectacular burled wood paneling, a little built-in desk, and so on, all very deco, right off an ocean liner. I knew queens in the city who hadn't done their studios as lavishly as Odysseus had that cabin.

"While I was taking all that in, I didn't really think right away how remarkable it was that he had summoned me at all, that he was sitting in this perfect little fauteuil and gesturing for me to sit in its mate not three feet away. Now that I looked, I could see in his face—but just barely, he nearly hid it—the same expression everybody else had, the usual fear and disgust. But, you know, I'd gotten so used to seeing that, I almost thought that was just the way faces looked. And even though we were at such close quarters, our knees were almost touching, he didn't flinch. I was kind of grateful, it almost made me trust him. Maybe what everybody said about how sneaky he was was just bullshit. Or maybe I was just taken in by the decor. Here at last was a man of refinement.

"He said, 'You know, we're all real sorry about what's happened to you. I mean, it's a terrible thing. If we knew which god was . . . implicated, there isn't anything we wouldn't offer up to . . . ' He let his voice trail off. Maybe he could only say so much of this stuff with a straight face, or maybe he could tell I didn't believe it any more than he did, that I could be cured by killing a cow if we slit its throat on just the right altar.

" 'It would be great to have you back the way you were before,' he said. 'I think I speak for everybody on this ship when I say: Whatever caused this, nobody's blaming you. We all just want you to get better.' Maybe I was the one with the sour stomach, but I think it was neck and neck which one of us was going to throw up first.

"I said, 'I'm not sure you speak for everybody.'

"He kind of cocked his head to one side and leaned back in his chair and smiled a little and said, 'No, I'm afraid I don't.'

"You understand: if Odysseus had said, You are evil and disgusting and I am going to get you off my ship the way I'd lance a boil, I might have bowed my head and half-agreed. I was so far along, if he had acted from his gut I would have accepted it, in my gut. But no: whatever he felt, and I guess he felt the same things as everybody else—he probably has feelings, even Odysseus—he put the whole thing in terms of morale, the good of the mission. He threw in other stuff, like how I might get better care on shore; he even joked about what a quack the surgeon was.

"Anyway, his main point was—he came right out and said this—that it wasn't my fault, that the way everybody felt was crazy and he didn't share it. If it were up to him we'd all just go about our business. But he had to deal with it. People were silly in all kinds of ways, he said, and if you wanted to keep an army together sometimes you had to make them stop being silly, but other times you just had to go with the flow, it was more practical. This was one of those other times.

"I didn't answer. I just sat across from him, real calm, in our nice little matching armchairs, and felt like I was looking straight at death. I don't mean the oarsman, but whoever it is that sits back in his armchair and sends the oarsman out to pick up his fares. I thought he was just as cold as that.

"Like I say, I'd started to hate myself; if he'd said it was all my fault I would have believed him. Instead he was so reasonable . . . I thought, you sonofabitch, this whole fleet should dash up against some rocks and everybody on it drown, the whole fucking army should go under before you tell me that screwing me is the practical thing to do."

At that he banged his glass on the bar. Pterelas looked over, startled, but then relaxed and turned away again. As if he were used to it, as if Philoctetes always marked his peroration in just this way.

"The funny thing is, I think the bastard saved my life. I don't know if I should be grateful or not. The way I'd been going, I was just sinking, I was ready to die. But from that day on I've kept going almost just to spite him. Like I hardly have to eat, I can just live on my hatred for Odysseus."

He was done. He lit a cigarette, signaled to Pterelas to freshen his drink, and it was as though he had just finished telling some little bit of gossip, what happened at X's party or who Y was seeing now.

"How *have* you lived?" Pyrrhus said.

"Huh? Oh, odd jobs, when I'm well enough. You know, afternoon shift in a T-shirt shop, sometimes a little gardening, that kind of thing. And when I'm sick, people . . . help out."

"Are you sick a lot?"

245

Philoctetes shrugged. "Now and then. It's the way it always was, comes and goes. It just doesn't go as much as it used to." He was quiet a second. "As a matter of fact, I'm not feeling too hot right now. You think . . . you think you could walk me home?"

Was this some kind of feeble pickup? "Sure," Pyrrhus said.

A stranger, practically a stranger, corners you in a bar and makes you sit through a protracted account of the injustices and indignities he has suffered. Every detail is convincing: you know Odysseus is a shit, you know how all the straight boys on the *Penelope* treated you, you know that the stupid superstitions about this guy have persisted, ten years later, you know he probably isn't making one word of it up. There is just something about hearing such a story in a bar. It doesn't matter if it's true, you can't summon up any sympathy. Because the teller is a boring old drunk who retails his story in a bar.

Worse, it was borne in on Pyrrhus that Philoctetes was sick. How different he suddenly looked!

We've all grown used to this frisson. Someone murmurs, "Melitus has been diagnosed." You look across the room at Melitus, and he is transformed. As sometimes you'll meet somebody of indeterminate ethnicity — plainly not Greek but not stereotypically anything else. Then someone tells you his provenance, he's Egyptian or Phoenician, and immediately all his features reshape themselves into your standard model of that group. So with Melitus: suddenly his forearms are not sinewy but wasted; that blemish is not, after all, a pimple.

How different Philoctetes looked: no longer trim but frail, a frailty that was possibly catching. Not through any ordinary avenue of contagion. Rather — the men on shipboard had it right — through excessive empathy. If you thought, This, but that the gods smile on me, this could be me, then the natural corollary was that it *could* be you, any day; the gods could frown any time. The only prophylaxis Pyrrhus could practice was to assure himself that it couldn't be he. He and Philoctetes were made of different stuff. Philoctetes was weak and maybe corrupt in his very substance. Charming, too, and maybe good-looking once, but nothing at all like Pyrrhus.

He was quite over whatever scruples he had about making this sucker fall in love with him. They weren't, couldn't really be, on the same side. He would be able to do his job.

They were at the edge of town, headed inland, near the point at which the shoulder of the road stopped being sandy and you started seeing trees. It was palpably cooler here: the cold came as abruptly as when you step through a door from the hot street into an air-conditioned building. The noise of the town, music from the clubs and honking horns and rowdy tourists, dropped just as rapidly into a background hum, while the foreground was taken over by the frenzy of cicadas.

Philoctetes said, "It must be hard to have a famous father."

He was back to that. If any other trick had tried this twice—using his father like a crowbar to pry a way into Pyrrhus's insides—Pyrrhus might have gotten nasty. Instead he said, neutrally: "He was gone, you know? I mean, since I was ten or so. I hardly remember him."

"Ten, that's not so little, you'd think you'd remember."

"I guess. I just don't think of him much."

"Really. But you came all this way to claim his stuff."

"Like I say, it was worth a lot."

"Oh. Well, that's a sight more than I got from my father. I don't think of him at all."

"Who was he?"

"Nobody. Poeas. He was an Argonaut, but I guess he didn't get any of the loot. Just came home and some nights, when he'd had a few, pulled out the roster and said, 'Look, I was on the *Argo*, there's my name.' I'd go 'Uh-huh' and pray he wasn't going to bring out the damn pictures. Dragons and things, used to give me nightmares."

They walked for a while without talking. It was uphill, they were approaching the center of the island; Philoctetes was breathing heavily. There weren't any houses or lights around. Pyrrhus hadn't noticed how far they'd come: his eyes, which had become city eyes, had already reacquainted themselves with the dark, like the dark of Scyros. He turned around. The little glow of the town, not a mile away, was an impotent arc at the base of a black sky filled with stars that never shone on the city.

When he turned back Philoctetes was looking at him. The way some guys at the Escapade would—not leering or about to grab him, but sadly, half-reproachfully, as a drunk will sometimes look at his glass on the bar. As if he were something they had meant to give up and couldn't. Philoctetes said, "You haven't told me anything about yourself."

The absolute worst line you could hear from a trick. Or at least right up there with 'Here, would you mind putting these on?' Pyrrhus had never known what sort of recitation was called for. My favorite color's blue, and I was born under this constellation, and . . .

"I mean, are you still living in Phthia, or—"

"I—" Admetus might have thought it was clever to pose him as Philoctetes' neighbor, but he wouldn't be able to sustain any long discussion of life in Thessaly. "I'm not actually from Phthia."

"No? I thought . . ."

Pyrrhus told him in as few words as possible the basic facts: his father's concealment and departure, his own life as the heir apparent on Scyros. He wound up, hoping to stop there: "Then I went to the city."

"Of course you did, as fast as your little fairy wings would carry you. And in the city you . . ."

"Waited on tables."

"Of course. But you also . . ."

"Also?" How could he know about Pyrrhus's also?

"No one just waits on tables. Did you model, or take singing lessons, or . . . ?"

Pyrrhus actually thought for a moment of saying, "I hustled." He knew it was a risk, knew that Philoctetes might conclude he himself was being hustled. The flip side, though, was that people like to get for free something other poor fools have to pay for. Nothing is more flattering than being courted by a hustler. Besides, Pyrrhus wouldn't have to make up some other occupation. Which, after a couple of Pterelas's ice cream drinks, he might not remember the next time they met.

But he felt—not ashamed of it, exactly; even Odysseus hadn't been able to make him ashamed of it—just that it was one fact too many. More than this stranger was entitled to. "No, I just waited. And dated a little."

"Ah. Waited and dated. Anybody special?"

"Naw. How about you?"

"What?"

"Do you have a lover?"

Philoctetes laughed, not heartily, not from his stomach, but from the back of his throat: willfully, the way you laugh when you are persuaded that you ought to find something humorous, your politics or your philosophy require that it be funny. You laugh, dry-eyed, and the very act of doing it—forcing that laugh from the back of your throat—can almost make you want to cough or gag or both.

Both in Philoctetes' case. Soon he was doubled over, the deep racking coughs coming from much deeper inside than the laughter had; now on his knees, convulsing as though he were about to give birth to something inside him; at last vomiting. The vomit—Pyrrhus could not turn away— flecked with blood. When he had finished he went on kneeling, breathing in gasps still punctuated with fainter coughs, face turned to the sky, in his eyes a mixture of terror and supplication: What are you doing to me, Chryse or whoever? Why can't you stop?

If at such a time you stand by, overrule any impulse—in Pyrrhus's case a dim and half-hearted one, easily mastered—to kneel down with the afflicted and hold him: if you stand apart, because you don't want to get drawn in, or because you are afraid of contagion, then you can slide quite easily from pity to contempt. The counsel for the defense that we have on constant retainer promptly enters his plea: Philoctetes isn't really sick, he's milking it, what an annoying display, why doesn't he just pull himself together. You know the feeling, we've all got very good at it now that the streets are overrun with panhandlers and we have lost even the flicker of a suspicion that one of them might be a god in disguise.

Pyrrhus just stood there, disgusted and a little angry, as if Philoctetes' coughing up his insides were a social blunder. He did not kneel and put his arms around Philoctetes. And this withholding of the most elementary human comfort made Pyrrhus feel, perhaps paradoxically, that Philoctetes, and not he, was less than human. Perhaps he had, there by the side of a road in the glowing dark, a vision of the world as it must have looked to Odysseus, a world where there was only one moving spirit and everything else was simply useful or useless.

Philoctetes stopped coughing but went on kneeling. Taking shallow breaths, so as not to set himself off again, at last looking over at Pyrrhus. Abashed, as if he, too, felt that his paroxysms were a breach of etiquette. Pyrrhus swallowed his disgust and helped Philoctetes up.

When they were able to move on, they walked in silence for a few minutes. Pyrrhus kept waiting for Philoctetes to initiate some new sub- ject—the older man's job. Maybe he was too winded. Pyrrhus would have to come up with something, and all he could think was that they'd better get to the main topic before they'd made it all the way to Philoctetes' house. He hazarded: "What we were talking about, last night. You think you might want to go home?"

"I'm sorry?" Philoctetes said, looking at him as if he were daft. "We're almost there."

"No, I—I mean, back to your country."

"Oh. That . . ." He frowned. "I don't think that's my country any more."

This was very bad news. "Uh-huh," Pyrrhus said. "You mean you feel at home here, on Lemnos?"

"I'm not sure. I mean—" Philoctetes stopped walking, turned around, as if to look back at the village and ascertain whether it was home. But they had crossed the hill and started the descent, Pyrrhus hadn't even noticed, they couldn't see the village any more. "I mean my illness is my country." He said this as plainly as one might say: I'm from Thessaly.

Pyrrhus wasn't just mystified, though he was that; he was also angry. Partly because he had expected everything to be so simple, and was frustrated by this dictum he couldn't understand. And partly because it sounded monstrously self-absorbed. Or self-pitying. As Pyrrhus didn't pity Philoctetes, he had no right to pity himself.

He must have seen something of what Pyrrhus was feeling. "I'm sorry, I didn't mean to sound so grand. I just mean, if you have to . . . some days I have to think about every breath, my inside becomes, like, my whole landscape. It wouldn't matter if I was here or Thessaly or . . . wherever."

"I understand," Pyrrhus said.

Philoctetes smiled. "You *are* a hustler, aren't you?"

"What?"

"I mean, you'll just agree with anything."

"Oh. Okay, I don't understand."

"Well, you shouldn't. I'm a little drunk, I guess, I'm not making much sense. Let's go on, we're almost there."

They seemed to be nowhere. The road was a forgotten intention largely surrendered to the sand; the landscape ahead was dunes and dune grass and—Pyrrhus could make it out now—some kind of shack, some distance from the road, on an elevation that must have been a little more permanent than a dune.

"You live there?"

"Yep. Nice, huh?"

"Did you build it, or—"

"Me? I may be butch, but . . . Some writer had it built. He was going to sit out here in grand isolation and write dialogue for the gods. But he kept getting lonely—and thirsty—and sneaking back into town. Until one day he said the hell with it and moved into town for good. This was years ago; he just abandoned it pretty much, and one night when he was pretty bombed he offered it to me. For nothing."

250

"It's . . . it's far for you, isn't it? I mean, with your . . ."

"It is, but the rent is right. And it's—for a shack not too bad. I actually have running water, heaven knows how far they must have had to drill."

"Electricity?"

"There's a little generator, but I can't afford to keep it going. It doesn't matter much. By the time I get home most evenings I'm ready for the sack. It would be nice to have a phonograph. Well, it would be nice to have a record."

They were at the place now, at the foot of a couple of steps that led to a screen door with no real door beyond it: nothing to steal. Philoctetes turned and said, quite formally: "This was awfully kind of you. Do you think you can find your way back?"

"Uh-huh." Pyrrhus didn't know what to do. Philoctetes probably wasn't expecting anything. The way he stood, hands in his pockets, seemed instead meant to ward Pyrrhus off. But Pyrrhus was in a hurry, wanting to move things along. If he did nothing, just headed back down the road, who could say when he'd get another chance? He swallowed, stepped forward, grabbed Philoctetes, and went to kiss him on the lips.

Philoctetes turned his face away and jumped back; he caught his foot on the first stair and fell, like sitting hard, on the step above that. He looked up at Pyrrhus with—Pyrrhus thought outrage for a second, but it was astonishment. He really hadn't expected it, maybe not ever again. Then he started coughing. Not the way he had on the road, turning himself inside out, but tiny rhythmic coughs that he tried at first to suppress— even managing a little apologetic smile—but that wouldn't stop, that came faster now, until he turned his head a little and Pyrrhus saw by the starlight the tears in his eyes and understood that he wasn't coughing any more, or rather that he was coughing and also sobbing.

Pyrrhus ran away, literally ran, on that winding, sand-obliterated road that snaked so gently he hardly realized that he was climbing the hill to the center of the island.

He should have moved in for the kill, he knew it. Right then, when Philoctetes was too surprised to resist. If he had ever fucking stopped coughing. Pyrrhus should have waited till the fit was over and then dragged him to whatever kind of pallet he must have slept on in that miserable little shack.

But for the tears, Pyrrhus could have done it except for the tears.

He used to be able to handle tears. Sometimes a trick would cry, or make himself cry. With a trick, if he got too heavy, well, you just had to cut him loose. Just shake him and remind him what kind of transaction it had been — as at the end of a tragedy the lights go down for a second and then come back up and the actors are smiling (though with dignified restraint) and bowing, even the corpse is standing up and almost smirking at you, What a chump, you thought I was dead. That's what lets you walk out of the theater and into the world where none of those things ever happened. When a trick got too heavy, you took the lights down and brought them back up again, and unless the guy was just crazy he found his way back into the world. And didn't call again, or if he did he knew what he was paying for.

That's how you handled tears. Except he hadn't been able to do it with Corythus. As for Philoctetes: of course Pyrrhus couldn't turn up the lights until he had Philoctetes on the ship. It was as if the tragedians had to stay in character as they left the theater, called a taxi, went out for drinks or home to bed. Pyrrhus was used to performances that ended, rapidly and conclusively, with somebody's ejaculation. Now he had signed on for a longer engagement.

He still didn't notice he was climbing, not till he got to the summit of the hill. He could look down one way at the village, almost dark, even the bars shutting up for the night, and back the other way at the wasteland in which, somewhere, was Philoctetes' shack, he couldn't make it out any more, and Philoctetes himself, maybe still coughing and sobbing. Pyrrhus was out of breath, hadn't realized how winded he was getting. The smoking, maybe — twenty-one and he couldn't even get up a hill.

He sat down right in the road, there at the crest of the hill, thinking about nothing but filling his lungs with air. He could suddenly see how, when that was all that mattered, everything else fell away, and you became a country of your own.

After a while, he made his way back down to the village, to the commercial pier. There was the launch, and the sailor who piloted it, substituting for Admetus. Dressed in civilian clothes so as not to draw attention, but of course he still looked like a sailor. The poor guy was asleep; Pyrrhus had to shake him awake. The guy opened his eyes and looked alarmed — not just the usual startle of waking up, but almost panicky, that he had awakened to find Pyrrhus touching him.

Pyrrhus hadn't recognized him before: the guy who wouldn't get in the shower. Pyrrhus drew back; the sailor recovered and started the outboard without a word. He didn't look at Pyrrhus once in their circuit around the island Pyrrhus had just traversed. It seemed to take so much longer, going around it.

Philoctetes sat on his steps and murmured, "My illness is my country." Pretty fancy, where did that come from? And what had been his country before? Not Greece. His homeland, the one from which he had been exiled, wasn't Greece.

Just a few weeks before Pyrrhus's arrival—or visitation, it almost seemed—another kid had sat down at Philoctetes' end of the bar, the shadowy tip of the left leg of the U. Halesus, or maybe Haliscus, Philoctetes couldn't remember.

Halesus was, needless to say, from out of town; no islander willingly sailed into Philoctetes' domain. Anyway, Philoctetes hadn't seen him before. No one so cute could have been in town twenty-four hours without Philoctetes' detecting him; Philoctetes might have lost his energy, but he hadn't gone blind.

Halesus wasn't in Pyrrhus's class, of course, and even less Philoctetes' type. Dark and—not fat, but broad in the hips, and his buns a little shapeless. If Philoctetes was turned on, he supposed it was chiefly by Halesus's eagerness: he was so pleased to be in Lemnos, this was all new to him, and he was thrilled to meet a year-rounder. Philoctetes would point out this queen or that one and tell his story, and Halesus would laugh and tell him about someone similar at home. They chattered away and Philoctetes was taken in, caught up by the kid's general openness to, interest in, life: Philoctetes even thought for a minute Halesus's interest extended to him. He couldn't see at once that Halesus was mostly gratified to have found a seat, and would have had just as lively a talk with any desiccated body that happened to occupy the neighboring stool.

He was only passing the time until his lover came in. Philoctetes saw the guy first, saw him come through the door and scan the room, and Philoctetes knew right away. Dressed not exactly like Halesus but similarly, roughly as cute as Halesus and about the same age, and clearly hunting for someone in particular: not just checking off the faces in the room, possible/impossible, but rejecting every one until his eyes settled on Philoctetes' neighbor. Philoctetes realized, the moment the guy came in, that he had expected it somehow, some part of him had known. It was almost as if the lover had appeared *because* Philoctetes had allowed himself, however briefly, to imagine there was something possible for him. He recognized the lover the way you might acknowledge a dismal fact about yourself.

Halesus introduced his friend; the guy smiled politely; then the two of them talked lovers' business—where were you, where shall we have dinner, I don't want to stay out too late, how about if we rent bikes tomorrow, and where shall we ride to? Halesus now and then including Philoctetes, as a native informant, but the couple closed together, not having to touch, their gravitational fields interlocking.

Actually Halesus's friend was, to Philoctetes' taste, the more attractive. Solemn and not quite so fussily groomed, his lips barely parted when in repose, his eyes dark and wise. Yes, the more Philoctetes looked, he quite eclipsed Halesus. Of course Philoctetes didn't look hard or often, afraid of being caught at it. Maybe he even overcompensated; the friend must have thought Philoctetes was ignoring him. And once, when their eyes met, the boy's glance seemed cold and half-accusing. As if he knew what Philoctetes had been thinking about Halesus before he came in. Or perhaps because this happened often—the less gregarious boyfriend often walking into a room and finding Halesus engaged with some stranger; perhaps he had reason to be watchful. After a little while Philoctetes disengaged and they turned in on each other, shutting Philoctetes out entirely.

Philoctetes didn't look at them any more, but he felt them next to him. A wan exuberance lit his heart. It felt right; they looked good together, better than either would have looked with Philoctetes. He blessed them, he hoped everything for them, and he even felt the first tiny surges of what might once, when he had more blood to spare, have become a hard-on. He yielded to the feeling: while imagining himself and anybody else only led to pain, imagining Halesus and his friend together seemed harmless enough. Philoctetes saw them naked, pictured one on top and then the other, but not at all sure, really—Halesus was a little larger, his friend a smidgen more butch, but Philoctetes wasn't sure.

Philoctetes was practically horny, or the closest he'd come in years, and real waves of happiness and excitement washing over him, one of those moments he hadn't had in so long, when he seemed at home in the world. What was it about this couple that pleased him so? That they were so natural together, what went on between them was right to its core, they had found each other and come together in defiance of everything that wanted to sunder them. It didn't even matter how long they lasted; they had come together. Philoctetes' mounting excitement was the thrill of the patriot; they were the legions of the only nation to which he would ever belong, and he saluted them, his short arm at attention.

Philoctetes had thought, when Pyrrhus just stood there and watched him heaving, not so much as saying "Oh dear," Philoctetes had thought he was disgusted. And then, astonishing, Pyrrhus had turned around and kissed him. Or tried. Oh, there had to be some god involved, to have racked him at that instant. One of the gods must have torn himself away from their endless revels and hurled the dart that left Philoctetes coughing and sputtering when he might have had a kiss. When the boy was on the very verge of sailing him home. Maybe he would come again. . . .

Philoctetes stood up, turned to go inside, and at that instant—perhaps just because the booze was wearing off—felt the pain in his ankle, not the abiding ache but a bite so sharp it threw him off the steps and onto the sand that was his dooryard.

Oh god, whichever one you are, how ever have I offended you? That I can't even, for one instant, dream of my homeland?

3

"You just left him there?" Admetus said. Not reproachfully, but as if incredulous.

Pyrrhus almost whined. "He seemed a little better, I didn't know what to do."

They were sitting side by side on Admetus's usual hatchway, near the bow. Admetus looked forward at the sea, not at Pyrrhus, as he said, "Well, you're the pro. I can't tell you."

Pyrrhus wasn't stung by this, as before. Admetus was just matter-of-fact; Pyrrhus was the pro. "This hasn't exactly been my line of work," Pyrrhus said.

"No?" Admetus said. Not interested, but willing to hear the next thing. As if he still hoped, but didn't believe, that he might after a century hear something new. He reached in his shirt pocket and got his cigarette papers and tobacco.

"You know, what I kind of feel like is — maybe one of those guys who plays up to rich widows? And then takes them for everything they got?"

"Uh-huh." Admetus shrugged. "Philoctetes ain't some widow with money and no brains. Just the opposite, kinda."

"You think he's going to see through me."

"Oh, that, I don't know." He lit his cigarette and then held it before him, not smoking it but as if reading something in its glowing end. "He'll see through you if he wants to, and he won't if he don't. Maybe the widows are the same way. But it ain't — if he don't want to, then he don't, it ain't your fault."

"So I shouldn't feel guilty."

Admetus shrugged. "Who knows? I feel guilty every day. In the morning, I wake up and I see the world and I feel guilty 'cause I know why I'm seeing it. But I get over it; by the afternoon I'm glad to sit out here in the sun.

"You know, sometimes you meet a guy whose mother died having him. That don't happen so much any more, but it used to. And you'd think he'd feel a little guilty, wouldn't you? Even though it ain't his fault, you'd think he'd worry about it some. But they don't, it's just the opposite. The guy grows up with this dead stranger everywhere, her picture all over the house, maybe the bedroom where she died kept just like it was. His father never mentions it, how the kid murdered this saintly broad on his way into the world, never talks about her at all. Until it seems like that's all they talk about. Any time they're quiet, all those times a father and son got nothing to say, it's like her name just hangs there.

"Then the kid, if it ain't just going to sink him, the kid has to just claw his way through to a life free of her, the same way he forced his way through while she was dying right around him. Well, we all got to do that, don't we, even if our mothers are still hanging around. You got to thank her nicely for all the shit she went through having you and raising you, just say thank-you-ma'am and get on with it. Because you don't ask to be born—you don't even get a vote."

This was probably the most Admetus had said in some decades. Pyrrhus didn't want to interrupt. Didn't utter, not out loud, the obvious rejoinder: You asked for life. Admetus seemed to have heard him, nonetheless, and replied. "Yeah, and if you had a vote you would've come in anyhow. Gangway, I'm comin' through. And don't you think Philoctetes wouldn't step right on your face if it would bring him back to life."

"Then I should step on him first, huh?"

"That's right," Admetus said, but half mumbling, as if he didn't mean any of it, was just saying all of it to make Pyrrhus feel better. Or himself; maybe this was a sermon he preached to himself every day so he could get out of bed. Or maybe he just wasn't sure, maybe a century hadn't settled the question for him.

Because you could see all around you the evidence that what he was saying was right, that people with superfluous scruples were just voting against their own lives. There was no life at all unless you were like a tree, sightless, willing to break the sidewalk and anything else that came between it and the sun. While you could see this everywhere and you knew it was true, a law of nature, there was a part of you that wanted to be the real outlaw and call a truce; the most subversive and unnatural thing you could do was to break that law and call a truce. But that would be like giving up. Wanting to spare Philoctetes: that was just like wanting to die.

"Are you going to take me in today?" Pyrrhus said.

"I'll run the launch. I ain't gonna hang out with you."

"For a little while, then you can split. I don't know, I—I'm still scared about meeting him alone."

.   .   .

258

They got to the bar around five. Pterelas was just getting ready for the après-beach crowd. He scarcely looked up as he sliced lemons with an ostentatious deftness. "He hasn't been in. Usually he's here by now. I don't know, maybe he's having one of his spells."

"You think he might be home?" Pyrrhus said.

"If he's not here. Nobody else will serve him." He looked up and said, with no apparent interest, "Where you guys staying?"

Pyrrhus remembered the name of a guesthouse they'd passed. "The Seaview."

"Oh yeah? That's a nice place."

"It's okay."

"It's a wonder you got a room, just passing through. Usually they're booked way ahead."

"Just lucky," Pyrrhus said. "They had a cancellation."

"Uh-huh. And they must have just changed their policy, I hadn't heard. About women only."

Serves me right, Pyrrhus thought. Admetus rescued him again. "Kid's too embarrassed to say we're just camping out on the beach. We ain't got a whole lot of scratch."

"I figured. You're probably okay, it's not full season yet; nobody cares much. In season, the cops'd be on your ass before the sun went down."

"We'll watch out," Admetus said.

"You gonna have a drink?"

"Nah, better not. We might go check up on Philoctetes. See how he's doing."

"You guys are awful interested in Philoctetes."

"We was in the war together, him and me, way back when."

"Yeah, he said."

"How long have you known him?" Pyrrhus put in.

"Since he got here," Pterelas said. "Of course I'd seen him, back in the city, but I never met him. Not till he got here."

Pyrrhus said, " 'Of course' you'd seen him?"

"Everybody knew Philoctetes. In the city . . . he was kind of a legend."

"Yeah? How come?"

"He—I can't explain it. He just was. I mean, up there with the guy in the cigarette ads. Not because he was so hot. He was; maybe you can't see that now. But he had something else, like . . . never mind." He waited on some customers and seemed to have forgotten Admetus and Pyrrhus.

But as they turned to go he said, "Let me know if you see him. If he's okay."

They could hear him — over the stirring of the dune grass in the breeze, hear through the screen door his stertorous breathing. They sat outside his shanty, Admetus on the little stoop, Pyrrhus on a log half buried in the sand. Pyrrhus felt like a little kid, sitting outside his parents' room in the morning, waiting for Mommy and Daddy to wake up. Listening to Daddy's snore, which was intimidating and at the same time somehow reassuring. As the snore of a monster in its cave tells you that a monster is present but at least it's asleep.

Far away, at the water's edge, a woman the size of a small bus was throwing a stick for her dog to fetch. She couldn't throw it far, not twenty feet, and the dog overshot it every time, sprinted past it and then had to turn around, hunt for it, bring it back to his mistress with a thwarted but still expectant air. The woman had to stop and catch her breath, each time, before rising to the great exertion of tossing the stick. The spectacle had the rhythm of a baseball game, long stretches of inactivity interrupted at intervals by a burst of pointless energy. Pyrrhus caught the rhythm, slowed down with it. When Admetus stood up, opened the screen door, and went inside, letting the door slap behind him, it was like a whirlwind culminating in an explosion. Only to Pyrrhus: Philoctetes' breathing didn't change. In a minute, Admetus was back outside. "I think he wet the bed," he said. Then he sat on the log with Pyrrhus.

The woman and the dog seemed to tire of their game simultaneously. Pyrrhus watched them shuffle along the beach toward home. The poor woman sinking into the sand so far with each step that she had to lift her legs as high as if she were walking through snow.

Philoctetes' breathing grew quieter and more regular, though they could still hear it if they strained. Pyrrhus went on watching the woman and the dog, advancing so slowly toward the setting sun they might have been on a treadmill; with what patience the dog adjusted his pace to hers.

"It's getting cool," Admetus said. "You shouldn't let him just lay there."

Pyrrhus nodded, but then didn't move.

After a while, Admetus snorted, "You don't want to touch him."

"I guess," Pyrrhus said. He shook his head. "The pro." He stood up and peered through the door.

At last Admetus dragged himself to his feet, went to the door, and pushed past Pyrrhus. Pyrrhus heard the bedsprings creak, then Philoctetes' protesting groan. Admetus said, "I just want to . . . freshen the bed a mite. Here, I'm going to lift you up, easy—"

"No, you mustn't!" Philoctetes shrieked.

"I ain't gonna hurt you. Here we go now, stop fighting me."

"You mustn't touch me." Then, almost whispering, Pyrrhus could scarcely hear it: "I don't know if you should touch me."

"I ain't worried. Here, you just lie still on the floor a second. You got any clean sheets, when's the last time you changed these?"

"I don't know. I . . . you think you could just dry me off a little?"

"Sure, I was gonna."

"You're a brave man."

"I don't get sick easy," Admetus said.

They were quiet. Evidently Admetus was changing the sheets. How could he—after his lecture about stepping on faces—how could he be so good to Philoctetes? Or to Pyrrhus, for that matter? Well, after all, he didn't have to claw for life; he just had to get through it.

At last Philoctetes said, almost inaudibly, "You're that one."

"Which one?"

"The one who can't die. Won't."

"Can't. Yeah, I'm the one."

"I used to hear about you."

"All right, up we go."

"Let me stand, I think I can."

"Okay. No, now let me help."

The bedsprings creaked again. Philoctetes said, "You're that one. I ought to hate you."

"Can't blame you."

"I don't. I mean, thanks. But . . . you'll never know how it feels. To be dying."

"I did once. I was going to die once."

"I remember, yeah. I remember the story now."

"And since I can't—that's what I wanted, I can't complain—but I ain't never felt alive. Not half as much as you are." There was a silence, then Admetus said, "Are you dying, d'you think?"

"Beats me. It comes, it goes. I think maybe each time, when I get better, I'm not quite so . . . better as the last time. I don't know, maybe I'm not dying any faster than anybody else."

He was, of course; we all know that now. Anyone today could look at him and see that we were in the last volume of his multivolume Life. But how could he have known? We forget this, sometimes, about Philoctetes and the other early ones. They knew they were awfully sick, but they didn't know just how fast the sand was falling through the glass.

Admetus came outdoors. "You need to go in there," he said.

"I know. This job is a little tougher than I thought."

"You don't need to go in because of the damn job."

Pyrrhus went in. Philoctetes was propped up on a couple of pillows, a fresh glass of water next to him on his orange-crate nightstand, the hygienic picture of a patient. From a long time ago, when the sick in bed were merely themselves, being sick, instead of pincushions. Against the white sheets his brown body looked startlingly healthy, giving Pyrrhus the illusion he had had when he first saw Philoctetes, that he was at some sort of apex and not the midpoint on a downward slide.

What must he have looked like before? Not flabby, probably; he probably worked out. Yet without *definition*, that chimera of the gym, where every muscle dwells in autonomous isolation and vessels blazon themselves across the thighs, the forearms, the lower abdomen, with anatomy-book candor. That's what Philoctetes had now, for a moment: definition, what we all have beneath the layers of skin and fascia that can be peeled away on the dissecting table.

He looked at Pyrrhus with mild interest. He didn't need anything else done just now; Admetus had done everything. Pyrrhus took his hand, cooler than Pyrrhus had expected, and horny like a workman's. Philoctetes let his hand be held, but didn't tighten it around Pyrrhus's.

"I'm sorry," Pyrrhus said. "I was scared."

"I don't know that you shouldn't be," he said. "Unless you're Admetus." Philoctetes took a sip of his drink, then said, rather lightly, "It's hard to think of yourself as something it requires bravery to approach. Like a sphinx or a hydra. I should be guarding some treasure."

This made Pyrrhus think of the bow, and he looked around the shack. It wasn't in evidence. Maybe that little curtained alcove, or the dresser? He had no idea how big it was.

Philoctetes didn't know what Pyrrhus was looking for. He smiled, "Yeah, some treasure. Of course, I didn't have much more than this back in the city. What did I need? A bed, my records, a few . . . toys."

"Fast life, huh?"

"I guess that's what people would call it. But it wasn't like, run here,

262

run there. You just did the next thing. You'd take four hours to dress for a party, and then you might not even get there." He leaned forward. "This is the fast life: I'm on edge all the time. As if I were racing toward something, or being chased, whichever, running anyway. Every day for ten years. Leaves you kind of fagged."

"I see."

"It must seem awful slow to you, hanging around with someone in a sickbed." Pyrrhus shrugged. "It's sweet of you, you and Admetus. I don't know why you bother."

He looked at Pyrrhus, not suspiciously, but with full attention: he wanted an answer.

Philoctetes looked at Pyrrhus as closely as Odysseus had. But it was a different sort of attention: when Odysseus pinned you in his heavy-lidded gaze, you felt as though he'd caught you picking your nose. Philoctetes looked as though he thought you might be about to do something wonderful.

"I—" It was time and, yes, Pyrrhus could say it. "I kind of have a crush on you."

Philoctetes closed his eyes, as if shutting out unwelcome news. Was he thinking that Pyrrhus was a fool, or that Pyrrhus was making a fool out of him? Then, eyes still closed, he squeezed Pyrrhus's hand.

Funny: Pyrrhus did, now that he looked down at the brown, cruelly definite body, have some kind of crush, or at least could imagine how people once did. What Pterelas had tried to say in the bar, and couldn't. If he wasn't the man in the cigarette ads, he had a sort of country charm — he must have been a kind of obbligato, a running bass under the shriek of the world he once dwelt in; it must have calmed down a room a little just when he walked into it. His slow smile and his perfect attentiveness, the calm eyes just looking at you, the honest, homely, almost rugged face before it was shaved to nothing: all of this must have promised, as he stood pulling on his beer at the edges of the frenzied half-naked mob on the dance floor, some sort of bucolic refuge. Long, slow hours of — not even lovemaking, but just stretching out together, such as might have soothed even the most ravenous queen. With him maybe you could just shut up.

Yes, Pyrrhus was attracted to him. That is the word, neutral, factual. Attracted, as perhaps iron filings might be attracted to a magnet that is too far away actually to pull them in; they would feel a distant arousal but stay where they were. It was, anyway, almost irrelevant. If a trick was truly repulsive, that was a problem. Otherwise, attraction was just something you were aware of. As a champion swimmer might note the temperature of the water but must plunge in regardless.

Pyrrhus had been sitting on the edge of the bed as they spoke. Philoctetes was still squeezing his hand. How should he proceed? The guy was sick, he couldn't do anything much. Better not to push too far, wait until his strength came back. If it ever did.

"I better go," Pyrrhus said.

Philoctetes let go of his hand. "Yeah. Admetus must be wondering what's keeping you."

"Oh, I think he has an idea what's keeping me."

Philoctetes smiled. "Holding hands. Pretty scandalous."

"It's the most excitement I've had in a while."

"You? Give me a break."

"No, I . . . I haven't really been out that long." Pyrrhus stood up. "Maybe I'll see you tomorrow night?"

"You know where to find me," Philoctetes said.

Sorry, at once, that he had said, "You know where to find me." As if underlining that he was an old, sick drunk who could be found in the same place every night, as if chained there. Yes: bound to his barstool like Prometheus to his rock, his liver ravaged not by an eagle but by Pterelas's overgenerous vodka-and-tonics. Well, one awkward remark wouldn't turn the boy away. Or would it? What was happening was so improbable, maybe the merest slip could kill it. Philoctetes could attest to the consequences of the tiniest missteps.

Still, it was happening, after the long drought: this twig of a divinity, so fresh that holding hands was a hot time, was falling for old Philoctetes. He looked down at himself, his brown body on the sheets. The body that had been for so long just a wasteland where pain waited to ambush him. He remembered the old days: dressing for a party, the preparatory pharmaceuticals washing over him. Looking in the antique cheval glass that had been the only real furniture in his bedroom, towering over the mattress and the—as he would joke—toy chest by its side. He remembered when he would look at his body in the full-length mirror and see: a gift to men. Not with narcissistic self-regard, just with joy that he had it to give, that it was built, every contour and concavity, for pleasure. How long since he had seen his body that way. But this boy saw it, saw right through the wasting and the drink and the self-pity. As if ten years were just a raggedy garment Philoctetes could now cast away, bringing to light again the naked gift that the hero of love once bestowed so freely on an enchanted city.

In the launch, Admetus said, "What went on in there?"

Pyrrhus was startled. He had been looking at the water, or rather his eyes had been turned toward the water but he had been seeing Philoctetes, the brown body against the sheet, wondering what it must have been like before. When he had been, as Pterelas said, a legend.

"What?"

Admetus blushed, a childish pink under his centenarian stubble. "I don't mean I wanted a blow-by-blow. Just, you was in there a long time."

"Nothing happened. We held hands."

"Ah."

"I know what I'm doing," Pyrrhus said, though he didn't.

"I'm sure."

Corythus was asleep in Pyrrhus's cabin, on his back and snoring cheerfully. Pyrrhus stayed at the door and looked at him for a minute; the square of light from the passageway framed his red arms and face, his pale chest, paler yet the belly still lightly ringed with baby fat. Not, objectively, as aesthetically pleasing a figure as Philoctetes, so hard and uniformly dark, as if he had leapt off a painted vase. Just young, young and healthy and — stirring awake now with the light, opening his eyes, grinning — ready. For something more than holding hands.

The next night, and the next, Pyrrhus would walk into Pterelas's and there Philoctetes would be, looking into his vodka and tonic as if reading something in the ice cubes. Funny, no matter how crowded it was, there was always a seat next to him.

Pyrrhus would take his seat. Philoctetes would go "Hey," as if they'd been barmates forever. He'd look up from his drink, only glancing at Pyrrhus, then look around the room, a little startled, as if he hadn't noticed there was anyone there. "What did you do all day?" he'd say, and Pyrrhus would answer, "Just goofed around," and they would look together at the crowd.

Some of whom would look back, wondering what kind of couple they might be, the gaunt but still handsome older man, the godlike youth. Not saying anything, so you knew they were an old married couple. Perhaps not so mismatched that you'd assume money was being exchanged, but far enough apart that some currency other than passion had to be involved. A little help with the career, travel, parties, the theater—the older guy looked a little scruffy, but he must have been taking the boy places he couldn't have got to on his own. Or maybe this was true only figuratively; maybe he could take the boy great distances in bed. Yes, you could almost see what kind of lover the older man had to be: composed, lingering, ruthless. If the boy looked sort of vacant, it had to be because he was thinking of nothing but the imminence of bed.

Pterelas would make Pyrrhus some sort of ice-cream drink. Pyrrhus and Philoctetes would watch the crowd in silence. Pyrrhus would think, I've got to get him back on the subject of home. But he couldn't, and he couldn't think of anything else to say.

He'd already used up his own little life story, or what he could tell of it. Stopping with the day he left Scyros, simply eliding the year that had passed since then, as if he had stepped off the ferry in the capital and stepped right on to a vessel bound for Troy. As if his sexual experience had ended with the chauffeur's son. He was like a used car whose odometer has been set back. Philoctetes seemed to be able to ignore the dings and blisters and rust.

Pyrrhus had nothing more to tell, so he would ask Philoctetes about his life. Just to end the silence, really, but he told himself it was kind of like doing research. The more he knew about Philoctetes the better.

"What were you doing going to Troy anyway?" Pyrrhus might say.

"I got a reserve notice. I mean, I'd been in the army before, when I was a kid. I'd almost forgotten about it when . . ."

"You were in the army before?"

"Yeah, that's what everybody used to say, just that surprised: 'You were in the army?' That was about all I got out of it, having something to amaze people with. Even then I didn't get as much fun out of it as Oxylus, this incredible queen who'd been drafted once. The idea of Oxylus in uniform was like, I don't know, a bearded lady. Anyway, I'd just about forgotten, and here—after ten years of *deeply* civilian life—here I was being called back. Of course I'd taken the oath like everybody else."

"The oath? About Helen?"

"Yeah, you know, the one everybody who dated her took. That we'd always be ready to help her and her husband, whoever she married."

"I know the oath. But you were one of the suitors? I mean, weren't you—"

"Yeah, I . . . I wasn't a real energetic suitor, maybe, but—I don't know, it took me just forever to come out. Way into my twenties I went on trying to make something happen with women."

"How come?"

"How come? I didn't want to be a queer. You never went through any of that?"

"I don't guess."

"You just found out about yourself and said, hey, that's okay."

"Sure," Pyrrhus said. Except that perhaps he hadn't been feeling entirely okay on the *Penelope*. "Or maybe not. Anyway, I never thought about chasing girls."

"We did back then, men my age. So I kept dating women."

"Including Helen."

"Well, shoot, I think every man in Greece dated Helen."

"Not my father," Pyrrhus said.

"No? Didn't he take the oath?"

"Uh-uh."

"Why did he fight, then?"

"He just wanted to kill people."

"Ah. Well, who doesn't, some days? Anyway, I went because I'd taken this oath."

He nodded at Pterelas for a refill, which meant there was probably more to the story. While they waited, Pyrrhus said, "Did you have sex with women?"

"Um . . . in a manner of speaking. I . . . did stuff. It was kind of like sex. I never actually, you know, did the deed."

"You did stuff with Helen?"

"Oh, yeah, Helen, she was about as close as I ever got. I mean, that's why I dated her in the first place, she was supposed to be pretty easy. And beautiful, of course—even I thought she was beautiful. I thought, hey, I'll make it with her and that'll be it. I'll prove I'm—" He snorted. "God, I haven't thought of this in so long. We went to some movie and then we parked; I mean, she had to tell me how to get to the place where everybody parked—I'm surprised she didn't have a mobile home set up out there.

"I didn't feel anything when I touched her. She was surprisingly big, it seemed like I could barely get my arms around her, and soft, but it was like her softness was only a quarter-inch deep. We kissed: that was . . .

interesting—I always enjoyed that with girls, just doing stuff with our tongues like some kind of little game to play. When I kissed her below the ear she made a noise, like when you squeeze a stuffed animal in the right place.

"I unbuttoned her blouse and got her out of her bra somehow and touched her breasts. I did feel something, some kind of little excitement. Not passion or desire, really. I was more aroused by the idea of it, that I was touching her, and that now she was opening her blouse all the way so I could lean down and suck at—at those things so many men have died for now. Imagine, all those guys lying dead, over those little titties I sucked twenty years ago. Well, I didn't know about all that, but I knew every guy in Greece threw a boner just thinking about her, and there I was.

"I even got a little hard, as if . . . as if all those hundreds of men who wanted her were just . . . flowing into my body somehow, wanted to be in my body as I nursed at those fatal tits. That's what I was thinking about, not her, but all those other guys. I got hard.

"Not hard enough. I knew it wasn't enough; when she reached for the waistband of my shorts I drew her hand away and just held her tighter, looking over her shoulder at the other cars. Out in the middle of nowhere, all around us these cars with couples in them. The guys just naturally doing what they naturally did. And I knew that wasn't going to happen, if we sat there all night I wasn't going to get hard enough. I said we'd better stop, and she buttoned up, and I started the car."

"Was she pissed?"

"No. No, she was almost happy. She didn't feel rejected or anything. Men had been chasing her since the day her little buds got big enough to cover up, I think she just took it as a given that every man wanted her. She must have thought I did, too, but was just showing a little self-restraint. She was nearly grateful. She thought I was a gentleman, and after that she even chased me a little. I mean, she'd have me to her parties and stuff; we didn't ever try anything again. I even went to her engagement party, where everybody took that oath. That we'd always protect the happy couple."

"That was dumb."

"Who thought it meant anything? I just forgot about it, till the notice came. Even then I thought, Come on, that was one long time ago. And this queen was not stepping out of her ball gown and back into olive drab. No way.

"It was funny, though, after a day or two of saying no way, I found a kind of calm setting in. Like, yes, this is the next thing. I was a little relieved, even, ready for it: what I'd been doing for the last ten years, since I'd left the service, was over. I can't even say exactly why. But it was — I wasn't the only one who felt it. The ball was still going on, but there were already people sitting this dance out, thank you. I'll just sit right here and have some punch, you go ahead and dance with someone else.

"Friends said I could probably fight it. Go down to the board and say: Hey, look, it was lovely being in the army before, but this funny thing happened, I have metamorphosed into an undesirable. I just had to tell them I was gay and . . . Though actually I hear that they weren't very picky just then; when they really needed the bodies they were ready to overlook little oddities that would have gotten you thrown out in peacetime. Flat feet, blindness, cannibalism. I might have wound up going even if I'd fought it. I didn't; I went sort of willingly — not exactly eager, but like, this is okay.

"Of course I wasn't eighteen any more. Unless you're the kind of moron who signs up for life, if you're much more than eighteen everything that goes on in the army seems pretty comical. I don't guess battle is, but I never saw battle. And even that must be kind of funny to the gods. I went along without making any noise, but once I was in I did keep this kind of distance from it all. You know, like I wasn't a soldier, I was a 'soldier.' " He made the quotation marks in the air with his bony fingers.

"Like you were playacting," Pyrrhus said.

"No, I don't know. It was like . . . back in the city I used to work out. You know, this was before they had all these machines — if a faggot wanted to inflate his boobs, he had to go lift weights in some smelly gym with a bunch of guys who had banana on their breath. Still, I stayed out of their way and did it. And then I'd come home from the gym and admire my new muscles. Except they weren't like other men's muscles. They were made of the same stuff and they'd been built up the same way: I grunted just like any other ape when I lifted those barbells. But they were different, like they didn't mean the same thing on my body that they did on some straight boy's. Like I had just slipped into them, the way Oxylus used to show up some nights in a little summer frock.

"That's the thing about being queer — you can put on things. Muscles or a dress or a cowboy costume or, when they called me up, a uniform. All these choices.

"Do you know how, sometimes at a restaurant, lots of things on the menu appeal to you, you just can't pick, and finally your dinner partner says he's going to have the veal, so you get the lamb, and it turns out you should have had the veal, he gives you one taste and it's to die for, while you wound up with blackened ribcage? This doesn't happen in the mess hall: you don't have to agonize over your choices, you just eat whatever the mess sergeant plops onto your metal plate.

"That's what it's like to be a straight boy, I think. It's sort of like they're in the army from the minute they're born. Or maybe they're born the minute they join the army, when the guy comes at them with the razor and shaves their hair off, all their personality falls on the floor and gets swept away."

"Yours didn't," Pyrrhus said.

"No. I mean, I got the haircut. But I was still me, playing dress-up. Naked, in the shower with them, I was still in costume."

Pyrrhus wanted to say, yes, that's how it was on the *Penelope*. Of course he couldn't. Besides, it wasn't just on the *Penelope*. He thought of asking: "When are you really you? When aren't you playacting?" Then he looked at Philoctetes' face, stripped of flesh as if he had taken off a mask, and was afraid of what the answer might be.

4

"I rented a room," Pyrrhus said, a night or two later.

"You did?" Philoctetes said. "Tired of sleeping on the beach?"

"No, I . . . I thought it wouldn't be so far for you to walk."

"For me to—" Philoctetes began; then he got it. He stared down at his drink and didn't say anything.

Pyrrhus wondered if he had been hasty. But how were they going to move on if, night after night, Philoctetes got drunk, Pyrrhus walked him home, that endless walk, and he got there and passed out? How else were they going to move on?

Philoctetes looked up at him, still silent. Pyrrhus wondered if he was going to start sobbing again. Instead, he grinned and said, "Then I'd better not have any more." He stood up, too quickly: Pyrrhus thought he could see the pain flit across Philoctetes' face the way the lights from a passing car cross your bedroom wall at night. But he didn't stop smiling. Pyrrhus stood up, too, thinking that perhaps it wasn't for Philoctetes that things were going too fast.

As they left, Pyrrhus glanced back at Pterelas; he had a look of consternation on his face. Was he worried about Philoctetes? No, Pyrrhus knew that face: it was the face a guy has when he's been cruising somebody forever and someone else swoops down and takes the prize. Pyrrhus registered this and just assumed: So, Pterelas was interested in me.

The room, at the Aeolian House, might have made a cubicle at the baths look overdecorated. An iron bed, the sheets clean but exhausted looking, as if the traces of other encounters had been beaten out of them rather than washed. Next to it, a nightstand with a lamp made from a porcelain figure of a shepherd boy, the socket and bulb rising from the top of his head as if he had just had a wonderful idea. Except there was only one possible idea in this place.

Pyrrhus sat on the bed, expecting Philoctetes to join him. But Philoctetes, who had been in such a hurry to leave the bar, stood now at the far end of the room—or as far as one could get in that tiny cell. The hero of love stood like a diffident schoolboy, biting his lower lip, hands planted in the front pockets of his jeans. As if he had forgotten what to do next, as if it were not at all like riding a bicycle.

Pyrrhus stood up and began to undress. Not as slowly as at the Escapade, nor of course with the urgency of a man in heat; just calmly unwrapping himself while Philoctetes watched, steadily but impassively.

He didn't step forward toward Philoctetes, suddenly couldn't. It wasn't revulsion; swallowing revulsion had been part of his job description. It was, more nearly, terror, but with an odd undercurrent of attraction. Philoctetes was beautiful, so dark and angular against the white wall of the cell, his gray eyes scanning Pyrrhus's body with slow attentiveness, as if reading it. Yet Pyrrhus felt that Philoctetes could kill him. Not just literally, with whatever venom might seep from his tiny paired wounds. Rather by draining his will to smash through to the sunlight. At last he made himself step forward. As, when the opposing armies face each other at a distance just greater than an arrow's flight, one man steps forward.

Can you picture what it is like to break ten years of celibacy? You can picture your first time, which ended some years of virginity that (unless you were awfully precocious) presumably also ran into double digits. Picture that, then, without quite the same rutting urgency and none of the awkwardness, try to recall it, and you might have some sense of the wonder and prayerful gratitude with which Philoctetes touched his hand to Pyrrhus's naked shoulder.

Pyrrhus could feel it. There had been boys for whom he had been the first—one was so young it seemed as though he must have broken his piggy bank, or gathered up all his earnings from the paper route, to come and visit Pyrrhus. Pyrrhus had been a little scared: such a responsibility, how could anyone be enough to repay so much pent-up longing? He did everything he could, got the kid off twice, let him stay way beyond an hour, even thought for an instant of letting him go without paying, so maybe he'd think better of himself. Still, he could see, as the kid left and started down the stairs—almost bumping into Leucon, Leucon had only agreed to be gone an hour—he could see the disappointment. The sad amazement, even, that after doing everything he'd ever imagined with the closest thing to a god he was likely to get, after that he still had to lift one foot and then the other to walk downstairs, he had not become an eagle. He called again, not a week later, and tried to negotiate a discount. Pyrrhus hung up on the little shit.

Philoctetes touched Pyrrhus's shoulder and emitted a low, guttural sound, some mix of wonderment and sorrow: he hadn't touched anyone in so long, touching Pyrrhus wouldn't turn him into an eagle. Pyrrhus just stood there, motionless, while Philoctetes' hand toured his body, his face, like a blind man's hand, coming to rest at last on his hipbone. It was almost like the Escapade: Pyrrhus naked, a clothed man groping him. Except that the customers at the Escapade didn't usually have tears in their eyes. Shit, again, tears.

Pyrrhus started to unbutton Philoctetes' unvarying flannel shirt, but Philoctetes squirmed away from him, headed toward the door. Was he about to run off? No, he was just going for the light switch. The body that had been a gift to the city could now be offered only in the dark. Philoctetes undressed himself, with a schoolboy's haste, then lay on the bed, waiting. Pyrrhus didn't move for a minute, let his eyes adjust to the dark; then he went and stood by the bed. Philoctetes looked up at him, with those wet, gray eyes, and his brown body stretched out before Pyrrhus was taut with expectation.

Expecting what? Pyrrhus didn't know what to do. Well, that wasn't unheard of, especially lately. Sometimes you needed a sign, or you just plunged forward, as he had with Corythus, and waited for assent or resistance. Philoctetes gave him no hint at all, and he couldn't take the chance of improvising and getting it wrong: he might spoil everything in an instant. As if the fate of Troy rested on what happened in the next few minutes (as, in the end, it did).

He took it as slow as Philoctetes did, matching caress for caress, pressing his lips to Philoctetes' only as hard as the answering pressure.

Once, back on Scyros, Pyrrhus tried out for a play. Just an amateur thing, directed by some friend of his mother's; he'd only done it because he thought the lighting guy was available. (He wasn't.) Pyrrhus got the part, even though he couldn't act—not on stage, anyway. He was the type they wanted. In rehearsals, they did stupid acting exercises. They would lie on the floor, trying to relax their whole bodies, starting with the toes. They would talk gibberish. They would play the game of mirrors. Another actor would start some movement or gesture, and you were supposed to mimic exactly what he was doing. At some point you were supposed to take over, and he would begin copying you. They didn't blow a whistle, or call out, "Now it's Pyrrhus's turn." It was just supposed to happen. But it didn't just happen, or at least not for Pyrrhus. When he took over, that was an act of will; when he surrendered

273

control that, too, was an act of will. It didn't just happen. Not in that game, and not in bed.

This night it did. There was no will in the room, no one was in charge. Pyrrhus had thought the music of love consisted of barked commands or whispered pleas. In contrast, that night with Philoctetes was one of silent interrogation.

Afterwards, Pyrrhus couldn't have said whether, in the hours they were together, either of them was ever really hard. Certainly neither of them came, or thought about it, or missed it. They did things Pyrrhus would have called moony: looked into each other's eyes, went oh, smiled until just the sight of each other's helpless, mirrored grins made them laugh. They didn't giggle so much as chuckle, as if looking down on themselves indulgently from some place of calm. Almost an Olympus: if the gods themselves were chaste, they might look down and chuckle just so at how two lumps of clay could make each other tremble and go Oh, surprised tears in their eyes. Until at last they didn't even go Oh any more.

The silence was broken by the cry of a gull. Pyrrhus looked up, and it was daylight: how many hours had they been in that silence? When he looked back down, he saw that Philoctetes had fallen asleep. That suddenly, as if he had just been an inch from it all along. Or as if they'd been asleep the whole time.

Shit, he thought, Admetus, how long had he been waiting at the launch? He grabbed his clothes and ran out, dressed in the hallway, so as not to wake Philoctetes. Shouldn't he wake him; wouldn't he spoil everything just running off? What could he say, though, how would he explain going so quickly after a night of . . . whatever it had been?

He started to run, but then he thought Admetus was probably asleep himself, down at the launch. Ten minutes more or less wouldn't matter. He slowed down, trying to think about whatever had happened, what it had been. And, funny, he did think about it. Every time he'd tried to walk himself into cogitation in the city he'd been distracted. Here there was just the silent town and the gray sameness of the houses.

He thought: I was blinded by Aphrodite, or wounded by Eros. It is customary to say these things, usually when you wake up and discover a monster snoring next to you, pinning you down with his hairy arm. But he had not been blinded. He had seen Philoctetes all night long. Seen quite clearly: that Philoctetes was old, and too thin, and . . . looking back at him. Maybe that was it, the way Philoctetes looked straight at Pyrrhus — not, say, at the ghost of some high-school crush, nor at some appliance —

and smiled with unreserved approval. As he ambled toward the launch, Pyrrhus realized that he himself was still smiling. He made himself stop, commanded his lips to form a grim, martial line.

Sometimes Pyrrhus had had a good time with a trick. Someone skillful and not too toadlike and with no bizarre demands. Even if he was only doing what the other guy wanted, he had nerves in the usual places. Sometimes he just couldn't help enjoying himself. As sometimes a barber must find that he's actually enjoying cutting somebody's hair. Or as a taxi driver might, on a pretty day, when the traffic's light, enjoy driving. But he doesn't turn off the meter.

There were hustlers—unprofessional, Pyrrhus thought them—who wouldn't make it with anybody too ugly or fat or old. One might suppose, on the face of things, that these boundaries would affect the bottom line, unnecessarily narrowing the market. Maybe there were tradeoffs; maybe the guys who wouldn't do it with just anybody were more enthusiastic with the clients who passed the entrance exam, and were rewarded accordingly. Still, their pickiness seemed somehow to adulterate the entire transaction. What they did was less honorable than straightforward prostitution. They never really earned their money; never, as Leo would have put it, gave good value. When they took their payment, it must have been like slapping the trick in the face. The trick who was almost, but not quite—the money declared—good enough to do for free.

Pyrrhus never picked. If, when the door opened, the guy turned out to be good-looking, that was a pleasant surprise. If he sucked like a virtuoso or fucked as attentively as a surgeon, that was a bonus. But one consumed in the receiving. Whereas, if a monster slipped Pyrrhus an extra twenty, Pyrrhus walked away with the twenty.

Which was a lot more durable, more fungible, than the silly smile he had already wiped off his face.

So long, it had been so long Philoctetes could scarcely remember why he had—when the reserve notice came—gone without protest, walked away from the city without regret. All these years on Lemnos, exiled, the party going on all around him and he unable to join: he had half forgotten that once he had been ready to walk away. That when the summons came he had almost been relieved. Happy to give up the discos and the drugs and even the sex.

He who had once lived for nothing else, back in the city. His whole life had been entirely about sex. Well, yes, maybe every life is, but I mean that Philoctetes himself, looking back, wondered at how entirely he had structured his life around it. Consciously and completely, the way a priest orders every minute of the day around his various obligations.

He supposed this didn't just happen to gay men; there were the hilarious straight playboys, with their bachelor pads and mood music, or their vans with shag carpeting. Yet even they did not spend every single night, as Philoctetes once did, in a world where the only subject was sex, every conversation was about acceptance or refusal, every joke about size or shape, every look about desire. And it wasn't true, not exactly, that he had tired of that; you couldn't really get tired of that. That is, you could get tired of Bar X, or of bars in general; you could feel, as they used to say, that the screwing you got wasn't worth the screwing you got. But no one ever got tired of sex itself. Remember the joke, so many men, so little time? Every man was different; if you paid attention every man had some gift for you, a ride to offer that might get you to the same place in the end, coming was coming, but the ride was always different. Even with a lover, if you paid attention. It wasn't that he had tired of sex; even in his years of celibacy, if he wasn't thinking about his wound, he was thinking about sex.

It was the people that fucked it up. Guys who thought that if they were on top in bed they could tell you how to have your eggs in the morning. Guys who wanted to remake you, or wanted you to remake them. Guys who wanted to play games, like one of you was a cop, or a football player, or a proctologist. Guys who wanted to hear you say you loved them, or wanted to hear themselves say it. Guys who wanted to be praised for the size of their cocks, or for their costly sheets. Guys who talked—not the ones who demanded or pleaded, but the ones who just supplied an endless play-by-play (always a beat behind what was actually going on, "I'm coming" when it was already dripping down your chin). Guys who looked for one million ways to evade or complicate the central mystery of skin against skin, of celestial games played with no uniforms and no equipment. It never stopped, not in the baths, not in the bushes at the island, not in the tearooms, just this endless currency of ego. Lives of foreplay and afterplay in which the main event passed by all but unnoticed, or was felt as an annoying interruption to the more important discourse. Well, if we have to . . . oh, wait, did I mention . . . ?

It was all a kind of blasphemy, as when a priest worries too much about his temple or his raiment. Here they had all taken a vow of unchastity, had in effect agreed to center their lives around sex, and they couldn't keep faithful. Philoctetes seemed to be the only devotee.

Of course Philoctetes had to wonder if maybe he was the crazy one. Or at least insufficiently acculturated, like somebody who answers literally when people ask, "How are you?" All the other stuff he deplored must have been what being human, being alive, meant: it couldn't be that Philoctetes was the only one who was alive. Maybe the silence Philoctetes sought was like being dead.

Now this mysterious boy had appeared and they had made a silence last all the way to dawn. Nothing had happened, really, they'd never got to the main event. Maybe he never had, the boy; maybe Philoctetes was his first one. Then they'd have to take it slowly. If he even showed up again—he'd disappeared so abruptly, Philoctetes had dozed just a minute and he'd vanished. But he had to come back. It wasn't possible that their perfect night, the most nearly perfect in five thousand nights of fucking, could be the end of it.

Corythus pushed Pyrrhus away and turned on the light to get a cigarette. Pyrrhus could see that there were tears running down his face. Not, like Philoctetes', tears of gratitude.

Pyrrhus was a little frustrated at the interruption and didn't, really, care what Corythus felt. But he didn't want to spoil what they had going, so he said, "Fuck, I'm sorry. Was I hurting you?"

Corythus just nodded and sucked on his cigarette.

"You should have said something."

"I . . . most nights I don't mind. I mean, I guess I kind of like it . . . a little rough. But tonight it was like . . ." He frowned, looking for the words; Pyrrhus waited. "Like you were trying to get to the other side."

"What?"

"Like I was in the way and you were trying to get through me."

"I don't know what you're talking about," Pyrrhus said, and perhaps he didn't. "You should let me know when I'm hurting you."

After a moment Corythus said, "Okay." The moment long enough for Pyrrhus to hear the unvoiced: You should know when you're hurting me. Pyrrhus didn't think this was fair, but leaned forward to offer an apologetic kiss. Corythus turned his face away and said, "Who's this other guy you're seeing?"

"What?"

"Every night you go into Lemnos and you—they say you go see some guy."

"Him? He's . . . just an old man. I go and we talk, we don't do anything."

This was true. He and Philoctetes had been together every evening, but they had never gone any further than that one night at the Aeolian House. Not even so far: of course it wasn't possible to repeat that night of interrogation and postponed answers. Answers would have had to be supplied.

They would get back to Philoctetes' shack, undress, and Philoctetes would fall asleep so fast there was barely time for a goodnight peck. While Pyrrhus—though he was usually pretty well done in from Pterelas's ice-cream drinks—would make himself stay awake.

Philoctetes would have his arms around Pyrrhus, the hot, damp arms of a man in perpetual fever. At last Pyrrhus would have to wrest himself free, pull Philoctetes' arms off the way you'd tear off some troublesome creeper. Philoctetes would protest without waking. Pyrrhus would sit up, look out the open window, feeling the cool air off the ocean in his face.

Pyrrhus almost wished Philoctetes would wake up, so he could—look in Philoctetes' eyes, feel the way he felt when Philoctetes' eyes rested on him, that he was about to do something wonderful. Instead of the kind of crummy thing he was actually doing.

Once he was sure Philoctetes was dead to the world, he would get up and hurry back to the launch.

When they would meet each night, Philoctetes never spoke of Pyrrhus's stealing away the night before. Of course it wasn't unheard of; we've all had tricks who couldn't stand to spend the night. They just don't usually come back again and again. Pyrrhus's constancy apparently outweighed this enigma: it was okay that he left as long as he returned.

Why shouldn't Philoctetes have imagined that they were some sort of couple? There Pyrrhus was, night after night, and not a penny had changed hands. Philoctetes had every reason to think Pyrrhus was there because Pyrrhus liked being with him.

And Pyrrhus really did like being with him. He liked the stories, the banter with Pterelas, he liked walking home, he liked being held in Philoctetes' wiry arms, until the heat overcame him and he had to pull away. He looked forward to going every evening.

Why did he run away, night after night? Hurrying from Philoctetes or to Corythus? Partly *from* Philoctetes: he told himself he was just afraid Philoctetes would do something . . . off-putting. Sweat too much or wet the bed or vomit in the middle of the night, something that would make it harder to go on, that even real lovers have trouble with, though they must swallow and deal with it. But also *to* Corythus, to their lovemaking, which was, at least, unambiguously what it was. No dissimulation, no mission, no unanswered questions. He really hadn't noticed that he had been so unambiguous as to bring tears to the poor little bastard's eyes.

"We don't do anything," Pyrrhus repeated.

"No?"

"If we did, how could I come back to you and . . . He's an old soldier. I'm trying—I'm supposed to be trying to get him to join up again. It doesn't have anything to do with you and me."

"Oh." Corythus put out his cigarette, turned off the light, and lay with his back to Pyrrhus. After a minute he said, "Why don't you take me to town some time?"

"What? I thought there wasn't any shore leave."

"You could swing it. I mean, you talk to Odysseus and all them. I'd sure like to get off this fucking tub, just for one night."

"I'll have to see," Pyrrhus said. Right: he was going to take this little cutie and parade him in front of Philoctetes, what a terrific idea.

"I won't be any trouble," Corythus said. "You can go ahead and talk to this guy, whatever. I won't get in the way."

"Okay," Pyrrhus said, just to shut him up. "I'll see if they'll let you."

Evidently satisfied, Corythus backed toward Pyrrhus, wanting Pyrrhus to enfold him. Pyrrhus was already nearly asleep and did not trouble to comply. Maybe Corythus left then, maybe in the morning, but when Pyrrhus woke up he was gone.

Corythus was gone, it was bright daylight in the room, and in the little chair across from the bed there sat Odysseus.

"Good afternoon."

"Is it that late?"

"It is. Even so, I'm sorry to waken you. I imagine, with your very complicated romantic life, you must require a lot of sleep."

"Um . . . my romantic life isn't so hot just now."

"No?"

"No. You want to hear about it?"

"Oh, very much," Odysseus said. "Perhaps you could start with Philoctetes."

"We're doing okay."

"Ah? Then it is the other one with whom things . . . aren't so hot?"

"That's right."

"You'll forgive my indifference to this development. Perhaps you might now concentrate more fully on the central target."

"I'm doing everything I can."

"Are you? It's been—what, now?—a week or more, at any rate."

"I guess."

"Have you . . . been to bed with him?"

"Of course."

Odysseus shook his head in mock amazement. "Well, I must admire you. I'm not sure, even in my first youth, that I could have sustained your very demanding athletic schedule."

"Philoctetes isn't really very demanding."

"No? Still, you meet such demands as he has?"

"I guess. I don't really want to go into this."

"This isn't a private affair. It is an affair of state, if you will. And a rather protracted one. I mean, either you're making some progress or we need some other stratagem."

"I'm making progress. I've . . . he's fallen for me. But I can't push him too fast, he'll get suspicious."

"I see. You will, perhaps, understand my impatience."

"No, I won't, perhaps. You've waited ten fucking years, what's a few more days?"

Odysseus smiled. "I am properly chastised. At least tell me this: do you know where the bow is?"

"No."

"You haven't even seen the bow?"

"You know, it's funny, I hadn't thought about it lately. But I haven't seen it."

Odysseus just sat for a second and covered his mouth with his hand, as if to keep some venom from spitting out of it. When he had collected himself, he said very softly, "Perhaps you might, just to reassure a faint-hearted old man, perhaps you might ascertain its whereabouts."

"Okay, I'll check it out. Now if you'll excuse me I need a little more sleep."

"By all means," Odysseus said. "I hope you will be at your most alert tonight."

When Odysseus had gone, Pyrrhus couldn't get back to sleep. He felt

280

a sudden dread; it took him a minute to identify it. He was being rushed along, he had to hurry Philoctetes to their destination. Any day now he would have to turn around and tell Philoctetes that the meter had been running all the time.

Philoctetes was at Pterelas's, at his usual corner — he wondered sometimes if it was something he could bequeath, practically his whole estate, that bar stool and a useless bow — waiting for Pyrrhus. They hadn't agreed to meet, never had, these last few nights. When would they have made a date? They stumbled home, went immediately to bed. Every morning when Philoctetes woke up Pyrrhus was just gone, as if Philoctetes had dreamt him. Yet every evening he reappeared, right after dinnertime — having figured out that dinner was seldom on Philoctetes' agenda, he always arrived with cheesesteak sub or pizza on his breath. A tiny bit sickening, really, until masked by the bouquet of Pterelas's ice-cream drinks.

If Philoctetes was confident Pyrrhus would show up, he was merely generalizing from a very few instances. For all Philoctetes knew Pyrrhus had already gone; any day he might just go without a word. Of course that's true of any couple: the expectation that your partner will be home for dinner may rest on a thousand occurrences and not three or four, but it's only a hypothesis. It can be falsified at any time.

Pterelas came over and freshened Philoctetes' drink: he did this often enough that Philoctetes never identifiably had more than one drink, although by the end of the evening his lime was all but pickled, as sodden and bereft of flesh as Philoctetes himself. Perhaps if Philoctetes had been absolutely certain that the boy was coming he would have slowed down, so that maybe one night he could show Pyrrhus he remembered how to do things other than cuddle and pass out. But Philoctetes wouldn't have wanted to risk, if Pyrrhus didn't show up, confronting that fact sober.

Pterelas said, "Your friend's a little late tonight."

"I guess."

"When's he supposed to be here?"

"He didn't say."

"Oh," Pterelas said. In that way he had, eyes half-closed, that suggested he had deciphered everything. So that — even when he probably had — Philoctetes found himself protesting, just because one had to believe that one's life was too complicated to be deciphered in a single glance by a bartender.

" 'Oh' yourself. Maybe he'll show up and maybe he won't."

"Uh-huh. You sit there all fidgety and now you get casual."

"Does it show?"

"Honey, you remind me of a girl on prom night. 'Ooh, what corsage will he bring?' "

"A camellia, maybe."

"Oh, I thought you went for cucumbers."

"I'm not sure he'd know what to do with it."

"Really? You mean you're just good friends? No wedding bells in the offing?"

"I don't know what we are. I mean, I really don't, maybe I've lost the hang of this. I can't read him at all." Pterelas went to take care of some customers, was gone a couple minutes. When he came back Philoctetes picked up right where he'd left off. "You know, I had—shit, I never counted, how could I?—maybe a couple thousand tricks. And I swear, there are guys I just blew in the dark, on the piers, never saw their faces, that I felt I knew better than I know Pyrrhus."

"Maybe that's 'cause you do all the talking."

"Do I? I guess so. He seems to want to hear all about my life."

"Maybe you need to start finding out about his."

"I have, I think. I mean, I haven't done *all* the talking. But he hasn't had much life."

"Honey, he isn't *that* young."

"No, but it's like he's . . . plastic. I don't mean phony, polyester. I mean he's pliable, kind of—just fits around all your hollows and bumps. Like he has no needs of his own."

"He's up to something."

"What are you talking about?"

"Where does he go all day? Where does he stay?"

"Oh, you mean that shit about the Seaview? He was just embarrassed about—"

"Where does he shower, Philoctetes? Where does he keep all those perfectly starched white shirts?"

Where indeed? Philoctetes had been thinking of him as some sort of divine visitation, not to be interrogated, any more than a man crawling out of a desert would insist on a particular brand of bottled water. But, the real mystery wasn't his arrangements for personal hygiene. It was what went on in bed. That he could join Philoctetes there again and again and want, apparently, nothing. A twenty-one-year-old, if he was that, content to kiss and sigh and look and go to sleep. When every man on the island, every one but Philoctetes, would have done anything Pyrrhus wanted, anything at all.

Pterelas continued: "He's after something."

"What could he be after? My money? My estate on the dunes? I don't have anything anybody could want. Just me. Of course I couldn't possibly be of any interest to anybody."

"Oh, touchy. Of course you're a prize, just by yourself."

"Aw." But he had to be, didn't he? There wasn't anything else the boy could want. And Philoctetes could, after all, remember the days when he could saunter into the newest club and have his pick of any man in the place. He wasn't what he was then—his affliction apart, if he'd never been bitten he'd still be ten years older. But he was still Philoctetes: the idea that the boy could care about him wasn't utterly outrageous.

He owed it to Pterelas to say: "It is funny, about the shirts."

"Oh, for all I know he has two of them and he brings one in to the cleaner's every morning."

"Maybe."

"Anyway, here he is. You can ask him."

5

Pyrrhus and Philoctetes sat side by side, in their usual silence, the boy cradling his ice-cream drink and looking around the room, Philoctetes staring into his glass and thinking: How can I ask him, how can I put the question? Which isn't even my question, but Pterelas's. I don't want to know anything more, not one more fact about him. There is no intelligence I could gather that would not diminish him. That in itself was kind of scary: sooner or later Philoctetes just couldn't help learning more than he wanted.

"You know, Admetus mentioned something about a bow."

"What?" Philoctetes said.

"He told me you used to have a bow. Something special, he thought."

"Oh, the bow, yeah. This was from the first time I was in the army. When I was a kid."

"You've never told me about that."

"Haven't I? I thought by now you'd heard about everything except maybe my toilet training."

"No. I mean, I know you were in before, but you never said why."

"There wasn't any big why, kids don't need complicated reasons to do stupid things. It was mostly just the only way I could think of getting away from home. I should have run off to the city like you did. But I was seventeen, and a hick, and I thought the army was the thing.

"After boot camp—you don't want to know—I tried to get into electronics. In those days they promised everybody who signed up they could get into electronics, later it was computers, so you could have an exciting career when you got out. Anyway, of course there were no openings in electronics, and I had a choice of cooks' and bakers' school or this special-forces thing. I was stupid, I couldn't see myself peeling potatoes for three years, so I took the other thing, which made boot camp look like a week on the beach. Anyway, by the time the training was over I had lost my baby fat for sure, and I had caught the eye of the unit commander. Who happened to be Heracles."

"*The* Heracles?" Pyrrhus said.

"The one and only."

"I always thought he was straight."

"Oh, pretty much, but he dabbled. You know, one of those guys who likes to split open a tiny androgynous blond once in a while. Well, I sure wasn't tiny, and I don't think I'm too androgynous, do you? Still, I guess I was the closest thing in that camp—the unit was full of huge hairy things that wouldn't have bent over even for Heracles. I swear I must have been there because of some clerical error. Anyway, like I say, I caught his eye. And then the rest of him just sort of descended on me.

"For a couple months we had this—I can't even call it an affair, he boffed me and I got little favors, a night off guard duty, an extra weekend pass. It was, thinking back on it, it was probably pretty horrible; he was always drunk. I don't mean he was drunk all the time, but it was only when he was drunk that he sent for me. So either he couldn't get it up, which was my fault, or he got it up but couldn't come, just went on and on until it seemed like I couldn't remember a time when I wasn't lying there with his great weight on top of me, enveloping me.

"It didn't seem quite so bad at the time. Partly because at least I wasn't getting jumped by some of the real simians in the unit; Heracles scared them away. Besides, he was divine, so it was, you know, like being fucked by a hamster. Except he was so heavy, and always on top, me on my belly, because it would have been sissy to fuck face-to-face. But it didn't seem so bad. Maybe partly because I was young and far from home, and getting anything was better than getting nothing.

"This went on, like I say, for a couple months, until suddenly one day the whole unit was shipped back to Trachis, which was Heracles' home base. His wife and kid were there, all of that, and of course he just dropped me. Wouldn't even look at me. Which was fine with me. I didn't need his protection so much any more; we were finally some place where I wasn't the only outlet in a hundred miles. There was a whorehouse in Trachis, the special forces went and patronized that instead of me. I even went—this was still that period when I thought I might go straight if I only had the opportunity.

"Anyway, we'd only been there a few days when Heracles got sick. You've probably heard the stories: how he was poisoned, maybe by accident, or he had an allergic reaction to a love potion. I've never been able to sort that out. However it happened, one day he was, you know, Heracles, and the next day he was dying. Of course it wouldn't do for Heracles to lie in some bed with tubes and monitors and things and modestly expire. No: he had to go out in flames. And everybody for twenty miles had to come and watch.

"There we all were, all his servants and hangers-on, around this huge tangled pile of firewood and brush. By the time I got there, Heracles was already on top of it—standing looking heavenward and murmuring something. Then he lay down and we all waited. Nothing happened. I don't know what we thought, that maybe a bolt of lightning would ignite the pyre, but nothing happened. Until finally Heracles propped himself up on one elbow, looked down at us with contempt, and rasped, 'Will somebody light the goddamn thing?'

"Nobody moved. We all looked over at his son, Hyllus—it was obviously his job, but he was just standing there paralyzed. He was a little nonentity; probably he was already picturing the pathetic future ahead of him, without his famous dad to protect him, just chased from one place to another his whole life. Anyway, he wasn't lifting a finger, and it was starting to look like rain, which might sort of put a damper on the old apotheosis.

"Heracles had with him his bow and arrows. I don't know if he had planned to do a little hunting in heaven or if he'd just absentmindedly brought them along. He raised himself up—you could see he was in pain—and threw them down at us: the bow and then the quiver, one or two arrows falling out on the way down, more fuel for the fire. The weapon lay at the edge of the pyre, not far from where I was. We all assumed he was giving it to Hyllus, and we stepped back to make way. Hyllus thought so, too; he was stepping forward to pick up the bow when Heracles called down, 'This is for the man who will step forward and send me to heaven.'

"Well, Hyllus just shrank right back, and nobody else was exactly rushing forward, butane lighter at the ready. It was probably a terrific offer, you don't see bows like that any more. But, I mean, who really wants a bow? We were all still just standing there when he called my name.

"I was humiliated. Half the people there must have known that I'd been his . . . I almost said *lover,* but *receptacle* is more like it. They all knew, and here he was singling me out. But I stepped forward, stood at the foot of the pyre. He called down, 'Philoctetes, I am begging you. Some day you will beg to be released from your pain.'

"I was a kid, I didn't see how that could ever be so. I felt in my pocket, there were matches, my hand closed around them. Still, I couldn't do it. Until he said, softer this time—I wonder now if maybe I was the only one close enough to hear, though at the time I thought everyone must have heard, I was so ashamed—'It's not too late for you to be a man.'

"I was so ashamed and enraged. I struck a match, lit the rest of the book with it, threw the thing on the pyre. It caught instantly. I barely had

287

time to snatch up the bow and the quiver before they were engulfed, and then I ran, through the crowd, just trying to get away from those terrible words.

"When I turned around to look, the flames hadn't reached him. I mean, the whole pyre was alight, burning away like a sonofabitch, and the flames weren't touching him. As if they didn't dare, as if he were already a god and it would have been some kind of, I don't know, sacrilege to consume him. He had to . . . crawl, on his hands and knees, crawl right into the fire. And he had this weird, eager look on his face. Like a bridegroom."

"What happened to it?" Pyrrhus said.

"What?"

"The bow. I mean, I've been over to your place all these times, and I haven't . . . I don't mean I've been looking for it, but I'm just curious, and . . ."

"Oh. I . . . keep it here in town."

"You do? Where?"

Philoctetes shrugged. "This is, I don't know, kind of embarrassing. I sort of hocked it."

"You pawned the bow?"

"Well, sort of. It's on consignment. You know that place the Green Peacock, little antique place right off Port Street?"

"I didn't notice it. I'm not much into antiques."

"You sure you're queer? Anyway, I was hard up, and I didn't see much prospect that I'd need a bow any more. Phyllis, who runs the shop, thought, well, it wouldn't fit just any place, but there might be somebody who'd want it, over their mantel or whatever. She felt sorry for me, I guess. She gave me a hundred and then we'd split whatever she got on top of that."

"Nobody ever bought it, though? It's still there?"

"I guess, someplace. Unless she sold it and never gave me my cut. But Phyllis is honest to a fault, what she's doing selling antiques is a mystery to me. I guess bows and arrows just aren't a big ticket on the objet d'art scene. Even if they're magic."

"Magic?"

"That's what they say, the arrows will hit anything you aim at. Which is a good thing—that's the only way I'd ever hit anything. I had to go through marksmanship four times before they passed me."

"And do they?"

"The arrows? Beats me. I never even used the damn thing."

Pyrrhus had about as much trouble swallowing this story about a magic bow as, say, you do. I hardly believe it myself: if it didn't show up in every single version of this old story I would simply have left it out, although Clio is subbing for my usual muse today, standing over my shoulder insisting that it is, too, part of the story—how dare I omit it? Very well, I have included the bow, as long as we understand that I don't really believe this part, either. It's a symbol or a metaphor or something.

The story starts with Heracles, and that's part of the problem, maybe. Really, I don't quite believe in Heracles. I mean, of course there was a Heracles; he died not twenty years before this story begins. But what with the tabloids and the made-for-TV movies and the first round of books— the encomiums by his friends—and the second round—the exposés—and finally the garish and pathetic exploits of the family he left, the Heraclids, that gilded doomed family: after all that there's nothing left of him. We have now all his exploits, his womanizing and occasional boyizing, his many policy errors, a few speeches written by other people, a handful of chance witticisms that may have been his own. We have that and the more recent news that he lived his life in unremitting pain, heavily drugged most of the time. Yet behind this mass of information there is no one, no one at all. We can't imagine what he *wanted*. We know what he got: high office, adulation, a princess bride, and so many other women that it was as routine as brushing his teeth. What he wanted, though, what drove him on, when he could have sat back with his money and his women and let the painkillers wash over him: this is irretrievable. We have learned to look at his once-sacred image and say knowingly: It was a mask. But we can't see beyond it. His intentions are as impenetrable as those of the gods. Perhaps that is the very reason that the credulous suppose he is one of them now.

Or, if I may put it another way: let us suppose we were going to make a movie of this story. (My agent is unencouraging on this point.) This is always fun, trying to think who might play Odysseus and Phoenix and the rest. But you're stumped, aren't you, when it comes to the Heracles flashback? You can picture the casting call — sides of beef in the butcher's freezer. Of course that isn't enough: there's a lot more to divinity than arms like dirigibles and six-pack abs. You might try to narrow down the list of candidates by specifying additional qualities. He should be — not brainy, but at least canny or quick, and charming and graceful and maybe even (some accounts differ from that of Philoctetes) good in bed. Still not enough: you want something more for Heracles. Dignity? Self-possession? A certain *je ne sais quoi* that separates deities from weightlifters, even when weightlifting was pretty much what they did.

Well, *je ne sais quoi*, but nobody in the lineup's got it. This doesn't just mean I can't shoot an Olympian movie. I cannot believe in the gods themselves unless there are mortals in their image. Zeus the Father of Heaven is unimaginable when Father means the softhearted patsy of situation comedy. Athena is a panelist spouting erudite witticisms; Aphrodite uses eye shadow; Hermes clunks around in winged sneakers. The gods were like people but better — I mean that their divinity was an indefinite extension of qualities we saw around us. And no one could wish the qualities we see around us to be extended. Picture the most beautiful and self-possessed man you know, and now imagine him *even more so*: do you have an image of Apollo, or even his shadow, something ready for your worship? No, you still have somebody who — in a phrase that was never uttered in the age of belief — shits like the rest of us. Of course, everyone always knew that heroes and kings did so, and it is true in a banal, clinical way that mortals shit and the gods do not. But it is only in our time, I think, that the commonality of the outhouse has overwhelmed the things that set some men and women apart.

All exploded, and I am left with the bow, a magic bow that is central to my story and that — I might as well warn you now — is in itself an unimpressive object, as diadems and scepters, in their glass cases, are rather a letdown now that we don't believe in kings.

Okay, it's just some kind of metaphor. Perhaps, as Phoenix remarked, it stands for Heracles, who conquered Troy in the previous war, coming to take Troy a second time. The old stories are filled with these merely decorative symmetries. Others say it has to do with the fact that the Greeks had abandoned the bow and arrow in favor of the sword, but they needed the bow to win, finally, as they needed other virtues they had also abandoned — abandoned on the way to Troy in the same way they abandoned Philoctetes. Or — well, if you're ingenious enough, you can provide your own exegesis. Who will contradict you, unless the author steps into the room? The author in this case being she who spins forth all the world's stories and never comments on them.

I, too, can play. Maybe the point, if there is one, is this: Philoctetes is the only living person who can draw the bow *and he has never bothered to.* Understandably: what was he supposed to do with the bow, shoot seagulls? Which happens to be against the law in Lemnos, as seagulls are an essential part of the ambience. Not to mention: have you noticed lately what seagulls eat? From the day Heracles handed it to Philoctetes, the bow has gone unused, languished first in Philoctetes' shack and now in a curio shop. Probably its string has gone flaccid, like the strings on a lyre that is never plucked. It is a capacity that has gone unused, the occasion for which has never arisen. The great occasion requires that each of us bring to it the bow that only we can draw. Not so that we can win, but so that we can discover why it has been given to us.

Maybe a more alert Philoctetes would have seen, in these sudden inquiries about the bow, evidence that Pterelas was right, that the kid was after something. But, really, the bow? That tacky old thing? It was just another anecdote. As for Pyrrhus's shirts: tonight's was a little wrinkled, and starting to fray. Leaving, really, only one mystery: why a healthy youth seemed to be content just to gaze in Philoctetes' eyes and cuddle.

Except that tonight he was more pointedly amorous. Which, too, might have been cause for suspicion, if Philoctetes hadn't been pretty horny himself. Maybe just from talking about the days when he lay pinioned under Heracles.

Remember the first time you were ever fucked? The guy making his way in, and you're going, even if he's gentle, you're going, oh, my god, god, why does anybody ever do this, oh god, is he going to finish soon? And then, probably not that first time, but some time, My god, this is why people do this, god, I hope he never stops.

Now imagine if you haven't been fucked in ten years and then you are. Pyrrhus's hand rested gingerly on Philoctetes' buttock as they kissed; Philoctetes pushed back and Pyrrhus grasped it more resolutely. Philoctetes pulled away from him and lay face down on the sheets. Pyrrhus was on his side, resting on one elbow, with his other hand lightly pressing at the perineum, then one finger venturing up and teasingly circling

Philoctetes' asshole. There wasn't a bone in Philoctetes' body. He was breathing so shallowly he was half afraid of blacking out. Pyrrhus's hand deserted him, then it was back, bringing the shock of cold grease, now working it around the edges, now the finger like a scout finding its way in, nerves that must nearly have atrophied coming awake, Philoctetes' whole body trembling in astonished welcome. Then the full weight of Pyrrhus on top of him, the immeasurable comfort of being crushed under the loving weight of a man, now a second finger, now Pyrrhus's knees urging Philoctetes' legs apart. The hand was withdrawn, Pyrrhus pulled back, paused, there was an Arcadian instant when he was just an intention, almost a question, hovering above Philoctetes, and Philoctetes was one shapeless puddle of yes. Then . . .

Lord, how it hurt. Gates that had not parted in a decade, that had rusted shut, battered at by a ruthless invader. There was a way once, if Philoctetes held himself at just such an angle, there was a secret way he knew that he could have taken a stallion, or a piano leg, smoothly all the way to his center. He had forgotten it, he couldn't get to the angle, and Pyrrhus wasn't waiting, just pushing forward as if oblivious of Philoctetes' involuntary resistance.

While Pyrrhus — Philoctetes was sure this was his first time, it had to be — Pyrrhus must have thought this was how it was supposed to be. Philoctetes was practically writhing, and Pyrrhus was just pushing, as insensible of Philoctetes' pain as a baby struggling to be born. Deep inside Philoctetes something was still beckoning Pyrrhus onward, as if remembering: Yes, come for me, tear your way through, I have waited so many years. But the gateway didn't remember, it went on meeting the intruder with outraged refusal.

At last, somehow, Pyrrhus was all the way in, still at the wrong angle. The pain somewhat abated, each forward thrust just a dull insult, the colloquy of Pyrrhus's insensate cock and Philoctetes' capitulating muscles all going on a million miles from the pleasure points that had been awakened only to be starved. Philoctetes opened up to meet each thrust and clenched around Pyrrhus at each withdrawal, in the old remembered rhythm, just to try to make him finish. That rhythm: it used to mean they were one body, Philoctetes and some anonymous fucker on top of him, pulsing together with one life. Tonight Philoctetes was manipulating Pyrrhus with perfect frigidity, as if Philoctetes were a whore.

Philoctetes was able to think almost as clearly as if this were all happening to someone else. What he thought was: I will have to do this again and again, if I am to keep him. Now that he's done it he'll want to do it every night. Maybe somehow I'll remember the angle, slow him down until I find the angle. Or maybe it will just be like this, always, until I grow to dread him. Why couldn't we just have gone on holding each other? Where is it written that you can't go on doing that forever?

Pyrrhus was tired already, his cock a little numb—too much to drink this evening, too much Corythus this morning, he felt like he might go on for hours like this. And Philoctetes would probably let him; he was moaning and pushing back. Pyrrhus thought the angle was funny, but it must have been working for Philoctetes, the way he moaned and clenched Pyrrhus on the outward pull. Pyrrhus was feeling nothing, just pushing forward, *whump, whump,* his legs starting to knot up.

He was going to have to fake it, the way he'd done now and then with a trick. Groaning, swearing a little, pushing far in and stopping, letting himself go limp on top of the guy, then panting for a minute or two. He didn't know if anybody was really fooled. Just one guy, deprived of the flood of warmth that ordinarily signaled conclusion, actually said, "You didn't come." Pyrrhus answered, "Sure I did. I'm sorry, I already came a couple times today, mustn't have been much left." The trick said, "Hmmp." Pyrrhus wondered if he was supposed to give the guy a discount, as if Pyrrhus's value were measured out in thimblesful.

Pyrrhus faked it. Pushed forward, grasped tightly at Philoctetes' shoulders, cried aloud, lay panting on top of him. Philoctetes gave a long sigh and didn't move. Pyrrhus put an arm under him, wrapped around his chest. The hairs on Philoctetes' chest were damp with cold sweat. Pyrrhus was still inside him, his cock going limp with unusual speed, but his balls aching a little in frustration. Next time he wouldn't drink so much, he'd really get off. For there would certainly be a next time; this was plainly Philoctetes' main event. Who would have thought it, this man so hard and taut he could seem like just one walking erection, like you practically expected to see some big vein running the length of him? But he was a bottom, and Pyrrhus would have to do this time after time, like going to work. He'd probably have to lay off Corythus a while. Even though Corythus was, frankly, a lot more fun to fuck.

• • •

293

When they met at Pterelas's the next evening, Pyrrhus had only a soda and announced he was going to tea dance, just to check it out. "I mean, I've been here all this time," he said. "I just thought I'd see what it's like."

What could Philoctetes say? "You ought to. There *is* more to Lemnos than Pterelas's. Although this is definitely the high point."

And of course there was more to Lemnos than Philoctetes. Many of the alternatives to be found readily at tea dance. Philoctetes wondered if their precipitous and ill-executed move to a new level, not necessarily higher, had brought this point home to Pyrrhus. Or maybe it was just that they'd been together more than a week, well beyond the natural life span of a Lemnos romance. It had been so long, Philoctetes had forgotten: people came to Lemnos with round-trip tickets. Every affair had an expiration date stamped on it, like a box of cereal, and somehow the arc of passion magically conformed to its allotted interval.

Pyrrhus seemed to know that Philoctetes was worried. "I'll just be gone an hour or so," Pyrrhus said. "Well, maybe longer, I want to get a hot dog or something. I'll see you at eight, maybe, no later. I want to . . . walk you home." This last in a sort of campy drawl.

Cute, flattering, reassuring. It would be enough just to be walked home. Except that the walk would surely be followed by another discordant fuck. "Okay," Philoctetes said. Realizing, as he watched the boy walk out, that he was feeling a certain relief; as if he were the one whose affection was expiring.

Still, as soon as Pyrrhus was gone Philoctetes wanted him back. And Pterelas was looking at him curiously: Why had he been left there? Was Pterelas witnessing an incipient breakup? Philoctetes knew that, the minute Pterelas got a break between customers, he'd drift down to Philoctetes' end of the U and start a nonchalant interrogation.

Philoctetes walked out—out on the street in broad daylight, only a little buzz on and no cash. Who in all of Lemnos would give him credit, who besides Pterelas? Otionia, maybe; he hadn't touched her for a dime in years. He went to Otionia's, the little second-floor bar with the open verandah overlooking Port Street. He started up the stairs and winced: of course, this was why he'd stopped coming to Otionia's. Still, it would be nice, up there on the verandah. From there he'd be able to see Pyrrhus; Pyrrhus would have to come by there on his way back from tea dance. If he was coming back.

Philoctetes would call down to him, Pyrrhus would look around in confusion and finally up, he'd be surprised, it'd be fun. A soupçon of fun, imagine! Then Pyrrhus would come upstairs, because he wouldn't have been headed any place else; Philoctetes was his destination. Somebody's destination again. He would put up with the clumsiness later, it was worth it, and maybe the kid could be trained.

Philoctetes looked steadily down at the street, even though he was making desultory conversation with Otionia, one of those dykes who had been in Lemnos forever, or at least since her own youth, long before Philoctetes arrived. She was talking about how different it used to be, back when it was a place of artists and fisherwomen and old drunks who might once have been one or the other but were then just drunks. In those days the fairies skimmed discreetly across the surface of the bohemian soup that was Lemnos; they didn't even have bars of their own. It was more fun somehow, an easy, tolerant mix. Or was it just that Otionia was young then?

Philoctetes didn't know; he turned to look down at the street as soon as he could without being rude. Looked down with patriotic affection at the crowd on Port Street. The vista hasn't changed much, even now. Perhaps the panorama was more various then, as people were. In those days, bodies were not yet uniformly gym-honed. People had ribs and bellies, appendix scars, body hair; above the seat of the skintight jeans or the ill-considered bikini, often as not, twin capsules of fat like secrets unknown to the teller. Really, there were not very many people who should have been wearing bikinis; not many such people have ever been born.

Today the bodies are better and the costumes more flattering. If you take a table at the terrace bar, the parade that passes before you is abstractly beautiful; you might be leafing through the pages of a glossy magazine. You cannot help but look, but you are not aroused. Perhaps because you do not even begin to imagine that you will ever have any of these men? Perhaps because any one of them, under the fashionable clothes and the equally fashionable physique, may harbor that unseen guest who will strip him of everything, leave him as naked and skeletal as Philoctetes? The body he has buffed to such intimidating perfection no longer belongs to him at all.

But Philoctetes was still the only afflicted one, that night, and that night it wasn't bothering him. He browsed the crowd with the smug neutrality of a coupled man: the passersby were either pleasing or not, but he didn't need to please any of them. He was engaged for the evening; any minute now Pyrrhus would appear in the street and Philoctetes would call down to him.

He was watching the crowd so carefully that he didn't even turn to glance at the stranger who sat next to him: just registered in his peripheral vision that someone had sat down, and hoped whoever it was would take over, willingly or not, the position as Otionia's audience. What ever happened to bartenders who listened to customers and kept their mouths shut? An ungrateful thought, from a man drinking for free.

"Do you have Green Label?" the newcomer was saying.

"Shoot, somewhere up here," Otionia said. "Yeah."

"On the rocks, with a glass of soda on the side, no ice in the soda." He said this as precisely as a bureaucrat issuing a purchasing order, as if he were a man used to specifying, then receiving, exactly what he wanted.

Philoctetes thought, What an asshole, and turned away from the street a second to give him a disapproving look.

Philoctetes didn't even recognize him at first. That is, he knew he had seen the face, years before. Or rather, the face as it had been: he could just make out, in the maturely handsome features before him, the traces, almost the afterglow, of some younger face. Where had he encountered that younger face? In the army? In the city? Had they danced together, had they tricked?

He kept trying to work this out while the stranger asked him about the best places to eat in town and which stores had the nicest sweaters — questions Philoctetes could only answer with hearsay, as he had almost never eaten out, and his most fashionable garment was a sweatshirt that said, *I went to Lemnos to find true love and all I got was this sweatshirt.*

"Everybody says the Café Europa is the best place in town," Philoctetes said.

"Ah. Would you like to go?"

"What?"

"I'm sorry. I'm all by myself, I'd be delighted if you could join me for dinner. My name's Paris, by the way." He stuck out his hand. "Yours?"

Paris, of course. So he had seen the face, not in person, but in the newsmagazines and the men's fashion magazines and, just before the army embarked for Troy, the propaganda film shown to all the troops. *Why We Must Fight,* with its footage of Paris masterfully edited, so that the amiable playboy was transformed into a rapacious fiend.

Paris's hand was still extended, like an ambassador who has not been received. Philoctetes shook it, half expecting it to be as cool and insub-

stantial as a photograph. But of course it was warm; the hand gripped
Philoctetes' with an easy firmness. The living creature before him was not
the dissolute fop of the newsreels but, well, a hunk. Who wanted to take
Philoctetes to dinner.

"Philoctetes."

"Philoctetes," Paris repeated, as if the very name were toothsome.

Paris has gotten, not so much a bum rap—much of what people say is
true—but an incomplete rap. His pictures tend to show a pretty boy with
pouty lips, whereas in person he had attentive eyes and a doleful, one-
sided smile that made you think he had derived some wisdom from all
his exploits, or that he was at least puzzled by them, a little bemused. He
had his perfect tan, of course, and like all men who pursue that toxic
chimera, he looked stupid. Or rather, people sometimes just assumed he
was stupid and vacant, because how else could you lie out there day after
day?

We're so hard, aren't we, on people who are given everything? If you'd
been given everything, you mightn't have wandered very far from the pool
deck, though perhaps you wouldn't have spent quite so much time in the
direct sun. It's as if, when someone has it all, we demand that he be
tormented by some pointless ambition for more. Here he is, rich and
handsome, beating off women with a stick, and he's supposed to go have
adventures, try himself somehow, scour the earth for some unhappiness.

Paris sat around the pool, he traveled—the sort of tourist who takes
in one new sight a day and then heads back to the spa in the hotel for
maybe a massage. He never for one instant let it bother him that he was
only nth in line for the Trojan throne. Policy bored him, not because he
was stupid—stop calling him that—but because he was just smart enough
to see that all the available courses of action would be painful and un-
popular. His one experience as judge in a beauty contest had taught him
that no choice was ever right. Let his brothers worry; he traveled. Spreading goodwill and getting okay press, really, until that last trip, that awful
tour of Sparta.

He took what life gave him, as who wouldn't? Until, at Sparta, the
most beautiful woman on earth practically leapt into his arms, and he took
her with perhaps inadequate premeditation.

Anyway, the point is that he was a perfectly charming man and that
when he took Philoctetes' hand and looked into Philoctetes' eyes and said

Philoctetes' name aloud—if Philoctetes' heart went pitty-pat, it wasn't because Philoctetes was a schoolgirl or a lousy judge of character. Even you would have fallen for Paris.

"I'm embarrassed," Paris said. "Imagine my just assuming that you had nothing to do this evening. But if you were possibly free for an hour or two, I do wish you'd let me take you to dinner."

As far as Philoctetes could recollect, he was free for the rest of the century. Even though Pyrrhus was, at that instant, passing on the street below Otionia's. Philoctetes' back was to the street, of course; he didn't see Pyrrhus or even think about him.

Otionia had extended Philoctetes only a little credit; for once he had made it to the dinner hour without getting plastered. He didn't feel dressed for the Café Europa. But Paris would probably be given the best table if he arrived in the company of a baboon.

"I'd love to," Philoctetes said.

In the besieged city, they were out of coffee and disposable diapers and sun-dried tomatoes. A committee of restaurateurs had visited the Zoological Park and devised the menu for a fantastical banquet—*hippopotame bourguignon, tournedos de zèbre*—while ordinary folk argued over how long to marinate a dog or whether you should butterfly a rat before you grilled it.

They couldn't go on forever; something had to be done. Which meant, King Priam's councilors insisted, that something had to be done with Helen. They had been bickering over her from the day the Greek ships first appeared on the horizon. Helen could be given back, one extreme party said, along with some objects of more durable value. Their opponents replied that she stood for a principle, that she must be defended to the limit lest Troy be perceived as pitiful, helpless. The centrists suggested that some accident or illness could be made to befall her. Conveniently removing the casus belli and giving occasion for a truce and a stupendous funeral party, with Paris and the cuckold Menelaus matching tankard for tankard as chief mourners.

The debate went on for years: although the number of adherents to each party dwindled after every battle, the survivors just shouted louder. Until one morning King Priam silenced the gap-toothed assembly and murmured that Helen didn't matter, there might as well be no Helen.

Everyone pretended not to have heard—the usual strategy when you're not sure if your monarch is joking or demented. Obviously Helen mattered: you could see her face, any week, on the tabloids in the supermarket. In fact, as there was scarcely anything else in the supermarket, her image might have been said to make up the entire gross national product of Troy. The face that had been so remarkable at the start of things and that still confessed only a handful of the years that had elapsed since her abduction or elopement, depending which paper you bought. The accompanying text rehearsed the interminable argument: was she a saint or a slut, a victim or a provocateuse?

No Helen? The stunning disproportion of the events this silly and headstrong woman had set in motion made her the center of Troy, indeed of the known world. What could possibly be more real than Helen?

Priam tried to explain. He understood perfectly well that there was a palpable Helen: she showed up most nights at his dinner table, picking at her *chat au vin* and laughing or crying inappropriately. But she was just a walking pretext. It didn't matter any more which side of the walls she was on, or if she existed at all. The massed armies of the world were whirling about a vacancy, and the battle would go on even if Helen were simply to disappear.

Oh, yes, the councilors said, we see now. And returned to their debate with renewed vigor. Especially the return-Helen party, whose simple, concrete proposal seemed all the more sensible now, in contrast to the monarch's distracted burbling. At last it was agreed: they would send one final embassy to the Greeks.

The ambassador—one of Priam's more expendable sons—came back a couple of days later, his striped suit in tatters. With the word—when he regained speech—that the Greeks demanded unconditional surrender. Priam was gathering himself for an especially regal I-told-you-so when his son added that, oh, by the way, he had been compelled after a modest degree of torture to reveal the oracles, the surprisingly detailed prophecies about the prerequisites to the fall of Troy.

The Greeks had discovered the oracles. The Trojans had always known them, knew from the very start all about Neoptolemus and Philoctetes' bow. You might suppose they would have found this a tad discouraging, that it would have been hard to strap on the armor every day and head out to the next battle knowing that sooner or later the Greeks were going to show up with their wonder boy and their secret weapon. Did they just not believe it, the Trojans? Or did they believe it the way you believe you're going to die? With certainty and utter incredulity so perfectly balanced that they fight to a draw, leaving the ignorant animal in you free to get out of bed in the morning.

It didn't matter what Priam believed. If he was not half the strategist Odysseus was, he must nevertheless have reached the same conclusion: that the prophecies were true precisely insofar as they might be credited by the ordinary foot soldier. Thus it was imperative that the Greeks be deprived of Neoptolemus or Philoctetes or both.

Of the whereabouts of Neoptolemus his intelligence service had no clue: the last anyone knew was that he had gained some small notoriety as a sort of dancer and had then disappeared from view. Philoctetes, on the other hand, was easy to find. He had, after all, spent ten years on Lemnos bending the ear of any tourist foolish enough to sit at the next barstool. Philoctetes was the prize, and the way to win him was as obvious, even to Priam, as it had been to Odysseus.

As always, Priam would send a son to do the job. But the younger ones seemed slight to him, somehow attenuated, as if the very seed he had persisted in scattering well into old age had been diluted by time and could now produce only the second-rate impressions that might be pulled from a worn-out lithographer's stone. He couldn't send any of those. And all the older ones were either not very attractive or very dead. All except Paris.

Paris was the only choice. Not merely by default: he was indisputably the hottest living Trojan, the obvious candidate for a commando mission of the heart. With just one tiny shortcoming: that he happened to be straight.

Paris actually pointed this out when his father first brought up the plan: the glider, the last one left, swooping silently off the northeast wall in the dark of night, maybe shot down, but if not then the submarine, then the rubber raft to the island. An enterprise filled with dangers, of which Paris focused on only one: "But I'm—you know, I don't . . ."

Priam said, "I'm not asking you to fall in love with him, I'm asking you to pretend to. If you're just pretending, it shouldn't matter whether your quarry is a homely woman or a handsome man or . . . or a frog, for that matter."

"I just don't know if I can pretend that well."

"You don't have to do it very well. He's a human being, he must be as vain as anybody else. If you tell him you adore him, he won't add up the reasons that you can't."

This wasn't, perhaps, exactly right. If Paris had arrived a few weeks earlier, Philoctetes might have had his guard up, might have recited a hundred reasons that no one would ever adore him again. So it was Pyrrhus's own fault, maybe; Pyrrhus had weakened him for the kill. For, having conquered such a handsome Greek, why should Philoctetes have been surprised that he was suddenly being courted by Troy's most legendary lover? Even if none of the legends Philoctetes could recall had ever suggested that Paris swung both ways?

So what if Paris didn't want to rush into bed on the first date, or the second? Their leisurely progress in this arena seemed of a piece with Paris's polished table manners and general urbanity. They would have cocktails — Philoctetes careful to have just the one — then dinner at Café Europa, at the table on the patio that seemed to have been reserved for Paris since the dawn of time. With its single white candle teased, but never extinguished, by a gentle zephyr, as they lingered over their cognac and Philoctetes listened to the stories of Paris's travels. It was funny: even though Paris was in fact doing all the talking, Philoctetes felt that he was being paid attention to. Paris's eyes never moved from Philoctetes'. His talk might have been soothing background music; they met above it.

When they would part for the evening — in town, outside the restaurant; for some reason Paris hadn't yet offered to walk him home — Paris would kiss Philoctetes on the cheek and give him that one-sided smile that could take on so many meanings, depending on the context. Right then it seemed to say: I am bursting with happiness, practically ready to smile with both sides of my mouth, but I don't want to frighten you or go too fast. We're just taking it easy, right?

That's what it said, and Philoctetes was ready to take it easy after the confusing and precipitous onslaught of Pyrrhus. Of course you think he shouldn't have been fooled: Paris was the world's most notorious heterosexual, a man who had had more women than you've had crabs. Of course it isn't unheard of for a man with a reputation for insatiability to make a few side excursions. But with Philoctetes? How could Philoctetes imagine it? That this walking magazine cover had gone gaga all of a sudden over a man who was, let's face it, middle-aged and . . . a little too skinny now, though thank god the foot hadn't acted up all week and there hadn't been a scene.

Philoctetes could pose these questions as well as you or I. Still, if his years in the city had taught him anything, it was: Don't interrogate happiness, of course it's going to leave. Probably not even as rapidly as you'll want it to, next week or the week after. Just take it. He felt that they had sort of arrived at the same place about things, he and Paris, even if Paris was a prince and Philoctetes was just a drunken veteran with airs. And besides, who really thinks he doesn't deserve a prince?

6

He didn't have any sense of actually dropping Pyrrhus. The first night, he and Paris finished dinner, parted, and Philoctetes drifted home on a cloud of cognac and surmise. The next night, after Paris left, Philoctetes went to Pterelas's for a nightcap — guilty, still feeling something for Pyrrhus, yet half hoping not to see him. But nobody was going to keep Philoctetes out of Pterelas's.

Pyrrhus was there, and quite cross. "Where have you been?" he said.

"I . . . an old friend happened to be in town, just for a couple of days. If there'd been any way to reach you, I would have let you know, that I was going to be tied up. But . . . I've never really known where you were staying. Maybe if you hadn't been quite so secretive."

This was good, almost made it Pyrrhus's fault. Except that Pyrrhus answered, "You could have told Pterelas where you were going to be. You could have left a message."

"That's true," Philoctetes said, unrepentantly. As if he were supposed to tell Pterelas every little thing about his life.

"Anyway, it's late," Pyrrhus said. "You ready to go?" As if they'd just had one night off and were going right back to their routine. Or, worse, to another demonstration of Pyrrhus's new bedroom skill.

Philoctetes hadn't seen him in this mood; the pugnacious thrust of his lower lip contrasted most unattractively with Paris's debonair half-smiles. He hadn't seen it before, that Pyrrhus was really little more than a petulant child.

"I'm going to have one more," Philoctetes said. He couldn't resist adding, "But don't let me keep you." Wondering, even as he said it, how he could be burning this bridge when Paris was a pretty vague prospect. Yet it didn't seem vague: he thought that he and Paris were in a very slow but definite courting dance, on their way to an encounter that would be as different from Pyrrhus's insensate assault as, say, cognac from an ice-cream drink.

Pyrrhus said nothing, but drew himself up with an air of outraged dignity. As if to say, Who are you to refuse me? As if he hadn't been interested in Philoctetes all along, as if it had all been just some kind of protracted mercy fuck. And, because Philoctetes still couldn't see what Pyrrhus could have hoped to get out of it, he found this unbelievable.

Flattering a little, that Pyrrhus should be jealous; it enhanced Philoctetes' redawning sense of self-worth and made him feel even more that he deserved Prince Paris. But he also thought: You lost, desperate, little thing, hunting for some kind of daddy, how could you have the gall to claim that *I* was the one who needed *you?* It made Philoctetes feel sorry for him. Just not sorry enough to take him home.

Any regret he might have felt diminished as, the next few nights, he and Paris kept running into Pyrrhus. They'd be at cocktails, Philoctetes nursing just one vodka and tonic, Paris ordering another Green Label and—his only annoying trait—repeating the tiresome specifications he had laid out at Otionia's. No matter where they went, Pyrrhus would inevitably appear. Sooner or later he would stroll into the place and up to the bar, order his drink, only after a few minutes affect to have suddenly noticed Philoctetes and Paris. When Philoctetes knew he must have peeked in the door of every bar on Port Street.

Pyrrhus would come over to their table and say, "Hey, how was your day?" stuff like that, all the while shifting his weight from one sneakered foot to the other, in a way meant to say, Here I am, youth, not to mention the first guy who gave you the time of day in ten years, and you've taken up with this . . .

This extraordinary man who was so considerate of Philoctetes' feelings that he was even pleasant to Pyrrhus, going so far as to invite him to sit down, when any less princely guy would have felt threatened, would have wondered if there was anything still between Philoctetes and Pyrrhus. Philoctetes thought: If Paris was taking it so easy, then there wasn't anything still between him and Pyrrhus.

Admetus ordered a banana split to go. The woman behind the counter, Evadne, looked at him reproachfully: why did she have to be an accomplice to this dietary crime, didn't he see their splendid variety of low-fat yogurts? Then she set about sullenly assembling the lethal confection. Evadne was cute, Pyrrhus thought, slim and brown-armed, one of those boyish dykes you look twice at before you're sure of their gender. Then you may find yourself staring, mostly bemused by the mysteries that separate us. She glanced up and caught Pyrrhus at it, looked cross. Maybe she thought he was straight and thinking impermissible thoughts. She rang up Admetus's order without looking at Pyrrhus again.

They sat at a picnic table. Admetus deconstructed his banana split with surprising punctilio, finishing the chocolate scoop completely before touching the vanilla. Pyrrhus smoked and watched the throng on Port Street. Presently Paris strolled by, resplendent in an eggshell silk suit. Philoctetes wasn't with him.

"Hey," Pyrrhus whispered. "There's the guy. The one Philoctetes has been seeing."

Admetus looked up, his mustache dewed with vanilla. "Shit," he said.

"What's the matter?"

"Don't you know who that is?"

"Uh-uh. I've talked to him once or twice, but—"

"Paris, it's Paris. Ain't you never read the papers?"

"From Troy?"

"I'll tell you, this town must've seen it all, if Paris can wander around and nobody say a thing about it."

"What do you think he's doing here?"

Admetus moved on to the strawberry. "Same as you, I guess."

"You mean he's . . ."

"Poor guy sits around here for ten years and nobody gives a fuck about him. Then all of a sudden he's got all these princes putting the make on him. It must make his head spin."

Pyrrhus thought about going straight to Odysseus. But he knew that, if he told Odysseus about it, it would all somehow turn out to be his own fault. He went to Phoenix's cabin.

Lieutenant Nereus opened the door. Pyrrhus was confused a second. Was this closet queen having an affair with Phoenix? Then he remembered: when he had commandeered Phoenix's cabin, Phoenix had been sent off to bunk with some junior officer. This poor sucker.

Nereus was wearing only his shorts, displaying a body that would surely have been put to better use in civilian life than shrouded in a navy uniform. He recoiled from Pyrrhus's neutrally appreciative once-over. "What do you want?"

"I was looking for Phoenix."

"He went to the head."

"Oh. Well, I'll wait a minute."

"He takes a real long time in the head."

Pyrrhus smiled. "You're a lucky guy, rooming with Phoenix."

"I don't know, he isn't much trouble."

"Bull, I bet he's been talking your ears off."

"No, he—well, he talks a lot, but it's kind of interesting. Stories and all."

"Yeah."

"Mostly about Achilles. He must really have been something."

"Uh-huh."

Even the lieutenant could discern that the subject of Achilles might not be a fruitful one. Still, there he was, practically naked, under the hot scrutiny of an overt homosexual, he had to say something. He blurted out: "You know, Phoenix—"

"Yeah?"

"He doesn't have any . . ."

How would you know? Pyrrhus thought. "Any what?"

"Beard. I mean, he doesn't have to shave."

"No? That's funny."

"If you're going to wait for Phoenix, you better come in."

Pyrrhus did, sat on Phoenix's bed while Nereus put on some trousers and a gray T-shirt, standard issue, *Achaian Fleet* on the left breast. Clothed, Nereus was a little more at ease. He said, "You go to the island every day."

"That's right."

"To see this Philoctetes guy."

"Uh-huh."

"And you're . . . what? Supposed to try to talk him into coming back?"

"Something like that."

Nereus was quiet. Maybe he was figuring out exactly what tools of persuasion Pyrrhus was using. Finally he said, "What's it like, on the island?"

"Like?"

"There are a lot of gay people?"

"Lots."

"What do they do?"

"Do? They have brunch and they shop and they go to the beach and they take a nap and they have cocktails and dinner and they go dancing and they go back to their rooms and fuck."

"Every day? That's what they do every day?"

"They're on vacation."

"Oh. What do they do at home?"

"They, you know, they have jobs. They live in the city and they work at their jobs."

"And nobody . . . minds them?"

"I guess some people mind them. But, you know, it's the city. There are plenty of weirder things in the city."

"I guess," Nereus said. "You know, I've been thinking, maybe when the war's over I'll . . . do something else."

"Oh yeah? I thought this was your big career and all."

"I think—I've been kind of paying more attention, and I think maybe I was kidding myself. I mean, that nobody suspected."

"I don't know, you fooled me."

"Did I? I don't think I even want to fool anybody. I mean, I've spent my whole life working so hard to do that, when I wanted to do just the opposite. I wanted to tell. Even with Pleione, my girlfriend, I wanted all the time to tell her."

"There really is a Pleione?"

"What do you mean? She still even writes and all. But I used to . . . there were times I'd be with her, and I really thought I was about to tell her. Like I'd have it right up there in my throat, ready to come out, I'd be practically shaking. Kind of leading the conversation, you know, so in a minute it would be just natural to say it and then it would be out and . . ."

"And then . . ."

"I don't know, it would clear things up somehow. Like—did you ever do a math problem, some equation you're supposed to solve, and you suddenly see that all the terms are multiples of some factor?"

"I was never too good at math."

"Oh," Nereus said. Disguising his pleasure, the way people do who are good at math. "Well, you see that there's some x, and if you just divide everything by x, just get it out of there, then everything's suddenly simple, you can see the whole answer. I thought, if she just knew this one little thing, then we wouldn't have all these stupid fights. If everybody knew, my parents and my friends and all . . . It's not the one lie you have to tell, nobody even asks you that question. Well, on the recruiting form, but nobody else. But you have to tell all kinds of different lies, all day long. I'm just not feeling well. I haven't met the right girl yet. We were going to, but it was her time, so we just . . . If everybody knew this one little thing life would get so simple."

Pyrrhus could scarcely remember—not a year away from it, and he could just barely recall the years of dissimulation, the feeling he too had had, that if he could just tell this one tiny thing . . . Well, if he had learned nothing else in a year, it was that factoring out this particular *x* did not make it any easier to explain yourself, did not put an end to dissimulation.

"It isn't so easy in the city," he said.

"It's got to be." Nereus was pacing now, as far as you could pace in the little space between the two berths, just a couple of steps before he had to turn. "Lately I feel all the time like—you ever see one of those clowns who takes a balloon and twists it around until it's some kind of animal? A rabbit or a duck? I feel like I'm doing that, doing it to myself. Twisting myself, all the time."

"You think you wouldn't do that in the city?" Pyrrhus said. "You've got to be some kind of animal, you can't just be a balloon."

He thought of Deucalion, the night Deucalion let him—induced him to—twist Deucalion's body into shapes it was never meant to assume, not rabbits or ducks but the monstrous hybrid forms you hear about in the old stories. A creature whose head was a footstool, whose rectum was a glove, whose mouth was a toilet. And Pyrrhus twisting himself into the even more improbable chimera whose parts were shaped to make use of Deucalion's. All this twisting—after you found you couldn't twist your body the one way the whole world said it should go, you didn't seem to be able to leave off twisting it, trying out shapes.

Nereus said, "I just want to be whatever kind of animal I am."

You can't, Pyrrhus thought. Nobody's that, not ever. Except, maybe, one night with Philoctetes. When they hadn't twisted one way or another, but had just lain there in animal silence.

He was wondering how he could ever get back to that night; he didn't notice at first that Nereus had sat next to him on the bed. Not predatory, just sitting there in a companionable way, also apparently lost in thought. His meditation leading to this conclusion: he put an arm around Pyrrhus. Didn't look, just stretched the arm around Pyrrhus's back and let his hand rest on Pyrrhus's shoulder, not even grasping it, just resting there.

They sat for some time in this fraternal pose. Pyrrhus wondered if this was all Nereus wanted, just to have his hand there. No, that was never all anyone wanted; no one stopped there, no one was just looking for a friendly place to rest his hand. He was waiting for Pyrrhus to show him what kind of animal he was. Pyrrhus felt almost sorry enough for him to do it. But angry, too: no one ever cared what Pyrrhus wanted, no one cared what kind of animal Pyrrhus was. Only Philoctetes was the least bit curious. A curiosity manifested by never asking, just waiting; why couldn't he have waited a little longer?

The hand had not moved. It was just a warm thing on his shoulder. Maybe he was all wrong: Nereus didn't want anything from him. Just to be there. Maybe this was the time when Pyrrhus could say aloud—

Phoenix came in. Nereus jumped up, but Phoenix was already shaking his head at Pyrrhus, as if to say: You insatiable child. Nereus stood for a minute with his mouth open. He must have been thinking: I was just toying with the idea of quitting the navy, going to the city. I wasn't planning on an undesirable discharge.

"I was waiting for you," Pyrrhus said.

"Ah. And occupying yourself in the meanwhile. I had heard you didn't go to the island this evening. I suppose, in your place, I should have spent my night off resting. But then, I shall never be in your place."

"We weren't doing anything."

"You needn't explain yourself to me."

"You bet I needn't."

Nereus must have concluded that he was in no immediate peril. He went and sat on his own bed. As each bed now had an occupant, Phoenix was left standing. Pyrrhus noticed this, but had long since stopped feeling the least bit uncomfortable about it.

Pyrrhus said, "You know, Philoctetes has been seeing this other guy."

"Really? I take it you have not reported this unwelcome turn of events to Odysseus?"

"Well, I kind of am now, aren't I?"

"If you wish me to tell him," Phoenix said innocently. Pyrrhus snorted, but Phoenix ignored him and continued. "How long has Philoctetes been entertaining this alternate suitor?"

"A few days."

"Has he been seeing both of you, or . . . ?"

"Just him."

"I see. That is, given your own evident ability to manage a rather complicated schedule, I shouldn't have been surprised if he . . . I suppose he lacks your youthful energy. He has concluded one affair before embarking on another?"

"He seems to."

"And have you any clue as to the identity of your rival, or successor, whatever he—"

"Paris. Admetus says it's Paris. I mean, once he said so, I could see it was."

Phoenix looked now as though he really did want to sit down. "Paris," he said.

"From Troy," Pyrrhus added helpfully.

"Here to thwart you."

"You think?"

"Why else? And evidently succeeding."

"Yeah, but if Philoctetes knew . . . I mean, if he knew why all of a sudden this stud was chasing him, then—"

"You mean, if he understood that Paris's motives were the same as your own?"

"But they aren't. I really . . . like Philoctetes."

"Ah. Absolutely, then, I am sure he will grasp at once the distinction between someone who is merely deceiving him and someone who *likes* him and is also deceiving him. You should go and elucidate this to him straightaway."

"Well, I wasn't going to tell him that," Pyrrhus said. "I don't know what to tell him."

"I believe this interesting impasse may require a more formidable intelligence than our own."

"You mean Odysseus? You think he'll know what to do?"

"Who knows? I doubt that he has ever devoted his tactical skills to the resolution of a love triangle. But where else can we turn?"

Phoenix said, "Well, but surely it's supposed to mean—"

Odysseus interrupted him, not sharply. "The very first principle of construction is to look at the plain meaning of the words. 'When Philoctetes' bow is brought to Troy,' that's all they said."

"Hence it doesn't matter if it comes with us or with Paris?"

"Not that I can see."

They were in the officers' mess, Odysseus and Phoenix at one end of the table, Pyrrhus as far away as he could get.

Odysseus went on, "I'm still not even sure if Philoctetes himself has to go with it. For all I know we could ship the bow to Troy by parcel post, if we could find the damned thing." He looked reproachfully at Pyrrhus, the pathetic whore who couldn't get one simple piece of information.

Pyrrhus thought of defending himself: he did too know where it was.

Instead he said, "This doesn't make any sense. Why would the Trojans send Paris to get the bow if once they've got it, they're finished?"

"Perhaps they're misreading the oracle. As I did, I admit it. Maybe they think it only counts if it comes with us. Given all the ambiguities, I suppose their best course, really, would be to kill Philoctetes."

Pyrrhus stood up. "What?"

"Kill him and hope nobody ever figures out where the bow is. That's what I would do, I think, in their place. But I suppose, if they were going to do that, they would have by now. Let Paris lead him off to Troy, him and his confounded bow. Then all the requisite parties will be at Troy, through one means or another. The prophecy will have been—"

"We can't let that happen," Pyrrhus said.

"We don't seem to have a great deal of control over events. You were . . . my only arrow. Now we've shot it."

"But Philoctetes—he might get hurt, we can't let them . . ."

"We're in the middle of a war. People get hurt. Maybe they really will kill him. But I shouldn't imagine his life expectancy is very long in any event." Pyrrhus didn't answer. Odysseus said, "What have you done, fallen for him?"

"I don't want to talk to you about it."

"As a matter of fact, the subject doesn't thrill me, either. Do you often develop these attachments to your clients?"

"No, not usually," Pyrrhus said. "Not ever."

"I see. Well, you've picked an inopportune time to begin."

"I couldn't help it."

Couldn't help it, Odysseus thought. Had he ever had that feeling? Even with Penelope—had he been helpless, would he have fallen in love with her if it had been inconvenient? The sort of hypothetical question he despised. This once he answered it: he would not. He did love her, had loved her unceasingly since the day they'd met, couldn't wait until they were done with Troy and he could sail back to her. But he would not have fallen, not even for Penelope, if there had been any impediment. There had never been one instant when he couldn't help himself.

"This has only to do with your ego. You don't care about hurting him, you have been about the business of hurting him. You just can't stand that he's going off with somebody else."

"That isn't so. I love him."

Odysseus drew back, startled. Then he laughed; this he couldn't help. "Good luck persuading him of that." He stood up. "I'm indifferent; I don't care what happens, as long as he gets to Troy. But you haven't got much time. Your rival must be moving in for the kill, literal or figurative, right now. Figurative, I guess. Either way, you'd better hurry."

Odysseus strode out of the room. Phoenix stood up, too, evidently meaning to follow him. But he hesitated and, after a minute, sat down again. As if, at long last, choosing a side. If there is one thing eunuchs are absolutely suckers for, it is a love story. "Do you really?" he said.

"What?" Pyrrhus said.

"Love Philoctetes?"

"I don't know. I hated saying that. I didn't want to say that to Odysseus, it's like it spoils everything. Like he has something of mine now."

"I shouldn't worry. He didn't believe you."

"No? I don't know if I believed me. Maybe he's right, it's just my pride."

"Nonetheless, you at least *like* him. I believe that was your word."

"It doesn't matter, there's nothing I can do. I mean, it's not even like fate's on my side. If Odysseus is right, it doesn't matter who Philoctetes winds up with, it doesn't matter if I win or lose."

"To history, you mean."

"That's right."

"Then I suppose what matters is what you want."

"What? I thought what mattered was my destiny and all."

"Which is going to occur. The only person who could possibly care just how you get there is you."

What Pyrrhus had always hated most about outcalls was the moment he got to a trick's door, when the guy opened the door. Partly, of course, because he'd see what sort of monster he was going to have to make it with. But also because the guy would in turn get his first sight of Pyrrhus. The trick would peer through the crack of the door as if peeping into a half-opened birthday present. Then he might, delighted, fling open the door and tear off the wrappings. Or he might, barely concealing his disappointment, step aside and admit Pyrrhus as grudgingly as one might a furnace inspector.

Just once, a trick didn't bother to dissemble. "I'm sorry, I . . . I'll pay you, but . . ."

"But what?"

"You're . . . a redhead."

312

Pyrrhus stepped into the foyer and looked in the mirror. "Gee, I guess I am." This was just to get inside, so the guy couldn't close the door. Because he was most certainly going to pay. "Is that so bad?"

"No, it's just me, just a thing."

Pyrrhus shrugged. He was already thinking, as he waited for his money, if he went home there might be a message on the machine and he could score again. More likely anyone finding him not home would have moved on to the next ad, and he would do better to make a personal appearance at Club 23.

He was thinking this through and was startled when the trick felt obliged, or entitled, to explain his *thing*: "I've never really analyzed it, but somehow the pale skin and the red hair, the pubic hair especially, when that's red, just gives me a kind of clammy feeling. It's like making it with a porcelain statuette."

Probably he had learned to be frank in some self-improvement regimen. He furrowed his brow, trying to think of some better way to articulate the revulsion Pyrrhus evidently aroused in him. Before he could Pyrrhus said, "Uh-huh. Anyway, I need a hundred bucks."

"Well, that's out of the question. I mean, I know you had to pay for the cab and all, but—"

"My name's Pyrrhus, asshole, what the hell did you think you were going to get?"

The trick recoiled. "I don't know what I was thinking."

Pyrrhus strode further into the apartment. It looked like the bridal suite at a casino hotel, all red and gold. And there was a surprising array of porcelain figurines.

The trick tried to block Pyrrhus's way. "Look, you're probably right, I owe you the hundred."

Pyrrhus shoved past and went to look at himself again, this time in the gilt chinoiserie mirror over the mantel. "I don't look like any fucking china doll." He was just playing. He made himself look mean and enjoyed the way the trick trembled as he stared over Pyrrhus's shoulder at the fierce image in the mirror.

"No, no, of course you don't. I wasn't talking about you." He pulled out a slender billfold. "I'm sorry. Here's that hundred. And . . . and twenty for the cab."

This outcome, for two minutes of effortless posturing, was so satisfactory that it wasn't until Pyrrhus got to Club 23, where the gray men at the bar eyed the lineup of punks, that he felt the full weight of the rejection. Scattered about the room were, undoubtedly, potential customers who took one look at Pyrrhus and got . . . a kind of clammy feeling. Men to whom any of the wasted kids posing at the far wall was more desirable than Pyrrhus. This didn't affect Pyrrhus's earnings: his overall market share wasn't dented by the handful of guys who perversely preferred Brand X. Still, it upset him, enough that he went home without even trying to score.

Most of us are familiar enough with the sensation that we might not be the prettiest creatures in the room. Poor Leucon, for example, back in the city, would spend most of his twenties trying to move up a rung or two on the ladder of beauty. Perhaps if he changed his hair, traded his glasses for contacts; perhaps a bulky sweater would camouflage his waistline, or lack of one. Until finally he discovered that there were men who found glasses sexy and who did not disdain a modest gut.

That is: for most of us, the inexplicable variations in human taste are a salvation. While, for Pyrrhus, they threatened the very foundations of his understanding of the world. It was not a question simply of envy, or of injured pride, or of any emotion familiar to mortals. His pain, that night at Club 23, rose from the part of him that was divine, and to understand it one must look for parallels in the special wounds that are inflicted only on the gods.

The reader will recall that, long before the war, Paris was enlisted to judge a sort of divine beauty pageant, in which the finalists were Hera, Athena, and Aphrodite, and the prize was a golden apple. Which had been tossed out by Eris, mother of strife, at the wedding of Pyrrhus's paternal grandparents, because—

Pardon me, I'm as bad as Phoenix. There was an apple, that's all. The three goddesses paraded, one at a time and naked, before Paris. Of course they were all perfectly proportioned, unblemished, and so on. Goddesses, in short. If there had existed, in a glass case in some celestial Bureau of Standards, a Rule of Beauty, they would all have measured up exactly. There was no way of ranking them. He might have awarded the apple to Miss Congeniality, but they were about equal on that measure as well, congeniality not being a usual endowment of goddesses.

Paris fell back on the talent portion of the competition. Each of the contestants, in her private audience with him, offered a stupendous gift that only she had it in her power to bestow. Hera brandished the deed to all of Asia. Athena promised him wisdom and victory in battle. Aphrodite offered him the love of Helen. He awarded the apple to Aphrodite, of course, incurring the wrath of the runners-up and thus bringing assorted miseries to Troy.

What were Hera and Athena angry about? They knew that, objectively, Aphrodite was no fairer than they, that she had only offered the judge the most appealing bribe. Yet it was a bribe they couldn't match. Their powers were limitless, but each on a single vector. Hera couldn't promise wisdom; Athena didn't have much in the way of real estate. Paris had, in effect, declared that their mightiest gifts were worthless. To him surpassing wisdom was a trivial attribute, like being able to wiggle your ears. Asia was a vacant lot he didn't care to build on. He had spurned all of this for some bimbo who was temporarily pretty, in a mortal way. In the face of this bizarre preference, as unaccountable and perverse as human preferences are, the goddesses were just losers.

So Pyrrhus, the most lustrous red on earth, when confronted by a trick who was pyrrhiphobic. It wasn't, as it used to be for Leucon, a matter of finding himself a rung or two lower on the ladder than he had imagined. Pyrrhus was at the top of his ladder, but it was the wrong one. Again: only the divine, I think, can know this particular style of futility. And it really pisses them off, makes them want to topple kingdoms and invent new plagues.

Faced with Philoctetes' apparent preference for Paris, Pyrrhus couldn't compete by developing his own debonair half-smile or compiling a repertory of amusing travel anecdotes. He could only put into the contest more of what he had, in the hope that he would somehow tip the balance. As if Hera could have won the apple by promising, not just Asia, but Europe and Africa as well: the whole world.

What he had, that Paris had not, was — what? Youth, vigor, a trimmer butt and more frequent and spontaneous erections. How, he wondered, could he display them to the best advantage?

Perhaps Athena, still harboring her grudge against Paris, granted Pyrrhus a moment of wisdom. Or perhaps he hatched his scheme out of the memories of the soap operas he used to watch, in the days when he sat by the phone waiting for some caller to answer his ad. The great plan was this: he would flaunt Corythus and make Philoctetes jealous. I myself am awestruck by the brilliance of this concept.

7

Corythus, dressed in civvies, looked a lot like a sailor about to go on shore leave. This might not have made him especially conspicuous some years later, when for a brief period the most fashionable queers in the cities strived for very nearly the same look. But it was, at the time of our story, a problem. Corythus was irrefutably a sailor. While sailors had a certain iconic allure that made them welcome ornaments in any gay bar, his sudden appearance on Lemnos would be difficult to account for.

Phoenix was the one who pointed this out. "Where is his ship?"

"What do you mean?" Pyrrhus said.

"I mean that, if I espy a duckling, I naturally look about for a duck. And if I see a sailor on liberty I assume there is a ship in the vicinity."

"Oh. Well, he could work on the weekly freighter."

"As I understand it, the men who work on the freighter tend to take their rest and recreation at the other end of the line. To disembark at Lemnos would arouse speculation about the style of recreation they preferred."

"Maybe he's an exception. Or, okay, people will be curious about him. That doesn't mean they're just going to figure out right away that he has a warship hidden nearby."

"At the very least he should have some explanation. In case he's asked."

Corythus had been studying himself in the mirror. He was wearing the immemorial outfit of sailors on leave: a loud, open-collared sport shirt and jeans so new they had a crease. He had put some gloop on his residual hair, in the vain hope of combing it into something, but had only wound up with a shinier flattop. Now he left off practicing expressions that might conceal his buckteeth and turned to face Pyrrhus and Phoenix. He didn't betray any annoyance at being talked about. On the contrary, he looked a little pleased, and mutely curious.

"He won't be talking to anybody but me," Pyrrhus said. "That's the point."

"The point?" Corythus said.

Phoenix looked over at Pyrrhus, eyebrows raised. Hadn't the child been told? "I believe I shall take a little stroll about the deck while it's still light," he said. Though he must have been torn between discreetly absenting himself and staying to listen as Pyrrhus elucidated *the point*.

When Phoenix had gone, Pyrrhus said, "You remember that guy we were talking about? The old sailor we're trying to get to join up again?"

"Yeah?"

"Well, I . . . I kind of want him to see us together. To make him, you know . . ."

"Oh," Corythus said blankly. Then, eyes widening: "Oh. We're supposed to act like we're . . . lovers."

"That's right."

"But we aren't?" This said with a surprising nonchalance, as if he were merely trying to pin down the situation. Pyrrhus didn't answer right away, and Corythus said, "What are we, then?"

What were they? They had slept together every night since Pyrrhus had boarded the *Penelope*—every night except the one Pyrrhus hadn't slept, but had lain awake with Philoctetes in silent astonishment, that night already long past. They had learned to sleep together: knew how to breathe, knew how to arrange their limbs so no one was paralyzed in the morning. If one of them woke up for an instant he knew, didn't wonder, who was beside him. Already Pyrrhus could hardly conceive of going to sleep without Corythus. As he could hardly conceive of spending an hour with Corythus awake.

"I think we're lovers," Pyrrhus said. He wasn't lying exactly—he wasn't sure what the word meant. He had always just supposed that he would understand the word on the day it actually applied. If he could say it without knowing if it was true or false, then it didn't mean anything, did it? Maybe not to anyone.

"You think we are?"

"Sure. What do you want, a ring or something?"

Corythus shrugged.

"We're lovers," Pyrrhus repeated. Because Philoctetes was going to go off with his Paris, and they weren't ever going to take Troy, and Corythus was all he had. Maybe this was all people got: just waking up next to someone and knowing who it was.

They kissed, but Corythus's lips didn't part; he was still thinking. It suddenly occurred to Pyrrhus that Corythus might always be thinking. That, in their long silences, Pyrrhus wasn't the only one thinking.

"If we're lovers," Corythus said, "why are we trying to make this other guy jealous?"

"It's politics."

"You mean it's over my head?"

"No." Pyrrhus actually thought about explaining it all. It wasn't over Corythus's head, he wouldn't blab to anyone. Why shouldn't he understand Pyrrhus's mission and the role he had now been conscripted to play in it?

Because it was shameful. Pyrrhus was astounded to discover this feeling, down inside where for so long there had been nothing, no shame the night he'd taken Lamus home or any other night of doing his job. Half the world had known that he was a whore, or had played at being one, if there was a difference. Why shouldn't Corythus know as well?

Maybe they really were lovers, maybe this at last was what the word meant: your lover was the one you had to shelter from the worst things you knew about yourself. Yes, this had to be it, the hot shame and, somewhere beneath it, a strange, hopeless sort of jubilation. He took Corythus in his arms. As, when you are first in love, you will take any willing bystander in your arms.

Corythus was sulky and silent on the trip to Lemnos. He looked at his feet mostly, even as the launch rounded the island and the town came into view; or he looked at Pyrrhus with the sort of unconsenting solidarity with which a convict regards the bailiff to whom he is chained. It didn't seem likely that he was going to carry his weight in the pantomime of exuberant young love Pyrrhus had hoped to stage for Philoctetes.

When they got to Pterelas's—crowded for once, a weekend mob that promised high season was coming soon—Corythus brightened. Pyrrhus was annoyed by the crowd, the trouble he had elbowing through to the bar to get their beers, the possibility that Philoctetes could be here and simply fail to notice them. But when he made his way back, he found Corythus looking around, wide-eyed and open-mouthed as a child. The stale vista of a gay bar was for him a scene of enchantment.

Do you remember? Loitering outside the disco, finally making yourself go in. You paid your three bucks to an improbably muscular man who looked at you with incurious disdain, got in return a little ticket good for one drink, then turned a corner and beheld: HUNDREDS OF US, under the flashing lights. Sometimes it can seem as though all the repression was almost worth it, because it made possible that explosive discovery: hundreds of us, in the disco, free, and you had turned a corner and were one of them.

319

Except that Corythus had the added thrill of seeing that hundreds, or at least dozens, were smiling back at him. A cute sailor: probably no one cared what ship he might have come from, no one was any more curious than you are when you luckily find a dollar on the sidewalk.

Corythus must have been enjoying a preview of the life he would have when his enlistment was up, when he got into civvies for good. All the wonderful men who lay ahead once he'd escaped the *Penelope*. Yet, oddly, the flattering attention from strangers made him draw closer to Pyrrhus. Maybe out of gratitude, that Pyrrhus had opened this world to him, or maybe because it was all, not just exciting, but a little scary. He reached for Pyrrhus's hand. An act of bravado — look, we can hold hands here — but his hand, when Pyrrhus took it, was shaking.

When they got to the next bar — calmer, more elegant, the bar with the piano player and the soft lights — Corythus pulled still closer. Maybe thinking it was all romantic. Which was good, because this of course was the bar where Philoctetes sat, nursing his single cocktail, at a corner table with Paris.

My. Pyrrhus had picked up some little sailor and was showing him off. How childish: Philoctetes had never been so convinced of Pyrrhus's raw innocence as when he beheld the poor kid trying to carry off this primeval maneuver. He would tease Pyrrhus about it when Pyrrhus came over to the table. As he would, any minute, the nightly game of imagine-running-into-you. He would let Pyrrhus know how transparent and silly he was being. Except that it was also sort of touching, the clearest sign Philoctetes had had that Pyrrhus really cared about him.

On the other hand: even if Pyrrhus was just exhibiting this kid for Philoctetes' benefit, there was a chance — no, a certainty — that Pyrrhus and his friend would take a cubicle at the Aeolian House and finish their pantomime. It had happened already; you could see it in the way the sailor walked, the legs stiff, not bending at the knee. The way a man walks who has very recently been screwed.

Fine, if the sailor wanted Pyrrhus's clumsy humping he was welcome to it. Philoctetes could picture it: Pyrrhus pushing forward like some relentless engine, the kid taking it. At the wrong angle. Well, he was young, young enough to be one undifferentiated erogenous zone. Maybe it hardly mattered if Pyrrhus aimed well: the kid was a target he couldn't miss.

Young: it was just natural for the young to be with the young. Maybe Pyrrhus had found this out; maybe he wasn't just putting on a show. Philoctetes thought of that kid he had met a few weeks before Pyrrhus arrived. What's-his-name—Halesus, the cute kid with the cuter lover. They had looked so right together, Philoctetes had had a moment's vision of the country from which he had been exiled. Now he was seeing it again. He had thought for a few nights that Pyrrhus offered a way back, a transit visa. Now he saw: that country was youth itself. No one could bring him back. He was old. If he hadn't gotten sick, he would be old.

Very well, he wasn't a kid any more, he would have to dwell in the country of grownups. Here at this table, with Paris. Who made maturity look pretty good, and who probably knew the angles. Yes: Philoctetes had the idea, though they'd never so much as kissed, that Paris would know just what to do. Even though no one had ever heard a hint of his being gay, the finest athletes can pretty much compete in any event. And Paris might be the very best in the world. After all, Helen had picked him, she who could have had anybody; he had to have some know-how, some finesse. Something he had acquired along with the crow's-feet and—Philoctetes just noticed, looking at Paris hard to avoid looking at Pyrrhus—the premonition of a double chin.

Philoctetes turned away for a minute. He was ready to sail, with Paris, toward the grown-up country where he could live again. But for a minute he looked at Pyrrhus, until finally Paris stopped talking—he had been telling a very long story about a trip to Egypt, Philoctetes had missed most of it—followed Philoctetes' eyes, and saw his competition.

"Oh," Paris said. "There's that kid again."

"Uh-huh."

"Hey, you know who that kid looks like?"

"Who do you think?"

"Achilles."

"Yes, he does."

"It's just amazing."

"Not so amazing," Philoctetes said. "It's his son."

"What?"

"That's his son. Neoptolemus, his real name is."

"God . . . um, excuse me." Paris went off to the men's room, stumbled off hastily, not at all his graceful self.

· · ·

321

"That's the guy?" Corythus said.

"Huh?" Pyrrhus said.

"The real skinny one?"

"How could you tell?"

"I don't know. You just . . . changed, the minute we walked in here. All tense."

"Am I?"

Corythus smiled, just a little, still trying to hide his sweet buckteeth. "Like I get when I see you. You want to kiss me or something?"

"What?"

"We can, can't we? We ain't on the ship. Don't you want to make this guy jealous?"

"We don't have to. This was stupid."

"Well, kiss me anyway. I just want to be kissed. In front of a bunch of people."

"Okay." Pyrrhus kissed him, perfunctorily, and pulled back. It was all right, they weren't on the ship. They were on an island, one of those islands where men can kiss. Yet Pyrrhus was uncomfortable. Partly because it felt kind of like showing off. And partly because shedding your inhibitions during a sojourn on a tiny, licentious island just reminds you how big the world is, and how few islands there are.

Corythus looked over Pyrrhus's shoulder. "That other guy left the table. You can go talk to your friend."

"That's okay."

"You might as well. I'm going back to that other place."

"What?"

"That other bar, I liked it there. I don't want to stay here and put on a show."

"Well, I'll go with you. Show's over."

"All right. But—" He looked down at the floor, swallowed, then looked back up at Pyrrhus, a huge and unself-conscious smile dawning on his face. "Maybe you're not the only guy who can make new friends."

In the men's room, Paris sat in the toilet stall, smoking a cigarette, his pants lowered to signal to any chance visitor that he was there for the usual purpose; not understanding that there were several usual purposes in that particular facility. He flicked the ashes into the bowl, carefully avoiding the famous member that had been where every man's (except Philoctetes') had longed to visit and that would now—there was no getting around it—have to be offered to Philoctetes himself.

His father had sworn that no such sacrifice would be required. But it would have to be done. There could be only one reason Achilles' son—even if he was, apparently, actually gay—would be hanging around an aging, fleshless hermit. Sooner or later Philoctetes would want—no matter how charming Paris was, sooner or later Philoctetes would require the attentions this boy had supplied and was evidently willing to supply again.

Too much, it was asking too much. If he could, say, just lie back and let himself be done, would that be enough? He could manage that. Just close his eyes and think of—well, not Helen; Helen had never done that for him, and the very picture of it was oddly threatening. Just think of someone; if he was still Aphrodite's pet she would send him some rousing vision to get him through the act. Except that Philoctetes would want more than—what did they call it? Trade, he would want more than that before he would actually pull up stakes and come along to Troy.

Whoever had been using the urinal was still there, though Paris had long since finished his cigarette and had been sitting for some minutes staring mournfully down at his soon-to-be-conscripted spearman for Troy. Whoever it was, he was still out there. Luckily, there was for some reason a hole in the stall door. Paris peeped through it and was startled to find that the man, who had oddly forgotten to return his own little recruit to his pants, was staring back. Paris got up, arranged his clothing, flushed his cigarette, and ran out of the room without even bothering—so great was his panic—to comb his hair.

It was asking too much, even for his father, even for Helen. Perhaps there was some other way? Philoctetes was still at the table, looking over at Paris with evident concern; he'd been gone too long. As Paris made his way through the crowd he tried to think of some other way. There wasn't any: he had too often been in the opposite position, going to dinner two or three times with some flirt who thought she could string him along indefinitely. He knew exactly what Philoctetes must have felt: sooner or later you have to give it up.

"Are you okay?" Philoctetes said.

"Yeah, I just . . . the last drink really hit me for some reason, I just had to sit for a minute."

"I saw Dolophion go in. I thought you might be having a mini-romance."

"You know that guy?"

"Dolophion's a legend. You almost have to admire somebody who shows off such a small gift with such high hopes."

"Huh?"

"Anyway, you're feeling better?" It was a sign of the high Philoctetes was on, maybe, that he could worry about someone else's health. As if he were not just in the midst of one more remission, but had returned to the country of the well.

"Yeah. I could use some air. How about I walk you home?"

"Um . . . I'm almost ashamed to show you where I live."

"I'm not too into interior decoration," Paris said. He didn't smile: a smile would have turned that tired line into a promise, and he was still trying to think of some other way.

As they walked, the village and its glow shrinking behind them, Paris said, "Achilles' son, huh? And you . . . got it on with him."

Philoctetes looked over at him. "Does that bother you?"

"No. No, I just thought you might be kind of, I don't know, mad at Greek people."

"Just some of them."

"Not him?"

"He's got his own grievances."

"Ah." Paris almost didn't say the next thing. They had scarcely talked about the war. That is, Philoctetes had of course explained his presence on Lemnos—briefly, not his usual account, and he had kind of forgotten to mention the snake. And of course Philoctetes knew who Paris was. But they hadn't talked about it; Philoctetes had been too polite even to ask how it came to be that Paris was holidaying in Lemnos while his family ate hippoburgers in the besieged city. To bring it up now would be to bring the war here, to Lemnos. (As they had done, Paris and Pyrrhus.) So Paris almost didn't say it. Except Philoctetes must have known, anybody who read the papers would have known. "You know I killed his father."

"What?"

"Achilles. I was the one who killed him."

Philoctetes stopped walking. He stood still, staring down at the ground, then finally and with evident reluctance looking up at Paris.

Philoctetes didn't know. He hadn't read the papers in years. They were such a disappointment, the papers, same shit day after day and Odysseus's name never on the obit page. Of course he'd seen pictures of Paris in uniform. Still, princes often wear uniforms, especially in wartime. It's just a gesture; you never think of them actually fighting.

Philoctetes looked at Paris. Paris's loosely draped silk suit giving way to the tight embrace of armor, in his hands the weapon, his eternal half-smile still in place, but a little scary now.

Of course there are, all around us, men who have killed. The veterans sit with you at business meetings, they drive you in taxis, on television they smile and sell lawn implements or dog food. They carry this within them, that they have killed, and for most of them it is no big deal, they don't think about it often. They were supposed to, after all; we sent them to a world with different rules and they did what they were supposed to and now they are back and all we really ask is that they not bring it up. That they not brag about it, or whine about what the government made them do. Or say, with an odd jauntiness: "You know I killed his father."

Philoctetes thought he should be appalled, but he wasn't really. It was rather as if Paris had committed a mild social blunder. As if this elegant man had farted or belched. That was all: it was simply rude to bring it up. Philoctetes didn't mean to let it spoil what they were finally headed for. He just said "Oh" and started walking again.

"It's kind of an odd coincidence," Paris said. "That we should both be after you."

"Are you after me?" Philoctetes said, more interested in that than in any coincidence.

"Of course, can't you tell?"

"I wasn't sure. Oh, look, we're here. My palace."

"Don't knock it. I often wish I could find some place simple, where I could just get off by myself. And, god, look at the view."

"Uh-huh." Philoctetes tried to see it as something other than the landscape of desolation in which he had lived. Here was a man of the world claiming to like the place. Maybe Philoctetes' world was upside down; if he could just rejoin the human community he would prize solitude and find the dunes beautiful.

As they watched, Paris put an arm around Philoctetes' shoulder. Philoctetes thought: God, it's going to happen, something out of a soap opera, genuine romance. He put his own arm around Paris's waist, but felt nothing except the rich silk jacket. He felt as though he were at some distance, looking at the pair of them, holding each other in the moonlight, as in a cognac ad. A coldly perfect parody of closeness.

You can have your pick of stories: Aphrodite sent Paris a vision, or Paris just found that he was naturally a whore, could do anything he needed to in service of father and country. In any event, he turned his head and entrapped Philoctetes in a deep movieland kiss.

Philoctetes was distracted by his cologne.

From the receiving end, indifference and uncontrollable lust feel almost exactly the same. Paris's groping hands, heedless of whatever sensation they were causing, his smothering and loveless hugs, might have come equally from playacting or ruthless desire: neither considers the other. Perhaps this was the way Paris made love. Would Helen have fallen for this? Maybe, maybe she was tired of being adored and ready for this manhandling. Even so—even if this was the way Paris always did it, it could still be mimicry: what could he feign except what he always did? Under the polished and almost effete exterior resided this fumbling lout, now playing the part of a lout.

What gave him away? Maybe—the simple answer—the absence of the one thing no man can feign. But he might have been granted a vision, or he might have been roused by the simple friction of his unfocused humping. He might have gotten hard. Perhaps there was something less palpably absent.

Maybe it was the lack of an agenda that betrayed him. Paris squeezed and clutched and never moved on, failed to focus on any particular one of Philoctetes' ins or outs, organs or orifices. He had no intention. So how was this different from the first idyllic night with Pyrrhus, equally lacking in a story line? It just was: with Pyrrhus, Philoctetes had been surprised to look over his shoulder and see the dawn, it might have been five minutes. While with Paris, every minute felt like a minute.

Philoctetes pulled away.

. . .

326

Paris said, "What's the matter?"

"I don't know."

Paris thought: Shit, I'm going through this, practically ready to throw up but doing the best I can. And it's not good enough for you? I'm not good enough, you washed-up faggot? He was stoking his own indignation; some part of him knew that he was not, either, ready to throw up.

Philoctetes said again, "I don't know. It's like you're not really interested."

"I—I think maybe I just had too much to drink."

"You're not gay."

Do you remember how, time was, someone would call you gay and you would blush and stammeringly deny it? Yes, you remember—I don't care how far out you are now, you remember doing this. Then you will forgive me if I revel in this moment, when a middle-aged straight boy must deny being straight. Paris blushed and stammered, just as you and I once did. "What are you talking about? Of course I am."

Philoctetes shook his head. "What's going on here? What are we doing?"

"I—I wanted you to come back to Troy."

"I was going to, maybe. I told you I can't decide. But now I don't know why you want it. I'm sorry, but I think you're really fucked up."

Perhaps Paris considered his dwindling options and settled on the truth, or perhaps he just had to respond to the allegation that he was fucked up. In any event, he said: "I'm *supposed* to bring you back."

"Supposed to?"

When Pyrrhus got to Philoctetes' shack, it was so dark he was almost to the front steps before he realized Philoctetes was sitting on them. "There you are," Pyrrhus said.

"Yes."

"I was afraid you wouldn't be here. I mean, I didn't see any light, and I thought you might have . . ."

"Might have . . . ?"

"Gone somewhere with that guy."

"You mean the Aeolian House," Philoctetes said. "Somewhere like that?"

No, Pyrrhus had meant somewhere like Troy; he was lucky to have been misunderstood. "Yeah."

Philoctetes smiled, a narrow smile Pyrrhus could barely make out in the dark. "I kind of thought *you* were . . . going somewhere like that."

"What, with Corythus? No, I was just trying to . . ."

"Make me jealous? That's sweet."

Pyrrhus knew he should leave it at that. But he said, "To tell the truth, I have fucked him." As if clearing a little realm of truth beneath the overarching lie, as if they could dwell in that.

"I know. I can't say I blame you. I haven't been much fun."

"Neither is he."

"No? He looks fun. What is he, a sailor?"

"I guess."

"From what ship? I wonder. The freighter isn't in. Not that they play much, anyway."

Pyrrhus sat next to him on the stoop, not close enough to touch. "He's off playing with someone else. What about Paris?"

"He went back to his hotel; he always does. For some reason, no one ever spends the night with me." He looked over at Pyrrhus. "You know who he is?"

"Well, sure—he's famous." Then, without sarcasm, "A famous lover."

"Right. He won't get any testimonials from me."

"Nothing happened?"

"Zero. You know, it's funny, I went through—years ago—this period when I went after straight boys. It was just a game; they were never very good, mostly just lay there, but getting them there was kind of fun. I mean, I'd go into a straight bar, one of those joints where everybody's watching basketball on the giant TV, and I'd just look around and say: That one, that one can be made. And I'd make him. Like I say, this was just for a while; I got tired of it. Some guys never get tired of it, they think there's something special about a straight boy. Even though they've just got the same parts as anybody else, except they, like, didn't get the owner's manual with theirs.

"Anyway, the point is that I could walk into a bar with a hundred mouth-breathing breeders with beer dribbling down their chins, and I could pick out the one guy who, after another pitcher or two, might be open to a little experiment. I don't know what it was, just something about a guy that told you his asshole wasn't sewn shut at birth. You could tell.

"But I went out with Paris every night for a week and I never once got any of those waves from him. He gave me long, soulful looks and all that, and I kind of got sucked in, I hardly noticed there was anything missing. It's just, thinking back, you know, I never for one minute got those waves."

"Huh," Pyrrhus said. Then, daring to ask only because it would have been unnatural not to: "What do you think he was up to?"

"Oh, I know what he was up to."

"You do?"

"He was trying to get me to come with him to Troy."

"Why would he do that?"

"This is . . . silly. There's this prophecy. It's stupid, but he says everybody believes in it, that the Greeks can't win the war unless I'm with them."

"You?"

"Like some kind of huge rabbit's foot." He gave a dry laugh, the kind that might have set him off on a coughing fit; it didn't, this once. "Silly, except it's just the kind of joke the gods would play. Don't you love it— they drop me off here, those shits, and in the end I'm what they needed?"

"Then you kind of believe it."

"Of course I don't believe it. I don't know, I'll probably go with him anyway."

"You'll—what?"

"Go. There isn't anything for me here."

"There's . . . me."

"Sure," Philoctetes said, flatly enough that he wasn't even rejecting a proposal, more just acknowledging a polite offer that wasn't meant to be taken seriously, as when people say you really need to come spend a weekend some time. He went on: "Hey, it would be funny, wouldn't it, if the Greeks lost, all on account of me? That would be funny."

"You're going to help the Trojans win?" Pyrrhus said. "I mean, I understand you're mad and all, but—"

"I'm not mad. Or, I am, but . . . even if it were so, this stupid prophecy, it's none of my business. I'll go with him or I won't. I don't have anything to do with the rest of it."

"But—I mean, just say it was so. Then you can't say it isn't your business. If your being there or not makes some kind of difference, then whatever you do is choosing one side or another. Objectively, I mean."

"Objectively," Philoctetes repeated. "What's that supposed to mean?"

"I don't know. It's just, you've got to be for your country or against it, don't you?"

"I told you it wasn't my country. It never was. Look: you know how, like when a football team or something wins the big event, their city just goes wild? People dance in the streets, waggling their fingers and going *We're number one*, as if they had anything to do with it. When it was just a bunch of guys who have nothing to do with one place or another, they just go anywhere they're paid. I could—I could almost see feeling that way about your high-school team. They at least sat next to you in class and, if you were discreet, you might suck one or two of them off. But I can't believe in a country bigger than a high school."

He had stood up during this speech. He was facing the water, and beyond it the island Sidheritis. "Anyway," he said. "I thought you were kind of mad at the Greeks yourself."

"I'm still a Greek."

Philoctetes shrugged. "You know, it's funny, Paris went on about what a beautiful view it is from up here. I hardly ever look this way, I never even noticed the view."

Pyrrhus joined him. "Not much to see, it's so dark."

"Yeah, but look, there's these little lights, way off the other side of Sidheritis. What is that, some kind of ship?"

Pyrrhus swallowed his alarm. "Beats me."

They stood for a while, looking out at the sea and the island and the little lights beyond it. There was no question about it: the longer you looked, the more clearly you could make out the outline of the ship.

Pyrrhus put his arm around Philoctetes. Philoctetes looked at him with neutral curiosity but did not shake him off.

"You know, I need to leave soon," Pyrrhus said.

"What?" Though this might have been the national anthem of Lemnos: I love you, I'm leaving.

"I need to leave soon. I'm almost out of money. I need to get home."

"Oh."

Oh. How silly, sillier even than some prophecy and Paris's offer of a life of leisure in an alabaster palace: Philoctetes had held somewhere in him the utterly deranged notion that this boy was the alternative. All because they had made calf eyes at each other for just one night. He blurted out: "You could stay here."

Ridiculous. Stay, and what? Join Philoctetes in his shack? Well, Pyrrhus could make money, waiting tables. He could get a place of his own as an ornamental houseboy at one of the guesthouses. He could come back some nights and watch Philoctetes, sleeping in a puddle of his own sweat. Or someone could swoop down on him, one of those guys with a villa at the far end of Port Street. It would happen; he would tire of Philoctetes and of privation and would let it happen. Imagine this innocent country kid turned into some sort of genteel whore. He needed to go.

Pyrrhus said, hesitantly, as if thinking it over, but in a way that told Philoctetes he was just being polite, "Well, I could, maybe."

"No." Which left one other opening, so ludicrous Philoctetes could not even say it.

The boy did, casually, tentatively: "Or maybe you could come with me."

Philoctetes had a catch in his throat. He was afraid he would start coughing, coughing/sobbing, and disgust Pyrrhus. Again. Sooner or later he would disgust this boy again.

"How soon are you going?" Philoctetes said.

Pyrrhus held him tighter, as if they had a deal. "Whenever. As soon as you're ready." With a rash eagerness, as if this thought he had tentatively thrown out was what he most wanted, as if he had just discovered it that minute.

How could it be, after just a few nights, how could Philoctetes think about giving up the life he had lived here, however barren, and returning to Greece with this enigmatic child? But the kid had said it; history had resumed in Philoctetes' life.

Too quickly. Philoctetes was a grownup; the last time he had acted this thoughtlessly he had wound up in the army. And thence here.

"How would we go?" Philoctetes said. "I mean, I couldn't even pay my own plane fare."

"Admetus got that figured out. You know, he used to be a sailor, still got a lot of friends in the merchant marine. He thinks he can get us on the freighter. Maybe just slip somebody about a hundred."

"That's a hundred more than I have."

"Don't worry, we'll scrape it up between us."

"The freighter's tomorrow," Philoctetes said.

"Is it?"

"I can't leave that fast."

"Why? Got to find a buyer for the shack?"

"No, I—" If he didn't seize the moment, if he put it off even by the week that would pass before the next freighter, Pyrrhus would get over it.

And if they went, so suddenly: then, too, Pyrrhus might get over it in

331

a week. Except they would be there instead of here. Wherever *there* was. "Where would we go?"

"I don't know. Back where you're from?"

"No." Philoctetes shook himself loose from the boy's embrace. "I can't—I'm too tired to think about this. I'll . . . I can decide tomorrow. We can decide. Can you wait till tomorrow?"

"Okay. Why don't we just go to bed?"

Yes, why didn't they? If Philoctetes wasn't going to go—and already he felt he wasn't, even putting off the answer by a day probably meant he wasn't—he could have one more night. Of what: the kid's mindless humping? Or just looking into each other's eyes again? As if he could look just one more time and figure out the mystery of this boy, the insoluble mystery of his wanting to be with Philoctetes. For Philoctetes had been disabused, hadn't he, of the momentary delusion that princes just naturally fell for him?

"No. You better go back . . . wherever it is you go. I'll see you tomorrow."

"Where?"

"The freighter leaves at three or so. I'll see you there. Or I won't."

"But—" Pyrrhus began, then gave up. He gave Philoctetes a little peck on the cheek, not unlike the cold kisses Paris had bestowed, then turned and left.

Philoctetes watched him as he went down the dune, then up the neighboring one—clambering with youthful effortlessness, up that dune Philoctetes could barely crawl up, some nights on his way to Pterelas's. The boy would have to slow down for him, would always have to slow down. Until Philoctetes came to a full stop: how much longer now? Impossible. He turned away and looked back out at the water. At what was, indisputably, a ship. Anchored out there, just beyond Sidheritis.

The longer he looked, the more clearly he could see it. A warship. A warship, here, when was the last time a warship had come anywhere near here?

Pyrrhus heard, the sound carrying across the dunes as if it were right next to him, the sharp cry. Shit, he thought, it must be Philoctetes' foot again. All this time with no problem, and now . . . He probably ought to go back. But what could he do about Philoctetes' foot? And maybe Philoctetes would rather be alone. He kept walking.

8

It was about a quarter of three when Pyrrhus got to the dock. He wasn't really surprised that Philoctetes wasn't there. Or rather, he hadn't thought the odds were good, but in his heart he *had* expected to see him; just as he had turned off Port Street and down to the quay he had had a mental image of Philoctetes standing there. Though he had felt even at that instant that it was only a picture, not a premonition. He wasn't so sharply disappointed that the actual vista before him was devoid of Philoctetes.

Wasn't really disappointed at all. Because, if Philoctetes had been there, Pyrrhus would have had some fast talking to do. The night before, brilliantly improvising the part about their running off together on the freighter, he hadn't thought ahead. Hadn't pictured the moment when Philoctetes would arrive with his pathetic belongings, a few worn-out flannel shirts and possibly—if he even thought to bring it—a bow. Then Pyrrhus would have had to explain that they weren't getting on, that he and Philoctetes had booked passage on another vessel entirely. One Philoctetes would never voluntarily board. Pyrrhus was in no hurry for that scene. It was just as well that he'd evidently been stood up.

Philoctetes might still come. Unless—what if the attack the night before was more serious than usual? He ought to have checked, ought to have gone back. How could he say, even to astonish Odysseus, how could he say that he loved Philoctetes when he could hear that cry and go on walking? Still: what could he have done about it, what good would it have done for him just to be there?

He understood, in the abstract, that some people didn't just walk away from the afflicted—Leo, for example, Leo might have hung around and tried to help even if he didn't care about Philoctetes one way or the other. But that meant, didn't it, that there wasn't any necessary connection between caring about somebody and staying to help? It didn't have anything to do with his feelings for Philoctetes. He just wasn't very good around sick people.

They were loading the last of the cargo. A few slender crates that might have held sofa-sized oils of the harbor; the artists must have used one giant tube of gray per painting. A box with holes in it, possibly some queen's matching terriers. On board, a geezer who was probably the captain was signing something on a clipboard held for him by an austere, clerical-looking dyke. Soon she lumbered down the gangplank and headed toward Port Street. In a minute the freighter would be gone.

Pyrrhus felt rising in him a hope that Philoctetes would, at the last, appear. Maybe just because he had always hated to be stood up.

Pterelas looked glumly at the empty bar. It was three-thirty, of course the place was empty; everybody was at the beach or napping, another hour at least before even the serious drinkers couldn't wait any longer and declared it party time. Except Philoctetes; Philoctetes was usually here to keep him company by now. He hadn't realized how much he counted on that, Philoctetes' wan face and the stories he'd heard a few thousand times. Until the routine had been broken, this last couple of weeks, by a bunch of princes. Out of nowhere, all these goddamn princes swooping down on poor Philoctetes. It was no wonder he was in the hospital again.

Otionia had told him that morning: Philoctetes had checked in again. Pterelas had stopped in just for a minute on his way to the bar. It wasn't a big deal—if you couldn't find Philoctetes at any of the bars you'd naturally check the hospital next. Maybe he looked a little worse than all the other times. Not any sicker, exactly, not like he was in more pain. Just kind of startled looking. As if it had sneaked up on him this time, as if after a hundred episodes almost as predictable as weather he had, this once, been surprised.

This once he didn't even to try to sit up, or worry if his visitor was comfortable, or apologize because he hadn't shaved. Or joke about being back at his old stool in time to check out the incoming crop of new cuties on Friday night. He was flat tired, from messing with all those princes. And awful skinny, lying there in his gown.

Pterelas had only stayed a minute; he had to hurry and open the bar. Maybe if he'd known how bad off Philoctetes was he would have come earlier in the day. Except that he was sort of relieved, only able to stay a minute.

There was nothing so dispiriting, Pterelas thought, as an empty bar at mid-afternoon. Even if he knew it would fill up later, even if he had the highest margin on Port Street, he could look around on an afternoon like this and have visions of bankruptcy court. If only it would rain: that would sweep the last queens off the beach. The place would be jumping in no time.

Pyrrhus came in. The strange kid who stayed nowhere and got his clean shirts from nowhere and had come from nowhere expressly to fuck Philoctetes up, raise his hopes and then walk away. Pterelas had seen him, the night before, parading around with some sailor. Looking all around, hardly paying any attention to his little bucktoothed catch, because he was so eager to show it off to Philoctetes. Leaving after one beer, dragging the sailor boy to the next bar, or the next, until he could make Philoctetes see . . . what? That he wasn't twenty any more? Philoctetes was the hottest man there ever was, at a hundred he'd be hotter than some little sore-assed sailor. Except that he wouldn't ever be a hundred.

Pyrrhus sat at the stool next to Philoctetes' empty spot and said "Hi." In that breezy way people have who think they're welcome anywhere. Well, he wasn't welcome here. Pterelas turned and began ostentatiously counting the money in the register, although it was only the change he'd just put in there. He was thinking of putting up a sign: No Princes. Except the glut was apparently over. The other one had left this morning, Philoctetes said so, he'd sent him away. One down.

Pyrrhus said, louder, "Hey."

Pterelas turned around, finally. "Now I see you in the daylight I've been thinking I should have carded you. You got ID?"

"Sure, I—No, I didn't come in for a drink."

"You're going to sit down you need to order something."

"Oh. Just a ginger ale."

Pterelas waited for the inevitable question. It came: "You seen Philoctetes anywhere?"

"That's a buck. You aren't on Philoctetes' tab any more. Yeah, I've seen him. He's in the hospital."

Pyrrhus stood up. "What?"

"The hospital. He checks in there every so often. When he wants to catch up on the soaps."

"Where is it?"

"Down across from the post office. Gray building, can't miss it." He had a nasty inspiration. "I wouldn't hurry. He's got a visitor. That other guy he's been hanging around with. What's his name?"

"Paris?"

"Uh-huh. The other prince. He's been there all day. Holding hands and all, feeding him lunch. Seemed like all the company Philoctetes needed."

Pyrrhus sat down again. "I guess he doesn't want to see me."

"I guess not." Pterelas already felt a little guilty: for all he knew Philoctetes did indeed want to see his little princeling. Well, and who wouldn't? He looked even better in the daylight. Why should Pterelas have hoped that, with the island rid of princes, Philoctetes' eyes would turn to him? After ten years.

Pterelas studied Pyrrhus without looking at him, as bartenders learn to do. Yes, he looked even better in the light, and also—

"Hey, I've seen you!"

"What?"

"In the city, last time I flew in. God, where was that? I know I . . ."

Pyrrhus didn't say anything, until Pterelas whispered, "Shit. Yeah, I saw a whole lot of you in the city. Just about all of you."

The kid looked satisfyingly alarmed, but still didn't answer. Pterelas laughed, a high, mirthless giggle. "The prince of the Café Tip-and-Grope. Wait till I tell Philoctetes."

"Do you have to?"

"Damn right I have to. He thought you were practically a cherry. All innocent in your little white shirts. A fucking hustler, I knew you were some kind of hustler."

"What could I have been trying to hustle from Philoctetes?" Pyrrhus said, in an irritatingly reasonable tone. "What could I have wanted?"

"What do you shits always want? Everything he had." This sounded so good Pterelas had spit it out before he remembered what Philoctetes had said: that he didn't have anything.

The kid drew in his breath as though he was about to make this point, but then just said, mildly: "That's right."

Was it hustling if the kid went after someone who had nothing? Maybe he was reformed, an ex-hustler. But there was no such creature. Pterelas's view was thoroughly Greek; the kid was a hustler for life. And if he was hanging around, there was—by definition—something left to steal. "I'm going to tell him," Pterelas said. Though with a faint uneasiness, as if to do so would make him an accomplice somehow, completing the theft, of whatever it was the kid had taken.

"Go ahead. Sounds like he's sort of settled on Paris anyway."

"Looks that way." Fine, let him think that and slink away. Let it be three weeks ago. Philoctetes would get out of the hospital and come back to his stool; everything would be as it was. Pterelas would get what little of him was left.

He turned back to the cash register to signal an end to the conversation. The kid got the point: after a minute he got up, said, "See ya," and started toward the door.

Pterelas said, "Paris is gone."

Pyrrhus stopped.

"I was just kidding," Pterelas mumbled, unable to look at him. "Philoctetes is all by himself."

The kid let out a breath and said, "I'm going to get him out of the hospital and off this fucking island. All these years, you people think you own each other."

Well, yes, they did. "It's too late now," Pterelas said.

"Yeah? Why is that?"

"Because he isn't coming out again. He's going to die." Pterelas realized, as he said it, that this improvised last shot was true. That's why he'd hurried out this morning, what he hadn't stayed to see. "He decided to die this time."

There is scarcely any need to describe Philoctetes in his hospital bed. The reader will have seen the image on a hundred vases. Heaven knows why this motif was so popular for a while. Drawing from the anonymous poet in the *Anthology* his famous reproach:

> *Even to paint Philoctetes is to make his misery perpetual.*
> *His skin is dry, and from his dry eye hangs a tear,*
> *Frozen, that the painter could have wiped away.*

Which is not, of course, about the underpaid artisans at the pottery factories, who paint whatever they're told. But about those of us who choose to tell this story, voyeurs who will not let the ill-starred fool rest, who would open his grave if we had to—because we have to have something to write about, and suffering is easier. Our only defense that, if we didn't make his misery perpetual, no one would remember him at all. With our help his name and his agony survive together, almost a tautology, while his body rots. The body that brought pleasure to thousands of men gone; all he has left to give is pain.

Anyway, he is wrong, the poet, about this: the tear does not hang forever but drops at last on the sheet. Philoctetes was through crying, was almost reviving a little, stirred back to life by the sovereign elixir that had kept him going so many years: hatred.

He himself was startled by it, the transcendent loathing that overcame him if he so much as pictured Pyrrhus's face. It wasn't, after all, as if this were the first romance that had ended in a betrayal. Philoctetes had been through plenty of those—the guilty party more often than the victim—and he had found over the years that it was better, really, to be the victim. Especially if it was the kind of affair that was in essence a promise to fuck until one or the other party got tired of it.

Philoctetes had always hated it when he had to break the news that, surprise, he was the one who got tired of it first. That was worse even than being on the receiving end of such an announcement: the stung look, the anger, it always made him feel that somehow he was declaring his own insufficiency, his short attention span. Instead of what was really so, that he and X just didn't fit, that the friction of square peg and round hole could excite one only for a while, before the peg visibly eroded.

What was the big deal, why had he lain all afternoon in this bed feeling sorry for himself, when really he *was* the one who had tired first? Knew, even as he pretended to entertain the boy's ridiculous proposal, the fantasy of shipping out together on the freighter, that it wasn't ever going to happen. Why had be been thinking, even, that he was ready to die? He had got through ten years of dying at a satisfactory pace. Why the big hurry? Because the kid had lied to him, because he'd thought for a few days that he was the darling of princes?

All just a lie, typical Greek subterfuge, except that this boy's having managed it made him the arch-Greek, made Odysseus look ingenuous. He had done it so well, you had to admire him. Philoctetes had almost thought they had become citizens of a new country, a country other than his disease. When they were only in Greece, all the time. That was funny, really. Philoctetes hadn't got through so much dying without knowing what was funny.

If what they had had was sex, ordinary sex, it wouldn't have astonished Philoctetes to learn that it was all fake. The one night they fucked: maybe Pyrrhus had even faked then. Philoctetes had faked it himself, once or twice. It was a sort of courtesy, really; if somebody really turned him off he wouldn't even bother to put on a show.

Still, how could Pyrrhus, how could even a Greek, have carried off that night when they shivered together and did nothing? What sort of monster could have faked that unreplicable night of silence? He had known it could never happen again, not with Pyrrhus or anyone else. But to learn that it had never happened, that the eyes into which he had gazed had been, all the time, darting about the room. Looking for a useless bow.

He didn't want to die. He wanted to get better—so that he could follow Paris, who had carried on a much more ordinary brand of deception. How foolish to have sent him away, sleazy as he was. Yes, he ought to go with Paris, and hope that the oracles were right for once. That without Philoctetes some awful destruction would rain upon the Greeks. Oh, not enough; he wished somehow the whole world could be destroyed. Since it had at the heart of it, or the closest Philoctetes ever came to the heart, nothing but Pyrrhus's lie.

The tears came again, frozen at the corners of his eyes.

As once Lamus, Pyrrhus's first trick, had looked up at Pyrrhus with tears in his eyes. And for the same reason. As if Pyrrhus had been put in the world just to make men cry, make a few unlucky souls understand the lie at the heart of things.

Philoctetes lay back, exhausted. Maybe he did, after all—even anger, this time, wasn't enough to bring him back to life, wanting to tear the world down wasn't enough, just somehow made him even more tired— maybe he did want to die this time.

"You mean to say that you came back without seeing him?" Phoenix said. They were in the officers' mess, Pyrrhus and Phoenix and Admetus. Who was pretending to examine the charts on the wall while the other two talked. He had never been in the officers' mess; even though Pyrrhus had invited him, it made him uneasy.

"I was . . . I don't know, scared," Pyrrhus said. "That weird thing Pterelas said. About how he'd made up his mind to die."

"Why should he do that?" Phoenix said. "Over Paris? Imagine anyone having his heart broken by Paris. Well, I don't know, goddesses have."

"But Philoctetes—I mean, he didn't, last night he didn't seem all broken up about that. I don't get it."

Admetus said, not turning from his chart: "Maybe Paris said more than you guys think."

"Like what?" Pyrrhus said.

"Or maybe he figured it out. Philoctetes ain't a stupid guy."

"You mean about . . ."

"Yes, perhaps that's it," Phoenix said. "If the Trojans came to fetch him, why not the Greeks?"

"But—I mean, he would have said something, been mad or something."

"Do you think you're the only Greek who knows how to dissemble? No, I should wager that he knows the whole story."

Pyrrhus said, without expression, "Shit."

"Come, he was going to have to learn the story sooner or later," Phoenix said. "Perhaps it's better—"

Admetus cut him off. "Maybe it was going to kill him whenever he learned it." Then more mildly, to Pyrrhus: "I don't mean it's your fault. I told you the first time we seen him: That ain't a man who's going nowhere. There wasn't a thing you could do to make him go anywhere again."

They were quiet a minute while Pyrrhus considered this bleak consolation. At last Pyrrhus said, "I can't imagine it, things being so bad you'd want to die."

Phoenix said, "That's because you're living in brackets. When you left Scyros you opened a parenthesis, and you've been dwelling to the right of that for some indefinite interval. But you can always close the parenthesis again and take up where you were."

"Uh-uh, not any more. I don't know what happens now—I mean, it doesn't look like we're going to need our street maps of Troy any time soon. But I can't go back. I've got to do the next thing. Maybe that's what I can't imagine: not wanting to know what happens next."

Admetus said, "I . . . can kind of imagine that." They looked at him. "I don't mean I'm in any hurry. I ain't ever in much of a hurry. But I can see—if you thought you was going someplace and then you ain't—how when you closed your eyes you might wish they wouldn't open again. So you wouldn't see the same shit again."

He shook his head. "Except, you know, people who want to die, or who want to kill themselves, whatever, I don't think they really believe it. That their eyes ain't gonna open again. They think, after the gunshot or a nice long nap on a hundred pills, they'll get up again. The way my wife did. Except they think everything'll be different, better—they'll be someplace else, they won't hurt any more. Only my wife . . . she came back and she was just where she set out from. We both was."

He laughed softly, as if he were just getting the joke of which he was the punch line.

Pyrrhus said, simply as a child, "I wish I could go see him."

"You wish?" Admetus said.

"Well, I mean, I can't. It would just upset him."

"I guess. But you want to?"

"He wouldn't want to see me."

"Who knows, he might. Or you might have to stand there and let him tell you what a shit you are. That's what you're scared of, ain't it?"

"I don't know."

Of course it was. Back in the city he had almost wanted it, dared people to call him a shit so he could say: You don't know me, you don't know anything about me. But to hear it from Philoctetes would be insupportable. The most terrifying thing that could happen to anyone: to have to stand there and hear, from someone who knew everything, the worst you've ever thought about yourself.

They were quiet for a while. Then Admetus said, "Time I headed abovedeck. This is about as much gloom as I can stand. Life's too short."

When he had gone, Phoenix coughed. Signaling the start of some interminable story. Pyrrhus thought of following Admetus but stayed where he was.

Phoenix said: "It will not surprise you to learn that I have rarely ventured into battle. Once or twice, early on, I accompanied your father. Just to fetch his water and so on. Oddly, I wasn't really afraid. That is, partly I was serenely confident that your father could defend me. And partly I was indifferent: I rather enjoy life, I greet each day cheerfully enough, but I don't care very strongly, one way or the other, if I ever see another day. Maybe there's something missing about me. Other than the obvious. Or maybe that's where it comes from, caring very much.

"At any rate, I wasn't afraid, but I was revolted. The first time, of course, by the terrible sights and sounds and . . . and the smell. I can't recall that I have ever heard a bard describe the smell of battle. It is unmistakable. An abattoir is an abattoir. The first time I was rather grateful we had set off without any breakfast. The next time was worse. Not that I couldn't get used to it, but that I could: by the second battle I was very nearly over my physical revulsion and was watching the combatants with a certain abstract interest, as if it were all an enormous spectator sport. Or as if I ought to be taking notes, so I could write a poem about it. I didn't go again.

"In the morning, I would help your father dress, see him off. He would turn, most days, just before leaving the tent, and give me instructions for dinner. He was very particular about his wines, your father."

"I never saw him drink anything but beer," Pyrrhus said.

"It was an acquired taste. After he had pillaged the cellars of some of the finest villas outside Troy, he became quite discriminating. In any event, on the last morning, when I had finished doing up all the little buckles on his breastplate, he turned and took my hand. I was flustered — this wasn't something he did and, besides, the whole camp was in a great hurry, there'd been a surprise attack on one flank, he needed to go. I pulled my hand away. He rushed out of the tent without saying anything about dinner.

"I went about my business, scarcely distracted by the familiar background noise of the distant battle. It wasn't until mid-morning, I think, that I suddenly understood — dropped whatever I was doing and simply stood there, realizing — he hadn't ordered his wines because he wasn't expecting to come back."

"He knew he was going to die?"

"I ran from the tent, toward the battlefield, but I wasn't halfway there when I could make out Ajax and Odysseus and . . . the body, already in the bag, but of course they couldn't fit the helmet in, or the shield — even from a quarter of a mile there was no mistaking the shield. They were already bickering over it, Ajax and Odysseus. As they got closer I could hear that they were already arguing about who would get the armor.

"I fell to my knees in the mud and . . . wept, of course. I cried bitter tears, more than on the day my father maimed me. Not because he was dead. I didn't care so much that he was dead. That is, I did, but of course we had always known, he and I, that this would happen one day. But because he had wanted to hold my hand, like a little boy, and I had pulled my hand away."

Pyrrhus said, "I don't think Philoctetes wants to hold my hand."

"Oh. Perhaps not. But you'll never know, will you?"

Odysseus came in. Behind him was Admetus, looking sheepish, like a man who has spilled something.

Odysseus was in mufti — more precisely, in the outfit a man of his age and station used to wear at resorts: a dark blue golfing shirt, yellow pants with ducks on them, deck shoes. He looked ten years older than he did in uniform, and impotent, or at least unmajestic. He didn't know what to do with his exposed arms, white and nearly hairless; he clasped his hands behind his back.

Pyrrhus could scarcely help laughing at him. "What are you dressed up for?"

Odysseus recoiled a little. "I thought it was about time I went ashore. I didn't wish to be too conspicuous."

"Oh. Well, I can promise you: no one on Lemnos is going to look twice at you."

Odysseus looked puzzled. And it wasn't true, anyway; gold diggers would look twice at him. The kind who did it for the money and not for the fatherland.

Phoenix spoke up. "May I ask why you are going ashore?"

"For the bow, of course."

"Ah, so you've concluded the bow is all that is required."

"It's all we're going to get, isn't it? The man is going to die, right here, he's not going with us or Paris or anybody else."

"I don't guess," Pyrrhus said. Looking reproachfully at Admetus, who just shrugged, as if to say: *You* try to keep something from Odysseus.

"Therefore the bow is evidently what we need."

"Without Philoctetes?"

"We got here and he was already dead, we found the bow, the prophecy is fulfilled. Where is it?"

"Beats me."

"You mean you never found out where it was?"

"Nope." Odysseus cocked his head, gave Pyrrhus his full attention. Pyrrhus was used to evading scrutiny. "I got kind of distracted. You know how flighty we are."

Odysseus's shoulders tensed with the effort of keeping his hands behind his back. Instead of around the little brat's neck. "Well, he can't have taken it to the hospital with him, it must be wherever he lived. You did find that out, didn't you? Where he slept?"

"Uh-huh."

"Yes, if there's one mission that can safely be entrusted to you, it's finding a man's bed."

9

They were there in a few minutes. It was strange for Pyrrhus, sailing straight toward the northern end of the island, instead of going all the way around Lemnos to the harbor and then cutting back across on foot. As the three of them—Odysseus, Pyrrhus, Admetus—piled out of the beached launch and made their way up the dunes, Pyrrhus looked back. The ship was so very close, and so conspicuous, how could anyone have missed it? Unless he had, after ten years, given up looking for it.

Pyrrhus hadn't ever been to the shack without Philoctetes, hadn't ever really looked at the place itself. It had just seemed part of Philoctetes' shabby raiment, like one of his worn flannel shirts. Now Pyrrhus saw it as Odysseus must have. A hovel, the shingles weathered to an even silver-gray and starting to drop from it like dead leaves, the cracked windows, the front steps like a broken-backed horse. Odysseus mounted them and stood for a second, as if reluctant to go in.

He said, over his shoulder, "I suppose this is what they call a warrantless search," and stepped inside.

The rest of the search party looked at each other. Neither wanted to go in, join in the violation, watch Odysseus turn over everything. Though Pyrrhus, at least, was a little curious. He followed Odysseus.

Odysseus was already rummaging through the little curtained alcove that served for a closet. Not just tearing through it, the way cops search a place, throwing everything out onto the floor. Slowly, deliberately, examining each object and putting it back. As if he weren't hunting for a single item, but just miscellaneously gathering evidence. Learning everything he could about how Philoctetes had lived.

He went on to the battered chest of drawers, orphan of some lost bedroom set, with its crazed veneer. Pawing through Philoctetes' underwear and socks and coming, inevitably, upon his stash of porn.

Odysseus pulled it out and set it on top of the chest, the little stack of old magazines. There, on the cover of the topmost one, was a face Pyrrhus knew from somewhere. Yes, it was Tydeus, one of the dancers from the Escapade. Small world.

Odysseus riffled through the pages, stopping at the centerfold, which provided a very close view of Tydeus from an angle familiar only to gay men and to physicians conducting prostate exams. Odysseus stared at it: possibly he had never actually beheld that part of a man.

Odysseus looked at the spread shot of Tydeus and, visibly, almost shook with revulsion. Now, Pyrrhus had seen magazines that showed parts of women that were just as unfamiliar to Pyrrhus. And not, objectively, much more captivating than Tydeus's little rosebud with its corona of down. He hadn't been repelled, he'd been . . . interested. The way you can be interested in a picture of an exotic destination you know you're never going to visit. Why should Odysseus have been so upset? Unless he realized that he, too, had one of those parts, and entertained the amazing delusion that some other man might covet it.

Odysseus replaced the magazines and went on to the next drawer, and the next. More hurried, hurling things around, as if he no longer wanted to take time to examine Philoctetes' world. Turning over the mattress, tearing aside the rag rug, ripping down Philoctetes' posters from short-lived cult musicals, in case there was something hidden behind them.

Finding nothing, of course, until Pyrrhus began to think: Maybe we'll just sail away from here now, leaving this ransacked hut and its ruined tenant. Maybe we'll just go.

Odysseus paused. "You haven't been much help."

"You seemed to be doing okay."

Odysseus sighed and sat down on Philoctetes' bed. "You knew it wasn't here."

"Well, there's no fooling you."

"You didn't—you don't have to tell me where it is. But you might have said it wasn't here, saved me a little trouble. I don't see the point."

Pyrrhus wasn't sure of the point himself. "I guess if you were supposed to find the bow, you would."

"Ah. And you'll be—what?—cleaner somehow if you don't lift a finger, just let Destiny take her course."

"Maybe."

"It's rather late for this minute scruple. After everything you've already done to him."

"Look who's talking."

"Oh, you're right, what I did to him was terrible, so many years ago. I'll live with it forever."

"Right."

"As you will. But you know—if you're robbing a bank, and you've already shot the guard and a couple of customers, then . . ."

"Then?"

"You might as well take the goddamn money."

The Green Peacock was the sort of antique store that has a million small, undesirable objects sequestered in dusty vitrines. No pictures or furniture — visitors to an island resort rarely buy sofas — just brooches and bud vases and other bibelots. Bows, too, maybe, though none was in evidence. Pyrrhus wondered if they were just going to overturn everything, as they had at Philoctetes' shack. He wished he were outside with Admetus, who was rolling a cigarette and eyeing the passing lesbians with an air of regretful surmise.

Odysseus affected to study a case filled with cut-glass candy dishes, relish dishes, whatever they were. Dispiriting objects, each of which had once disappointed a bride-to-be who had opened the box with such anticipation. How had all these things migrated to Lemnos, as if it were the inevitable destination of the rejected?

Phyllis, the owner, said, "Were you looking for anything in particular?" She had that nobody-ever-comes-here-but-you're-not-welcome tone that antique dealers must learn in a school somewhere.

"Oh, not really," Odysseus said. "Just browsing. Except . . ."

"Yes," she said, leaning forward. What could she mark up?

"I do sort of collect . . . well, antique weapons. I guess you wouldn't have any."

"Weapons?"

"Old pistols — dueling sets, you know — or swords. Bows. I don't know."

"Oh. Well, I do . . . I happen to have a bow."

"Really?"

"It's in the back somewhere."

While she went to fetch it Odysseus calmly resumed his scrutiny of the cut glass. Even when she returned, he didn't look up right away; she had to clear her throat to get his attention. As if he hadn't been waiting forever.

The bow was tiny. Well, not tiny, but no more than an arm's length, and unornamented. Pyrrhus had already gotten used to the idea that every killing device should be encrusted with golden foliage and historical scenes; this looked naked and homely in comparison. Maybe the more vicious for that: it wasn't meant to hang over a mantel, all you could do with it was kill somebody.

347

"There's a quiver, too, and some arrows." The quiver of pressed cardboard made to look like leather, a handful of arrows with tattered, dun-colored feathers. The whole package a most unprepossessing assortment of objects; how could this be the key to everything?

Odysseus himself couldn't believe it. "Well, that's . . . interesting. I mean, of its kind. You don't have anything else?"

"No. I just happen to have this one, on consignment. I don't do a big business in bows and arrows."

"I imagine not." Odysseus held it, looked at it with evident disappointment. He sighed: this was it, it had to be it. Why did he look so crestfallen, as if this little anticlimax betokened a larger letdown to come? "Well, I suppose it will do for my collection. I really don't have anything just like it. How much?"

"I don't know. You probably know what it's worth better than I do. Make me an offer."

"Oh, goodness. A hundred?"

"Well, like I say, it's on consignment. Maybe I should try to get in touch with the owner. He thought it was worth—"

"No, no, don't bother. Oh, what's this tag, is that when it was left here?"

"Where? Let me see."

"Ten years ago?"

"One fifty," Phyllis said.

"One twenty-five."

"Will that be cash or charge?"

"GeoCredit," Odysseus said. "Here, hold these a minute." He handed the bow and the quiver to Pyrrhus. Who slung the quiver over his shoulder and hefted the bow. It was even lighter than it looked, and it bent easily, like a child's toy.

Pyrrhus nearly knocked Admetus down as he ran out of the shop with the bow.

Ran isn't exactly the word. You couldn't run down Port Street in the early evening, what with the lingering clots of tourists and the bicyclists and the men who loitered like windows waiting to be shopped. You couldn't even walk at a normal pace. Pyrrhus was really just strolling; but running inside, his heart going as fast as if he were running, pumping that extra blood that had to go somewhere, he felt as though his head was swelling from it. He tried to just move straight forward, as if the crowd would part for him, but the crowd was made up of a thousand people, all of them with little intentions and destinations of their own. How infuriating, to be rushing somewhere and have so many people, obviously headed nowhere, in your way. His head was pounding. All these jerks; once again he saw the world for a second the way Odysseus must have seen it every day.

He tried to dodge around one especially irksome clot of tourists and came face-to-face with the enormous woman he had seen, days ago, playing on the dunes with her dog. There was no getting around her. She said, softly, "What's your hurry, sucker?" before letting him pass.

What *was* his hurry? He looked back. Somewhere in that crowd were Odysseus and Admetus, probably not hurrying at all, just inching along with the tourists. They knew where he was headed; they had all the time in the world to get there. Philoctetes wasn't going anywhere.

He slowed down. Passersby couldn't help noticing that he was marching down Port Street toting a bow and arrows. He felt like an idiot. What had he been thinking? People in Hell didn't need bows. Or in Heaven: even Heracles had given the damn thing away en route to his apotheosis.

Pyrrhus stood still, clutching the bow. He knew what he had been thinking. That he would simply thrust the thing into Philoctetes' hand and it would make Philoctetes a soldier. The way Pyrrhus was a soldier when he put his father's armor on. Philoctetes would rise up from his bed, a new man, and they would march off together. Hero lovers, ready to make history side by side.

Which was either the most idiotic fantasy he'd ever had, or the truth. Maybe Odysseus was wrong: the two halves of the prophecy were inseparable. He and Philoctetes marched together or nobody marched.

The hospital was, like everything else in town, gray shingle with white woodwork. While the getup was pleasingly quaint on cottages and shops, on larger buildings—the town hall, the bank, the hospital—it seemed unreal and even a little overbearing; the very number of shingles some unfortunate souls had had to nail up made you think of pharaohs.

Inside, though, the hospital had the homely, low-tech air of a college infirmary. Back then, it catered mostly to tourists who got sick on the whale-watching cruise or who had eaten bad mussels; back then, it wasn't the center of the island.

A male nurse sat at an old steel desk beneath a chipped plaster bas-relief of Chiron, the healer. Next to him was a wooden wheelchair with cane seating.

"I want to see Philoctetes," Pyrrhus said.

The nurse eyed him disdainfully, like the night clerk at the Palace Hotel. As if the nurse knew anything. "I don't know, I don't think he should have any more visitors today."

"I really need to see him."

"Everybody really needs to see him. But nobody seems to make him feel any better. Anyway, there's somebody with him now. You better wait."

"I . . . Okay." Pyrrhus looked around for some place to sit. There wasn't anywhere, just the wheelchair. He sat there. The nurse was about to protest, but let it go.

They would come any minute, Odysseus and Admetus, they would come right in and find him there and he would never have a moment alone with Philoctetes. Which was maybe just as well. Because it occurred to him suddenly that maybe Philoctetes would just let him have the bow. Not rise up, not forgive, just send him off into battle alone. With the stupid bow, accompanied by its indecipherable instruction manual, Heracles' final sneer: *It's not too late for you to be a man.*

He saw, down the hall, Philoctetes' visitor emerging from a room. Pterelas, of course.

"My, my," Pterelas said. "The invalid prince. What happened, get your draft notice?"

Pyrrhus got out of the wheelchair. "Is he alone now?"

"Yep. Probably wants to stay that way."

"Oh. Did you . . . ?"

"Everything. He knows all about you."

Pyrrhus had the old familiar thought, that knowing he was a whore wasn't the same as knowing all about him. He didn't feel sure of that, not enough to say it out loud. "Then you've saved me a lot of breath."

Pterelas gave a surprised little laugh. "Oh, you were going to come clean."

"Yep," Pyrrhus said. "I think that's best, don't you? I mean, if people are dying, somebody really ought to make sure they don't go out with any illusions."

That shut Pterelas up for a minute. Then he said, "I don't know if he's dying after all. He seems a little better this evening."

"Yeah?" A little better: a tiny upward tick on Philoctetes' chart. Pyrrhus could imagine the line extended all the way to health.

"Yeah. Not that it's going to do you any good. I think he'd be just as happy never to see you again."

Probably so, Pyrrhus thought. Probably everybody would be just as happy if he went outside right now, waited for Odysseus and Admetus, turned over the bow, went on with them to Troy. Odysseus would be happy, Philoctetes would be happy. Why, even Pterelas would be happy. Such a contribution he could make to the sum of happiness in the world. If you didn't count the likely distress of a few Trojans.

"Well, see you around," Pterelas said.

"Uh-huh."

"Except not at my place." He added, flatly as if reciting from the bar owners' code, "I don't let hustlers in my place."

When he had gone, Pyrrhus started toward the room from which Pterelas had emerged, third door on the right. He felt a strange exultation, even though he was headed to learn the worst about himself. Because everything was about to be decided. Or maybe just because he was going to see Philoctetes again.

"Wait," the nurse said. "Are you . . . are you taking that . . . thing in there?"

"What?"

"I mean, this isn't the big city, we don't have metal detectors or anything. But I don't think I'm supposed to let you take a weapon with you."

"It's his, Philoctetes'. I'm just bringing it to him."

"What's he going to do with a bow and arrow?"

A good question. Pyrrhus ignored it and hurried down the hall. The door was open, but he knocked on the jamb.

"Shit, who is it now?"

Pyrrhus didn't answer, just stepped into the room.

Philoctetes looked like . . . an underweight man in a hospital bed. Ordinarily, when confronted by this all-too-familiar spectacle, one may be diverted by the gifts and knickknacks with which the sickbed has been surrounded—stuffed toys and flowers, cards with little jokes meant to impress upon the recipient that it is poor form to make too much of one's little problems, foodstuffs the very sight of which makes the invalid retch, and so on. As Philoctetes' room contained none of these things, there was really nothing to look at but Philoctetes himself. His gown so oversized he seemed to dwell within it rather than wear it. His scant hair damp, darker than its usual dead gold, one matted strand forming a little curl against the sun-dark forehead traversed by a single prominent vein like a railroad across a steppe.

He looked at Pyrrhus the way someone with indigestion watches television: it isn't interesting, it's kind of making him sick, but there it is, he can't help looking at it.

"You stood me up," Pyrrhus said, as lightly as he could, and with a hundred-dollar smile.

Philoctetes smiled back at him. "I was indisposed." A colorless little smile. Yet enough to give Pyrrhus the idea, for a second, that they were just going to laugh it off, everything that had happened.

"I was all set to take you home," Pyrrhus said.

Philoctetes' smile vanished. "Right." But still he looked at Pyrrhus, not with disbelief or anger, just with a terrible weariness.

From which, Pyrrhus thought again, he might somehow be stirred. "Look, I've got your bow."

"Great. I hate hospital food, now I can kill something."

Pyrrhus held the thing out to him; of course he didn't take it. Feeling foolish, Pyrrhus sat down in the visitor's chair.

Philoctetes was still looking at him. Well, if there was one thing Pyrrhus was used to, it was being looked at. Except that Philoctetes didn't stare at him the way the men at the Escapade had, stopping at the skin. Or, like Achilles, peer into the weakest part of him. Philoctetes still seemed to look at Pyrrhus the way Pyrrhus looked at himself in the mirror. As if he believed that there was a hero inside there, one who would sooner or later manifest himself.

What was amazing was how very much he looked like Achilles, could have been his son. For that, too, was evidently a lie. If Pterelas was to be believed—and you had to believe somebody, finally—this kid was just a hustler they had dug up in the city, found in some go-go bar. Quite a stroke, really, casting him as an aggrieved prince and then dressing him up in those innocent white shirts. They must have hunted high and low before they could find a whore who could pass as a prince.

You could see it now, though, how very ordinary he was. Nothing divine about him at all: just a street kid they'd dressed up and maybe taught how to hold a fork. What had they promised him? Philoctetes wondered. He had a sort of desolate look; they must have promised him a lot. Which he wouldn't get now, having bungled the job. He almost wished he could give the kid a reference, tell his employers what a very good job he'd done, right up to the end. Nobody could have done it better, got him as close as this kid did, inches from boarding their ship.

In fact: he was more interesting now, a more tantalizing mystery, than he had been as Pyrrhus, son of Achilles. Where had he come from? How had he lived, before they came and recruited him for this imposture? What would he do afterwards, when they dumped him back on the street from which they had plucked him? What was his future? Well, that was easy enough to guess; you didn't need any oracle to read the future of a hustler. He'd be used up soon enough.

Philoctetes felt a sudden outpouring of pity and affection for this lost boy, who had only been doing a job. Maybe the lonesomest job there was. He had a momentary fantasy of rescuing Pyrrhus — if even that name was real — before he caught himself. For one thing, he was scarcely in a position to rescue anybody. Besides, he'd had friends, in the city, who'd had delusions about saving hustlers. Boys like this were dead weight, they always dragged their rescuers down with them.

Still, the more he looked at the boy the more he was enchanted by him, the more he wanted to know all about him. The more he felt himself sinking into the most ludicrous delusion of all: that in one night of silence someone, under that mask, had been looking back at him. He made himself turn away.

Philoctetes turned his head away, as if he had tired of waiting for Pyrrhus to manifest his divinity.

"Look, I'm pretty beat," Philoctetes said. "Why don't you go away now?"

Pyrrhus thought: Why don't I? I've done my duty: I've faced him, given him every chance to tell me what a shit I am. I've even offered him the bow. But here it is, still in my hands. And I guess I'm going to Troy with it; this is how it is supposed to be.

"Pterelas said you were better."

"What?"

"I mean, first he said he thought you kind of wanted to . . . Then he said you were better."

"Ah. Telephone, telegraph, tell Pterelas. He's right, I was kind of plan-ning to . . . But it mustn't be time, I do feel like I'm getting better."

"Good."

"I don't want to. It's like my body is getting better just to spite me. Another little prank."

"Maybe it's supposed to get better, maybe you're supposed to—"

"Go to Troy? With my little bow? Don't tell me they have you be-lieving that shit."

"I—I don't know. I'd rather believe that than . . . that you're just going to lie here and die."

"You don't exactly get a vote."

"No. But you're getting better, you said so."

"I might be better for a while. I might be able to get back on my stool at Pterelas's and wait for it there. It doesn't matter: I've got a one-way ticket, and it's not for Troy."

"You could still come with us. Or, I don't care, go with Paris. Do something."

"I don't want to." Philoctetes sat up, with surprising energy. "Us? They're taking you with them?"

Pyrrhus couldn't fathom this bizarre question. Hadn't he figured every-thing out? Well, at least he was sitting up; that was something. Pyrrhus went and fussed with his pillows so he'd stay sitting up a while. Philoctetes accepted the attention.

"I'm part of the prophecy, too," Pyrrhus said. He returned to the visitor's chair. "You're supposed to go to Troy, or your bow is, or some-thing. And I am, too. I mean, if you believe this stuff. We're sort of sup-posed to go together. Two big rabbit's feet."

He was, too, the son of Achilles. He hadn't been lying, except for that one little fib, the one about caring for Philoctetes. A lie Philoctetes had heard from lots of guys, some of whom hadn't even known they were lying. Philoctetes was trying to digest this disquieting news—that Pyrrhus was exactly who he said he was—and just starting to realize that he still knew nothing about the kid, when Odysseus entered the room.

Followed by Admetus, and then the nurse, who was saying, "Listen, this is too many people, he can't have more than two . . ." Odysseus didn't even need to look at him, just willed him out of the room and stood before Philoctetes' bed.

Odysseus was older, Philoctetes thought; he had aged more than Philoctetes himself. Well, maybe he had been through more. Philoctetes had had his attacks and all, his weariness, but Lemnos *was* a resort. Life there hadn't asked much of him. Or rather, he had asked so little of life that he hadn't bumped up against it much. Apparently men who wanted great things took quite a beating for them.

Odysseus just stood there, waiting for Philoctetes to hurl some vitriol at him. With a patient expression: he was going to take whatever Philoctetes dished out, as perhaps he might have taken a scolding from a trial judge. Just part of the job, it wouldn't touch him.

The only satisfaction Philoctetes would get was to say what he felt. Utter to the man's face all the imprecations he had hurled into the sea behind his shanty, all these years. Ten years of rehearsal; Philoctetes had pretty much got the speech down. But—it wasn't just that it would all roll right off the bastard. Philoctetes didn't, looking at him, feel any of it.

Because Philoctetes realized, looking at him, that Odysseus hadn't done anything to Philoctetes. Philoctetes didn't even exist for him. Odysseus thought that he was the only being on earth, that anyone else who said the word *I* was misusing it somehow.

No, that was backwards. Odysseus hadn't robbed him of the pronoun; he had mislaid it somewhere. For ten years, at every twinge, he had looked up and seen Odysseus's smug face; he had imagined he dwelt in the shadow of Odysseus's unceasing, vigilant malignity. When the man hadn't been thinking of Philoctetes at all, just going about his business, his deluded mission.

While Philoctetes had been cast away in paradise and had spent ten years cursing the gods, that he had not been privileged to join the poor bastards who died in the mud.

Odysseus looked down at the floor. Philoctetes had managed to make him uncomfortable just by saying nothing. That was, sort of, satisfying.

At last Odysseus looked up and said—not imploring, more as if repeating an obligatory ritual phrase—the words he had once spoken to Achilles. "Come with us."

"No, thanks."

Philoctetes waited for the speech. For Odysseus, too, must have been working on his speech, if not for ten years.

Odysseus just nodded, as if for once in his life he would take no for an answer. "Then you won't mind if we take the bow? Pyrrhus."

He stepped over to Pyrrhus, still in the visitor's chair, and reached for the bow. Pyrrhus sprang up and darted around him to the doorway.

Admetus was right next to the door, silently watching, as if this were the most interesting scene he'd witnessed in decades. He stepped aside to let Pyrrhus pass. But Pyrrhus stopped, clutching the bow, unable to think where to run with it next. And not sure why he was running with it again, what instinct made him want to keep it from Odysseus.

"Admetus, grab it," Odysseus said. Admetus just stuck his hands in his pockets and went on watching.

Pyrrhus still wasn't going anywhere. The bow was so light in his hand, it was hard to believe it could matter to anybody.

Philoctetes lay back and said, "Let him have it."

"But it's yours," Pyrrhus said.

"I don't care. It's just something I have. Used to have. I'm tired of having things people want." He seemed to lie back even further—as if, in his weariness, trying to melt into the bed. "You spend your whole life trying to peddle your . . . attributes, and one by one they go. Your looks, the energy to try to charm people, the bow. Everything goes, and you're just a body lying in a hospital bed with nothing. All this attention I got, princes tripping over themselves to court me, because I had some lousy bow. You want to know who cares about you, you give away your bow and kind of watch the crowd thin out."

Pyrrhus was appalled. No wonder he had never wanted to look very far ahead.

Odysseus said, quietly: "Now you know what death sounds like."

"What?" Pyrrhus said.

"Your father's body has gone up in smoke, some day my tongue will be silent, some day your beauty will have worn away and you too will be in a hospital bed. So why bother? You might as well crawl in with him right now."

Pyrrhus wondered if this was so. He felt tired, almost as tired as Philoctetes was. He wished he really could just crawl into that bed with Philoctetes, let himself be clasped in those frail, damp arms, and not think about the future. Having a future—foretold or not—was the most tiring thing of all. An attribute, useless as a bow.

"And you will never know what you could have been. You will never know what you had in yourself, what you were meant for."

Philoctetes said, "He's right. You'd better give him the bow and head on back to your ship. Troy's waiting."

"I don't want to go anywhere," Pyrrhus said. "Maybe I want to stay with you."

Philoctetes smiled. "You can't even bear to spend a whole night with me. Now, what, you're going to sign on for a lifetime? Even a short one? You want to go, you're just scared."

Was that it? It was, Pyrrhus was scared of something. Not that he would be killed; he couldn't believe that anything would cut him down next week. But at the same time it did feel like death he was headed for.

"Go on," Philoctetes said. "Go kill yourself some Trojans. Get a few for me."

Pyrrhus tried to picture it, his arm raised, then the sword descending on the supplicant king. He could see himself going through with it. But it seemed like a chore, all of it: feats that would be celebrated forever seemed like some impossibly tedious assignment.

He sighed. "If I have to."

"Have to?"

Pyrrhus shrugged. "I guess it kind of goes with the armor."

Philoctetes sat up. He looked closely at Pyrrhus. Not the I-still-think-you're-wonderful look Pyrrhus had hoped for. More a who-is-this-lunatic-and-how-did-he-get-into-my-room? look. Philoctetes said, slowly, as if talking to an infant, "It isn't incidental, you know. People put on the armor so they can kill people; they don't kill people so they can put on the armor."

Pyrrhus wasn't sure of this, but he said, "Then okay, I want to kill people. I want to do whatever it takes."

"Takes to . . . ?"

"I don't know."

Well, the answer was obvious enough, Philoctetes thought. You could have ordered your degree in psychology from a matchbook cover and still filled in the blank: whatever it took to be like his father. He had to keep from saying it aloud. For what good would it have done to supply this answer for Pyrrhus? He would just have turned away. Not because it wasn't true; even Pyrrhus would have to acknowledge the tiresome truth of it. But it was the sort of generic insight that might be true yet doesn't get you anywhere. Like telling a short person he's petulant because he's short. After which he's still short. And feeling especially petulant toward the messenger.

There wasn't any point diagnosing wounds he couldn't heal, any more than he could heal his own. Oh, and why should he want to heal this boy, who was Pyrrhus after all, who had been prepared to walk over Philoctetes or anybody else to get to his precious future? Let him have a future as endless as Admetus's; let him live forever the way he had lived so far, dead to the present, always looking toward the next thing. That was the real ending to Pyrrhus's unfinished sentence. Not something about his father, though his father was mixed up in it somehow. *I want to do whatever it takes* to be: somebody else, somewhere else. Anywhere, just not here.

Philoctetes looked at him and saw again, for an instant, the anonymous whore they'd recruited from somewhere to carry out a mission he knew nothing about. Saw that innocently dissolute youth they had picked up on the streets of the city. Who called himself Pyrrhus, who had no past worth recalling and no destiny other than, probably, the park bench. Beautiful and empty, a vessel for your dreams.

He knew that boy wasn't in the room. That, inside, Pyrrhus was nothing like that boy. He understood suddenly that wishing for that boy was a kind of murder—that he wanted to lobotomize Pyrrhus somehow, or scrape out his guts and mount him like some taxidermist's specimen. Leave him as mysterious and empty as the Pyrrhus who had courted him. Then he could have long silent nights looking at nobody in particular, gazing into eyes with nothing behind them.

Pyrrhus would thank him, Pyrrhus was just waiting to be obliterated. He must have thought, as Heracles did, lying on that sky-high pile of kindling, that if someone would just kindly incinerate him he could become a god.

Philoctetes lay back. He was too tired to do anyone that favor again.

This is the point in the drama when Heracles is lowered from the rafters on pulleys. From the wings a mortal voice—mine—is supposed to utter the great promises, as if they came from the mouth of the understudy who dangles uncomfortably a few feet off the floor. Greater singers than I, having to get the essential couple to Troy, have resorted to Heracles. No other way out of that hospital room: Heracles must order them to go. And must promise the cure.

Here is what is missing: no one has mentioned the cure. Philoctetes is supposed to obey, unthinkingly, the command from the recently deified hulk who used to boff him, so long ago. Now Philoctetes will leap out of bed and go with Neoptolemus to the ship. When they get to Arisbe, at the foot of Troy, Machaon, son of Asclepius, will dress Philoctetes' twin wounds with divine salves. He will bathe Philoctetes and anoint him with oil. Until his whole body shines, that body that was a gift to the city, shines as though it had returned from the dead. Then he and Neoptolemus will crawl inside a giant mock-up of a horse and—

But I didn't promise to get us to Troy; I said I would get us to where we are. Even if I believed in Heracles—even if I thought Philoctetes would believe him, hop out of bed and head to Arisbe with his divine prescription—I cannot do it. Maybe some son of Asclepius is, right now, concocting that miraculous salve. But he did not do it for Philoctetes, Heracles did not appear, we are where we are. If I owe nothing else to the dead, I can at least refrain from wheeling out Heracles.

Besides, the really big lie Heracles has to utter isn't the ugly fib about a cure. It is the lie he has already spoken once to Philoctetes, in that last minute before the fire transformed him. And which it now falls to Odysseus to repeat.

Yes, let us assign the great speech to Odysseus. Who was alarmed. So much futility in the room: he had to dispel it, or he would never get the boy to Troy. He didn't see that futility was the engine that would drive the boy there. He thought he had to argue. Or maybe it was instinctive to argue; he couldn't stand there silent, even when he was winning.

"It isn't about killing," he began.

They used to say that, if the very Furies were in the jury box, Odysseus could get you off with time served. They used to say that, when Odysseus really got going, you weren't hearing his voice at all, but Athena's. Some yokels even swore they saw her standing behind him, working him like a ventriloquist's dummy.

Before a battle, he would address the armies gathered before the ships—speaking so softly each man thought Odysseus was talking only to him, king or foot soldier hearing Odysseus utter the very thoughts he'd just been having. And then turn them around: the bad omen twisted into a promise of impending victory, your longing for home transformed into a headlong eagerness to scale the ramparts of Troy, even the churning of terror in your stomach rediagnosed as hunger for war. Men on the very brink of desertion, all packed and ready to sail, would, after a few whispered words from Odysseus, throw down their duffel bags and run naked and heedless toward death.

"It isn't about killing," he began, and taking that classic lie as his theme, improvised a dazzling series of variations—first the brass fanfaring glory and honor, then the strings countering with the plaintive theme of Pyrrhus's lonesome boyhood, then the winds with their velvet promises of luxury and wealth, now a solo horn hymning the pride and jubilation of the ghostly father who was at that minute watching them from Hell. Under all of it the drums, beating out the hollow days and years that lay ahead for Pyrrhus and that would all be empty if he did not take up his father's lance, strap on the armor that fit him so well he might have been born in it.

Philoctetes couldn't even listen to this shit, just watched the boy drinking it all in. And thought about the enormous irony, that Odysseus had thrown Philoctetes off the fucking ship and was now expending his last reserves of bullshit luring Pyrrhus back on it. Couldn't he have spared a little of that eloquence for Philoctetes?

Philoctetes was almost jealous. There: somewhere under a decade of anger, buried under the grievance that had been almost a religion, was the jealousy and hurt of a little boy who has been barred from the club-house, left outside to play with the girls and their dolls—or to die, for all the boys cared.

He needed to explain it. He couldn't match Odysseus's rhetoric, but he needed to get it through to the kid somehow. Because Odysseus was just about finished rendering Pyrrhus the great service Philoctetes was too tired to perform: incinerating him.

Odysseus had reached his peroration, his manner suddenly casual and intimate. "It isn't about killing. It's about doing something bigger with your life than . . . counting how many people you can sleep with."

"Counting?" Philoctetes cut in. He flapped his hand in the imme-morial gesture of the swish. "Honey, I lost count when you were still dating your fist."

"There," Odysseus said. Pleased, as if exhibit A had just entered it-self—flung itself into evidence. And the boy looked satisfactorily annoyed. "You can be like that, or—"

"Or be one of the guys," Philoctetes said.

"I meant to say—"

"That's it, isn't it? It's like—when I was a kid I wasn't much of an athlete, you know?"

"Me, either," Pyrrhus said.

"No? With your build? I would have thought you . . ."

"I guess I was kind of a sissy."

"Ah. That is the word, isn't it? I've always been scared to say that word. I was a *sissy*. Whiny and clumsy and—not just clumsy but also scared, afraid to be hit by the ball, afraid to fall down. Now that I'm older, I know I wouldn't break. I think sometimes, if I could be eight or ten again, I could play their games, I'd be the best. Graceful, fearless. Except, you know, they must have come out of the womb knowing they wouldn't break. Maybe that's the difference between real boys and sissies.

"Anyway, once in a while I'd accidentally hit the ball, or catch it, whichever I was supposed to be doing. And I'd feel like they accepted me for a minute. Still making fun of me, but . . . the way they would make fun of each other. The next day in school I'd be as restless as they were, waiting for the three o'clock bell, when I could go with them and play again. They had short memories—they wouldn't think of all the times I'd screwed up, they'd just remember that one good play yesterday. So, just for once, someone would pick me for their team. Pick me before I was the last kid left."

Odysseus just stared at him. He couldn't figure out what this little reminiscence was about. But Pyrrhus seemed to be spellbound as Philoctetes went on.

"You were picked for the team finally. Here you thought you were a sissy, and you were picked for the team. By Odysseus, no less. Or the Fates, the Fates finally signed you up so you could play with the big boys. But honey: you are still a sissy."

Perfect, he couldn't be doing a better job if Odysseus had handed him his lines. Odysseus had merely to say, quietly: "Nowhere is it written that you have to be a sissy all your life."

"But you do, honey. That's just what's written." Philoctetes was suddenly screeching; Odysseus had never seen a queen in such full feather. The boy was plainly disgusted; he was standing there with his mouth open. "It is the most important fact about you, you can't just get rid of it. You can put on a uniform and line up with the rest of the boys, but when they take the team picture there you'll be, anyone could pick you out, the sissy in the second row.

"You can dress up in your daddy's armor. And if you do just what you're supposed to, the straight boys will say, 'Man, that sure took balls. Burning that city, killing those babies. That kid's *got* a pair.' Oh, do it: I bet those Myrmidons will hoist you up and carry you on their shoulders just like you hit the home run. They'll all want to be buddies with you. For an afternoon. Why, honey, if I had the strength, I'd get up and join you."

Apparently he didn't have the strength; he sank back again. Giving Odysseus time to think of the answer to this bizarre oration.

Philoctetes hadn't said anything Pyrrhus didn't know. He had never articulated it: he wasn't in the habit of screeching at himself in his internal monologues. But no one could really tell him anything he didn't already know about himself. Maybe not even an oracle. He knew the armor couldn't change him; he knew that if he were to conquer the world he would still be scared of little crawly things. He knew that he would still be Pyrrhus when he got to Troy. Some part of him had already, long since, started thinking ahead to the next thing after that. The more distant future, the farther place where he would be out of his father's sight forever.

He understood all this; or if he hadn't, he understood it as soon as Philoctetes said it. What he could not understand was why Philoctetes should hurl it at him. Here, in front of Odysseus and Admetus. Or why he should have turned into some awful parody of himself, nellier than Pyrrhus had ever seen him. Here, in front of the straight men. It was almost funny.

He started to laugh.

The boy was laughing, and after a moment Philoctetes joined him, the two of them perversely laughing at some joke Odysseus couldn't get. He felt—not just excluded, but even a little stupid. It was time to intervene, get past all this noodling about who was a sissy and who wasn't, and bring the boy back to the real point, the great things that were coming to him, soon, the glory and the loot and the father beaming up at him from Hell. Remind him that this fairy with whom he was sharing some impenetrable joke was going to die, any day now. It was time to leave him behind. How could he word this sensitively enough, the most important summation he had ever delivered? Perhaps if he just reiterated: It's not too late for you to be a . . .

Philoctetes stopped laughing and said — not screeching any more, suddenly calm. "I used to feel the same way, honey. Used to? I got over it about ten minutes ago.

"God, I've been so mad all these years. When Odysseus was just some little team captain who wouldn't choose me. They start so early, getting you ready, making you think it's the only way to be a man. And it goes so deep inside. Even after I grew up there wasn't ever a time . . . when I could walk into a disco and watch a hundred heads turn, I didn't ever feel as proud, or as *whole*, as on those few magic afternoons when a bunch of snotty fifth graders let me into their world. They get so far into you, and it never goes away.

"You can wear their uniform as long as you promise to be *straight-acting.* You can join them that way — or if you can't hide it, if you walk funny, you can carry their dirty towels. Or you can just lie in your shack and beat off looking at pictures of men with bodies of death, men dressed to kill. It doesn't matter; they win every way. You can't even defy them, even your defiance just tells them they're the real men. It's all a big circle, and they fence you inside it the minute you're born. They look between your legs and sign you up.

"So when you're big enough they can send you into this war that isn't going to end next week, next week's glorious battle is just one inning. Guys will go on bleeding in the mud as long as they can just be picked. Please don't leave me out.

"Until somebody says no. No, I'm going to start my own team."

"Country," Pyrrhus murmured.

Philoctetes looked perplexed, shrugged. "Country," he repeated. Then, casually: "Now, give me the bow."

"What?" Pyrrhus said.

"Give it to me, I've had it all these years and I never knew why. I never knew what I was supposed to do with it."

Odysseus lunged for the bow. "Don't do it, he's crazy!"

Pyrrhus eluded him.

"Just hand it over," Philoctetes said.

Pyrrhus did, handed him the bow and a couple of arrows from the quiver.

"What the fuck are you doing?" Odysseus cried, in an unmartial treble. He hesitated: Philoctetes was pretty feeble—even Odysseus could probably lick him. On the other hand, there was the slightest possibility that the bow really was magic, that Philoctetes could send an arrow your way just by thinking unkind thoughts about you. Probably nonsense, but Odysseus tactically retreated to the safest place he could think of: he cowered behind immortal Admetus.

Pyrrhus stayed where he was, by the bed. He wasn't at all sure who Philoctetes was going to aim for, with that bow only he could draw. Though it would have to be Odysseus, wouldn't it? Philoctetes was going to sit up and shoot Odysseus. The first blow for their team; Pyrrhus wished he could strike it himself. He cried out, "Admetus, get out of the way!"

Admetus didn't move. "The kid's kind of a slow learner," he said.

"Isn't he?" Philoctetes drawled. "I just hope I stick around long enough to drum it into his divine little head. This is what I was supposed to do with the bow."

As if with a sudden resurgence of strength, Philoctetes sat up. And broke the bow over his knee.

ISLANDS OF GRIEF

Tourists in the capital may buy a little atlas whose successive maps depict the city as it might be seen by a congeries of monomaniacs. One map shows only hotels, another theaters, another temples, with everything else rendered as empty squares of gray bounded by avenues and cross-streets. As if, on the unchanging topography of the street grid, a series of dynasties had erected their own cities, one on top of another: a city of transients, a city of playactors, a city of worshipers. Nothing in the atlas suggests that it is possible to stroll from the Grand Hotel to the Majestic Theater, or thence to the Temple of Hera, that these things coexist in time. To discover this, one would have to hold in his head all at once plates 7, 11, and 19, a feat of multiple perspectives of which few of us are capable.

Every citizen, of course, could devise a plate of his own: apartment, office, grocery store, dry cleaner. The corner where he glimpsed his unattainable love, the restaurant where the affair he settled for instead was broken off. As in the atlas, every irrelevant landmark or edifice, all the things the citizen merely passes by on his way from one point of interest to another, would be reduced to gray vacancies. There could be a million such maps. And to see where one person's map coincided with another's would require a stretch of sympathetic imagination as great as moving from plate 7 to plate 19.

There are also maps that could be constructed for an entire class of citizens, maps omitted from the atlas only because of the parochial interests of its intended purchasers. There is the city of the homeless, for example: the warmest grates, the least secure foyers, the best corners for panhandling. There is the city of adolescents: high school and movie theaters and malls and safe places to park, if there are any left. There is the city—maps of this one are in fact procurable, despite its omission from the atlas—of queers. Bars, mostly, and the residual discos; bookstores and peep shows and leather shops and gyms; cruising spots for differing tastes; strip joints and, if you can remember where they were, the ruins of back rooms and baths.

Some people live entirely in that city—Pyrrhus came close, early in his career. Others drop into it only occasionally, stealthily creeping onto its map from another map of wife, job, children, temple. Most of us, like Leucon, have inscribed a few of its landmarks—a favorite bar or two—

onto our personal maps and never visit the rest. But it is still there, the queer city, places whose ads we see in the gay paper and have never bothered to go to. It is there, our implicit community, it never entirely recedes into the gray area with everything else.

Except that a few of the other plates have gradually bled into the gay one. Five or six years after Odysseus and the other Greeks sailed home, leaving behind an unconquered Troy, the gay map already showed, here and there, temples and cemeteries. And hospitals, like the one where Leucon sat, waiting to see his old friend Gelanor.

Gelanor, the last classic queen, the one who called men *numbers* and *did* them. When Gelanor was gone, nobody would talk that way ever again.

Leucon was, as often in idle moments, thinking about love, in a green place, Corydon and Alexis, sheep, but he looked up and saw only the green walls of the waiting room. It occurred to him suddenly that somebody had *picked* that green. It was so familiar you thought of it as a law of nature, but it wasn't. Someone, probably a fairy on commission, spread out the paint chips, every hue imaginable, and selected it. Maybe he didn't really choose it; maybe the hospital accreditation people demanded this particular shade, in the same way they specified the minimum equipment for the ER. Or maybe the decorator thought it was soothing, could somehow turn death's anteroom into a pasture. The great joke for Leucon's generation being that the pasture was death's anteroom. Not that they were the first to learn that. But he thought it would never be unlearned now; no one would, as they had, forget it for one moment.

That same decorator must have decided to carve up the waiting room into what used to be called conversation groups: a table and four chairs there, a vinyl sofa and matching easy chair there, by the window the single chair in which Leucon sat and looked out at a day startlingly sunny for February. The layout allowed families to be miserable together yet isolated from everyone else, little islands of grief as far apart as possible. Only one other island was occupied just now: a couple in, maybe, their sixties, he in corduroy trousers and a green blazer—ivy green, mind you, not the color of the room—she in a tan skirt and a tattersall blouse. They might as well just have dressed in bank notes. Or: even naked, you would have known the heft of their portfolio just by the way they murmured to each other, so decorously, no more displaying their grief than they would fling back the bedroom curtains when, if ever, they fucked. Here with their son, of course, on this floor, and not his first admission: they were too calm, this was already routine for them.

Leucon was, as I say, waiting to see Gelanor. Leucon had thought he was one of Gelanor's very best friends. He didn't know how many friends Gelanor had, so many that he had exceeded his quota of visitors and they wouldn't even let Leucon in until somebody had left. So many that it occurred to Leucon that he was kind of peripheral and maybe he could get away without seeing Gelanor at all. Except he hadn't gone to see Linus and he's always felt guilty about that, even though he and Linus weren't bosom buddies, guilty just knowing everybody else had gone simply as a matter of decency and Leucon had stayed away.

Thus he was here to see Gelanor as a prophylactic measure, to forestall future remorse, rather than for any comfort he might bring. Leucon wasn't going to cheer Gelanor up; he could barely make conversation with a well person. He was afraid he might wind up just staring. Thus replacing his memories of vibrant, silly Gelanor with a terminal memory of Gelanor disintegrating. He wondered if he should just go home.

He read a *Reader's Highlights* for a while. Not the reactionary political articles—"How the Greeks Lost Troy: Destiny or Subversion?"—or the ones on ten ways to tell if your husband thinks you're sexy, but the little joke fillers, cute remarks by celebrities, embarrassing incidents at work. All the jokes were about minor disjunctures in a white-bread world: in smiling at them you were supposed to confirm the basic order that was momentarily and without lasting effect disturbed. Leucon started imagining what it would be like if our stories were to creep between these covers like an invasion. "The other day, I was at the hospital waiting to see an old fuck buddy . . ." "One night at the baths a man's towel slipped off and . . ."

Leucon looked up, probably with a subversive grin, and there was a new guy in the room, at the next island, looking steadily over at him. Leucon thought: Oh, he's cute, and he's looking straight at me. Leucon let his grin settle into a smile, which the guy did not return. But he didn't look away, either; he was definitely cruising Leucon. Right there fifty feet from Gelanor's deathbed, twenty feet from that decorous couple—what would they think, if Leucon managed to pick this guy up right before their eyes? Would it be like witnessing the night their son, all unaware, betrothed himself to the unseen?

What would Gelanor think—would he bless Leucon, would he forgive if Leucon went away without even seeing Gelanor because he had scored with this guy? Who wouldn't take his eyes off Leucon, some hunk from straight out of a magazine cruising Leucon, and who looked a lot like . . . was. Pyrrhus. Was Pyrrhus.

It had been—what?—five or six years? He really hadn't changed so much, Leucon should have known him right away. It's just that Leucon hadn't thought he would ever see Pyrrhus again. No, that's insufficient: it was one of the organizing principles of Leucon's life, one of the ways he made sense of things, that he wouldn't ever see Pyrrhus again. Leucon was at first simply disoriented, as you might be if you were to walk into your apartment and find the furniture rearranged. Or the way you feel when you walk up to a car that looks just like yours but isn't, and your first thought is, Why won't my key fit?

Anyway, Pyrrhus had too changed. He was, as Phoenix had thought so long ago (prematurely), a man now. Leucon had thought he was a man when he left. But no, the Pyrrhus Leucon remembered was a youth; this was a man. So Leucon was, too. This was what being a grown man was like. Though he would never stop feeling like a youth inside—his friend Amyclas assured him, and Amyclas had to be seventy, you never stopped feeling like a kid, playacting at being a grownup.

Pyrrhus said "Leucon?" and Leucon said "Hi," but he was still sort of confused. Almost as if he were dreaming, but that's just backwards. In a dream he took for granted the wildest incongruities; he carried on perfectly normal conversations with his dead parents half the nights of his life, and it wasn't unprecedented—though not so common, either—for Pyrrhus to show up on the other nights. He never felt strange about such things when he was dreaming, no one does. Only when you're awake can you feel as though you're dreaming.

"God, it's so good to see you. I never thought I'd see you again."

"Me either," Leucon said.

"How are you doing?"

"Me? I'm fine." Too emphatically, meaning he was . . . fine. He tried to cover it with a shrug. That's how decent people say it, never with relief or, god forbid, triumph, but with a shrug. As if it were an undeserved and slightly embarrassing bit of good fortune, to be fine. "How about you?"

"Okay." Great: both negative, an island of negativity there in death's anteroom. Some part of Leucon was already spinning out their negative future together when Pyrrhus added: "So far. I haven't, you know . . . checked."

The future grew a little murky. Pyrrhus hadn't been tested. After his year in the city as—practically a public utility, and then whatever new adventures he'd found in the intervening years, he hadn't been tested. Maybe Leucon wouldn't have, either, not if he'd had Pyrrhus's career;

maybe he wouldn't have wanted to know, either. Because there wasn't much chance, was there, that Pyrrhus was fine?

Even I don't want to know. I suppose he probably wasn't. I mean, if it were possible to trace the course of things, the most direct chain would surely be snake to Philoctetes, Philoctetes to Pyrrhus, Pyrrhus to Corythus, Corythus to: the HUNDREDS OF US he glimpsed that night at Pterelas's, the great world that waited to embrace him when he got out of the navy and into civvies for good. That would be the simplest tree: Philoctetes the root, Pyrrhus the trunk, all the myriad branches traceable finally to Corythus, who stepped off the ship one day and, with his innocent, bucktoothed smile, brought the unseen guest to the great party that was still going on in the city.

Perhaps this was all written somewhere. But all Destiny's scribblings, if compiled into one unimaginable volume, would not yield a message. She has no point to make. Corythus was innocent. Even the snake was innocent. Philoctetes innocently misstepped, the snake innocently bit.

Anyway, Leucon didn't suppose the odds were very good for Pyrrhus, unless there was some sort of divine immunity. But even Achilles died. Still, Leucon grasped at whatever tiny chance there was and, for a minute, built a future on it. One chance in a hundred that Pyrrhus was okay: this great gamble obscured for a moment the fact that there wasn't a chance in a million Pyrrhus would wind up with Leucon.

They were quiet a minute; Leucon knew he was staring, but couldn't stop.

"How come you're here?" Pyrrhus said.

"See a friend."

"Oh. I'm sorry."

"You?" Leucon said. "A friend?"

"Um . . . lover." A little abashed. As if he had seen Leucon plotting out a future and was letting him down gently. Or maybe just because it was rude to be too obviously pleased about having a lover. Even if this was evidently a transitory bit of good fortune.

A lover. Every chance gone, then. Not just because he was taken — he might, Leucon thought guiltily, be on the loose again soon enough — but because having a sick lover sort of multiplied the odds that Pyrrhus was positive.

Every chance gone. Leucon knew that his face must have proclaimed his disappointment. He was ashamed that Pyrrhus could see it. What must it have been like for Pyrrhus, to go through life knowing that everyone wanted to capture his future, hold him prisoner? For that is, isn't it, what Leucon had imagined for an instant? What he had wanted since the day he had stepped into the living room of a vacant apartment and beheld Pyrrhus. Just to keep him there, to behold him always, blind to all the ways the years would transfigure him.

He was transfigured already. He looked more divine than ever, but he was a dying man, and he would die far from Leucon.

"I ought to get back," Pyrrhus said. "I mean, Phoenix is with him, but he gets tired of Phoenix pretty quick."

"Phoenix? That old guy?"

"Yeah, I never could shake him. I guess they'll be okay for a few minutes. I just wanted a cigarette, you have to go all the way downstairs and outside."

"It's cold."

"Yeah, what you have to go through for a fix. You'd think—everything else people have to go through here—you'd think they could take a minute out from improving us and just let us have a goddamn cigarette." He looked toward the elevators, then back to Leucon. "I'll be back up in a couple minutes, if you're still here."

"No, let me come with you." Leucon recalled the last time he had said that to Pyrrhus, and hastily added, "I mean, I'm getting out of here. I'll see my friend tomorrow, maybe."

"You sure?" Pyrrhus said. Meaning what? Sure he wanted to go downstairs, or sure there would still be a friend?

It might have been sunny for February, but it was bitter cold, there outside the hospital entrance. Leucon had put on his coat, while Pyrrhus had come down in just his shirtsleeves. It wasn't going to be a long talk; he'd be heading back up as soon as he'd had his fix. Leucon didn't even smoke, there wasn't any excuse for hanging around. Nothing would ever happen between them again, even if Pyrrhus's lover was on his way out, even if Pyrrhus should miraculously turn out to be healthy. They couldn't even be friends; even now they could scarcely make conversation.

"Um," Leucon said. "Your lover's name is—"

"Philoctetes."

"Uh-huh. What's he like?"

Pyrrhus smiled. "Kind of a queen."

"Oh." Leucon didn't know what to say to this. He couldn't imagine loving a queen. "Where did you meet him?"

"Lemnos."

"Oh. I've always wanted to go to Lemnos. When was this, lately?"

"A long time ago. Right after I left . . . here."

"What, on the way to Troy?"

"Yeah," Pyrrhus said. He took a last drag of his cigarette and stamped it out. "Well, no. I mean, it turned out I was never on my way to Troy."

He looked at Leucon for a second and then spread his arms. Meaning he was willing to let Leucon have a farewell hug. Out here with everybody passing by, doctors and patients and all. Leucon stayed where he was. He managed to say — not decency but unfelt manners compelled him to say — "I'm sorry about your lover."

Pyrrhus dropped his arms. "We had a long time. I don't know, it seems like a minute." He shrugged, then said, "See ya," and headed inside.

Leucon remembered the night when he had thought, if he wanted only one memory, it had to be of Pyrrhus inside him. He remembered thinking that. He couldn't remember Pyrrhus inside him.

A NOTE

The story of Philoctetes and Pyrrhus, or Neoptolemus, has been recounted for almost three millennia. The *Philoctetes* of Sophocles is the most familiar, and I have drawn from it more than may be immediately evident, though I have also used some ideas from André Gide's version and snatches of Seneca, Quintus, Cicero, and the *Greek Anthology*. A useful compendium of primary sources is Oscar Mandel's *Philoctetes and the Fall of Troy: Plays, Documents, Iconography, Interpretations* (Lincoln: University of Nebraska Press, 1981).

Most of the mythology in my account is attested by one source or another. I might note at least three deviations:

1. Phoenix was blinded by his father, not castrated.
2. In some accounts, Paris is already dead by the time the Greeks learn that they need Philoctetes; in others, Philoctetes himself kills Paris. In a lost *Philoctetes*, however, Euripides allegedly has Paris arrive on Lemnos and seek to lure Philoctetes to the Trojan side.
3. Some sources contend that the war ended differently.

As for my geography: readers bound for the Aegean might wish to bring along a second guide, in case this one should sometimes prove unreliable.

It should be unnecessary to remark that Greek sexual attitudes and practices, even in the classical period, were very different from those depicted here. What the Greeks did many centuries earlier is lost to us. The classic Greeks themselves argued about the sexuality of the archaic heroes—who was the top, they wondered, Achilles or Patroclus? And there were evidently a few persistent rumors about Philoctetes. Witness Martial, as late as the first century of our era: "The hero son of Poeas was an effeminate who yielded easily to men" (*Epigrams*, 2:84). This is not the place to join the debate about whether there have always been gay people. I am not arguing for this view, any more than I am suggesting that the ancient Greeks wore blue jeans or hailed taxicabs.

Finally, readers may notice that there are almost no women in this story. This is true of Sophocles' version as well: his *Philoctetes* is the only extant Greek tragedy with no female character. Hence it is also the only tragedy in which none of the actors wear drag.

It has only lately become common to tack acknowledgments onto works of fiction, as if favoring the reader with a preview of the acceptance speech to be delivered at some future awards ceremony. While I think this new custom is nearly as pretentious as ending a novel by reciting the places of its composition (Washington–New York–New Jersey, if you care), I will take the opportunity to thank a few people I may not have thanked adequately in person. Robert Dawidoff, Richard Howard, Patrick Merla, and Michael Nava, in alphabetical order, provided comments and encouragement. My editors, Keith Kahla and Christopher Potter, took a chance on a rather eccentric manuscript, while my agent, Leslie Breed, has qualified for sainthood by actually returning my calls. Several employers have made allowances for my dual vocation. Bob Ashe has made countless allowances, living through the second-novel blues and making the next novel possible, as he makes every day possible.